Praise for

"Based on a true story, a debut Victorian-era novel explores the life, loves, and losses of Colorado's notorious Silver Queen, Baby Doe Tabor.... Burns paints a vivid portrait of late-19th-century America, capturing the bold, reckless, and ever-shifting social conventions of the Wild West and its aftermath. Baby is a captivating and complex character, both sympathetic and flawed and always straining against the confines of her status and sex. With witty prose and a third-person narration that shifts easily between perspectives, the author pays equal care and attention to the people around Baby, whether they adore or despise her. The result is a book that unpretentiously explores the pitfalls of luxury, the desperation of poverty, and the hazards of being an ambitious woman in a world ruled by men. A thoughtful, immersive, and deeply human look at one of history's most famous social climbers."

—*Kirkus Reviews*

"Burns pays loving attention to period detail.... the story's twists and turns and larger-than-life personalities will leave fans of historical fiction breathless while offering a welcome glimpse into a captivating past.... A whirlwind tale of triumphs and tragedies celebrating the Colorado gold rush era through the eyes of an infamous lady."

—*BookLife Reviews*

"From Wisconsin to the gold and silver mines in Colorado, Kimberly Burns skillfully spins a quintessential American story of one woman's determination to join Colorado's moneyed elite during the 19th-century boom years. Told with compassionate insight and a fine-tuned sense of humor, Burns' historical Baby Doe is a fully-realized, complex character who dares to break social conventions. The author's careful balance of historical details enriches this fast-paced, captivating novel so that Baby Doe's story is also Colorado's. A pleasure to read from beginning to end, *The Mrs. Tabor* is historical fiction at its best."

—Ann Weisgarber, award-winning author of *The Glovemaker, The Promise,* and *The Personal History of Rachel DuPree*

"Well researched with descriptions of events and setting that will draw you right in."

—Linda Ulleseit, award-winning author of *Under the Almond Trees* and *The Aloha Spirit*

"An excellent and balanced job of portraying Baby Doe's life, the scandalous choices she made, and the world she lived in during Colorado's early years. From mistress to wife to wealthy social outcast to mother and, finally, to widow and pauper, the author successfully portrays the life of a complex woman, humanizing her and bringing her richly to life ... Baby Doe's story is fascinating, appalling, and heart wrenching."

—J.v.L. Bell, award-winning author of *The Lucky Hat Mine, Elizabeth Byers: Denver Pioneer,* and *Denver City Justice*

the MRS. TABOR

Based on a true story

KIMBERLY BURNS

The Mrs. Tabor
Published by Thomas Bard Publishing LLC.
Leesburg, Virginia

Many contradictory stories surround Baby Doe Tabor, and many factual details have been lost in the mists of time and legend. This is a work of fiction that attempts to follow the truth as the author's imagination perceived it. The names and some details of historical figures have been used, but the characters are fictional creations. Actual events, business establishments and locales have been depicted; however, in a fictitious manner.

Publisher's Cataloging-in-Publication data

Names: Burns, Kimberly, author.
Title: The Mrs. Tabor / Kimberly Burns.
Description: Leesburg, VA: Thomas Bard Publishing, 2021.
Identifiers: ISBN: 978-1-7368169-0-5
Subjects: LCSH Baby Doe, -1935--Fiction. | Tabor, Horace Austin Warner, 1830-1899--Fiction. | Frontier and pioneer life--West (U.S.)--Fiction. | Women--Colorado--Fiction. | Women--Colorado--History--Fiction. | Love stories. | Historical fiction. | BISAC FICTION / Historical / Romance | FICTION / Romance / Historical / American
Classification: LCC PS3602.U76635 M77 2021 | DDC 813.6--dc23

Cover and Interior design by Victoria Wolf, wolfdesignandmarketing.com

QUANTITY PURCHASES: Clubs and other organizations may qualify for special terms when ordering quantities of this title. For information, email info@thomasbardpublishing.com.

Dedicated to my father, Gene Coleman, who never let the facts get in the way of a good story.

CHAPTER 1

February, 1935 – Leadville, CO

"WHO IS THAT?" she called. A ghost? No, ghosts came to haunt her in the night, and the sun was bright on the mountain today. The tiny old woman squinted, trying to make out if the figure trudging up the mountainside was friend or foe. She'd never had many friends, so most likely foe. There was nothing of value inside her rickety one-room shanty. It was, of course, the fabulous treasure of silver buried in the Matchless Mine that everyone wanted to steal. She had stood guard on this mountain for over thirty years; the mine was more valuable to her than just the vein of silver running through it. It was her legacy, her life.

She stood in the open cabin doorway, holding an old Winchester rifle at her hip. She made her voice deep, tried to sound taller than her five feet two inches and younger than her eighty years. "You're trespassing on private land. Turn around now and go back to town."

The figure gave a friendly wave and kept walking toward her.

"Stop right there." She raised the rifle to her chest as if she might take aim. "I know how to handle claim jumpers."

The young man paused and held up both hands in surrender. His wide eyes stared at the gun.

She looked hard at the young man. He was soft, a bit round in the middle and his fair cheeks pink with exertion. His hair was the color of fall wheat. Was that Harvey Doe? She hadn't seen him in more than fifty years. No, of course, it wasn't Harvey. He would be in his eighties, probably dead by now. It was the blonde hair and tenderfoot look of him that reminded her of her first husband.

"Mrs. Tabor, my name is Wesley Meyers." It came out in gasps. The air was thin here at ten thousand feet above sea level.

"Did Merle Greene send you? You tell him I am not leaving." That blackheart claimed he owned the mine; he had conspired with the government to steal it from her at a foreclosure auction. The Matchless Mine had belonged to her second husband, the great Horace Tabor, once Colorado's richest man. On his deathbed he had made her promise to keep hold of it and years later she was doing just that. Merle Greene could reopen the mine over her dead body. She would join the other ghosts that haunted this place and guard the Tabor silver, so he'd never find an ounce.

"No Ma'am. Mr. Greene didn't send me. Mr. Eugene Hawthorne did."

Eugene Hawthorne, she hadn't heard that name in years. Her hatred of that scandal-mongering yellow newspaper man was like holding onto a frozen metal spike, cold and painful, but she couldn't let go. Hawthorne had made a living painting her as a low woman with overreaching aspirations, a vain conniving opportunist. He didn't know the first thing about her.

"Hawthorne," she said through gritted teeth, "what does he want? Why are you here?"

"I'm a reporter with the *Denver Star Ledger*. I'd like to tell your true story and get your response to the movie *Silver Dollar* that dramatized your life. My editor, Mr. Hawthorne, sent me."

A shriek ripped from her, and she ran toward young Wesley howling like a banshee. She swung the rifle like a club at his head. He ducked and bolted back down the hill, sliding and skittering in the gravel.

"Lies, all lies," she screamed, hot on his heels. She picked up a rock and threw it at Wesley's retreating back

Eugene Hawthorne was the devil incarnate. He couldn't tell the truth if his life depended on it. He already knew the facts; he knew her entire life's story. He had been there to see it all unfold, hounding her every step, following her and Horace, then printing fantastic fabrications with sensational headlines. That bastard would say anything to sell a newspaper. She should have known he would never leave her alone, after all these years sending a young man up here to find something sordid to write, some way to humiliate her when she was down on her luck. Hawthorne should have known she would not have forgotten him either, or his lies.

She missed Horace. Her second husband may not have been a sophisticated man, but he was an admirable man. He had used his silver fortune to help civilize the Wild West. He opened post offices and firehouses, created water and gas companies, and his opera houses brought culture to rough towns. Most of all, he loved her.

He was kind and generous and treated her with respect. Living here alone for all these years, keeping her deathbed promise and working the Matchless, was the only way she could think of to honor him. Her loyalty proved her love for him. She would never let Eugene Hawthorne and his filth taint the memory of Horace Tabor and all he accomplished in these mountains.

She threw another rock at the distant figure running down the old mining road and walked back to the shanty. She looked at the mountains that surrounded her like protective arms. Mount Elbert and Mount Massive, frosted with a thick layer of snow, dominating the imposing skyline. These peaks never failed to awe her. They had bestowed great blessings upon her, and even now they held her fortune, hidden and patiently waiting for her in the mine below.

She could still clearly remember the first time she saw the Rockies rising up from the plains. It was over fifty years ago, summer 1877, and she was on a train bound for Colorado with her first husband, Harvey Doe. It took three long days from Oshkosh, Wisconsin, rocking along in that hard seat. She had watched out the window across the endless prairie for Indian raiding parties and great herds of buffalo. But as the miles wore on it became clear that Bill Cody had killed all the buffalo, the Cavalry had rounded up all the Indians, and sitting like a proper lady on a rumbling train would make that lady's bottom hurt. Then she saw them, the peaks rose over the distant horizon, a faint shadow, a blue silhouette at first. With each passing mile, they grew in size and intensity, eating the previously boundless prairie sky, and the locomotive, which had dominated the grass sea, became increasingly diminutive. Brown-green foothills knelt like handmaidens before the growing majestic mountains. The late afternoon sun shone like a halo above the white snowcaps. Cool wind blew down from above and kissed her cheeks like a benediction from the Madonna. She knew then that these mountains held her destiny.

But that train ride West was not the start of her story. It was all a long time ago now, before she was the crazy old woman, before she became the femme fatale known as Baby Doe. In the beginning she was just pretty Lizzie McCourt.

CHAPTER 2

1877

MOST OF OSHKOSH THOUGHT Lizzie McCourt had done well when she married into the Does. She had met young Harvey in her father's clothing store where she spent afternoons telling gullible middle-aged men how dashing they looked in a new hat or helping them choose the more expensive tie. From behind the shop counter, the McCourt's favorite daughter had taken an inventory of the town's eligible marriage prospects and found Harvey Doe was the most attractive, both physically and financially. When the Doe men visited the haberdashery, Lizzie made sure she was on hand to assist with their purchases. She focused her many charms on Harvey—her angelic face and vivacious curves—and he was powerless to resist. She would straighten Harvey's tie and smooth his lapels, letting her hand linger a moment too long on his chest. She would boldly gaze into his eyes until the young man began to blush, only to dip her head and lower her lashes in feigned innocence. Harvey gaped when, on warm afternoons, Lizzie fanned her smooth, white neck, and on cold mornings she pursed her Cupid's bow lips to blow on her fingertips. Although his father did most of the talking, Lizzie was sure she saw infatuation in Harvey's face.

Colonel Doe was a self-made man with a confidence that Lizzie found very attractive. He had made a small fortune in the Colorado gold rush and then returned to Wisconsin to live a respectable life. The Colonel had been the mayor and Mother Doe, his wife, was the president of the Saint David's Episcopal Church Ladies Aid Society. The elder Doe was not involved in the war but had earned the moniker Colonel because of his decisive manner in business and politics.

Lizzie thought the nickname was more appropriate for Mother Doe given the way she commanded her fair-haired son, Harvey. Mother Doe had not been pleased with the match; she had aimed higher for her only son. Lizzie's family were Catholic, with hordes of children, and the father was a common merchant. In an effort to appease her future mother-in-law, Lizzie had agreed to be married in the Doe's Episcopal Church. She was sure the union would be blessed no matter where it took place. She was also betting Harvey had inherited more from his father than good looks, but his strong will and business acumen as well.

As the last guests left the wedding banquet, Colonel Doe called the young couple over. "It is time I gave your gift," he announced, rubbing his beefy hands together. "I own half of a mine, called the Fourth of

July, near Central City, Colorado. I've leased my partner's half for two years with an option to buy. Harvey, you will work the mine with a crew and receive half the profits. If all goes well, we will buy out my silent partner and deed the mine to you."

"Oh, thank you. Thank you." Lizzie gasped. Young Mrs. Doe jumped up and kissed her father-in-law on the cheek. She bounced back into the settee beside Harvey and squeezed his hand. "Harvey, can you believe it? We are going to be millionaires."

Harvey sat silent.

Lizzie nudged him. "Isn't this a generous and thoughtful gift?"

After taking a long swallow of whiskey, Harvey said, "This certainly is a generous gift, but Lizzie and I would prefer to live in Oshkosh nearer the families."

"No, we would not prefer that," she said. She took a quick breath and with a smile tried a different tack. "We can follow your father's path, make our fortune in Colorado and then return to Oshkosh."

Harvey turned to face her, but his gaze fell to the floor. He could not meet her deep blue eyes. "Darling, mining is hard and dangerous. The boomtowns attract the roughest sort of people. To say nothing of the fact that I am uneducated in the whole business. And there is no guarantee that the mine is anything more than a hole in the ground. I could work like a donkey for two years and end up with nothing but calloused hands."

Lizzie blinked in disbelief. She couldn't imagine anyone wouldn't grab this opportunity with both hands and run to get a shovel. "Well, I think it is a wonderful idea. A little elbow grease and we can live a very grand life."

"Listen to your wife, Son. I'm giving you quite a leg up, with nothing at stake. You'll have to work hard, but that kind of self-determination will give you great satisfaction when you reach my age."

Harvey stared gloomily into his whiskey as if his future lay drowned at the bottom of the glass. Perhaps, she should have seen it, but Lizzie was already looking forward.

"Fourth of July is such an auspicious name. I feel it is a very good sign." Lizzie gave the Colonel a bright smile.

"That's my girl." The older man patted his son on the back. "You'll see, a man can't be in a mining town too long before catching gold fever." The Colonel leaned over and took Lizzie's tiny hand in his. "And I'm counting on you to. . ." He searched for a word. "Encourage Harvey along."

The rail line stopped at a small, rough mining camp called Blackhawk where they bought tickets on the stagecoach, up the steep one-mile ride to Central City and their mine. Lizzie held onto her seat and stared out the window at the strange new world as the coach bounced up the gulch. Only stumps, covering the slopes like a stubbly beard, remained of the forest here, sawed down in the frantic efforts to quickly build sluice boxes, cabins, stores, stables and mine timbers. The naked hillsides were ulcerated with mine shafts, reduction mills and ore dumps. Cascading yellow piles of slag, like small rockslides, marked the opening of each mine.

The easy days of panning for gold from streams were long gone; now miners blasted into the mountains, following veins of white quartz, which encircled thin ribbons of gold. Blast rubble was picked and crushed and finally sluiced in a backbreaking process to pluck Mother Nature's most valuable treasure from her bosom.

Lizzie stepped off the coach into a beehive of activity. In Central

City, saloons and banks, tin-roof shanties and charming Victorian homes and shops of all make and manner formed a crazy quilt pattern. The boomtown lacked the planning of a more civilized city like Denver. Miners laid claims and merchants built stores wherever they wished then connected them with streets and boardwalks that jagged and jogged to meet them. The surrounding hills rumbled with thumping pumps and shrieking steam hoists. Soiled doves called to customers. The dry air smelled like dust.

She noticed females in town fell into three categories: the miner's wife, dirty and worn to the bone by hard labor; sporting girls, painted and a little plumper, but tattered at the edges; or one of a handful of true ladies, wives of bankers or successful mine owners. In a town where men outnumbered women five to one, young Mrs. Doe was pleased to find she was in a class by herself.

The next day Lizzie had insisted on going with Harvey to see the mine. That morning they joined clusters of men making their way to the many mines in the surrounding hillsides. She overheard the lilting accent of Cornishmen, recently arrived in America to work those mines.

"Oh, Lord, 'tis it a vision? An angel here on earth?" a young man called out, as Lizzie passed by. "She has the bluest eyes I've ever seen. And the purest white skin, like those china baby dolls."

"Quit your gawking." An older man cuffed the cheeky lad. "That be the wife of the new owner at Fourth of July Mine, Harvey Doe."

"I think she be a china Baby Doe," said the young man with a grin, pleased with his play on words. "Baby Doe, bless me with a smile."

A hungover Harvey frowned, but said nothing. In a small fit of pique at her husband's apathetic response, Lizzie turned and flashed the miners a dazzling smile.

She had smiled often during those first long summer days in 1877, sure of their glittering future. But Harvey turned out to be a mama's boy and a drinker who couldn't get out of bed in the morning without being told how to do it.

The newlyweds' first home was a two-room house in Blackhawk, which wasn't even a town, just a mining camp where the train tracks stopped and the rent was cheaper than in Central City.

"The end of the line," Harvey had called it.

"Or the beginning," she offered. But Harvey couldn't be cajoled out of his disappointment. He had expected more—more guidance, more money, nicer cabin, easier mining and better weather. Truthfully, living in a windowless, ramshackle log cabin where the wind blew through bread-loaf-sized gaps in the chinking was not what Baby Doe had expected either. Yet if she shut her eyes, she could see the beautiful Oriental rug, the flocked wallpaper, the gleaming polished furniture. They just had to pull the gold out of the ground and it would all be theirs.

It had been August when, after a few weeks of shoring up timbers and making a couple of exploratory digs, Harvey had taken the first samples of ore from the Fourth of July to the assay office over in Nevadaville. Baby Doe spruced up the house as best she could and made dinner while waiting for him to return with a report of the mine's potential payoff.

Harvey shuffled in and silently hung his hat and coat. Baby Doe clasped her hands at her throat, a nervous finger reaching up to pull on a low-hanging curl. "Harvey, I've been thinking about this all day. Please don't keep me in suspense."

"It's worthless," Harvey mumbled. He tossed a chunk of ore onto the table.

"What?"

"Worthless," Harvey spoke up. "The assayer says the quartz lode we're digging is too poor to even bother taking out of the ground." He slumped into a chair at the table.

Baby silently dished up shepherd's pie, and Harvey began eating. Baby stared hard at her plate and thought of her father. Pete McCourt had lost his clothing store when fire destroyed most of Oshkosh, but he built it anew from the ashes. A few years later, fire again destroyed his business. Baby had watched Mama stand in the soot and smoke and weep, "What will we do?" Papa had answered, "The only thing there is to do, try again." He always told his large Irish brood that in America hard work would pay off.

At last Baby spoke to Harvey, "What else did the assayer say?"

Harvey shrugged, "Well, he said we could sink our shaft deeper or take another angle and hope to strike a richer vein. But it's a gamble."

"I say we do it. We've got 500 feet on that claim; I say we don't give up until we have mined every inch of it." She tapped the table. "We need to sink a second shaft."

"It could turn up nothing. Besides I don't have the money to blast and timber another shaft and hire miners to work it. As it is, I'm running out of money to pay the men I've got."

"Well, what can we afford to do, Harvey? Sit in this little house and drink until all of your father's money is gone? Then what? Go back to your mother?" She spit out each question as an accusation. Harvey's cheeks flushed and she knew that was his greatest desire. "No, we're staying and working the mine until we find the gold," she said. "We can ask your father for more money or get a loan. The mine will serve as collateral."

Harvey shook his head and continued to eat. "I can't supervise two crews at the same time."

"I'll work the second crew."

Harvey's fork stopped in mid-air. "No. You cannot work in a mine. It is dirty, dangerous work that can kill a man." His protests were lost as she got up from the table and began digging through trunks and drawers, looking through Harvey's work clothes for items she could wear. He followed her around the cottage. "You'd ruin your hands, your back," he said, "I must insist. What will people think? What will they say?"

She stopped pulling things from a trunk and looked at him, "Honestly, Harvey, I don't care beans what people say."

Harvey walked back to the supper table and looked at his dinner, grown cold. He went to the cupboard and pulled down paper, ink and whiskey. He pushed aside his dinner plate and began his nightly letter home to his mother.

CHAPTER 3

THE NEXT MORNING BABY DOE used a piece of twine to clinch Harvey's canvas pants around her waist. She rolled up the pant legs until she could see her tiny feet peeking out and then tucked her curls up under a cap. She filled Harvey's pie-tin with two ham sandwiches and an apple to share. Harvey glared at her but said nothing. They stepped out of the house and joined clusters of miners making their way up the hillsides in the early morning frost.

Baby Doe had a figure that an hourglass would envy, and walking past the men on their way to the morning shift she caused as big a stir dressed as a man as she would in a gown. "Tis that the beautiful Baby Doe?" the miners called. She cheerfully tipped her hat and blonde curls fell around her shoulders.

"Honestly, you're making quite a spectacle of yourself," Harvey whispered. "And I don't like that nickname, Baby Doe."

"I don't see you doing anything about it," she replied.

As they passed the window of Sandelowsky-Pelton Clothing Store, Baby peeked inside. It was early, but she could see a figure working in the back. "I need to stop in here. You go on and get started; I'll be along shortly."

She rapped at the door, putting her face to the glass. The figure looked up and then, just as she had hoped, the owner hurried over and opened the store for her. Jake Sandelowsky was good looking in a roguish way with coal black hair and eyes, a small moustache and lazy smile that showed straight, white teeth.

"Good morning, Baby Doe," he said, taking in her unusual get-up.

Using all the techniques of persuasion she had practiced in her father's store, she dipped her chin and looked coyly up through her lashes. "Tell me, Mr. Sandelowsky, how do you know about that nickname?"

"The only man in this town who hasn't noticed you is Blind Bartie McManus, but no doubt even he's heard the fellows talk about the china baby doll strolling about town."

He had a habit of tilting his head to the side and raising a single eyebrow, very charming she decided.

Jake asked, "What can I do for you this morning?"

"Well, I'm becoming a miner and I have one small problem." She lifted the baggy, rolled-up legs of the pants she'd borrowed from Harvey. The pointed toes of tiny, button-up boots in soft calf leather peeked out. "I need work boots."

"I think I can help you." He disappeared in the back and quickly returned with a sturdy pair of boy's brogans.

"May I open a personal account with you, Mr. Sandelowsky?"

"Only if you call me Jake and promise to return for a visit," he said with a rakish grin.

Life in a mining town was as far from genteel as one could get and still be around human beings. Since coming to the American West, the Cornishmen had witnessed riots, lynchings and shootouts. They saw friends go blind from drinking rotgut in the shanty saloons and witnessed death in numerous horrible and strange accidents. They took turns sleeping in shifts, in living quarters no more substantial than tents. They had come to expect to pay outrageous prices for the fine luxuries of life, like a bath or a clean shirt. They had lost fingers to sledgehammers and toes to frostbite. There was little in this harsh life that would give these rugged men pause. But that morning when Baby Doe announced she was taking half the men to begin work on a second shaft, bushy eyebrows flew up. The men stood, rooted to the spot, glancing at their buddies, as she strode off to the other end of the claim. She stopped and called back to them, "Anyone who doesn't want to work will be paid for his last day." She turned and kept walking.

The men hurried to catch up with her. As they walked, the men poked at James, the unofficial leader of the group, and sent meaningful looks at Baby Doe's back. He took his hat off. He put it back on.

"Begging yer pardon, ma'am," James began in his broad Cornish accent. He took his hat off again as he fell in step with the petite woman in overalls. "Meanin' no disrespect to ye, but..." He paused; his ruddy face deepened a shade.

"You don't think I'm going to be bad luck, do you? A woman in the mine?" She gave him a half smile.

James was almost purple now. "No, ma'am, no. Yer charms would prob'ly quiet the wildest tommyknockers. It's just, well, ma'am, have ye ever been down in a mine?"

Baby Doe stopped and calculated the best answer. It would quickly become clear to these veterans of the underground that she didn't have the faintest idea what to do. There was nothing to be gained by lying to them. She turned and faced James. "No, I haven't. I don't know the first thing about mining. But I do know that the Cornish are the best miners in the world."

"Aye, we're born to it. Most of these chaps were digging in a tin mine in England by the time they were twelve years old."

"Then I'll have the finest teachers. Now, how do we begin?"

James blew out a breath. "This is whar ye be wantin' to dig, eh? Well, first the boys need to drill five or six blasting holes. I'll pack those with black powder." James clamped a huge hand, the middle finger missing its tip, on her shoulder. "This be the most important thing ye learn today—when ye 'ear 'fire in the hole,' run for cover. It means I'm blastin."

Baby Doe nodded solemnly and James quickly pulled his hand back as if it had been resting on a stovepipe. He cleared his throat. "Aye, right. So, then we pick the muck from the blast. The quartz will be loaded in the wagon and taken down the gulch to the stamping mill. Those men will grind the quartz fine and then wash it down a sluice. Any gold will sink to the bottom of the sluice box."

"How do we know which direction to dig?"

"That be the real secret to mining," James said. "We should look around for any outcroppin's of quartz. They be easy pickin's and then we could folla' the vein into the mountain. But barrin' that, yer guess is as good as any old forty-niner. I'd be thinking we should dig toward the other shaft. Then we can blast a drift 'tween the two."

"A drift?"

"It's a horizontal tunnel 'tween two downward shafts. It'll help circulate the air."

"And the men can travel between the two shafts."

James shook his head. "A man could get through in a pinch, but a drift should be small. Ye don't want to weaken yer ground support or spend time breakin' rock that can't be mined."

The first swing of the pickaxe fell softly into the dust covering the mountain. Petit Baby Doe pitched her weight to heave the pick again. This time she hit rock. The stone sent a quake up her arms, through her shoulders and into her head. She clenched her teeth against the rattle and swung again and again. By midmorning, she and her crew had cleaned away a face for blasting.

A combination of exhaustion and fascination held her stare as the double-jack team drilled blasting holes into the rock. With unfailing rhythm, two large men traded blows on an iron rod held by a fearless soul who turned the bit a quarter turn with each blow. James stuffed the holes with dynamite and laid the fuse. "Firin'," he bellowed, lighting the cord and trotting away for cover. A dull explosion echoed off the hillsides and dirt fell like rain.

The men grabbed their shovels and began tossing the rubble into wheelbarrows pushed to slag heaps by two boys. Baby tried to get herself off the ground. The muscles across her shoulders seized up in revolt and the back of her arms quivered. She landed back on her fanny.

"Ma'am?" Big James bent down, trying to see under her hat. "Are ya' alright?"

"I'm fine. Just catching my second wind," she said. She held up a hand, and Big James pulled her to her feet.

"Why don't you call it a day, Ma'am?" asked James. "Me and the boys will give you an honest day's work."

"I know you will." She gave James a weak smile. *It's not you I distrust,* she thought. *It's Harvey. I think he'd give up, just quit and head to the saloon if I wasn't here to shame him into working.*

Baby Doe picked up a shovel. Her forearms felt like hundred-pound weights and her hands seemed too weak to grasp the handle. She picked up a pitiful scoop. *This isn't the life I had imagined as Mrs. Doe.* Sweat ran into her eyes making them burn. She considered her choices. Their cabin was too small to take in boarders and she wasn't much of a cook. She could do laundry for the miners or be a shop girl for Jake Sandelowsky. Neither of those ideas would bring in much money, probably just enough to keep Harvey in whiskey. Or they could do what Harvey wanted—go back to Wisconsin and live with the Does. *No, never. Keep shoveling,* she told herself.

Work continued through the fall. As her crew's shaft began to dip into the earth, Baby Doe drove a team of horses, hauling timbers to the mine to shore up the mine walls and hauling quartz down to the stamping mill. In November the days grew short and the weather more turbulent. Gray clouds would build over the mountains and sink down into the gulch, bringing a numbing chill, only to be chased away by howling winds, clear skies and breath-robbing cold. Baby walked to the mine each day, a scarf wrapped over her hat and around her face to keep the wind from scraping her cheeks raw. Inside the tunnel, she and the men would ask Saint Barbara to protect them and then begin work by the flickering light of candles set on the brim of their hats or pushed onto spikes hammered into the walls.

Baby Doe's hands, once pale white petals tipped with shiny pink nails, now looked like a dog had chewed them. Her nails were chipped and broken, fissures appeared at her fingertips, her knuckles were red and chapped. Each evening she tucked her tender hands into the deep pockets of her work pants and walked home with the Cornish miners, singing snatches of songs they taught her. Harvey glumly trudged behind. Back at the cottage, she would gingerly wash with chilly water in the washbasin. At bedtime, she rubbed tallow over her sore hands, wrapped them in flannel, and then pressed them together, as she prayed, "Dear Heavenly Father, watch over Mama and Papa and my brothers and sisters. And please, God, help me find gold tomorrow."

Leaning against timbers at the mine opening, Baby sat trying to catch the occasional snowflakes that were beginning to materialize out of the evening gloom. She had been working ten-hour days, six days a week with the men for almost three months. She was proud that her shaft now reached down sixty feet into the earth. Her crew hadn't reached a vein of whitish quartz laced with a magically golden ribbon yet, but she knew it was down there. Each morning she would whisper a prayer to the spirits in the shaft to lead her to the gold and, someday soon she knew they would. She had seen omens in the mineshaft, rocks shaped like rainbows and the letter G.

"Well, that's it," Harvey handed the last miner his pay for the week.

She pushed her sore, tired body up, "End of a long week."

Harvey sighed, "No, end of the Fourth of July."

Baby Doe stood up straight, "What do you mean?"

"This is it. We're completely out of money, Father's and the bank loan. There's nothing left to pay the miners. I have to shut the mine down."

She felt like a tap had been driven into her chest and the life drained out of her. "No, Harvey. You can't."

"The gold isn't just sitting around, waiting to be picked up. It's very hard work and those Cornishmen aren't worth a tinker's damn. They never worked as hard as they could."

She shook her head at Harvey's arguments. *They worked harder than you ever did.* "Just what are we going to do?" she demanded.

"I have a job working at another mine."

"Fool. How much could you earn digging a hole for someone else, maybe ten dollars a week?"

"This is not my fault," Harvey said. "Father didn't give me enough guidance before he left. When I wrote Father for more money, he suggested I get a job working for his friend at the Bobtail Mine. He said it would be an opportunity for me to observe how a mine is operated." He gave his chapped lips a lick.

She kicked a rock at the mine entrance. "You're wasting your time working for someone else while a bonanza is in there. We've got to keep working this mine." Their future, their fortune lay buried a few feet away, she was sure. How could he not see the potential?

"The Bobtail pays good wages. And if we're careful with the money we can pay off the loan and other debts and maybe reopen the mine in the spring."

Baby Doe's blue eyes narrowed. "What do you mean other debts?"

"The first shaft didn't get timbered quite right, and the

Cornishmen wouldn't work the mine until I hired a guy to come and redo the work."

Timbering the mine had been Harvey's first job after his father left, but he had botched it. She wanted to shake him.

"Like I said, working at the Bobtail Mine will give me a chance to learn more about mining. The men I hired gave me nothing but bad advice." Harvey picked up his shovel, pick and lunch pail. The snow was sticking to the ground now. "Now you can stop acting like a man. In Mother's last letter, she was very upset about your behavior, working with men, digging in dirt, wearing pants and so on. It's quite disgusting."

"If you acted more like a man, then I wouldn't have to." She turned and stomped away into the whirling snow before she gave into the temptation to scratch out his eyes.

CHAPTER 4

HARVEY'S JOB AT THE BOBTAIL MINE didn't last long. He was too busy drinking to make it to work every day. Baby Doe went to see Jake Sandelowsky to explain why she had fallen behind on the payments for the work boots and other necessities that she had been blithely buying on credit for the past weeks. She was hoping a big smile and fluttering eyelashes would smooth things over.

"Our mine is temporarily closed for the winter and my husband is busy exploring other opportunities, so I fear it may be spring before there is cash available to finish paying my account," she explained. It may not have been the complete truth, but it was close.

Jake arched an eyebrow. "I see your husband around town, and all he is exploring are whiskey bottles. I'd be surprised if there was any more cash come spring than there is now. I think we need to set up a little barter."

"I don't have anything of value to trade."

"You underestimate yourself."

What exactly was he saying? Yes, she had hoped to charm him into dismissing her debt, but this seemed a step beyond gracing him with a big smile in order to get her way.

"In truth, you have almost paid for the boots. I think a kiss would suffice to close your account." He took her chin in his hand and gently put his mouth to hers. His tongue languidly touched her Cupid's bow, and slowly their lips pressed together, ever so gently, then more firmly.

Jake pulled away and with a rakish smile said, "I'll mark your account paid in full."

Stunned into an uncharacteristic silence, Baby Doe managed to nod and walk out of the store. Her mind wobbled like a top. That was really too much, how very crass of him, how insolent. Thank goodness, no one was in the store to see. She took a few steps and paused. She was dizzy and breathless. Well, of course she was. She had been holding her breath. Jake's kiss was unlike anything she had ever experienced. She had kissed Harvey twice when they were courting, chaste kisses with lips extended in long puckers, nothing else touching. These days, Harvey rarely kissed her except when they made love, and then he smashed his drunken mouth against her teeth. She had imagined kisses that made the heart beat wildly, that left one giddy, but had thought that was just the fancy of young girls and penny dreadful novelists. She knew now those types of kisses did not exist solely in the imaginations of over-heated young women. Those kisses came from rogues like Jake.

Baby spent the next week ranting to herself about that scoundrel and his brazen behavior. He had *stolen* a kiss from her. But her nights were spent thinking of his lips on hers, reliving the moment and dreaming of something more as Harvey snored beside her.

Only a handful of coffee beans lay at the bottom of the tin, maybe enough for a weak pot. Baby Doe knew they were getting low on other kitchen supplies, like flour and soap, too. There were still beans in the larder, but she had been cutting off smaller and smaller bits from the hunk of fat back. They hadn't eaten fresh meat or vegetables in a long time. Harvey received a few dollars from his mother each month, but that letter wasn't due for several days and his father's letters kept suggesting that Harvey find a steady job. She felt along the back of the shelf for the small tin box that held her household money. It had been moved from its hiding spot behind the sack of sugar, under a bottle of Scott's Cod Liver Oil. She knew it was empty before she opened it. Harvey had drunk it up.

A desperate plan began to form in her mind. She pulled off her apron, grabbed her hat and headed to Sandelowsky's store. She wasn't sure what she would do once she saw that rascal Jake, but they needed food, and she had an account to settle. He could not just steal her kisses; he would have to pay for them. Jake owed her an apology; she would take cornmeal and coffee instead. Taking a deep breath, Baby Doe turned the door handle to pull it open when a wind gust ripped the handle from her hand and flung the door wide, crashing it into the side of the building. Baby decided it was a sign that she should march in and boldly ask for all her needed provisions.

"Good afternoon, Jake, I've come to do my household shopping." She read off several items, more than she actually needed, but she had decided to ask for the moon and see what she got in return. Jake and a stock boy hustled around gathering items. "I would like to put these items on my account," she added.

Jake paused and stared at the floor for a moment, as if gathering his thoughts, then asked the stock boy to deliver a newly arrived twenty-pound bag of peanuts to Belle, the madam at the Shoo Fly Saloon.

"Take a cake of that lavender soap that Belle's girls like, too," Jake told the boy. He turned and smiled at Baby Doe, "He will dawdle around trying to get a peek at the girls. We won't see him for another hour."

Baby Doe tried to steady her wildly beating heart.

"I am glad you came back to the store. I was afraid I had scared you away. I was very forward."

"Yes, you were."

"I am not making excuses, but the men are pretty rough around here and there aren't that many true ladies. It makes a man forget about the delicate nature of the fairer sex."

"You can fill my order as a way of making amends."

That lazy smile crawled across Jake's face. "Very well. I'll pack your basket with the light things, and I'll send the boy over later with the flour and the bacon."

He held the door for her as she left, "I sincerely hope you will continue to patronize my establishment, Baby Doe, but one thing before you go..." That rogue's grin again. "Did you like my kiss?"

She turned and stared straight into his dark eyes. "Yes," she whispered. "But the next one will be on my terms."

Discretion and caution had never been companions of Baby Doe, and she began to make regular shopping trips to Sandelowsky's store. Jake's first delicious kiss led to more kisses and those kisses led to caresses. As soon as they were alone, one strong arm would wrap around her tiny waist and pull her close to his chest while his other hand gently cupped her head, and his thumb traced the outline of her shell-like ear. His lips first gently, then firmly pressed hers. His tongue tickled her bottom lip then, with the lightest of touches, he kissed her jaw, her neck and her collarbone. Baby Doe gasped and leaned into him. With every kiss the passions stirred hotter, with each caress the stolen moments lasted longer until Baby did not want to pull away, could not pull away. On a purloined spring afternoon, when the warm weather made her giddy, she became Jake's lover in the rooms above the store. She had not known that a woman could enjoy lovemaking. Jake kissed and touched her in ways and in places as never before. His gentle strokes of her most secret place caused her to spasm with pleasure. Then he stuffed her basket with groceries before she headed home.

Baby Doe wondered if passers-by would know what she had just done and tried to appear composed as she walked back to the cabin. She hoped her cheeks weren't overly flushed. She held her head high and endeavored to walk at an even pace. Inside her mind pitched and reeled like a schoolyard teeter-totter. *That was wonderful. Now I understand, that must have been ecstasy.* In the next breath, *No, no, no. This is terrible. I am going to burn in hell.* She closed her eyes to say a short prayer for forgiveness, but Jake's dark eyes filled her imagination. His touch still lingered, the pressure of his fingers on her thighs, his lips on hers. Her secret place began to tingle just thinking of their intimacy. She opened her eyes and looked around, but no one noticed her condition. It was clear, she was under a spell. She had read about the power of unbridled passions in romance novels. If God didn't strike her dead, she knew she would return to Jake's bed. She could not resist his lovemaking or the fresh meat that filled her ice box.

For the next few months, Baby Doe waited to be struck down. But she never was, so she continued on a carnival ride of deception, delight and denial. Jake began to act more like her husband than Harvey. He made love to her in stolen moments at the store, and then sent her home with supplies to stock her pantry. When Harvey was working, Jake visited her cabin for a quick rendezvous and to replenish her wood box.

Harvey was in and out of work, in and out of saloons, never questioning where the ham and beans came from. Baby was sure he wasn't ignorant of what was going on; he just seemed not to care enough to gather the energy to do or say anything about it. Baby Doe stopped going to Mass. She could never confess what she was doing with Jake, and perhaps since she hadn't been married by a Catholic priest, it wasn't quite so sinful. In fact, Jake had become her savior when Harvey was out of work and her little tin box was out of money. It seemed that both God and Harvey turned a blind eye when the cupboard was bare.

CHAPTER 5

1878

THE SUN WAS JUST PEEKING OVER the mountains when Harvey left to go to work; however, he did not come home as the sun set at the end of the day. When he was still missing the next morning Baby set out hunting the saloons for him. On the edge of town she looked in the canvas tent saloons where bartenders served something called Taos Lighting from behind bars made of wooden planks set on whiskey barrels. She stopped at the more established drinking and entertainment institutions in Central City proper. Some featured girls who danced with miners for a dime; others were more luxurious affairs that advertised women talented in the forbidden arts. The sun moved lower in the afternoon sky and a chill came down the mountainside. With tired feet and a nose pink from the cold, Baby Doe headed to the one person in Central City that she could count on, Jake Sandelowsky.

"Rumor has it that he got on the afternoon train for Denver yesterday," he told her.

Baby Doe tried to figure out how to make the best of the situation. Harvey hadn't provided for her in months. She didn't like his whiskey breath blowing in her face when he managed to climb on her at night. She wanted to scream at his lazy ways and his endless talk of how his mother would do things. Now it appeared that he had deserted her. What should she do? Return home to Wisconsin broke and abandoned? Never. She wasn't going to give up on this Colorado dream; she knew her future was here in these mountains. She just needed to keep body and soul together until her destiny arrived.

"Rent on the cabin will be due in a few days," she said.

Jake nodded. "I could help with that." He took her hand and looked into her eyes with uncharacteristic concern. "Do you think he is coming back?"

She shook her head. The admission made her sad and angry, but self-pity was not a luxury she could afford.

"Then come live with me."

Jake brought her to live in his little gingerbread trimmed Victorian, and they played house—pretending to be husband and wife. A blizzard of gossip blew through the town in the days following Harvey's run and Baby's immediate move to Jake's. It soon passed. Life in the high country was too hard and kept most people too busy to give the new couple more than a passing curious thought. For the next few months, she hopped out of bed to make a breakfast of eggs and toast and to give Jake a kiss as he headed off to the store. Baby beat his feather tick mattress, swept his floors, starched his shirts and fixed his dinner. She even helped out in the store on busy Saturdays. The more proper matrons of the town treated her with stony disdain. Baby had never been friends with any of them anyway. She was warm and safe and eating well, but if she were completely honest, being a shopkeeper's mate was a dull life and a lot of work.

"I'm so tired I could fall asleep on my feet," Baby said through a yawn as she cleaned up the supper dishes.

"It's not even nine o'clock," Jake said. "I'm going to round up a card game."

Jake hadn't given up his bachelor ways when Baby moved in, making the rounds at the gaming houses, playing cards and such into the night which piqued her. She wasn't jealous precisely, but she could not afford to lose another man. She needed to know whom he was playing with and what games were being played.

"Tomorrow night, I want to go with you when you go play cards."

"You can't come with me to a saloon."

"Why not? Do you think it might tarnish my reputation?" Her laugh was mirthless. "That train has left the station. I'm bored, and I get lonely when you're out. I've got no reputation to lose. I might as well have some fun."

The next night, after they had eaten a bowl of soup and a skillet of cornbread, Baby Doe got her coat, hat and muff and announced, "I'm ready to go out."

Jake hesitated. "All right," he said slowly. "I guess I could take you to the Shoo Fly. It's a pretty nice place. Belle runs a tight ship. It's clean, and there's rarely any trouble. You can visit with the girls. They are the nicest ladies in Central City, Baby. They aren't always treated very nicely by the local matrons either; so I'm sure they'll be very sociable to you."

As they walked to the saloon, Baby thought about women who received money to let men have their way. Everyone made it sound like it was the most terrible thing, but most women had to do it anyway and didn't get paid a nickel. Baby thought if you could pick men like Jake, handsome, gentlemanly, clean and talented in those things, it wouldn't be that bad.

They stopped in front of a big brick building.

"There's a side door over here." Jake pointed.

"No point in sneaking in. By morning, everyone in town will know I was here."

The Shoo Fly housed various entertainments. A broad set of stairs led from the street to the main entrance on the second floor. At the top of the stairs, a covered porch spread out along the front of the building, holding a porch swing and several chairs covered in small snowdrifts. Mud and tobacco juice surrounded the spittoon and boot scraper guarding at the door. Guests were received in the front parlor, decorated to look like a fine Victorian home. Tatted doilies and ceramic knickknacks topped every surface and heavy velvet drapes covered the windows. The rooms beyond held a dimly lit bar, dance floor and stage. Tucked quietly downstairs were two large gambling rooms and four small bedrooms.

Three young women, lounging in the parlor, stopped their amusements when Jake and Baby Doe walked in, shaking off the December cold. In the lamplight, further veiled with smoke and dust, the women were as pretty as dolls. Upon a closer look, Baby noted that these dolls had seen some rough play. She was secretly relieved to know that she was the most beautiful woman in the room; she wouldn't lose Jake to one of these competitors.

"Hello, Jake Darlin'," drawled a petite, raven-haired girl. Her lips were painted a deep crimson and her dress was a yellow cotton, too thin for the winter weather. Her pale face framed startling blue eyes with a sprinkle of freckles across her tiny nose. A front tooth had a small chip. Baby Doe was stunned; this girl couldn't be over sixteen, but it seemed she had been working at the saloon for a while.

"Hello, Lilly. I'd like to introduce you to a friend of mine," Jake said. He took off his hat and gloves.

Baby drew up her height, as little as it was, and held her breath. An unusual feeling of shyness blushed her cheeks. It was one thing to be shunned by the few old matrons in town, but if these girls of easy virtue snubbed her, she was unlikely to find a friend anywhere.

"Everybody in town knows Baby Doe." Lilly's Southern accent warmed her words. "Pleased to meet you," she said with a smile that Baby could see was genuine.

"Don't leave them standing in the doorway, Lilly. Show them in." Into the center of the parlor strode Belle. She had been a beauty in her day, but that was quite a few days ago. White face powder had settled into the wrinkles around Belle's eyes and jowls. She was round as a barrel; the fine green satin of her gown strained to reach around her middle and her ample bosom spilled over the top of the low neckline. Her plump hand toyed with the emerald pendant resting on the soft crevice of her chest. Matching earbobs dangled below Belle's dry peroxide blonde hair. In the mountains, all rare commodities were wildly overpriced, women included. The flashy-dressed madam had succeeded in the business of pleasure.

"Belle, you look lovely as always," Jake said. A tall, thin Negro woman had appeared silently behind them. She helped Baby shed her coat, and then held out her hand to take her scarf and muff. "Hello, Ester," Jake said as he handed over his things.

"Belle, Baby has been having some tough times here in Central City," Jake began.

"Are you looking for work, dear? With those looks, you could do real fine in this business. I'd be glad to take you on here. Twenty-five dollars a poke; you keep ten."

Baby Doe was shocked by Belle's frankness, but could see no hint of malice in the madam's face. The woman was offering a simple business proposition.

"No," Jake answered for her. "I'm seeing that Baby is taken care of these days. We just thought it might be good for her to get out. Perhaps she could watch tonight's stage act or have a little visit with the girls while I play Faro," Jake said.

Belle let out a laugh. "So you brought her to a parlor house?" Belle shook her head and patted Jake's arm. "Ah, I wouldn't let her out of my sight either if I was you. I just don't know how you're going to concentrate on your cards and keep the fellas away from her at the same time." She turned with a great rustling of skirts and petticoats. "Make yourselves at home. I need to speak with tonight's act. He's a ventriloquist. Makes me talk to his doll." She belted out another laugh and swept into the bar, her dress swishing side to side like an enormous bell.

Jake gave Baby a nod and a grin and headed to the gaming tables downstairs.

Little Lilly pulled Baby to the chaise. "Come sit with me and meet the other girls. That's Meg, over there playing solitaire and forgetting her manners."

A redhead paused with a card in mid-air. A blue robe draped loosely around her shoulders revealing that she wore nothing but a corset and bloomers beneath. She regarded Baby from the corner of amber eyes for a moment. "I can't chat now, I'm in the middle of a game."

I know those cat eyes. I've seen her in Jake's store, and he couldn't offer her enough help. Tweaked, Baby replied, "Are you winning?"

Meg looked at Baby head on. If she was looking for signs of argument, Baby Doe didn't give her one, just a pleasantly bland smile. "Yes," Meg said in an Eastern accent dressed in sarcasm.

Lilly smothered a giggle with her hand and introduced the woman on the settee looking through a stereoscope. "This is Caroline."

Caroline was the plainest of the three soiled doves. She looked like someone's sister, with a tired face, dark brown eyes and hair the color of a mouse. Freckles were sprinkled on a crooked nose that must have been broken in the past. A cameo brooch held together a bodice that was missing buttons.

"Nice to finally meet you, Baby Doe." Caroline's voice was quiet as a lullaby. "I've seen you around town. I've often thought about you; we're in the same boat. My husband was a miner, who ran off and left me with a pile of debts and winter coming on. I was in dire straits when Belle took me on here."

Baby couldn't believe she would have anything in common with this plain-faced prostitute. "Oh no, no, my situation's not like that."

Meg shot a knowing look at Lilly, "I told you she'd be full of airs."

"Meg," Lilly scolded.

Meg slapped down a card. "If you ask me, she's better off without that momma's boy."

Baby Doe's mouth fell open. "You know Harvey?" She knew he spent a lot of time at saloons, but she had never imagined him desiring any woman but her.

"We know most everyone in town," Caroline added in her soothing way. "Mr. Doe just came in to have a drink occasionally."

Caroline was obviously trying to ease Baby's mind regarding this revelation, but Baby couldn't find an ounce of care about it in her. "It's all right. I'm really not upset; surprised, I suppose, but not upset."

Caroline gave her a sad smile and held out the stereoscope. "Would you like a look? Meg likes to collect views of famous cities. This is a picture of Paris."

Baby held the viewer to her eyes and the double image became one. "I'm going to travel there someday. I'm going to visit the entire European continent."

"Like a high-born lady making her grand tour, eh?" Meg asked.

"Yes." Defiance lowered Baby's voice to a growl.

The two beauties stared at each other in a silent battle of wills, when the door flung open and in strode a bear of a man. A buffalo-hide coat wrapped around his wide girth and his head and face were covered with a bramble of black hair and whiskers. His smell of old grease and sweat was so bad Baby thought he could wilt flowers.

"Come on in and shut the door, Tiny," Caroline said. "It's a cold night out there."

"Yes ma'am, it is," Tiny said. "I've come looking for something to warm me." He slapped his belly and gave it a rub as he looked around the parlor. He pointed a dirty finger at Baby Doe. "You're new."

A shiver of disgust ran down Baby's back.

"Oh no, Baby Doe isn't working; she's just visiting," Caroline quickly intervened.

"Well then, Little Lilly will do just fine," Tiny said with a leer.

"You need some whiskey. You know, to get warm from the inside out," Caroline said. "Meg, could you get a bottle from the bar?"

Meg dropped her cards and hustled to the bar just as Ester slid silently into the room. Tiny shrugged off his coat and tossed it at her. Ester held his coat at arm's length and walked, not toward the armoire that held Jake's and Baby's wraps, but to a back porch. Tiny walked over to Lilly as she rose from the chaise. His red tongue poked out of the black tangle of whiskers and licked his lips. Baby held her breath to keep from gagging at his stench. *How can Lilly possibly lie with this beast? Let him crawl on top of her? I could never let him touch me.*

"We haven't seen you around here lately, Tiny. You been prospecting up in the hills?" asked Lilly. Her head didn't reach the big man's shoulder.

"Can't tell ya," replied Tiny. "Don't want anybody sniffin' around my digs."

Lilly just smiled. "Town isn't the same without you."

Meg rushed back into the parlor with a bottle of whiskey and a shot glass, pouring as she walked. "Here you go, Tiny. Get this one down and let me pour you another."

"Tiny," Belle called as she swished into the room. "Glad to see you're back from the mountains. Have the girls gotten you a drink?"

"Yes ma'am." The man gulped two more glasses in quick succession.

"Ester is warming water. Lilly will bathe you, no charge," said Belle.

"Let's go," he ordered Lilly. "Evening to you, Miz Belle." He nodded to the madam with what Baby suspected were his best manners. Lilly picked up the bottle and led the hairy man downstairs.

The four women sat silently until they could no longer hear the clomping of his boots.

"How can she do that with him?" Baby cried. "He looks and smells like a wild animal. I'd rather die than lie with him."

"Sometimes those are the choices," Caroline said. A self-conscious hand slid over her rough nose.

Meg furiously fanned at the air with her scented hankie. "You'd be surprised what you'd do when you get hungry enough."

"You know, Baby Doe, there are some people who would think that the way Jake takes care of you puts you on the same ladder as these girls. A different rung maybe, but the same ladder," Belle said.

Baby's face flushed and her chin jumped out.

Belle wiggled a plump finger. "Now don't get your Irish up, little girl. We won't judge you here, but we expect you not to judge us. These girls know that out here a woman has to do whatever it takes to get along. A woman alone can mind her manners, act like a lady, conduct herself with the highest decorum and, in the end, she will politely starve to death. Or," Belle paused and spread herself where Lilly had been sitting, "A woman can do what needs to be done, even if it's not according to Hoyle, kinda like you did when you were digging your mine." Belle nodded at Baby Doe.

"I'm not ashamed of that. I don't want to do that again, but I will if I have to," Baby said.

"There are easier ways to make money, dear." Belle smiled and gave her hand a pat. "Really it is just a matter of figuring out what a man needs and how can you get him to pay for it. Does he need cooking or clean laundry? Or does he need female companionship? Then the choices become yours: do you make a man pay cash for those services or marry you for them. Out here men outnumber women, which is advantageous no matter which plan you choose. Now, I have paying customers I need to attend to." The big blonde heaved herself up and started toward the bar. She turned and faced Baby once again. "There is something you need to understand if you are going to live in Colorado by yourself, Baby Doe. The laws of survival always trump the rules of etiquette."

Baby sat silently, reflecting on the lessons the madam had dispensed when Caroline leaned over and whispered, "Don't worry about Lilly. Tiny usually passes out after a warm bath and four drinks, and we know the real reason for his nickname."

CHAPTER 6

1878

AS FALL BECAME WINTER, Baby Doe and Jake fell into a routine of working together in his store during the day and then spending the evenings at the Shoo Fly Saloon. Some nights she would watch Jake as he played cards in the smoky tables back by the bar. Other times she would watch the new stage act which most often involved young women with little talent wearing little clothes.

Baby's favorite times were the nights when a crowd of business-men, investors and bankers from Denver or back East came to sample the variety of entertainments at the Shoo Fly. Unlike the miners, trappers or cowboys who wanted to quickly get drunk and screw, these men could spend the entire night taking their amusements. They asked the girls to dance and conversed with them like courtesans. Sometimes Meg would sing love songs. On these busy nights, Baby would act as hostess, pouring drinks and making small talk with the men waiting their turn with the girls. Baby Doe was talented in these arts, and enjoyed herself at these parties. Belle let her keep any tips she made, but as the night wore on, she would leave the dirty business to the working girls. Occasionally, Belle would raise an eyebrow and nod toward a gentleman, a silent inquiry if Baby wanted to service a customer. Baby could never bring herself to accept the employment. It wasn't the act she objected to, but the quality of the men. The thought of pawing drunks, sweating and breathing on her made her nauseated. And all for so very little; a good roll and a high-priced girl would earn ten dollars, but there wasn't much left after she paid Belle for room, board and clothing.

She suspected that if Jake thought she was servicing other men, he would drop her like a hot rock. No, the wiser move was to be Jake's girl right now. He kept her fed and clothed. He was clean and more pleasing to look at than most men who frequented the Shoo Fly. However, he was, in the end, just a merchant. The more thought she gave to her plans for the future, the less sure she became about Jake's place in it. Her mother, a shopkeeper's wife herself, had told her time and again, she could do better. Jake was paying the bills right now, but she had bigger ambitions than being his shopgirl.

Baby Doe tore January's page from the calendar that hung in the backroom of Jake's store. February lay clean before her. The growing crescents leading to the black circle of a new moon caught her eye. Her monthly courses should have started—started and ended. She looked at January in her hand. When was that course? She couldn't remember having it. She couldn't recall using any of her feminine things since she moved in with Jake four months ago, since before Harvey left. "Oh, my God," she prayed. "Oh, my God," she swore. "Oh, Mary, Mother of God, please no." But she knew it was so. It explained her tiredness, her hunger, and her contrary moods.

"Baby, can you get some vinegar and water and clean the display counter?" Jake said, sticking his head in the backroom door. "What's wrong? You have a funny look on your face."

"Nothing's wrong," she lied. She looked at a sketching of roses on the calendar. "I was just longing for spring flowers."

He smiled. "Winter has a long way to go yet," he said and headed back into the store.

Jake had headed straight for the card tables when they arrived at the Shoo Fly that night. Little Lilly and Meg were in the bar hustling drinks, while Caroline had a regular downstairs. Baby sat alone in the front parlor, her mind and stomach spinning and bouncing like buggy wheels. What would she do with a baby?

"Oh Lord," Belle moaned as she plopped her broad bottom on the horsehair sofa. "Mind if I rest here with you for a spell?" Baby simply nodded. "Quiet night," Belle said to herself as much as to Baby. "Quiet here, quiet everywhere. I walked down to the Lady Luck and they only had a handful of drunks and one table of card players. Ain't that pitiful?"

Baby simply nodded again, but Belle continued to stare at her, as if expecting more conversation so Baby finally said, "Those bankers in here last week said that the gold in Central City is drying up and we are on our way to a bust. They said silver had been found in a new town called Leadville. It is the new place to be."

"Hmm, maybe. Winter's always a little harder. Things always pick up in the spring. But that's not what's making you blue, now, is it?"

Baby admired the way Belle seemed to handle every situation. Jake joked that Belle could cut cards, stop a catfight and count her money all at the same time. Baby knew she had no one better with whom to share her secret. "I'm with child."

"You know, my girls can show you how to keep that from happening. We'll make you a sponge on a string or order you a Dutch cap for next time," Belle said. "Have you told Jake?" Baby shook her head no. "Oh," Belle said as if Baby had said more. Belle reached to the end table and rang the bell for Ester.

Silent as always, the black woman slipped into the room.

"I think Baby Doe needs a cup of your special herb tea, Ester," Belle said.

Baby sat there dumbly as Ester's large hands reached out and felt her belly then cupped and squeezed her tender, swelling breasts.

"When was your last flow?" the Black woman asked.

"I'm not sure, at least four months ago," she stammered.

Ester straightened up. "It's too late for my herbs to help. I could give her a wash of arsenic and mercury, but it can cause problems if she wants to be a mother later down the road."

"Perhaps she could go see Doc Towson," Belle suggested. Baby Doe began to understand what the women were talking about.

"He is a butcher," Ester glowered. "He fills girls with whiskey and sticks a dirty hook in them. He'll run away and let a girl bleed to death."

Belle shook her blonde head. "Then maybe it's best if she has the baby."

Visions of blood and dead babies filled Baby with horror. Vomit pushed up her throat and out onto the rug at her feet.

CHAPTER 7

1879

BABY DOE SAT DOWN AND WROTE a short letter to her parents. She hoped everyone was well and, by the way, she was with child. She was feeling better now, just tired. The baby would be born in early July. She wrote a second letter to Colonel Doe announcing that he would soon be a grandfather and, by the way, Harvey was missing; could he send money to help her prepare and care for the new baby? Although secretly Baby Doe wasn't sure who the father might be, she was sure Harvey's father would not want any grandchild of his to go without.

She suspected Harvey had gone home to let his mother care for him. She could only imagine the scene her letter must have caused when it arrived in Oshkosh. Baby didn't think Harvey's father would drag him all the way back to Central City, yet a month after she had written, the two men were at the door of Jake's little house. As usual, the Colonel took charge.

"You look well," he kissed her cheek. "Harvey asked me to come back to Colorado with him and help get you all re-established." Baby Doe tried not to roll her eyes. "We stopped by Mrs. Porter's on the way here. She has a clean, large room for let that we can have this afternoon. We paid for it through the summer so you don't have to worry a wit. Harvey, help your wife get her things together. I'm sure she doesn't want to impose on Mr. Sandelowsky any more than she already has."

There was little choice in the matter. She was Harvey's wife; he owned her. She was his chattel in the eyes of God and the law. She could think of nothing to do but obey as she had sworn to do. She loaded dresses, shoes and hats into her trunk as Harvey and a hired man loaded her hope chest and a few home goods into a wagon. The Colonel took the opportunity to catch her alone.

"I still have friends in this town, and I have heard all the rumors. I know that Harvey wasn't a very good provider and maybe you had to," he paused, "lean on others. This stops now. Harvey is here, and I got him a job working in a mine. I am moving back to Colorado. Mother Doe will be coming this summer. We will provide for you and this child."

"Mother Doe is moving to Central City?" *Oh good grief, no. Harvey will never cut the apron strings now.*

"Well, the mines around Central seemed to have played out. So I am going to spend the spring looking at other business opportunities, maybe in Idaho Springs," the Colonel replied.

"I hear of a silver strike in Leadville."

"Leadville is booming, but it is wild. There is not much law there.

The saloons never close. The drinking and carousing go on all night. Completely unsuitable for Mother Doe."

All the more reason to move to Leadville, she thought.

Spring came screaming down the mountain with the Chinook winds, powerful enough to blow down rickety wood buildings and send canvas tents sailing, like giant white birds, for the Kansas border. Old timers said the Chinooks were the whispers of the devil, the breath warm enough to melt a three-foot snowdrift in a day. The ceaseless blowing and tugging and pushing caused even pleasant people to fuss and animals to nip at their owners. Morning would dawn crisp and clear. By afternoon the winds would shift directions and blow up the mountain, bringing feet of snow. The next day would be lovely and warm, as though a storm had never tracked across these skies. The snow would begin to melt, and Baby would believe spring was on its way. A few days later, the winds would kick up and the snow would fall knee deep again. Baby Doe had never seen such volatile weather.

Baby Doe's emotions were equally unpredictable. Some days she stormed at the unfairness of it all. Everyone was leaving Central City for richer ground elsewhere and she was stuck in the boarding house, snow falling outside and her with a big old belly and Harvey Milquetoast. Some days were sunnier, dreaming of a baby to love and be loved by, imagining a gurgling cherub with blue eyes and curls. Baby Doe refused to acknowledge the slight chill of fear skirting round the edges of her day dreams, for she had no idea if those curls would be the color of Harvey's blond or Jake's raven hair.

A small cramp grabbed her belly, waking Baby from sleep. She lay still. Harvey snored softly beside her in the gray predawn light. *It's nothing,* she thought, and tried to roll to the other side to get comfortable. There was no comfort to be found. Her back ached in every position, the room was too hot and her belly stuck out like a ribbon-winning pumpkin at the state fair. Her belly gripped again. She had a sudden desire to rock in the rocking chair Mrs. Porter had put in the room. She waddled over and began to rock, at first slowly then she rode the chair like she was making a get away from a bank robbery. Harvey snorted and rolled over. The sky began to lighten in the east and rays shined into the little room and woke Harvey.

"What are you doing up?" he asked as Baby hauled herself out of the chair.

"It's time," she answered. Another contraction rippled through her and stole her breath. She didn't understand why, but she thought it would feel better if she climbed onto the bed on her hands and knees.

"What are you doing? Lay down. You look like a dog, panting on all fours like that."

"Go get help," she growled.

The light dawned in Harvey's eyes. He hopped up, pulled on pants and boots and hurried downstairs, shouting, "Mrs. Porter, my wife is having her baby. Come help. Come help."

The round little woman bustled out of the kitchen. "Oh my, Mr. Doe, I don't know much about children. I've never had a baby. Doesn't she have a midwife?"

Harvey was out the door and down the street before he realized he couldn't remember the name of the woman Baby wanted, and he didn't know any midwives. He stood helpless in the street for a moment before he turned and ran toward the only man left in Central City that he knew, shouting, "Jake, the baby is coming."

Mrs. Porter wasn't pleased to see Harvey and Jake arrive with Ester, the taciturn Negress maid from the Shoo Fly Saloon. A disreputable air followed the Does and their womanizing friend. Now they were bringing the Black help from a brothel. Since Central City's mines were petering out and people were busting and leaving, Mrs. Porter had taken in the Does and their father's money. Beggars couldn't be choosers.

"No men in the ladies' rooms," she declared.

"But it's my room." Harvey was confused.

"Let's stay here in the parlor. Let the women take care of this business," said Jake, gently moving Harvey to a settee. Together the two men waited as morning turned to afternoon, which turned to evening.

Ester walked slowly down the stairs, solemn as usual, carrying a silent bundle of blankets. Jake and Harvey jumped to their feet.

"Little boy, stillborn." She handed the bundle to Jake. "Take him to the undertaker on Third Street." She turned and went quietly back upstairs to the mother.

Harvey collapsed into the settee and fought back tears. Jake carried the tiny baby outside and carefully pulled back the blanket to reveal a small head cover with jet-black hair just like his.

A few weeks after they buried the baby, Harvey stopped going to work. His father arranged for him to meet another foreman, but Harvey didn't show up. Word got out that Doe was not dependable, and there were plenty of other out-of-work miners to choose from. He and Baby spent their mornings sitting in gloomy silence in Mrs. Porter's drawing room. After lunch Harvey would make an excuse and wander out. Baby was always relieved to see him go.

"Where are you going?" Baby Doe asked one August afternoon as Harvey pulled on his hat and headed out of the boarding house. He didn't answer. It didn't matter; she was sure he was going to a saloon. She just didn't care what Harvey did any more. *Lord, why are we going down this path again?* She asked God, *I just want to live my life, a life without Harvey holding me back. I want a good life. How do I do that? Show me a sign. How do I get off this path?* God was silent.

Baby Doe moved to the window and watched Harvey wander down the street. It was a crisp day. The dry mountain air was so clear the world seemed to be in sharp focus. The humidity back in Wisconsin had softened the air, giving life a slight blur. Or maybe it was just her memories that were blurred. She could see everything so clearly here in the mountains. She could count the pine needles on every branch outside the window. She could see for miles in the distance and the thought struck her she could see all the way to Leadville. This was the omen. She had asked God for a clear sign about her future, and now it was crystal clear. There was no point in living with Harvey. They didn't love each other anymore. Her dreams had never been his dreams. She needed to leave him. *I need to get to Leadville, that's where I can make a life.* There was nothing except Harvey holding her here she reasoned. Perhaps God was displeased with her marriage outside the Catholic Church; perhaps the baby's death was a blessing. A sliver of guilt ran through Baby like an icy knife. *Lord, I didn't mean that about the baby. Please, show me how to get away from Harvey and on the road to Leadville.*

On the dusty street below, Harvey paused, looked around, and then ducked into a building.

A policeman with a new blue uniform walked slowly around the corner. Baby Doe felt as though he were looking at her, through the window and into her soul. An idea started to form and with each of his long, slow strides she developed another step in her plan. He stopped, as if waiting for her, under the sign for Eureka Street. What she was thinking was not within accepted conventions. There was no going back if she did this. When her father's store had burned down, he told the family they had to try again; she needed to try again, to start her life over. If she didn't act now, she would rot here forever. She flew down the stairs and out into the street without even stopping to get a hat or wrap.

"Officer, officer! I need your help." She pulled him toward the building Harvey had entered. "My husband is inside Maddie Preston's bawdy house with the intention to commit adultery."

A few months later, with the policeman's statement, Baby Doe was granted a divorce.

CHAPTER 8

End of February 1935

THE WIND BLEW HARD during the night, stirring up the ghosts that lived near the mine. Baby Doe heard them. Some beckoned her to join them; some howled of injustices and loss; others relived the moment of their death and, in anguish, begged for help. The dawn was lavender in the east before she had finally slept. Now with the sun high in the sky she wasn't sure she had the strength to pull some rock out of the mine. She decided to run the electric pump to clear the water from the flooded deeper shafts.

That blackheart Merle Greene had brought the new pump and hooked up the electricity when he announced to Baby Doe that he had bought the mine for back taxes at an auction on the courthouse steps. He told her she had to leave the property. He said he planned to reopen the mine in the spring as soon as weather permitted. Come spring he could just try and throw her off her property.

She walked to the mine's head frame, clumping along in the oversized men's work boots she had bought at the nuns' charity shop. She had stuffed newspapers in the toes for warmth and to keep them from falling off her feet. She wasn't sure how to start the pump and was looking for a switch of some kind when she heard a burro bray.

Claim jumpers, she thought. She ran to the cabin, boots flapping, to get her gun, wishing for the second day in a row, that she knew how to fire it and that she hadn't sewed the buckshot into the hem of her skirt to keep it from blowing in the wind. She grabbed the gun, but remained hidden in the cabin. She peeked out the window and realized it was the young man from the day before. He was leading a short-legged burro carrying large bundles on each side. *What was his name?* She couldn't remember, but she did know he had been sent by the devil himself. She opened the door about an inch and stuck the rifle barrel out.

"Get out of here!" she shouted. "And tell Eugene Hawthorne he can take the next train straight to Hades."

The young man paused then bent over with his hands on his knees to catch his breath. "Please don't shoot me, Mrs. Tabor. I just want to show you something." He proceeded cautiously to the mine head frame and began to unpack the little animal.

Wesley, that was his name. "I am not buying anything you're selling, so just pack that animal back up and get on out of here," she shouted from the door. She shut it as hard as she could. The slam made Wesley jump, but he kept right on opening bundles and setting out equipment. Baby Doe lifted a curtain corner and watched as he turned an old crate on its side to make a table just inside the mouth of the mine and placed a box of some kind on top. He ran a wire to the electrical box and fiddled around. It looked like he had tacked a bed sheet to a framing timber inside the mine.

What is he up to?

Finally, he took two silver discs from a saddlebag. He attached one to the box and fished film through the machine. He bent over the machine and, a moment later, it shuttered to life and gray images began to dance on the sheet hanging from the mine rafter.

Baby Doe stepped out of the cabin and hollered to him, "You can't show movies here. Mines are dangerous places. I can't have children running in and out of the Matchless."

Wesley just smiled and waved to her to come closer.

The pictures jerked as the sheet ruffled in the wind; it was hard to figure out what she was seeing but then her beloved mountains came into focus and made her stop. The film cut to a street scene. It was clearly set in the past. The streets were not paved and men drove buggies, not cars; ladies dresses were pinched at the waist. She picked up a fist-sized rock and placed it on the bottom corner of the sheet to hold it taut. "What is this?" she asked, staring at the makeshift screen.

"It's *Silver Dollar*, the movie they made about your life."

Baby Doe had been invited to the movie's premier, but she had not attended. She was sure the dramatization would portray her as a woman of low morals, a home wrecker or worse. She wanted the past to remain as she remembered it now with more good times than bad and her love for Horace untainted by scandal. Yet, as the pictures paraded before her, she could not look away.

They watched in silence for a few moments, the clattering of the projector the only sound. "The theater owner down in Leadville let me rent his old projector, but it doesn't play sound and he wouldn't give me the sound discs and player. He said they were too fragile to take up the mountain on a mule."

"Burro," Baby Doe corrected, without looking away. "Who is that?" she asked as a tall older woman with a deep frown entered the scene.

"Augusta, Tabor's first wife. Looks like she is eating a sour pickle during the whole movie."

"Well, they got that right," Baby Doe said with a soft laugh. "Is that supposed to be Horace? It looks nothing like him."

"Yes, that's Edward G. Robinson playing him. There are a few things that got changed in the movie. I personally think your real life was more interesting. That's why I want to write your true story." They watched the two characters hold a silent conversation.

On the bed sheet screen, two miners entered a general store. "That is supposed to be Hook and Meyer," Wesley narrated.

"They are too clean and well fed to be prospectors," Baby Doe said. Back when she was still in Central City, she had first read newspaper articles about the two Germans who used Horace's grubstake to start one of the most fabulous fortunes in America. She had heard Horace tell the tale many times to hangers-on gathered at the elegant mahogany bar of his Windsor Hotel. She knew the story by heart.

Baby Doe leaned forward as a petite light-haired young woman strode across the screen. The actress looked over her shoulder and pursed her painted lips into a small bow.

"That's you. Or supposed to be you," Wesley said. "Her name is Bebe Daniels. She is very beautiful."

Baby Doe arched an eyebrow at Wesley, but did not comment.

The tail of film thwacked through the projector as the first reel ended, startling her. Wesley carefully placed it in the silver container and threaded the second reel through the machine.

"I am sorry for the lack of sound."

"It doesn't matter. I know what was said. I was there."

CHAPTER

9

1877

IN THE SUMMER OF 1877, a geologist named Alvinus Wood traveled to a hard-luck gold mining camp to help a friend solve a problem at his sluicing operation. Colorado's prospectors had long cursed a heavy black sand which settled with the gold at the bottom of sluice boxes, damming the flow of water meant to wash clean the precious metal. "What is this?" Alvinus asked. "A pain in my arse," his friend replied. "Get rid of it and help me boost my gold take." Alvinus gathered samples and performed an assay. When the results were clear, Alvinus rushed to his friend, pulled him from earshot of the men working the sluice and whispered the most wonderful secret. The black sand was lead carbonate. His friend did not understand. "It means," Alvinus told him, "the sand you have been throwing away can be smelted into silver. We are going to be rich."

The two men tried to keep their discovery under wraps, but the workers manning the sluice questioned why the black sand was loaded onto wagons and taken to the smelt works. Word got out that a fortune lay waiting to be picked off the ground and the rush was on.

The population of the mining camp tripled in the few weeks that remained that summer. A new town sprang up overnight and was christened Leadville in honor of the metal that held such promise. Deep winter snows then covered the high mountain roads to the Shangri-La. Nearly twenty-five thousand fortune hunters, miner, gamblers, conmen, whores, rubes and merchants waited for the winter to pass so that they too could make their way to the next bonanza.

The two prospectors had not fared well over the winter. Their burro had died. They were thin and dirty; whiskers grew like wild scrub brush around their gaunt faces. Their clothes were filthy and threadbare. George Hook's coat might once have been a cavalry blue, traded for years ago, its brass buttons lost. Twine woven through the buttonholes held the coat shut against the wind. August Meyer's feet had worn holes in his socks and were now making their way through his boots. The men's hair stuck up in unruly, greasy clumps when they removed their battered hats and entered Tabor's store. A mangy dog with every rib showing wobbled in with them.

Merchandise was stacked to the ceiling against all four walls and the aroma of wood smoke, tobacco and coffee beans welcomed patrons. The Tabors sold Leadville miners everything they could need: hams, handkerchiefs, cheeses, chaw, molasses, mouse traps, tea, tin cups, bullets, blankets, shovels and shoes. Barrels filled with apples, beans and dried fruit filled the center of the room along with a potbelly stove. A counter ran along the back of the room. One end, sectioned off with wire, displayed a sign: POST OFFICE. A door at the opposite end of the counter led to the Tabor family's living quarters.

"Good afternoon, gentlemen. What can I do ya for?" Horace Tabor boomed across the small room where he had been holding court with his cronies, sitting around the stove swapping stories of stupid tenderfoots. Horace was a tall man with a slight slump. His wrist bones hung out of his shirtsleeves and his ham-sized hands were always slapping people on the back. His brown hair was starting pretty far back after forty-seven years, but he had a full moustache that hung to his jaw and danced when he got going on a story. The skin around his eyes and cheeks hung in loops and pleats. Horace loved to tell tales and would lead the laughter with a loud guffawing. His gregarious ways had gotten him elected mayor of Leadville.

"Sir, are you the proprietor of this store?" Meyer's polite speech spoke of a fine, long-ago education.

"Yup," Horace nodded. "Best in town."

Horace's wife Augusta was actually the business mind and the driving force behind the merchandising business. She kept the books, ordered supplies, paid bills, sorted the mail, baked fresh bread and took in laundry. In her spare time, she cooked for her family and stray miners, tended a vegetable garden, sewed their clothes, and taught her son to read, write and do sums. Horace liked to keep his time freed up to do a little prospecting or politicking.

"It looks like you boys are a little down on your luck," Horace said. "Why, that dog you got there is so skinny that it has to lean against a rock to bark." His cronies haw-hawed.

"Sir, we own a claim on Fryer Hill. We're sure there is a vein of silver there."

"Oh, boys," Horace said, "If I had a dollar for every time a fella came in here with a sure thing, why I could vacation in a fancy Denver hotel for a month." The cronies chuckled and nodded. He didn't want to be unkind, but he'd heard it all before. Besides, Augusta would skin him alive if she found out he was handing out credit to strangers.

Hook spoke up; his accent was German. "We are offering you a third of any profits if you would grubstake us. We just need some equipment to get started."

Horace looked into their eyes. In spite of, or maybe because of, not having had a decent meal in months, the miners' eyes gleamed in their hollow sockets. Horace had seen that look many times in his twenty years in the Colorado gold fields. It was ambition, eagerness, naiveté, hope. He, too, was a dreamer, who had chased elusive treasures from Maine to Kansas to Pikes Peak. He had never found much gold though; Augusta's cooking and washing for the other miners in camp had been their main source of income. Horace reluctantly shook his head no.

Hook stepped forward. "When I was a boy in Germany, I learned a proverb, 'A lode will cut rich and fat, when it wears an iron hat.'" He leaned across the counter close to Horace's ear. "Sir, we have seen the iron hat. The lode is there."

Horace had seen men become millionaires overnight; he had heard many stories. Things like that happened in Colorado all the time. Leadville was booming. There was silver in these hills and men were making new strikes every day. A prospector just needed a sign, something to nudge him in the right direction. Horace had not heard any iron hat tales, but it sounded reasonable. If ever there was a time and a place to get lucky, it was here and now. Augusta wouldn't like it; of course, she didn't like much. Sometimes a man just had to take a chance, had to place a bet.

"Gentlemen, I feel lucky. You have a deal." Horace helped them get shovels, picks, a pan, an eight-pound driving hammer, black powder, rope, some coffee and flour. He threw in a little hardtack and whiskey for which they were very grateful and then hustled them out the door before Augusta got back.

Augusta passed the men as they went on their way. She strode into the store calling, "Horace." She pointed a scowl at the cluster of men gathered around a checkerboard that lay atop a pickle barrel and the men hushed like scolded school children.

No one wanted to be on the receiving end of Augusta's sharp New England tongue. Every man in Leadville had already heard Augusta's lectures on idle hands being the devil's workshop, a penny saved was a penny earned, and the basic tenets of Puritanism. However, she was the only respectable woman in the area, so the men treated her with a mix of fear and deference usually reserved for religious figures. Augusta had been the only white woman when she arrived in the territory a decade ago, and she had gotten right down to work. She directed miners to build her a seven by nine foot cabin, which became a general store. She added a post office and got Horace named postmaster. She bought a scale to weigh the miners' findings and a safe to keep it secure. Horace may have been elected mayor of Leadville, but Leadville grew from a mining camp into a town because Augusta willed it.

"Horace, those two men that just left, they paid for that merchandise, didn't they? You didn't give them a grubstake, did you?" Augusta's hands were on her hips. Time and hard labor had worn away any softness in Augusta, leaving her all sharp edges and raw bones. Small round glasses pinched her nose and her thin lips drew a straight and disapproving line across her narrow face.

"Now, Augusta. . ."

"Oh, Hod! It's just like throwing money away. How many miners have you grubstaked over the years?" She didn't wait for an answer. "Dozens. And how much money have we made from them? Not a nickel." Augusta sighed and shook her head. "Did you, at least, record it?" Horace just smiled and shrugged. She marched behind the counter and pulled out a ledger. "How much did you give them?"

"About sixty-five dollars' worth. Augusta, I have a good feeling about these fellas."

"Nonsense. We will never see a penny from those men. Just like all the others."

One month later, Horace and his twenty-year old son Maxcy were minding the store, while Augusta went to meet a freight wagon loaded with new merchandise. Hijacking was becoming common in the boomtown; and she wasn't about to let her goods get shanghaied.

The door to the store busted open and in strode Meyer and Hook. They were still as thin as rails, but Horace could tell they'd had a recent bath and shave. Huge grins arced across their faces. "Mr. Tabor," Hook began, "we have good news."

"Just good news or 'get the whiskey' good news?" Horace asked, catching the men's infectious smiles.

"Whiskey good news," shouted Meyer. "A thirty-foot drift of high-grade silver ore. We made eight hundred dollars in our first load."

"Hoorah!" Horace hollered. There were drinks and backslapping all around as the two men told how they had found the vein of silver and counted out Horace's share of the take.

Horace stuck the sixty-five-dollar grubstake in Augusta's strongbox and the rest in his pocket. He grabbed a pick and shovel from the wall. "Maxcy, watch the store," he called over his shoulder. The three partners headed toward Fryer Hill and the thirty-five-foot hole in the ground, now called Shaft One of the Little Pittsburg Mine.

"Where's your father?" Augusta asked as she walked briskly into the store a short time later. "We need to get this wagon unloaded. The driver is sitting shotgun so that nothing grows feet and walks away."

"Mother, they found silver." Young Maxcy had gotten caught up in the excitement of the strike like his father. "I want to go help them dig."

"What? No, I need your help here. Who found silver?" Augusta barely paid attention; she was busy pulling out a ledger book, inkpot and pen to record the incoming goods.

"Those two skinny prospectors," Maxcy answered.

"Every man who comes in here is a skinny prospector. What are you talking about? And where is your father?"

"Remember, the two men Pop grubstaked last month? They came in a little while ago, all cleaned up and carrying a big wad of cash."

Augusta sighed. "Your father left with them?"

Maxcy nodded. "Yes, and I think I should go help them, too."

Augusta shook her head. "No, Maxcy. You were right to stay here with the store. Those claims usually turn out to be flashes in the pan. This store is our steady mainstay. It will continue to support our family long after the gold and silver runs out. Now, come on and help me unload the wagon."

The young man sighed but did as his mother directed and carried boxes into the mercantile; Augusta meticulously recorded every item and its cost. She'd have a talk with Horace that evening about keeping his priorities straight. She knew that she would be talking to the wall; Horace would have to get over this itch, just as he had so many times before. Augusta had married Horace until death do them part and several of their adventures had nearly done that. She had followed him from New England to Kansas and all over Colorado as he looked for the pot at the end of the rainbow. She couldn't count the number of times she was left alone to man the camp while Horace went off on a hunch, and she roughing it with only a baby as company.

Augusta had imagined she and Horace would face life as a matched team, pulling the load together. Horace turned out to be a plunger, diving into one venture and then another. He worked hard, but he always had an eye to the horizon for something better. In the braces and hitched to him for life, Augusta got dragged along. She could deal with his impetuous behavior, because she knew that behind the braying laugh was a good man who would stand by her forever. She knew, however, that she would have to be the partner that planned for that eventuality.

The Little Pittsburg Mine was soon producing $20,000 each month. Horace Tabor was rich. Augusta continued to run the store.

CHAPTER 10

Spring 1880

BABY DOE TOOK TWO TRAINS, twisting, dropping, climbing and clinging to mountainsides and then a teeth-rattling, neck-jerking, bottom-bumping stagecoach to travel the fifty-six miles from Central City to Leadville. Peering out a train window into a deathly deep gorge or hanging on for dear life in a jarring coach did not allow for deep contemplation about the new life she was about to start. That was fine because Baby had already thought enough about it. It was time to start living the life she wanted. She wanted a wardrobe of beautiful dresses, fancy hats spilling over with flowers and plumes, and velvet slippers with delicate needlework, lovely and useless. She wanted to spend hours having her hair brushed, curled and pinned. She wanted to go to the theater and parties. She wanted to laugh every day.

To live that kind of life would take money. She wasn't afraid to work, but every job acceptable for a woman provided only enough wages to ward off starvation. Washerwomen, maids and cooks didn't live the life she sought. She didn't have the money to buy and operate a mine and she didn't relish the idea of traipsing through the wilderness, panning the streams searching for the next elusive strike. Baby took stock. She had a few dollars courtesy of Colonel Doe, two house dresses, two nice dresses, her good looks and a barrel of gumption. She needed to work with what she had. Momma always said her looks were a gift from God and wasn't it sinful not to make the most of God's gifts? It wasn't immodest to believe she was the most beautiful woman in any town in Colorado. Rich men like to collect beautiful things, like art and horses and, sometimes, women. Belle said the French called them courtesans, women who were not just beautiful to look at, but pleasant and entertaining to be around and therefore, valued, kept in a quality way. Not like the girls at the Shoo Fly who were used by all manner of rough men and had little money to show for it. No, she needed just one man, but he had to be wealthy enough to provide a place for her to live, buy her stylish clothes and entertain her. History books were full of kings who married off their princesses to replenish their treasury or increase their kingdoms. Why couldn't she marry herself off in order fill her own coffers? Leadville was full of men who could do that for her. She had been reading the newspapers; and Horace Tabor was the biggest fish in that pond. She decided to set her sights for him first, but there were several millionaires in town if Tabor didn't bite.

She had thought a lot about Jake, too. He had moved to Leadville, anglicized his name to Sands and opened a new store shortly after the baby had been born. He wrote to her that he had heard about her divorce and encouraged her to join him in Leadville. Baby agreed to come but asked him to arrange a room in a boarding house for her, not in the same place he was staying. She enjoyed his company, and he had done so much for her; she felt like she owed him, but Jake could not afford the dreams she had, not as shopkeeper. She wanted more than spending every evening at sporting houses, talking with the working girls while Jake played cards. She was, of course, grateful for all he had done for her, and she did need him to help her get established in Leadville. Well, that knot would have to work itself out.

The stage slowed and Baby heard a growing chaos. She stuck her head out the window, craning her neck to see down the road. The streets of Leadville were jammed with every kind of wheeled conveyance along with men on horseback and men leading mules. A tourist guide published by the local Chamber of Commerce boasted the town had nearly seventy-five hotels and lodging houses, forty restaurants, more than eighty saloons and twenty-one gambling houses. There was every kind of establishment along the boardwalk: grocers, cobblers, mining supplies, bakeries, laundries, and booksellers all stood hip to hip with Faro halls, luncheonettes, banks and bawdy houses. A gun fired in the distance, only one skittish horse seemed to notice. Baby Doe had never seen anything like it. Freight wagons and stagecoaches sloughed down the center of the street, past rivers of well-dressed businessmen with fine-boned horses and grubby miners with rough-coated mules, as eddies of shoppers and greenhorns swirled the storefronts.

Everyone, everything seemed to be moving. There was an energy fizzing in the dust-choked air. The Chamber of Commerce guidebook called Leadville "The Magic City." It would be magic for her, she knew it. She was no longer Mrs. Harvey Doe, married woman.

So long Mama's Boy; she would never think of him or see him again. This town was where she would remake herself. This was where she would find her lucky break.

Jake had been true to his word and his nature. He had not only gotten Baby Doe a room and arranged for her things to be delivered, he also had secured an invitation for "Jake Sands and Lady" to a spring ball for the following night.

Baby wore her favorite blue taffeta dress. It, of course, set off her eyes and fair skin beautifully, and she liked the way the dress bustle bounced saucily when she danced. There were plenty of potential dance partners; Baby guessed there were seven or so men for every woman. Most of the females were older than her, and although they were cleaned up and well-dressed, they had that worn look that comes from years of rough living in mining camps. Their hands, spotted and gnarled, told the tale of days spent digging and nights spent freezing. There were a couple of young ladies about Baby's age. "I recognize those girls," Jake said, when he noticed her staring at the girls' short skirts and low décolletage. "They work in a parlor house on Harrison Street, probably got paid to come."

Baby Doe thought back to the Shoo Fly girls. Central City's proper matrons would have thrown a hissy fit if the girls had attempted to socialize outside the parlor houses or saloons. "Seems to be that in Leadville things are a little less formal than Central City," she said.

"Things are surely wilder. I imagine that in a year or so it will settle down and all this money will start buying some respectability." Jake smiled at a lanky man making his way toward them. "Jim Parson, let me introduce you," he started.

Jim grabbed Baby's hand. "Everyone knows who this is, Baby Doe, the famous beauty of Central City. I'm Jim Parson, but not a preacher." He leaned forwarded and laughed at his little joke.

"You are from Central City, too?" Baby Doe did not remember him.

"No, I was living in Denver before this, running a lunch counter. When the boom hit, I figured I could sell meat pies and sandwiches for a better price up here. I'm mining the miners." Again he leaned in and laughed, although Baby wasn't sure what the joke was. "Yup, the real way to make a good living up here is to sell something—purt' near anything—to the miners. Jake knows. They pay top dollar, and I don't get my health ruined in an old dirty mine. My new place is a couple of doors down from Jake's store. Most of my customers these days are fellows who busted in Central and are now chasing their luck here. They all tell a tale about a woman so pretty you would think she was a china baby doll. Jake, would you mind if I danced with your lady?"

Baby reached out and grabbed Jim's hand. "Of course I'll dance with you."

Jim swung her on to the dance floor. He two-stepped her around the room with a gusto that set her bustle bumping.

As the song ended and Jim and Baby Doe made their way back to Jake, a ruckus came in the door. A tall man with a drooping moustache and receding hairline whooped and hollered, "Happy spring, everybody." The crowd shouted back a "Hoorah." People began moving toward him like moths to a flame, each receiving a handshake or clap on the back. The two parlor girls made their way to his side, batting their lashes so hard Baby was sure she could feel the breeze.

"That's Tabor," Jim said, nodding toward the center of the crowd.

Oh my goodness, thought Baby, *he looks like a hound dog*. The bags under his eyes, lengthening ears and slight jowls all gave the impression that he might bay at the moon. The newspaper artists had been flattering to the great man.

"He's one of the richest men in the entire United States but no airs about him, still just as friendly as can be," Jim said. "Of course, the same can't be said about that wife of his."

"Which one is she?" Baby Doe asked. She peered around Jake, but could only see a couple of women near Tabor, and none seemed like the stiff-necked New Englander that she had read about in the newspapers.

"She wouldn't be here. She is not one for this kind of frivolity."

"She has airs?" Baby asked.

"No, it's just that she's no fun. Ha," Jim leaned in and laughed in Baby's face. "I think Tabor would like his wife to put on a little bit of airs. He just bought a big ol' mansion in Denver, four stories high, seventeen rooms, and she acted all put out by it. Made a big pout about moving in."

"So Tabor lives in Denver now?" Baby hoped she sounded nonchalant. Jake slid a sideways glance at her.

"Only part-time, when he is doing government business. You know he's lieutenant governor. Mrs. Tabor is down there full time, but Leadville is more his kind of town." Another funny thought struck Jim. "He may live in Denver, but he lives it UP in Leadville. Hahaha." Jim brayed so close to Baby that she thought she could count his molars. "I hear he is making time with a little gal named Alice that has a juggling act over at one of the variety houses." He surveyed the room. "I don't see her here either. Would you all like an introduction?"

"Oh no, he is about to drown in admirers. Let's not add to the fuss," Baby said. "Jake, would you ask me to dance?" She asked with a teasing smile.

Jake took her by the hand and guided her in a waltz. "Not interested in meeting Tabor, eh?" he asked, his eyes not meeting hers.

"I admit I have read about him and he seems to be a likeable fellow, but I don't want to appear to be an opportunist."

Baby Doe wanted an introduction, but not with Jake at her side, who would then be forever linked with her in Tabor's mind. Besides, Tabor was so drunk, he might not even recall their conversation. No, she would make sure her first meeting with Tabor would leave a lasting impression.

CHAPTER

11

BABY DOE SPENT THE NEXT FEW DAYS, becoming acquainted with her new town and learning about Tabor's lifestyle. It wasn't hard. Everyone she spoke to knew the richest man in Colorado and seemed eager to tell her all about their friendship.

To Mrs. May, the cook at the boarding house, "This Sunday roast is so delicious that Mr. Tabor himself should have the good fortune to dine here."

"Oh, Mr. Tabor eats at only the fancy restaurants," said a blushing Mrs. May.

"Which restaurants are those?"

"I hear the Saddle Rock Cafe is one of his favorites. He eats there most nights."

To the waiter at the Saddle Rock Cafe: "Everything is so lovely, the decor and the music. I hear the food is fit for a king, that even Tabor comes here."

"Yes, ma'am, Mr. Tabor is here several times a week. I am afraid you are too early to see him tonight. He usually has a late supper after the end of the show at the opera house."

"Just bring me a small cup of soup."

To the ticket seller at the opera house box office: "Do you have a seat available for tonight's show? Something on an aisle near Mr. Tabor's seats?"

"Mr. Tabor comes in through his private entrance. He has a walkway up above the alley that connects his suite at the Clarendon Hotel to his box here at the opera house. I have a real nice seat halfway back on the right side."

Baby Doe didn't want to waste her money on a ticket to just be a face in the crowd. "Never mind, I don't need a ticket. What time does the performance end?"

In order to get close to Tabor, the plan would be to have a late supper at the Saddle Rock when he was likely to drop by.

When Jake told Baby Doe he would be out playing cards until late, she knew it was the night to put her plan into motion. No gentlewoman would ever dine alone, but there were very few gentlewomen in Leadville, and she was guessing that Tabor, accustomed to the mining boomtown life, would not be shocked by this tiny breach of accepted manners. She put her sharpest hatpin in her reticule to use as a weapon, as the Shoo Fly girls had shown her, if she had to walk home alone. She made a long study of herself in the mirror, liked the way the mauve dress added a light color to her cheeks, and set off to create her destiny.

Arriving a little before the après-theater crowd, Baby Doe asked the waiter for a table for one near the center of the room. She had already decided that oysters on the half shell seemed like the most glamorous and seductive item on the menu. She winced at the price. Well, if she played her cards right, she wouldn't have to pay for them.

The restaurant had begun to fill up when her oysters were placed before her on a dish of glittering chipped ice. Baby turned to nod her thanks to the waiter when she recognized Billy Bush being led to a reserved table. She knew the Central City businessman had moved to Leadville and was involved in several ventures with Tabor. And then there he was, Horace Tabor in the flesh, following Billy to the table, stopping to say hello to most everyone. Baby pulled her eyes back to the dish before her and feigned great interest in the bivalves.

Damn! Billy Bush undoubtedly knew her whole history, all the Central City gossip, how she had worked like a man in the mines, that her husband was a lazy drunk. She was sure Bush had seen her dining with Jake and probably heard about her spending time at the Shoo Fly. The whole town knew about her divorce. *Damn!* Billy Bush could spill the beans and ruin her chances with Tabor before she even got to say hello.

She could feel their eyes on her. Baby bowed her head to wipe her lips and tried to look from the corner of her vision. She could see Bush looking at her and then back at his dinner companion, but Tabor was out of her line of sight. What were they saying? She couldn't hear over the growing crowd.

Bush waved the waiter over, handed him something and pointed in the direction of Baby's table. The waiter brought over the playbill from the night's theater production, *The Marble Heart*. On it was written, "Won't you, please, join us? Billy Bush."

"Mr. Bush from Central City?" Baby Doe tried to sound surprised. "Why, I'd be delighted to renew our acquaintance."

The waiter helped her from her chair and gathered her oysters as Baby turned and gave Billy Bush a wide smile. The men rose as Baby swept over to the table offering her hand, "Mr. Bush, fancy seeing you here."

"Governor Tabor, may I introduce Mrs. Harv—," Billy began.

"Miss Elizabeth Doe," she stated offering her hand to Tabor.

"Everyone knows the famous beauty of Central City. I hear most people call you Baby Doe," Horace said, bowing slightly over her hand.

"Yes, it is how I am known now," she said, tucking her chin and looking up at Tabor through her lashes. Yes, this was who she was now. Lizzie McCourt and Mrs. Harvey Doe were long gone. Baby Doe from this moment on.

"How do you like Leadville, Baby Doe?" Horace asked.

"It's a little quiet for me," she answered with a sly smile.

He stared at her for the length of a heartbeat and then burst into a full belly laugh. "That's funny. Billy, order champagne for the lady. Baby Doe, do you like champagne?"

Baby had never actually drunk champagne, but naturally she said, "Why, of course, what lady doesn't adore champagne? That is like asking if I like diamonds. Or should I have said silver?"

Horace laughed again, slapping his knee. "Waiter, champagne and keep it coming."

The champagne began to flow and making conversation was easy. The table chatted about mine owners and businessmen they knew in common; however, two names never came up, Harvey Doe and

Jake Sands. Horace told stories about drunken miners and ignorant tenderfoots. Baby laughed and laughed; she was having a delightful time. Horace Tabor, Colorado's Croesus, was very entertaining company. He was genuine and unassuming. He did not judge himself better than others, just luckier. He tended to say what he was thinking, although not always in the most artful manner. The small theater of etiquette was completely unknown to him.

Unlike Tabor, whose thoughts and feelings were displayed in plain view, Baby Doe was not sure where she stood with Billy Bush. In contrast to Tabor, Bush was a graceful man with neat dark hair and clean, fashionable clothes, somewhat of a rarity in a mining boomtown. Dark brows hooded narrow green eyes that took in everything. He was polite but distant, as if making small talk with a beautiful woman was an expected part of his job which he would complete adequately. He seemed to be listening in all directions at once, scanning the crowd, like a cougar prowling for the weakest lamb. He perked up when Horace talked about plans to open new businesses and bring culture and civility to Leadville. "But not so much civility as to ruin the good times," Horace said and gave Baby a wink.

Billy took this as a cue to excuse himself. "The staff should be finished closing up at the opera house. I need to go review accounts and put the night's receipts in the safe. I shall see you at the Clarendon tomorrow, Governor."

Baby and Horace bid Billy a good night and turned to face each other. Horace took Baby's tiny hand in his large boney one. "Now, tell me all about you."

Baby hesitated. She didn't know how much Horace knew about her. All could be lost if she was caught in a lie, but all could be lost if she told the truth. Like the Cornishmen who taught her about mining, she decided Horace was not afraid of a dirty truth, but would detest a shiny lie. It would catch up to her sooner or later, so it would be better if she were the one to tell her story to Horace. She began. She explained to Horace how she had married a beautiful young man and was sure their future was golden. She recounted the awe she felt upon seeing the Rockies and how she knew these mountains were God's providence for her. Horace nodded with understanding; he had felt the same. She told how she had come to realize that her husband was hollow inside, without thoughts of his own, no gumption and, ultimately, no future. When she remembered how she had worked the mine, swinging a pick and digging dirt, Horace gently stroked her hand. When she described how she would have gone hungry if Jake Sands hadn't taken a shine to her, worry and hurt furrowed Horace's brow.

"You gonna marry this fellow, Sands?" Horace asked. He leaned close to her and looked deep into her eyes.

"I don't want to," Baby said. Her eyes were damp. "I do feel obligated to him. He did so much for me back in Central City. He is paying for my room and board here. I just don't know how to end our association."

"Let me give you the money to square things with Jake and carry you along for a while."

"Oh, I don't know," Baby pretended to protest.

"Hear me out. I know money doesn't buy happiness, but it can give you choices. Having a choice can bring you happiness. I am not a very learned man, but I do know that the ability to make your own decisions is a powerful thing for the human spirit. I want to give you the fresh start that you are looking for."

"I don't know how I would ever pay you back."

"Baby Doe, haven't you heard of my famous Tabor luck? I grub-staked men and it made me a millionaire many times over. I'll grub-stake you, 'cause I got a good feeling about you. Waiter, bring me paper and something to write with."

Horace quickly scratched a note and handed it to her. "Take this to Billy in the morning. He'll write you a draft for five thousand dollars. You can pay Sands what you think you owe him and give him one thousand dollars as a parting gift. You should have a little left over to buy some pretty clothes. Billy can arrange to have your things moved into the Clarendon. You deserve to live somewhere finer than a boarding house."

"Governor Tabor," Baby leaned even closer and fixed her clear blue eyes on his wrinkle-lined brown ones.

"Call me Horace."

"Horace," her voice was a deep whisper. "Are you asking me to move into your suite? To become your mistress?"

"Yes," Horace's own voice was hoarse.

Baby smiled slowly, "Well, let's toast our new friendship."

The conversation had been more like a business deal than the romantic seduction that Baby had envisioned, but she wasn't complaining. She had a note good for five thousand dollars in her reticule, she had a beautiful place to stay and Horace was a nice man.

Perhaps, given time, she could make him love her and better secure her future. After all, she knew marriage didn't have to be forever and a mistress could become a wife.

"To happiness," Horace said.

She raised her glass to meet his. "To happiness."

One night later, the couple consummated their arrangement, and Baby Doe thought it wasn't that bad. Horace wasn't as good looking as either the fair-haired Harvey or the swarthy Jake. He sagged from his eyelids to his knees. The muscle of his youth had been worn away leaving a bag of skin hanging off big raw bones, even his manhood hung low. His recent good living had given him a little pooch belly of which he seemed to be proud and rubbed lovingly. Baby had learned a few tricks from Belle's girls to get things going and then speed them to conclusion. They suggested that most men didn't like a dead fish. The girls' professional opinion was to begin with a slow rocking of the hips and then follow the customer's lead. She and Horace were a little drunk when they climbed into Baby's new bed at the Clarendon, and Horace acted like it was a party, loud, fast and cheerful. He didn't caress her the way Jake had, but she happily gasped and smiled through it all. Afterward he asked Baby how she felt, if she was all right. Oh yes, she gushed. The fact that he had bothered to inquire struck her. Jake had asked how she liked it, but it really was more of an opportunity for her to compliment his lovemaking. Harvey had never asked if she liked it, sometimes acting as if Mother Doe could now check marital relations off his list of chores. Horace Tabor was a considerate and gentle man; being his mistress would be easy work.

CHAPTER 12

THE AIR IN LEADVILLE was thinner and even more invigorating than in Central City. Baby Doe couldn't keep from smiling as she sauntered down the wooden walk. It was Leadville's quiet hour, if there was a quiet hour here. The all-night revelers had eaten breakfast and gone to bed. The prospectors had started into the hills at sunrise and the working miners were already deep underground. The stagecoaches from Denver had not yet arrived with eager tender-footed dreamers. The dust settled on the rutted street. Leadville's more respectable citizens were out doing business. She nodded greetings to everyone she met.

Her first stop was at Billy Bush's office to trade Tabor's note for a check. Billy didn't bat an eye when she handed him the note and explained that Horace would like him to write her a check, as if it were just another business transaction. She stopped at a bank and deposited most of her "grubstake." She put the money she owed Jake and a little walking around change in her beaded purse and set off to set things right with him.

On the way to Jake's store, she passed a storefront proclaiming *William Peabody-Photography-Portraits* in bright yellow paint. On a whim, Baby stepped inside.

"How may I help you, madam?" asked a short man in a red brocade vest and matching sleeve garters.

"I would like my portrait made, now if possible."

"Yes, of course. Is there a special occasion that you wish to commemorate?"

I just became the mistress to a very rich man she thought. "Well," she began carefully. "Things are going well for me, it's a beautiful day, and I have a new . . . friend, whom I would like to give a cabinet card."

If Mr. Peabody thought there was anything indelicate in her request, his face did not give it away. "Of course, this way to my studio." The little man gave a slight bow and then bustled toward the backroom. It was a simple room with a camera and hood standing in the center; a stool and white plaster pedestal stood off to the side and a painted backdrop with a mountain scene hung on a wall.

Peabody pushed away the backdrop and pulled forward a pale curtain, "That scene is for the prospectors. Something softer, more feminine for you." He fetched a pillow with gold braid and fringe. He placed it on the pedestal and arranged Baby Doe's elbows on it. "Madam has lovely round arms." He pulled out two yards of embroidered lace and draped it around her shoulders. He took her chin in his hand and tilted it just so. "Very good and hold still," he said hurrying back to the camera.

Baby Doe smiled broadly.

Mr. Peabody popped from behind the camera, "Madam," slight shock tinged his voice, "your teeth are showing."

"Yes, it is how I smile."

"One generally does not smile in a portrait."

"I am told I have a beautiful smile."

"This is quite true, madam, however, it is not done in photography. Subjects usually want to appear dignified. Perhaps closed lips with a slight upturn at the corners. As if, one has just smelled a delicate rose." He demonstrated.

"But I'm happy, I want to appear happy."

"Madam, it is not traditional."

Baby Doe stared at him for a long minute and then said, "Mr. Peabody, I do not believe my life will be very traditional." She tucked her chin in her hand, tilted her head saucily and displayed all her pearly whites. Mr. Peabody sighed and gently squeezed the shutter.

Baby Doe walked slowly toward Jake's new store, practicing what she would say to him. She would tell him that she thought highly of him. She would thank him for all that he had done for her. She would explain that he was right that this was a good time to start over, start fresh.

Jake was stocking shelves in his new store when she walked in. He climbed down from the ladder. Baby Doe forgot everything she had planned to say and the two lovers stood silently for a long moment.

"Jake," she began and paused.

"I know," he said. "I know all about it." He didn't sound angry, but resigned. "The whole town's talking about Tabor's new girl." He sighed and pushed that rebellious forelock out of his eyes. "Can't say as I blame you."

Baby Doe hand him the envelope thick with money. "Is this one of Tabor's famous parting gifts?" he asked. She nodded. "Well, take care Baby. I hope it turns out to be everything you want."

CHAPTER

13

June 1880

LIFE AS TABOR'S MISTRESS was delightful, an endless carousel of midnight champagne suppers and leisurely mornings in bed. Meanwhile below ground, away from the brilliant summer sunshine, miners worked long and brutal shifts to pay for Baby's shopping sprees and Horace's opera house.

The workers on the night shift at the Chrysolite Mine had spent most of their time re-timbering and cleaning up after a small fire had shut down work on the earlier shift. There was not much damage and no one had been hurt, but now the bosses were calling for extra effort to make up for lost digging time. The usual grumbling about hard work and low pay had grown through the night, and several men wondered aloud about approaching Tabor regarding the working conditions. Good Ole Hod had thrown a pick; he understood how tough the miners had it. Now he had more money than God, surely, he could raise wages a little bit.

Everyone agreed Michael Mooney would be the best man to approach Tabor. He could read and write and had a logical mind. The young Irishman was often the de facto supervisor when problems occurred deep underground. He was a natural leader, a hard worker and wasn't afraid of much.

By the time the men spilled out of the mouth of the mine at sunrise, several were shouting suggestions for Michael to take to Tabor. Most wanted $3.75 and an eight-hour workday.

"Ask for four dollars a day. I heard miners in Gunnison are getting that."

"And it will give you negotiating room."

"Don't forget about improving safety."

"Mining is dangerous. It ain't never gonna be safe. Don't fuss about safety. Work on getting more money."

"We want a hospital for miners."

"Hey, hey. What goes on here?" asked the mine superintendent. George Daley was stocky man who liked bowler hats. He was perpetually red in the face as if on the verge of a temper tantrum, but his competence had earned him the respect of both miners and owners all over Leadville.

"Mr. Daley, we'd like to talk to Mr. Tabor about work in the mine," Michael began.

"No. He is a busy man. Clear on out, and let the day shift in." Daley turned and waved at the day shifters to get in the bucket and get to work.

"Mr. Daley," Michael said, his voice stronger this time. "Mr. Tabor needs to hear us out about wages and hours. We can't work for this pay. We won't work for this pay."

Daley turned back to Michael and squinted at him. "Are you threatening to strike?"

Michael took a breath, "Yes." Shouts went up from the miners surrounding him. "What we are asking is reasonable. We want four dollars a day and eight-hour shifts and . . ." he faltered not quite remembering all the things that most could agree on. "And a few other items that we will describe in writing to be presented to Mr. Tabor. Until we can talk to him, we will not work."

Some of the miners began chanting, "Strike, strike."

"Ah, by God," Daley took off his bowler and ran a hand through his few remaining hairs. More men took up the chant. "Alright, I'll go tell Tabor what's going on. You fellas keep running those pumps. Otherwise, the mine will flood and none of us will have a job." Daley bustled off down California Gulch toward town.

Michael turned to the group, "We have strength in numbers. We need to get word to all the mines that we are striking and ask them to join us. We will meet here tomorrow morning at eight and march into town together to present our demands."

Michael sent runners to the other mines on Fryer Hill, west to Carbonate Hill, north to Iron Hill and east to Breece Hill. Then he hurried down the gulch to find a printer who, supporting their cause, would print handbills detailing the meeting at Chrysolite and the march afterward. He also needed to write down what the miners wanted so he wouldn't get flustered and forget when he met the great Mr. Tabor.

It was still cool the next morning as miners from all over the area gathered at the Chrysolite. The turnout exceeded Michael Mooney's most optimistic hopes, he guessed about six thousand men were waiting to march into town. These men had come to Leadville to find their own fortune, but found themselves performing backbreaking work for low wages while owners were rich beyond belief. There was little chance to get ahead, and many wondered if they should have just stayed back East at the factory in Chicago or the burnt-out farm in Mississippi.

Michael stood atop of the mine's frame entrance and addressed the crowd. "Thank you all for coming today. This strike started here at the Chrysolite, but we have more leverage if we stick together. Let's march down Harrison Street to the courthouse steps where I'll read our list of demands."

"Just what are those demands? I ain't going nowhere 'til I know this ain't a wild goose chase," said a voice in the crowd.

"We printed up these handbills," Michael waved his in the air. "I will read them now." He knew probably only half the miners could read. "We, the United Miners of Leadville request the following: First, no man shall be allowed to work for less than four dollars per day. Second, that hours for work shall not exceed eight. Third, no one will work, in any mine, unless these conditions are met for all workers. Fourth, we request a pledge from owners that there will not be retribution for participating in the strike. We promise to conduct ourselves in good order and negotiate in good faith." He looked up from his paper, "That last part is important. No violence and no mayhem. That can only hurt our cause." He held the paper aloft again. "Now, let's go."

A cheer went up as Michael jumped down and led the men down California Gulch. The men grew quieter as they approached the edge of town and by the time Michael climbed onto the courthouse steps the men were silent. Usually-bustling Leadville was hushed. It seemed as if the whole town was hiding indoors and peeking from behind curtains. Michael knew some of those watching eyes belonged to mine owners.

In a strong, clear voice he reread the strike proclamation, then said, "We are having copies sent to all the mine managers and any owners who are in the area. We'll meet again after we hear from the owners, so watch for posted bills. Now, everyone, go home and keep your noses clean."

The next afternoon C.C. Davis, a newspaper man with an oversized handlebar moustache and a sense of self-worth to match, stood on the stage of the Tabor Opera House, banged the butt of his pistol on the podium and called to order the first meeting of the Committee for Public Safety. Davis had invited those whom he deemed the one hundred leading citizens of Leadville to discuss the miners' strike. All the mine owners and bankers had shown up, as well as dozens of other concerned businessmen and a couple of women, saloon and brothel owners that hadn't rated an invite.

"Gentlemen, as you are all aware, yesterday miners from around the area declared a strike and stopped work. In an audacious display of hubris, they marched en masse through our gentle streets and issued demands from the courthouse steps. They are expecting four dollars pay for a day that ends within eight hours."

Disgruntled sounds rose from the mine owners in the audience. "Hell, no!"

"I was lucky to make four dollars in a week when I first came to Leadville."

"I say, let the bums walk. Every day a hundred new men arrive in town, and they are all looking for work."

Davis held up his hands for quiet. "Gentlemen, I think we all agree these outrageous demands will only hurt our illustrious mining industry and, by extension, the whole of Leadville business and citizenry. While it is possible to replace all the workers, I suggest a more efficient method."

A voice called out, "Michael Mooney is the leader. Run him out of town."

"Hang him from the courthouse rafters," said another.

Horace squirmed in his chair; vigilante justice was not unknown in the mining towns, but it made him uneasy. He had hoped to just quickly hire several replacement workers, welcome back any miners who wanted to work and end talk of striking. After all, when the mines were closed no one made money, not him, not the miners, not the dancehall girls, nobody. Now, the whole situation was threatening to get out of hand, like a rockslide that started with a few stones, it was gaining momentum. Horace knew they had to stop the slide now, before it buried them all, but he certainly didn't want anybody hanged.

The theater again began to fill with the rumble of indignation when a small man rose from the back of the crowd. "Mr. Davis, I am Mr. John Ellis of Ellis' Mercantile. May I have the floor?"

Davis banged his pistol on the podium again, "Speak, sir."

"I believe many of the merchants and business owners are of the same mind as I. Sir, the streets of Leadville are full of wildness and disorder. We are mightily concerned that it wouldn't take much for the striking men to turn riotous, causing harm to persons and property. With all respect, the Leadville police cannot maintain order on any given Tuesday, let alone a tenuous situation such as this. They are not even here at this meeting," Mr. Ellis said.

C.C. banged the pistol yet again. "Mr. Ellis is right. We cannot let the strikers believe they have the upper hand. We must meet their show of force with an even greater force." He banged the pistol for effect this time. "It is our sacred duty to protect the life and property of the good citizens of Leadville against this hoard of rapscallions. We must be the champions of law and order," Davis' voice rang through the opera house.

"Hear! Hear!" a hundred voices shouted.

Horace, too, was caught up in Davis' oration. *Now is the time for strong leadership*, he thought. *We need to show the strikers who's boss.*

C.C. Davis thundered on. "I have taken the liberty of telegraphing the governor and requested that he declare Leadville to be under martial law. He telegraphed his agreement a short time ago. The cavalry is on its way with munitions for 1,000 civilian volunteers. I call on all of you to assemble your employees and march to the courthouse steps tomorrow at noon. We will greet General Cook and his troops and show the miners that the citizens will not be intimidated."

Horace realized that C.C. Davis had done some work before this little meeting and come up with a very prudent strategy, a demonstration of strength, backed by professional soldiers. The miners would not want to wrangle with the United States cavalry. The mine owners' authority would remain unassailable, and the strike would be quickly and quietly busted. Impulsively, Horace jumped up. "As the lieutenant governor, I and the Tabor Light Cavalry will lead the march." Horace had founded the militia to march in the Fourth of July parade. There were a couple of old veterans of the Civil War, but most did not have a lick of military training. Their focus had been on wearing smart uniforms and stepping in unison. "Let's show them we are not to be trifled with."

The Citizens' March did not go off as planned the next day. An overturned wagon had blocked the road and delayed General Cook and his men. Meanwhile in Leadville, Horace and C.C. Davis decided that postponing the march would look indecisive. So Tabor's Light Cavalry, in all their glorious regalia, led a band of mine owners and businessmen, followed in turn by a hodgepodge of shopkeepers, bartenders, tailors, bakers and errand boys from the opera house to the courthouse.

The miners had gotten wind of the march and the coming troops and were waiting in an uneasy silence at the courthouse. Tabor's militia pushed through the crowd so that Davis, Tabor and a few other mine owners could climb the steps. Most everyone in Leadville was there, supporting one side and sizing up the other. The air tingled with tension like the moment before a lightning strike.

Baby Doe edged through the crowd to get a better view of the speakers on the steps. Earlier Horace had told her there would a short parade, a few speeches, and with the miners firmly in hand, work would resume tomorrow. He had said the troops would be mostly for show, just to make sure the miners went peacefully on their way. She could feel the agitation in the men's arms and backs as she gently pushed passed. It was unnatural for these rough men to be so still. They were like feral dogs, bristling and alert.

She could see Horace now, standing beside that newspaperman with the waxed moustache. He looked so serious. His arms were crossed and his head high. It struck Baby that Horace would make an easy target for someone with a gun. Everyone had a gun. Her heart thumped in her chest.

She had been his mistress for only a few weeks, but she was becoming genuinely fond of Horace. He had proven himself thoughtful and considerate, lively and generous. Standing on those steps was a Horace she hadn't met yet. This man was fighting for what was his, standing up to thousands of angry men. *Harvey didn't have the nerve to stand up to me, let alone a mob like this,* she thought. A wave of admiration came over her. Horace had grit.

Suddenly, an arm wrapped around her waist, picked her up and dragged her away. Baby kicked and hit as a large man in a gentleman's suit shouldered his way through the crowd.

"Stop it," hissed the man. "This is for your own good."

Baby squirmed to see his face when he turned down an alley and dropped her. Billy Bush stepped from a doorway, grabbed her arm and pulled her into the dim light of the backstage of the opera house.

"What are you doing?" Baby shrieked. "How dare you grab me off the street? I will tell Horace about this."

"Calm down. Horace asked me to keep you out of the crowd today, in case things got dangerous. I believe he told you to stay in the suite at the Clarendon," Billy said arching one eyebrow. "Follow me. I will take you back there through the private walkway."

"I am not your child, to be taken to my room. Where I am and what I do is none of your affair." Baby pulled her most imperious face.

"You are wrong, Baby Doe. Your *affair* is very much my business. I work for Governor Tabor. It is my job to find good investments, protect assets and get rid of liabilities. That includes you. Currently, you are an asset; therefore, I will protect you. I advise you, don't become a liability." He turned and walked toward the walkway.

Baby was so fuming mad she couldn't think of a response, so she just stomped along behind Billy, her thoughts spinning. What did he mean, don't become a liability? She'd like to knock him right off that high horse he was riding. On the other hand, he was Horace's most trusted man, and she was just the new mistress. She knew Billy would be a dangerous enemy.

They crossed from the opera house into the hotel in silence. They reached the door of the suite before Baby got a rein on her temper and her thoughts arranged. "You look at me and think you see a witless doll. I assure you, Mr. Bush, I am not a fool. You and I both work in service to Horace Tabor. You keep his books, and I keep him happy. Do not think for one minute that I am less diligent than you in performing my duties."

She swallowed and forced herself to say, "So, while both of us have influence with him, it would not be productive for us to be at odds. I suggest we make peace."

"Oh, I have nothing against you, Baby Doe. I have been on good terms with many of Tabor's girlfriends. It is just that they usually don't last very long. I intend to be at the lieutenant governor's side for a long time."

"Me too, Mr. Bush. Me too." She pushed past him into the suite and gave the door a satisfying slam. She suddenly understood why she didn't trust Billy Bush. He wasn't infatuated with her.

Baby greeted Horace at the door when he returned that evening, wrapping her arms around his neck and slathering him with kisses. "Oh, thank God you're alright. I was worried sick about you. Horace, you looked so fine and brave up there. I was so proud of you."

"Well, this is quite the welcome," Horace said with a tired smile.

"Just what the doctor ordered after a hard day." He picked her up and kissed her. "A big heaping helping of sweet Baby."

She helped him out of his coat and tie. "I've ordered a couple beef steaks and baked potatoes be sent up. We can have a quiet dinner here tonight."

"That sounds just right by me," Horace flopped onto the bed. Baby pulled his boots off and propped his head with another pillow, then snuggled up next to him. "Besides there is a curfew with the town under martial law. General Cook closed the saloons and said he'd jail any group of three or more men that weren't on their way to work or home." Horace hugged her tighter and stared at the ceiling. "Lord, I don't like this strike and all the bad feelings it has caused. Augusta is usually the one speaking with a sharp tongue and standing hard on a point."

Baby stilled; this was the first time Horace had ever mentioned his wife to her.

He didn't seem to notice and continued, "I can usually get along with anybody. But, damn it, if we give those guys an inch, they'll take a mile. If we give into those strikers just once, it will never end. They will call strike after strike for every little thing." He let out a long unhappy sigh. "We have to bust this."

"Horace Tabor, don't you feel bad about this hullabaloo. You didn't start it." She pushed herself up so she could look in his eyes. "You are right to stand up to those men. You have been working these mountains for years. You risked life and limb, not to mention your own money to develop your mines. Why, this town would be nothing without you. It was your grubstake that let those two old diggers strike the mother lode. Without you, there would not be a silver rush. You built the post office, the opera house, started the fire department and created the militia." She took his saggy old face in her hands. "You are a great, great man. Now I am going to kiss you until you forget about any old strikers."

CHAPTER

14

"HORACE TABOR, you are the biggest fool in all of Colorado."

"Hello, Augusta. It's nice to see you, too." Horace had barely made it into the grand foyer of the Denver mansion when Augusta began firing with both barrels.

"What were you thinking, using soldiers to break a strike, declaring martial law? You are an idiot. I read it in the papers, Horace. I know how you and that poppin' jay, C.C. Davis, nearly caused a riot."

"The strike was broke in three days. Not one shot fired. Not one concession given. Everyone is back at work at the same wage. If that is not success, I don't know what is," he shot back.

"You could have accomplished the same thing by waiting them out. Everyone would have gone back to the mines when they got hungry."

"Enough, Augusta. You weren't there."

But Augusta was not finished. "Not only did you almost blow up Leadville, you probably blew up your future in politics. The governor did not like being pushed into sending the cavalry to stand against his own citizens. And to think of all the money you threw around, trying to buy friends and votes." Augusta wiped at a stain on her apron. "What a waste."

Horace noticed for the first time what Augusta was wearing, a homespun skirt and blouse that had to be as old as Maxcy, sleeve covers, a dingy scarf neckerchief and an apron with a streak of gray ash crossing her waist. The neighbors' maids were probably better dressed. Amid the luxurious furnishings, thick rich carpets, drapes and gleaming marble floors, Augusta looked like a weed in a rose garden.

He sighed; he just wanted to wash his neck and have a small whiskey. Horace pointed to his valise and carpetbag. "Can you ask the house man to take these upstairs?"

"You'll have to take them yourself. There are no servants. Maxcy and I have no need of them." Augusta stood with her hands on her hips daring him to fight. Too weary to argue, Horace merely picked up the bags and started to climb the stairs. "You will be by yourself up there," she called after him.

Horace turned, not sure what to say that wouldn't just prolong the argument.

"I sleep in the servants' quarters. It is good enough for me, and it's near the kitchen where I can do the cooking."

"Who the hell are you cooking for, woman? I have enough money that you never have to raise a finger again." Just then something moved outside the window, catching Horace's eye. "What the hell is that?" He moved down the stairs to the window and stared face-to-face with a black-and-white cow. She blinked her big brown eyes and then licked the window glass. Horace turned to Augusta, his mouth hanging open.

"I need her," Augusta said, crossing her arms, "for milk and butter."

"You don't! Augusta, do you know who our neighbors are? The finest citizens of Denver, millionaires, every one. Here you are running around acting like a farm hand. Are you going to wear that outfit when we have dinner with the governor and Mrs. Pitkin? Do you think people are going to elect a senator whose wife wants to bring a cow to Washington? You are just trying to embarrass me. You and your damn cow are the ones shitting on my chances for higher public office."

"I embarrass you?" Augusta shrieked.

But Horace wasn't listening. He had grabbed his bags and was headed for the door.

"I know what is going on in Leadville," she called after him.

Horace slammed the door.

Augusta opened the door and shouted after him. "You need to end this wildness, Hod. Stay here in Denver."

She quietly closed the door and leaned her forehead against it. "Oh Hod, you old coot. Don't you know, I'm the only one you can trust?"

Irritated with his wife, Horace decided to live in the luxurious Windsor Hotel in downtown Denver while he was performing his duties as lieutenant governor. He came with a coach to pick up Augusta when they were to attend formal public events. She was always the New Englander, proper, polite, but utterly unable to make small, gay conversation. The necklines of her somber dresses were buttoned to her ears. She wrinkled her nose to hold a pair of pince-nez to her eyes, giving her the appearance of smelling something foul. She was a dun-colored hen compared to the society ladies, peacocking in bright dresses of the latest fashion.

Augusta may have been lacking in social graces, but she was smart. She was right about the governor being unhappy about the breaking of the Leadville strike and right about Horace needing to stay in Denver with the political bigwigs if he were to advance to higher office.

Fortunately, Governor Pitkin had a task for his lieutenant that would take him back to Leadville and give him a chance to soothe sore feelings there and, if all went well, it could help Tabor make headway in Denver and Washington. Ulysses S. Grant was touring the world after winning the Civil War and serving as president of the reunited country. One of his last stops would be to see the fabulous riches that were pouring out of the Colorado mountains. Governor Pitkin would greet him in Denver, but Tabor would show him Leadville.

Augusta sent word to Horace to come to the mansion so she could go over plans for the presidential visit to Leadville. "Grant is a plain man, a soldier and, I'm told, very humble. We shouldn't plan anything extravagant for his visit. He just wants to see the silver mines, but he should also visit a smelter and an assessor's office. It can't be just anybody. Ernest Johnson, he runs an honest assess office, and he cleans up pretty well." Her library desk was covered with paper. She was writing multiple lists—things for Horace to do, for Billy Bush to do, for her to do, things for her to pack, items to be sent from Denver and guest lists.

"Yea, Johnson would be fine. I'll ask him tomorrow when I get up the mountain," Horace said. He sat on the edge of a beautiful brocade chair, admiring the furnishings that someone he didn't know had picked for a house he didn't live in.

"No, I'll handle that. You find a nice coach and matched pair to bring him from the train station to the welcoming banquet at the Clarendon. I hear Grant appreciates fine horses so it's probably worth the splurge to get the best pair around." Augusta picked up a different list and scribbling said, "Mr. Bush is handling all the arrangements at the Clarendon: the banquet, the food, seating arrangements, and decorations. Oh, and the president's sleeping arrangements, he really should have the suite you have been using at the Clarendon, it is the most elegant."

Horace pulled at his moustache, dragging his whole face into a worried frown. That was the suite in which Baby Doe was now living.

"Of course, I will go over all of it with Mr. Bush when I get there," Augusta said, dipping her pen into the inkwell.

"Augusta, you're not going to Leadville," Horace said abruptly.

"What?" Augusta was so surprised she dropped her pen. Ink puddled on the list she was writing for Horace.

Horace stood up, trying to be more authoritative, but he was having a hard time looking her in the eye. "I think you should stay here in Denver and greet Grant with the governor."

"No, Hod. Absolutely not." Augusta jumped up, horrified. "You cannot entertain the president with your latest fancy girl. It is a presidential visit, not a mining camp bacchanal. You must act respectable, with dignity and decorum. The whole town needs to act respectable."

Pink had begun to creep up Horace's neck to his oversized ears. "I know how to conduct myself. I'm the lieutenant governor."

Augusta gave a snort.

"You seem to forget that I can get along with people. I'll be just fine with Grant. Hell, he and I will probably end up buddies." Horace jammed his hat on his head and headed for the door.

"There will be reporters from all over with Grant. You won't be a fool in just Leadville; you will be a fool in every state in the union."

Horace was already gone. Augusta sat back down at the desk looking at all her lists, an ink stain blotting out her planning, black spreading across the page. She carefully folded the paper's edges making a small box. She folded the edges again as if to shut the box, enclosing and then covering the ink. "Oh, Hod," she said to herself, "who will clean up your messes if I am not there?"

CHAPTER

15

THE CITIZENS OF LEADVILLE were a coarse bunch, whose idea of formal entertaining might be getting a clean glass before passing the whiskey bottle. There were no social doyennes to advise Billy as he made arrangements for the presidential visit. He felt like a circus juggler keeping so many plates spinning on thin canes; and when Horace got off the train without Augusta, Billy was sure he heard plates crashing all over town. Organizing the reception and tours for a former president and war hero was a monumental feat, and Augusta was just the field general for the job. She wasn't shy about bullying others into helping, and she didn't mind rolling up her sleeves and doing the work herself. Furthermore, she was quite literally the first lady of Leadville. Her little store and post office had made Leadville a town, not a fly-by-night mining camp that was abandoned when the weather turned bad or the minerals got scarce.

Billy had one of the bellhops from the Clarendon with him. "Get Mr. Tabor's bags, boy. And does Mrs. Tabor have bags?" Billy asked, his voice cracking with desperate hope.

"I told her she couldn't come. But if I know her at all, she'll be on the next train anyways." Horace stomped toward Billy's buggy as Billy hustled to keep up.

"I do believe she would be invaluable helping organize everything," Billy said.

"Aw, hell. I just got tired of her banging on my ears."

Horace stopped and looked down at the fine coating of dust that now covered his recently polished boots. He knew Billy was right. He knew he needed Augusta's help, but dang gum, she was unpleasant to be around. He would need to keep her away from Baby Doe. Now there was a different story, Baby was a joy to be around, never criticizing, always happy and she never pulled back when Horace wrapped his arms around her tiny waist and kissed her lips. Augusta had been batting him away for years. He didn't want either woman to be mad at him. Baby Doe had only been his lover for a few weeks, but he had taken quite a shine to her. Augusta had been his wife for over thirty years, and she was hard on people even when she wasn't mad. It was the difference between drinking vinegar or wine.

"Aw, hell," he repeated, climbing into the buggy. "Send Augusta a telegram and get her up here on the next train. She'll be in her glory, bossing the whole damn town."

An excited Baby Doe giggled with delight when Horace walked into the suite. "Oh, Horace, President Grant! And you will host him." She pulled him onto a velvet chaise lounge and snuggled up, kissing his high, white forehead. "I've been thinking and we must make Leadville the grandest stop on his world tour. How about a banner at the train station that reads 'Leadville - America's Treasure Chest'? Then maybe a red carpet, like they have for Queen Victoria, all the way down Harrison Street. And lights all through town. And flags and bunting on every building. With flowers everywhere. Do you think Grant knows how hard it is to get flowers up here in the mountains? How expensive they are?"

"Slow down, little missy," Horace tried to unwind himself from Baby and sit up straighter. With a quick shift of her hips and a hug, he was upright and she was in his lap. Horace leaned awkwardly back searching in vain for the back of the chaise. Baby looked beautiful lying on this thing, but it was not built for grown men to sit on.

"Oh, both the Tabor Fire Hose Company and the Tabor Light Militia want to host a ball. Of course, we have to have entertainment at the opera house, too. That is your crown jewel." Baby didn't miss a beat amidst all the wrangling and wiggling.

"Now, Baby," Horace took her tiny hands in his and continued to shift in his seat. "This visit by Grant is a pretty big deal. It's a political thing and, you know, it has to be just so, all high falutin'. It has to be ... well, I mean, we can't ..." Horace ran his hand over his thinning hair and sighed.

Baby clearly heard what Horace wasn't saying out loud. *I have to escort my wife. I can't be seen with my mistress. I have to be respectable.* Disappointment slapped her in the face. Of course, a wife would take precedence over a paramour at such an important event. She had been a fool. Baby took a deep breath. Throwing a hissy fit wouldn't change the facts. No, better to keep her place, remember her role and continue to play the sweet young ingénue. If Augusta was the burr under Horace's saddle; Baby wanted to be the sugar cube treat that enticed him. Baby willed the corners of her mouth to turn up in a small smile.

"I understand, Horace." She reached over and held his hand. "I will be the soul of discretion. I am just excited for you."

Baby Doe had to admit Augusta and Billy had done a fine job planning the welcoming parade and banquet. Baby joined the huge crowds cheering as President and Mrs. Grant, accompanied by Mr. and Mrs. Tabor, rode by in an open-air barouche pulled by gleaming black horses whose hunches sparkled with gold dust.

As soon as the carriage passed, Baby headed to the Clarendon Hotel. She knew Horace insisted that Billy reserve a seat for her. She also knew that seat was in a dark corner at the far back of the room. While everyone else was waiting on the front steps or in the lobby for the former president and first lady to make their way into the hotel, Baby weaved her way surreptitiously to the banquet room. She walked directly to Ben, the headwaiter.

Ben knew Baby Doe was a special friend of Mr. Tabor's who lived in his suite at the hotel, and she was always pleasant to him and the rest of the staff. When a new waiter had been so stunned by her beauty that he tripped over a chair, spilling a tray of food and causing a ruckus, she merely laughed and told Ben not to be hard on the young man.

"There has been a mistake, Ben. The table in front, just to the left of the dais," she pointed, "it is missing a chair and setting. Quickly now, before Mr. Tabor arrives with the president."

When the guests of honor entered and sat down at the dais, Baby slipped gracefully into a seat at a table at the front of the room. She chatted lightly with her crowded tablemates about the decorations and weather. When all eyes turned to the head table to hear Lieutenant Governor Tabor toast their esteemed visitor, Baby felt two sets of eyes settle on her. She gave the president a small smile, then turned to meet Augusta's stare with an unblinking gaze of her own.

If Horace wasn't forty-eight years old with a miner's aching back and size thirteen feet, he would have skipped up the stairs to Baby Doe's new small room at the Clarendon. Staying in the little house on Chestnut Street with Augusta was exhausting. She spent three days hissing in his ear and every sentence started with "don't'" or "no" or "stop": "Don't slouch," "No more drinking," "Stop talking about yourself." Hell, she even told him that he chewed his food wrong.

Horace flung the door open without a knock, "How's my best girl?"

Oh Horace, I know I am not your best girl; I'm just your right-now girl. When it was important, you turned to Augusta. But I am going to change that. "Happy to be with you," was the answer she said aloud.

Her rose colored dressing gown was cinched tight at the waist and pulled so low on her décolleté it barely clung to her shoulders. Baby had waited for Horace for the better part of two hours, trying out different poses, draping the gown this way and that. Subtle didn't work with Horace, and so she carefully orchestrated every moment of the scene. She lifted her skirt slightly and walked slowly toward him with long steps, showing softly curved calves. "I was so proud of you. The president's visit went very well."

He grabbed her and planted a sloppy smooch on her perfectly painted lips. She gently nibbled on his hairy upper lip, then stopped and gave a dramatic sigh. "I'm going to miss that moustache."

"This caterpillar is not going anywhere, but right here." He landed a strong kiss, and she indulged him, flicking her tongue against his and licking his bottom lip. She pulled away again.

"After this success, Governor Pitkin will want you in Denver more and more. You are bound for higher office now. I will be left here in Leadville." She pretended a small pout while tracing a seductive line around his mouth and down his neck. She loosened his tie. "I just wish there was a way I could be near you." She kissed the hollow of his throat. "Always." Another kiss on his neck, his earlobe. "I don't want to be out of sight and out of mind."

"I could never forget you, Baby," Horace said, fumbling with his shirt buttons.

Baby pushed Horace's hands away and slowly, slowly unbuttoned his white dress shirt. She pulled his suspenders down, holding them at his hips. "I don't want to be just in your mind." She pressed close against him. "I want to be at your side every day as you conquer the world. And I want to be in your arms, in your bed every night."

Words abandoned Horace, so he picked her up and carried her to bed.

Morning light streamed into the Clarendon suite as Baby Doe rolled over and lazily opened one eye. Horace was standing at the window. A small frown wrinkled his face. "Silver dollar for your thoughts," she teased.

"I was just watching people going to church. Augusta is probably on her way, too."

Baby remained silent. She tried to never say the woman's name or utter a word about her in front of Horace. She wanted her bedroom to be a world where she and Horace were always happy and Augusta didn't exist. Now, just when Baby had begun to plan the expansion of their little world to the outside, that woman intruded.

Horace sighed. "She isn't a bad person, she's just unhappy. Everything I do makes her bitter. I think she was happiest when we first came to the territory. Life was so hard, we lived in a tent, we moved from camp to camp. She was the first white woman in this area. She was alone a lot," he talked on, almost to himself. "Augusta made a little money running a store and boarding miners in our tent." He turned to face Baby, "She feels that hard, plain living is godly. It is the Puritan in her. So, the more successful I become, the more money I have, the more unhappy she is."

Horace sat down in a stick chair. Baby silently got out of bed and settled herself at his feet, resting her head on his knee. "You should see the way she acts. She won't sleep upstairs, says it's too fancy. She sleeps in the servant's room off the kitchen. She milks a cow on the front lawn. The lieutenant governor's wife milking a cow! When I give her pretty clothes or jewelry, she practically throws them in my face, like I'm the serpent from the Garden of Eden tempting her into evil." He paused and looked at his large hands. "Augusta believes that God is demanding and vengeful, but I think He wants us to find happiness where we can."

Horace cupped his hands around Baby's smooth white cheeks. "I find happiness in you," he whispered.

That afternoon Horace told Billy that he would be moving to Denver full time. His mining and business interests in Leadville were running smoothly and could be left under the watch of capable managers. His future now lay elsewhere, Denver and beyond. He instructed Billy to start looking for new business ventures and to arrange for new living quarters for Baby Doe in Denver. "Something grand. Baby Doe likes grand."

CHAPTER 16

BABY DOE GOT THE IMPRESSION that Billy was trying to throw cold water on her plan to move to Denver. She and Horace were both bubbly with excitement when they arrived at Billy's office on the first floor of the Clarendon; but sitting across the broad mahogany desk, she soon felt like a high-spirited child being lectured to mind her manners in front of important guests.

Billy had given them quite a talking to about the growing morality crusades and how different life was in refined Denver compared to rough-and-ready Leadville. He had several suggestions to assure the Tabor name be accepted in the highest circles. The Mile High City social scene was dominated by women determined to wipe away the dusty origins of fortunes made in mining, railroads and timber. These nouveau riche ladies polished their thin veneer of respectability with many public acts of philanthropy and civic involvement. They were doing their best to ensure the world saw Denver as the glimmering jewel of the West, a city of refinement and sophistication, even if that meant importing the culture from Europe and hiding the unseemly origins of their own fortunes.

"A gentleman in your political position must be very careful of appearances," Billy said. "You can't be seen publicly with any," he paused, "disreputable characters."

"I don't know any disreputable characters, unless you mean Democrats," Horace answered with a laugh.

Although sure that some people would describe her so, Baby was touched that Horace defended her. She gave him a smile before shooting a hateful glare at Billy.

Ignoring her and speaking to Horace, Billy said, "I have arranged for you to arrive in Denver by private rail car. David Moffat is happy to lend his. There will be newspaper reporters to greet you at the train station. You can say a few words about being able to better serve the people and looking forward to becoming a Denver citizen. Two days after your arrival, I am planning a small reception at your house. You can formally announce that you will be living in Denver year-round and starting new business enterprises there. I think a nice touch would be to make a donation to one of the many organizations dedicated to improving Denver values. The Temperance League is well known and the Denver Protective Society is also respected."

"What do they protect against?" Horace asked.

"Well, their full name is the Denver Protective Society against Tight Corsets, but..."

Horace and Baby both burst out laughing.

"No siree," Horace said. "I like a gal with a tiny waist. I am not giving them a dime." He winked at Baby.

"They do other work as well." Billy looked a little indignant.

"Like what, cutting the heels off of women's shoes?" Baby guffawed.

"They are concerned with improving the character of the city and preventing local madams from parading their girls through the street on Sunday afternoons," Billy sat straighter in his chair. "There are many well-placed ladies in that organization." He pulled a paper from a folio on his desk. "Here is a list of a few other civic and charitable groups to whom a donation could enhance a reputation."

Baby felt a twinge between her shoulder blades like a stab in the back. She wasn't sure Billy had looked her in the eye since they arrived. She peeked over Horace's shoulder at the list. There were several groups trumpeting their causes with ridiculously pious names, such as The Moral Purity Crusade against Urban Vice and the Vigilance League to Stamp out Moral Deficiencies, as well as a few Episcopal and Protestant benevolent groups. Billy Bush, that wily fox, was going to make Denver society ladies do his dirty work. Baby decided she needed to let Bush know she would not be pushed away once they got to Denver and that he wasn't the only person to whom Horace listened.

"Horace, could you please consider the Society of St. Vincent de Paul? I don't see them on the list. I don't see any Catholic charities at all, but St. Vincent's does great work for poor women and children, and so many of your miners are Catholic," Baby asked, all round eyes and innocence.

"Of course," Horace grabbed the pen from the inkwell and wrote "St. Vincent" at the bottom of the page.

"Perhaps you should not give to a religious organization. That might put off voters from other churches," Billy pulled the list away from Horace.

"Not if he gives money to them too," Baby countered. "Horace, I just had a wonderful idea. What if you gave donations to one hundred organizations? That would make a big splash in Denver's fish pond."

"One hundred and one!" Horace declared, slapping the desk. Baby laughed and clapped her hands. She gave Billy her biggest smile, although he did not seem to like the idea.

"I want to help build a new post office for the city. A town can't thrive without a good postal system. Write post office on the list, Billy, and invite the postmaster to that reception at the house."

"How very astute, Horace. You have a fine business mind," Baby said.

"Speaking of business," Billy said, trying to regain control of the conversation. "You asked me to find new ventures in Denver, as well as find new living quarters for Baby Doe. I think I might be able to kill both birds with one stone. Do you remember Charles Hall?"

"Sure, struck a nice load of high paying ore last year. Then sold out and moved to Denver. I think he owns the Windsor Hotel," answered Horace.

"That's right. He renovated it top to bottom and now finds himself a bit short of cash. I propose that you purchase a one-third share in the hotel, and Baby Doe can make her residence there."

"I read about the Windsor in Denver newspapers. It sounds extraordinary," Baby said.

"Sold," said Horace, throwing his hand in the air as if at an auction. "Baby needs all things extraordinary."

Baby Doe leaned from her chair and wrapped her arms around Horace's neck, kissing him on the check. Horace smiled and patted her knee.

Billy busied himself making notes, looking away from the garish display. He would insist the two lovebirds take separate trains to

Denver on separate days. He also wanted Baby Doe to wear a veil to cover her face when in public in Denver. Her looks drew stares everywhere she went and the woman did nothing to discourage them. Better to not have Tabor's name associated with such a memorable female. Horace's behavior was colorful enough.

With all of the couple's antics, Billy had not found the time to tell Horace that he, Billy Bush had also purchased a one-third interest in the hotel and that he would be managing it. Billy and Baby Doe would be neighbors at the Windsor.

CHAPTER 17

Denver

THE WINDSOR HOTEL was the most exclusive residence in a town where gold and silver came in by the trainload, where bankers outnumber horse traders, and safes were a common commodity shipped in from the East. Baby's calfskin boots sank into the hotel's thick carpets covering the glossy parquet floors. The twenty-foot-high ceilings were painted with frescos of cherubs playing among clouds and trimmed in elaborate baroque molding like a European castle. Ladies lounged on fine velvet settees and sipped tea from tiny bone china cups in the lobby, while gentlemen enjoyed whiskey from cut glass at a sixty-foot mahogany bar before indulging in a steamy Russian bath or a dry Turkish one. Dozens of elaborate crystal chandeliers twinkled above the lobby and ballroom.

Horace had Baby's suite prepared in advance. The bellhop tied back the heavy burgundy curtains from the tall windows in the sitting area and sunbeams filtered across a Persian rug. An intricately carved mahogany headboard dominated the bedroom. The pink satin bedspread seemed to softly glow. Baby, amazed at the grandeur, moved slowly through the suite, touching each item: the delicate writing table, the gold lacquered chairs, the enormous armoire, the brush of the velvet curtains, the smooth pillow sham. A bubble of laughter rose from her belly. She tried to stifle it.

"Madam? Is everything to your liking?" asked the bellhop.

The laughter popped out as she flung off Billy Bush's hated veil and flopped into the deep feather mattress on the high bed. "Oh, yes. It is so lovely to be home."

The Windsor Hotel bar was the gathering place for Denver's politicians, bankers, wheelers and dealers. The joke about town was if a man needed something done in Denver, he should first stop by the Windsor for a drink. Newspaper reporters realized that there was little need to run all over town researching stories, investigating leads or interviewing subjects; all could be done in the comforts of the Windsor bar while sipping whiskey neat. Horace's brand of political activism fit in well at the Windsor. He believed there were few issues that couldn't be resolved with a funny story, a slap on the back or a stiff drink, and his open tab made him a crowd favorite.

"Baby, let's stop in the bar on our way to dinner and say hello to some of the fellas. It seems that the Colorado state legislature pretty much meets there every night before going home to supper," Horace said as he waited for Baby to finish pinning her hair. "I can introduce you around."

"Will there be other ladies there?" She knew sporting girls, like her Shoo Fly friends, did not frequent the elegant Windsor. She was unsure if Denver ladies, who proclaimed their sophistication by flaunting memberships in morality committees, would accompany their husbands to the bar for a small sherry before heading into the dining room.

"I don't know," Horace replied. "I know I see them in the lobby having tea."

"That's different."

"Aww, it'll be fine. You'll have all those men eating out of your hand in no time."

Baby Doe knew Denver would not be as fancy-free as Leadville; but most of the town's millionaires had found their wealth digging in the dirt of the rough mining camps; and there wasn't an established upper class of well-bred aristocrats here. Those that thought of themselves as the city's elite had just been down from the mountains a little longer than she. In the West, gentility did not come from one's linage, but one's accomplishments or one's bank account. As the companion of the state's wealthiest man, Baby Doe hoped the male citizens of the town would receive her with some degree of regard. She was less sure of her reception by their wives. She pushed any doubts from her mind and nailed a smile on her face, determined to have a lovely first evening in her new city.

Dozens of male heads turned to stare as the couple entered the bar.

"Evening all," Horace called. "Oh, hey there, Mr. Easker. Come and meet Baby Doe. She just moved down from Leadville. Mr. Easker leads the state legislature."

"Pleasure to meet you, Miss Doe."

"Oh, and over here is the head of the state Republican party, Ambrose Smith. Ambrose, come and meet the city's newest resident, Baby Doe."

"How do you do, Miss Doe?"

On it went. Baby shook hands with several men, carefully reading their faces to gauge her reception. Most seemed slightly stunned to see her, but she was unsure if it was because she was a woman in a bar or if they realized her position as Tabor's mistress. Some were pleasant, others merely polite, only a very few intently studied their drinks determined not to notice her and Horace. No one was blatantly discourteous.

She didn't even feel out of place standing alone at the bar for a brief moment when Horace was pulled into a conversation with other Republicans about finding new candidates for office. She smiled and chatted with the burly bartender, Jaime, whose muscled arms strained at his shirtsleeves as he daintily poured more champagne into her glass. She didn't notice the short, stocky young man, standing amid a cluster of reporters, who stared at her with naked admiration.

Eugene Hawthorne was completely bewitched by the pocket Venus sipping champagne just a few steps from him. Eugene's mother had assured him that his abbreviated stature would not matter to ladies of substance; they would all be enamored by his towering intellect, his forceful personality and Adonis-like good looks. The ladies that Eugene had encountered so far compared his appearance to a bulldog rather than a Greek god and, while his tenacious personality was an asset to his burgeoning journalist career, the fairer sex did not seem to appreciate it. Of course, no woman could ever be impressed by his mental agility, it was beyond the female capacity. He was sure that the slights he suffered at the hands of foolish females were due to his squat limbs. The petite blonde before him would be the perfect complement to his compact frame. When he offered his elbow, it would fall delightfully at the curve of her waist. Her tower of curls would not top his own thinning crown. Her slight hand would fit flawlessly in his. She was exquisite. Together they would be the most handsome couple in all of Denver.

"That's quite a dish," a deep voice interrupted his imaginings. Lester Graham worked with Eugene at the *Denver Star Ledger*. They weren't exactly friends, more like competitors. Lester came from a fancy East Coast family and carried himself with an air of pretentious prissiness. He was annoyingly tall.

"She's lovely," Eugene's voice had oddly gone hoarse.

"You can't afford her, Hawthorne. She's Tabor's new dolly, bought and paid for."

"Get lost, Graham," Eugene said pushing him aside and walking up to this seraphim come to life.

"Allow me to introduce myself, I am Eugene Hawthorne, reporter and writer for the *Denver Star Ledger*."

He put out a soft, pudgy hand that Baby found slightly moist. His tight smile pushed his small eyes into a squint above a turned-up nose. She thought he looked a little like a pig, and remembered that pigs are smarter and meaner than most people give them credit. She would tread carefully with this little man.

"How do you do? I am Baby Doe, most recently of Leadville."

"Yes, yes, so I understand. It's Miss Doe, correct, not Mrs. Doe. Is that right?"

Baby's stomach clenched. She was not sure where the conversation was headed, but she gave him a small smile and replied, "Yes, I am not married."

"What brings you here, Miss Doe?"

For all her mulling in preparation of meeting new Denverites, she had not been able to think of a satisfactory answer, so she pretended not to understand. "The roast pheasant. I hear it is delicious."

A small chuckle and shake of the head, "Charming. No, Miss Doe. What will you be doing in Denver?"

"I intend to make Denver my home," she began.

"And where do you plan to reside?"

"I am currently staying here at the Windsor. Really, Mr. Hawthorne, so many questions. Do all reporters make conversation in this way?"

"Yes, yes. Tabor has put you up here for now." He continued in a most impatient way. "But I am sure you will be seeking more youthful and sophisticated friends. Where will you be receiving gentlemen callers? Surely not here at the hotel?"

"Excuse me? I cannot possibly understand to what you are referring." Baby became aware of the group of reporters moving up quietly behind her, the young bucks leaning into listen. She felt a trap begin to close around her. What was he implying when he asked if she would receive gentlemen callers? Did he mean like the Shoo Fly girls? *How dare he*? Hawthorne's beady eyes glistened and his faced pulled into a forced smile that seemed a smirk to Baby. She could feel her temper start to rise and she forgot about caution.

"Where can I call on you? Here at the hotel? I think you will find me quite good company."

Baby stuck out her chin and looked down her nose. "Mr. Hawthorne, I only keep company with men of a certain standing and," she paused and allowed her eyes to slowly run up and down his small frame, "a certain stature." She turned her back to him with a flourish as his mates burst out laughing.

Eugene gaped in surprise.

"Hawthorne, old boy," Lester Graham clapped him on the back. "Perhaps if you stood atop Tabor's wallet, you could achieve a *certain stature*." The howl of laughter grew.

"I think she wants a man with a bigger . . . *pair of pants*," jeered another.

Fresh bays of mirth arose from the callow group and Eugene's face flushed deep red. He grabbed Baby's elbow and whispered in her ear, "Now see here, you whore."

She turned to slap his ugly pig face, but she wasn't as fast as Jaime who leapt over the bar and clocked him in the jaw. Eugene crumpled like a used hankie. Donald, the other bartender, came around and grabbed one arm and the seat of Eugene's pants. Jaime picked up the other side and they carried the would-be suitor like a sack of potatoes through the lobby with Eugene's friends following. The young reporters held their sides in laughter when the bartenders threw Eugene into the street.

Donald brushed his hands and headed back inside, but Jaime leaned over the smaller man. "I heard what you called her. You are not welcome back at the Windsor."

"You can't keep me out of there," Eugene cried as he struggled to his feet. "I am a political and business reporter. It is important that I remain in close contact with these people, the people at the Windsor."

Jaime pointed a sausage finger in Eugene's face and simply said, "No," before turning and walking back inside.

CHAPTER 18

EUGENE'S EDITOR at the *Denver Star Ledger* had heard all about the previous night's hullabaloo and decided that Eugene was going to have a very difficult time writing about Colorado politics after insulting the lieutenant governor's paramour and getting banned from the capital city's favorite watering hole. In disgust, he reassigned Eugene to the society page, where the brash young reporter could work on his manners and diplomacy.

It was humiliating. Eugene's writing skills, his superior intelligence and his keen insights would be wasted on such a demeaning assignment, an assignment so meaningless that even a woman could do it. Eugene had to get out of this assignment and back into the Windsor. His most savvy diplomatic move would be a conversation with Tabor's right-hand man, Billy Bush. If anyone could get the ban from the Windsor bar lifted, it was Bush.

"It was a terrible misunderstanding. I didn't realize to whom I was speaking, Mr. Bush," Eugene said, sitting in the manager's office, hat in hand, contrite expression on his face.

Billy brushed his small moustache with a finger then held it up. "Do not continue with this story. I know it's not true." He closed his eyes in thought. "My advice to you is to use your new position to its greatest advantage. There is much to be learned in the drawing rooms and ballrooms and, even the halls of the capital building." Billy leaned forward, as if in confidence, "Baby Doe will not be Tabor's mistress forever. Another pretty face will catch his eye, she will be given a parting gift and you can come back to the Windsor."

Eugene's reporter instincts were beginning to understand this gossip trade. "Oh? Is there discord in the suites at the Windsor? Something I could mention in the next edition?"

"No, it is quite the happy little love nest," Billy leaned back in his chair. "But, you know, readers might be interested in Baby Doe's history, who were her friends in Central City, her first husband ..."

A week later, Baby Doe gasped as she read the *Denver Star Ledger*:

TABOR'S VEILED WOMAN IS A DIVORCÉE!
WHEREABOUTS OF HUSBAND UNKNOWN

Silver King, Horace Tabor, has installed a young divorcée in a luxury suite at the Windsor Hotel.

Elizabeth McCourt Doe, now calling herself Baby Doe, first arrived in Colorado with husband Harvey Doe, a mine owner in Central City three years ago. Baby Doe was well known among the townsfolk for her remarkable beauty and libertine ways. When Mr. Doe's mine did not prove immediately profitable, Baby Doe sued for divorce. She soon departed for Leadville in the company of another man. It was in Leadville that the gay divorcée met Mr. Tabor and appeared on his arm at several dinners and local balls.

It is rumored that the hapless Mr. Doe may have succumbed to the temptation of alcoholic spirits.

Eugene was doubly satisfied with his story. Not only did the erupting scandal tarnish the haughty harlot, it also had the other young reporters scrambling to catch up.

Billy read the paper with a silent smile.

A couple of weeks later the *Denver Star Ledger* newsies shouted on street corners, "Tabor's Woman Lives in Luxury. Read all about it. Get your paper here."

THE LUXURIOUS LIFE OF
TABOR'S KEPT WOMAN!

Horace Tabor is keeping his other woman in high style while the miners he employees make less than four dollars a day. It is purported that Baby Doe, a divorcée originally known as Elizabeth McCourt Doe, resides in

> the grandest suite at Denver's most prestigious hotel, the Windsor. Mr. Tabor is a part owner of the Windsor and it appears he is financing Mrs. Doe's lifestyle. It is rumored that the woman drinks champagne, bathes in cream and rose petals and insists that only silk touch her skin. Tabor has hired a special seamstress to make an entire wardrobe of silken unmentionables for his latest friend. Although the woman is not frequently seen in society and wears a veil to hide her identity when out of doors, it is thought that she uses paints and powders on her face which are ordered at great cost from Paris, France. According to people familiar with the hotel goings-on, a certain jeweler, reputed to be an expert in gemstones, is a frequent visitor to the hotel suite.

"Not true! Not true," Baby shouted at the latest edition. "I do not paint my face." She did like champagne, but was careful not to overindulge; she had read it caused bags under the eyes. Milk baths were the latest rage in beauty treatments, but she had only tried it once and it wasn't cream, it was milk. Horace ordered the lingerie and she hadn't met any jeweler. It was as if the writer was just making it all up.

The editor of the *Star Ledger* was so pleased with the salacious stories that he gave Eugene Hawthorne a byline. "Baby Doe is selling more papers than your political stories ever did. The public can't get enough of her," he declared.

The next week the *Star Ledger's* headlines were closer to the truth:

TABOR'S MISTRESS A GOLD DIGGER,
DRESSED AS A MAN

By Eugene Hawthorne

Baby Doe, the current companion of Silver Baron Horace Tabor dressed as a man and worked inside a mine with a crew of Cornish miners while living in Central City. The young woman, surrounded by rough mining sorts, descended into the depth of the dark tunnels each day for over two months while living in Central City. Locals say her husband, Mr. Doe, tried to dissuade her from the dangerous work.

That evening Baby shouted at the paper, "I am not ashamed of that."

Horace asked, "Who is Eugene Hawthorne?"

A month later the *Denver Star Ledger* sold out when the headlines read:

TABOR'S WOMAN SEEN AT HOUSE
OF ILL REPUTE

By Eugene Hawthorne

This reporter has it on good authority that Silver Baron Horace Tabor's doxy, Baby Doe, was a frequent visitor to a saloon and brothel while living in Central City. The Shoo Fly Saloon is owned by Madame Belle and, in addition to serving alcohol, features gaming tables, stage

> shows and fallen women. Mrs. Doe was escorted to the palace of sinful pleasures by a local shopkeeper, Jacob Sandelowsky. It is suspected that Mr. Sandelowsky is of Jewish descent. While it is not known what activities Baby Doe engaged in while at the Shoo Fly, it is noted that she returned on several occasions.

"It was a parlor house," she railed, "not . . . not . . . not that!" She wadded the paper and threw it across the room. "They were my friends."

The editor of the *Ledger* handed Eugene a cigar, "Tabor's man, Billy Bush, came to see me. Seems to be, Horace Tabor wants you fired. You've got a real knack for this kind of reporting. Keep up the good work."

CHAPTER 19

IN HIS LATEST STORY, Eugene Hawthorne listed several "colorful female companions" from Horace's past. "I already know about these women, you little swine," Baby Doe muttered as she read the newspaper. She suspected Billy, in an effort to unseat her, had provided the reporter with the women's names; however, the article merely bolstered her resolve to strengthen her ties with Horace. She needed to weave her way into all parts of his life so he would be unable to lightly toss her away. She would be his confidante in all matters, from romance to business, from bedroom to boardroom, from kisses to claims.

With the move to Denver, Horace threw himself into becoming a successful business baron. As the Windsor Hotel humming along as the premier place to lay one's head, Billy cast about for other ventures.

Denver was growing; a new building dedicated to commerce would have no problem finding businesses to fill it. So, Horace's first project became building Tabor Block. "Not just a building—an entire block," he declared. The six-story granite and iron building in the center of town would be the first in Denver to boast of an elevator

As the building began to take shape, both of Horace's women inserted themselves into the project. A routine began to develop: Horace would propose an idea, Augusta's sharp tongue would slash it to ribbons while Baby Doe would pump it up like a hot air balloon. The two women were never in Billy's office at the same time, but they seemed able to sniff out any touches of the other on the construction plans. Billy was pulled like a schoolyard tug-of-war rope between Augusta's demands to see the latest construction costs and suggested economies and Baby's proposals for ever more elaborate detailing, such as marble stairs and fitted flagstones in front of the building rather than the usual wooden boardwalk. When called upon to make a decision, Horace used the axiom: "If it pleases Baby, then do it. There is no pleasing Augusta, so don't worry about it."

Tenants included a jeweler, a law firm, an insurance office, ticket counters for the Kansas Pacific and Central Colorado railroads, a bank owned by Horace's friend, David Moffat and, of course, an office for Tabor Enterprises. The $325,000 construction costs made headlines and the friendlier newspapers described the edifice as ornate, but tasteful. The capstone was carved, at Baby's suggestion, with Tabor's totems: a miner's prospecting pan, pick, and shovel, and the phrase "Dies Faustus" — lucky day.

"Tabor Block is finished and I'm ready for another project," Horace announced to Augusta in the study of the 14th Street mansion. Augusta insisted on knowing the goings-on within the Tabor Empire. In an effort to keep his women separated, Horace began visiting the house, or frequently sending Billy, to provide his wife with updates. "I am going to build an opera house for Denver, the likes of which has never been seen," he declared. "I'm sending men to Europe to get ideas from the Vienna State Opera and Covent Garden in London and whatever fancy theater they have in Paris."

"I don't see the need," was Augusta's characteristically blunt answer, not even bothering to look up from the sock she was darning. She sat in a rocking chair taking advantage of the tall windows and the bright Colorado sunshine streaming through.

"I don't see the need of you patching up that old sock when I could buy you new socks every day of your life," Horace said. Augusta shot him a look, but didn't bite. "This will put Denver on the map," he continued. "It will show those society bitties that Ol' Hod has some culture."

"How much is this latest vanity project going to cost?"

"One million dollars!" Horace said with huge grin and a slap to his knee.

Augusta was aghast. She couldn't tell if he was teasing, trying to get a rise out of her, or if he was serious and this was an actual planned budget on a palatial scale. He certainly looked proud as punch.

"No, Horace, you can't, you just can't," she stumbled, this was wrong for so many reasons. "It is vulgar to flaunt wealth like that, like this." She swept her arm around the drawing room with its high ceilings, mahogany furniture and gas jet lighting. "Hod, for reasons I cannot understand, God has given you one of the greatest fortunes in all of the United States. Now, you must take care of that gift. Invest and save so that Maxcy and our grandchildren and great-grandchildren can live respectfully and, if there is excess, help those that cannot help themselves. Small philanthropies for righteous causes are far more favorable in God's eyes." She resumed her darning, "No million-dollar opera house."

"Woman, you do not know what God favors, and you do not make business decisions for me," Horace said, rising from the brocade armchair. "You accuse me of not knowing my social place. Well, know your place, Woman." He punched the crown of his hat and headed for the door.

"I know where you are going. I know who you see," Augusta leapt up and followed. "You cheapen yourself in the eyes of your son, in the eyes of all of Denver with that blonde. Then you try to buy respectability with a post office and a theater. Why, Hod? Do you actually believe that she loves you? Look at yourself. You are a podgy, wrinkled old man who is losing his hair. The only thing she finds attractive is your wallet."

Horace stopped. "Shut your mouth. You go too far."

Augusta caught up with him and placed herself between her husband and the door. "I have overlooked a half dozen harlots over the years because I knew in a couple of weeks they would be gone. But this one is too much. It has been six months of her parading around in satin and jewels and that ridiculous veil, as if it can hide her wantonness. Tell me, Hod, what does this one have?"

"She is nice to me," Horace said through gritted teeth. He pushed Augusta from the door and went out to his waiting buggy.

"Give her one of your parting gift checks and get rid of her," Augusta called after him.

Horace climbed into the buggy and plopped down so hard the whole contraption shook. He whipped his horse hell bent for leather all the way to the train station. Inside, he scribbled three messages and handed the notes and three silver dollars to an errand boy with instructions to deliver them to the Windsor Hotel.

To Maxcy he wrote: Went to Leadville. Come pick up the horse and buggy at the station.

To Baby Doe he wrote: Went to Leadville to see to about some business. Will return soon.

To Billy he wrote: Tell David Moffat I borrowed his private train car for a trip to Leadville. Will return soon.

It was dull without Horace, so Baby Doe decided to enjoy the lovely Indian summer weather with a little stroll about. She grabbed the hated veil that Billy insisted was critical to the Tabor reputation and headed downstairs.

"Good afternoon, Mrs. Doe," Billy called from the doorway of his office near the Windsor front desk.

Baby pinched her lips at the married woman's honorific. "Everyone calls me Baby Doe now."

"Yes, I know." Billy said. He stepped aside and waved a hand toward a chair in his office. "I'd like a moment of your time. I want to tell you about some personnel changes here at the hotel."

Baby sat down and considered Billy warily. Although she had tried to make herself useful offering her opinion and suggestions in

Horace's business affairs, she never said a word about the Windsor. She knew that Billy owned a one-third interest in the hotel and felt a proprietary pride in the Windsor. He would think her overstepping her place by offering any comment. She disliked Billy but she would not make the mistake of purposely stepping on his toes.

Billy sat down behind the desk and cleared his throat. "I have been discussing the Tabor legacy with the family and it has been proposed that young Maxcy come work here with me and further his education in commerce. His title will be assistant hotel manager, but I anticipate that he will begin attending to some other Tabor interests and eventually oversee business affairs on his own."

Like a chess master, Billy had used a minor piece to corner the queen. Horace always wanted to keep Baby separate from his family, now by bringing Maxcy into the Windsor office, Billy locked Baby out of any business discussions and into her room.

"What a grand idea," Baby said, not feeling that way at all.

"Yes," Billy agreed, "of course, Governor Tabor and I will work out the details when he returns from his little holiday to Leadville." Billy paused. Baby realized he said holiday to describe what Horace had told her was a business trip, but she kept her face still. Billy continued, "I know Tabor told everyone it was business, but the town's Fall Ball is really more of a bacchanal, a last hootenanny before the snow flies. You know how revelry can deteriorate into a debauchery in Leadville. I am told Tabor had a bottle in each hand and a girl on each knee." Billy shook his head in mock sadness.

"Why are you telling me this story, Mr. Bush?"

"I am greatly concerned with Tabor's reputation and wellbeing."

"Your success being tied so closely to his," Baby said tartly. "I'm aware that you don't like me, Mr. Bush, but this attempt to drive us apart will fail. You see, I'm very different from Augusta. I will not be goaded into a jealous fit, and I'm not going to harangue Horace for any indiscretions. In fact, if the topic does arise, I will take the position that a man whose habit it is to work very hard needs vigorous entertainment as well."

A thin sarcastic smile eased across Bush's face. "Very shrewd, Baby Doe, but you will need to be a powerful actress to pull it off. Women are possessive and demanding creatures by nature. When you next see Tabor, you will not be able to prevent yourself from henpecking him."

"I'm sure Augusta will, but not me." Baby had already figured out that her caresses to Horace's bruised spirit were as welcome as her caresses to his body. "A cad like you may not be able to understand the subtle differences between Augusta and me. We both want Horace to be faithful. Augusta will demand it. I will never make such claims, but I will achieve what she has never been able to. I will make Horace *want* to be faithful to me." Baby stood to leave.

"Be sure to wear your veil, Mrs. Doe. It will be hard enough trying to stop the gossip from Leadville without adding more scandal of your own making," was Billy's parting shot.

The next afternoon there was a timid knock at Baby Doe's door. She opened it to find a pale and shaky Horace, eyes bloodshot, skin the pallor of old dishwater, twisting his hat in hand. *He looks like death warmed over,* she thought. *It must have been quite a bender.* "Come in, darling." She took his hand and led him to the settee. "It's a little early for supper, but would you like me to order some tea and sandwiches?"

"That would be good." He stared at his shoes.

Baby Doe patted his shoulder and briskly made her way downstairs to the dining room and ordered a tray be delivered as soon as possible. She sent a bellhop out for Seidlitz powder to calm Horace's stomach and willow bark tea for his aching head. Billy caught her eye as she started back upstairs, but she would not give him the satisfaction of a dramatic reaction.

When she returned to the room, Horace patted the settee beckoning her to sit. "Baby, I didn't behave well in Leadville. You may hear some stories." He shook his head, "I don't know why I put one on like that, but I do know that I am powerfully sorry about it and I'd even be sorrier if you were mad." Horace finally looked into her eyes. "I promise you I won't behave like that again."

Baby held Horace's sagging, whiskery cheeks in her hands and said, "Horace Tabor, you are the best thing that ever happened to me. And I promise you, I won't ever forget that."

Horace put his head in her lap and wept. Baby stroked his head and knew she had played that hand just right.

CHAPTER 20

TABOR AND BILLY were finishing up the day's business in the dim gaslight of the December early evening. The men had spent the afternoon settling accounts for the Windsor and the tenants of Tabor Block. They discussed briefly the plans for the next project, the Tabor Grand Opera, named by Baby Doe so that Coloradans would not confuse it with the original Tabor Opera House in Leadville. Although these meetings always went more smoothly without the attendance of either of Tabor's women, Augusta's endless criticisms or Baby's unbridled enthusiasm, Tabor's extravagant impulses were enough of a challenge for the methodical Bush. When the two men had seen samples of beautiful Honduran mahogany to be used at the new opera house, Tabor was so impressed with the gorgeous colors and whorls of the wood that he ordered Billy to buy all the finished wood needed for construction and then purchased the whole damn forest that it was cut from. He ended up purchasing nearly half of the country of Honduras.

"Oh," Tabor said casually, "there is one more thing I need you to take care of. I'd like you to give Augusta a parting gift."

Billy paused, unsure what he meant. He had given cash or checks to a few tarts after Tabor had tired of their company. He knew Tabor had not been sleeping in the family's mansion on Broadway since fall, shortly after Baby Doe had moved into the Windsor, but Billy was sure that, sooner or later, Tabor would go back to steady Augusta. "You mean Baby Doe? Give Baby Doe a parting gift?"

"No," Horace cleared his throat. "I'm leaving Augusta. I'd like you to suggest to her that she file for divorce. Tell her that we need to keep this gracious and quiet. The state legislature will be voting next year on who to send to Washington as the new senator. I don't want a big hullabaloo in the newspapers."

Billy could not believe his ears. "You will be marrying Baby Doe?"

"Yes, but we don't want that made public yet. I want any gossip to die down before Baby and I announce our intentions. I think that is kinder to Augusta." Horace nodded his head in agreement with himself. "And politically wiser, too."

"What parting gift will you be giving Mrs. Tabor? The usual one thousand dollars?"

"No," Tabor seemed piqued by the question. "She was my wife. I think one hundred thousand dollars is a fair amount."

Billy could not imagine Augusta's response. She could respond sharply when passers-by commented on the lovely weather. To truly cross her was to risk being flayed alive. "What if she doesn't wish to divorce?"

"I don't think that will be a problem. Billy, you know Augusta and I haven't been what you would call happily married for some time now. She'll probably be relieved to be rid of an old scoundrel like me."

But Augusta did not seem relieved when Billy visited her the next morning with Horace's gift and suggestion of divorce. She pressed her lips tightly together as if holding back a spew of vinegar and her eyes lost all color becoming black holes of anger. Her hands, clenched in tight white fists, trembled in her lap.

Billy had prepared himself for a vicious tongue-lashing, but Augusta's strangled silence was even more frightening. This was the worst errand Billy had ever performed for Tabor.

When Augusta did speak, her voice was low and controlled. "Tell Horace there will be no divorce. Good day, Mr. Bush."

The abrupt end to the conversation was fine with Billy. He stood and reached for the one-hundred-thousand-dollar check lying on the table between them, but Augusta was faster. She snatched the check and deepened her icy glare. Billy pulled his empty hand back, mumbled goodbye and bolted for the door.

A few days later, Billy sat in his office at the Windsor Hotel. Tabor and Baby Doe had not taken Augusta's response well, but it was their problem to solve. Billy eyed his calendar. No doubt, with all the palms he had greased, Tabor would be elected senator and move to Washington next year, taking Augusta, Baby Doe and all the drama with him. Then

Billy would buy out Tabor's third share of the hotel. Billy would be majority owner, the boss, not Tabor's errand boy. Charles Hall, the other shareowner, rarely came around, trusting Billy to care for the business. Oh, he would take very good care of this grand dame. He loved the Windsor with its glamour and excitement.

Maxcy Tabor knocked on the office door. He was turning into a fine assistant. Maxcy was a nice blend of the best of both his parents, inheriting Augusta's business sense and Horace's pleasant nature. Billy wouldn't mind if the young man stayed in Denver and worked for him after the soon-to-be-Senator Tabor moved to Washington.

Maxcy's face peeked around the door. He was flushed. "Mr. Bush, I need to speak to you right now."

"Come in," Billy said waving him in.

"Mother's bought out Hall," Maxcy's explanation was cut off as Augusta pushed him aside with her parasol and strode into the room.

Billy was on his feet, "Mrs. Tabor, how fine to see you. How may I be of service today?"

"You heard my son. We are business partners, Mr. Bush," she said. "I used the one hundred thousand dollars that my husband so generously gave me to purchase Mr. Charles Hall's share of the hotel. I am here to learn more about my investment. I would like to begin with a tour of the building."

Augusta obviously knew Baby Doe was the hotel's most famous guest. Billy and Horace had always worked to keep them apart, but the two women had each developed a sense for sniffing out anything the other had touched.

"Perhaps the best way to start examining an investment is to look first at the financials," Billy suggested. "Maxcy, would you please review the accounting records with your mother?"

"I want to inspect the rooms."

"Yes, of course," Billy replied. "After you review the financial records, I will personally give you a tour of the building. The lobby and the ballroom are the most lovely this side of the Mississippi and the men's salon is quite popular. We have both Russian and Turkish baths."

"I want to see the guest suites."

"I can show you any of the unoccupied rooms."

"I want to see all of the rooms," Augusta persisted.

"We mustn't intrude on our guests. We like them to think of their accommodations at the Windsor as their own home."

Augusta clearly was not satisfied, but she let the matter rest. "Fine. Maxcy, get the books."

Billy silently sighed with temporary relief.

CHAPTER 21

1881

ALONE AT THE WINDSOR on a cold January afternoon, Baby Doe lovingly opened the new scrapbook that Horace had given her to record the progress of the Tabor Grand Opera House. The cover was hand-tooled leather and the pages gilt-edged, waiting for newspaper clippings, plans, notes, fabric swatches and sketches. Baby was delighted when Horace said she could help decorate the new opera house. She needed to keep making more ties between them, threads woven into all parts of his life. Augusta would always be connected to him through Maxcy; however, Baby wanted Horace to look to her in all other areas, from the bedroom to the business office. She would entertain him and advise him, soothe his soul and engage his mind, make herself invaluable. She grabbed her glue pot and gently dabbed paste on the article she had cut from yesterday morning's *Rocky Mountain News*.

A knock at the door startled Baby Doe; she couldn't imagine who it might be. Horace was at the opera house building site with Billy, Maxcy rarely crossed her path and, honestly, she didn't have a single friend. She opened the door to a bellhop holding a silver salver with a calling card reading "Mrs. Horace Tabor."

Baby knew Horace would not want her to receive Augusta; and it didn't seem a coincidence that Augusta chose this afternoon when he was not around. Be that as it may, this might be the opportunity to press for the divorce. Characteristically, Baby Doe took the chance, "Please send her up."

The two women dominating Horace Tabor's life could not have appeared more different that day. Baby Doe was not expecting any visitors but always planned her appearance as if a party could break out at any moment. This afternoon her hair was piled high and held with a diamond studded comb. The neckline of her emerald green velveteen dress plunged to show a snowy white bosom. It pinched her waist, flared at the bustle and narrowed at her ankles so she could take only the daintiest steps. In contrast, a man's tailor could have made Augusta's dark gray dress. The high neckline encircled her throat and buttons ran down to a comfortable waist followed by a straight skirt.

Baby Doe gestured to the high-backed chair across from her own. "To what do I owe this visit?"

"I assure you it is not a social call. I have come to provide you with an accurate history of my husband's affairs so that you can better assess the situation in which we find ourselves," Augusta spoke slowly and carefully. "My husband is a good man, amiable and generous to a fault. His greatest character flaw, however, is his attraction to women of ill repute. He has been associated with numerous bad women."

Baby's eyes narrowed. "In the past," she said.

Augusta continued as if she had not spoken. "You may have known Alice Morgan from Leadville. She performed an Indian club swinging act at the Grand Central Variety Hall. She was a favorite of Horace's. Before her, there was Willie Deville, a common prostitute from Chicago. He liked to take her on trips to St. Louis and New York. She drew a lot of attention to herself, talked to newspaper reporters, so Horace let her go. Being of a generous nature, he gave them each a parting gift."

Augusta seemed ready to list all of Horace's sins but Baby interrupted, "Why are you telling me this? What do you want?"

"I want you to know how easily Horace tires of these women. He will tire of you too, eventually, but I think you should leave now, gracefully retire from Colorado, and become a distant memory before he begins campaigning for Senate next year. I will make sure that you are given the customary parting gift."

Baby Doe's cheeks flushed with anger and she struggled to keep her voice even, "I will never give him up. I have nothing else to say to you. Good day."

"I do not understand this hold you have over him, this spider web in which you have him trapped. The scandal you cause is hurting him. The disgrace of your company will kill his political career. End this embarrassing spectacle now," Augusta's voice was rising.

"I am not the source of his embarrassment," Baby leaned out of her chair in a most unladylike way and pointed her finger right at Augusta's face. "It is you. You and your cow. I am helping him to make his mark, to build his empire. I am trying to do what is best for him."

"I know what is best for Horace," Augusta's voice now shook with anger. "I have always taken care of him, even when his impulses and passions run away with him. I am his wife."

Baby stuck her chin in the air. "I hear you don't take care of *all* his passions," she shot, "like a good wife should."

Augusta gasped. "For shame," she whispered. "For shame." Her voice built into a shrieking crescendo. "You care nothing for him, you hussy. You only love his money!"

"I do love him. I love him more than you ever have!" Baby screamed back. "Get out, get out, get out!"

Augusta hurried to the door and down the hall. Baby slammed the door as hard as she possibly could and stomped her feet in fury. *That cow, that shrew, how dare she presume to come here and tell me . . . anything . . . I am going to . . . Why, I should . . . Horace is going to hear about this . . . How dare she say that I don't love him?* Gasp . . . *I told her I love him.*

Baby Doe spent most of the afternoon in a frenzy. She had been furious and was going to demand that Horace rein in that old nag, buy out her share of the Windsor, have the sheriff evict her from the mansion and put her on a train for the farthest reaches of Maine. After some time to calm down, and though she loathed to admit it, Baby realized Augusta had made a valid point. A mistress might be heavy baggage for a new senator to take to Washington. The morality committees were growing in popularity and influence, and the ways of mining towns were looked down upon here in Denver. She imagined Washington to be even stuffier. She wanted—needed—to be Horace's only woman—his wife—by election time. She would not act like Augusta, with shouting or insults, but she needed to make it clear to Horace that things could not continue on this way. When he arrived home from the opera house building site, Baby Doe was ready.

Baby helped Horace out of his coat and kissed his shaggy moustache. "How was your day? Were they able to dig on the foundation for the opera house?"

"I had a fine day, my darlin' Baby. The ground is still too cold to do much more with the foundation. Billy and I looked at plans for the backstage area and I was told I need to commission an artist to paint a scene for the curtain. Come with me tomorrow and put your womanly touch on things."

"I would love to do that," Baby said as she poured a small shot of whiskey for Horace from the heavy crystal decanter. She sat down on the chaise lounge and patted a spot beside her.

Horace plopped down. "It is good to be home."

"It makes me so happy to hear you call this home. Although, it's not a house, just a hotel suite. It would be lovely to have a real home, wouldn't it?" she asked wistfully.

"Baby, do you want a house? I'll buy you a house. It would put some elbow room between you and Augusta. That might make everyone happier."

"I don't think elbow room will satisfy Augusta. Horace, she paid me a visit today."

Horace looked a Baby and then around the room. Baby wasn't sure if he was looking for Augusta or for the busted furniture that must have resulted from the face-to-face meeting of these two women. "I've told Billy to keep her out of here, but once she latches onto something . . ." Horace began.

"She told me you would tire of me and it would be best if I left you."

"Oh no, Baby. You are the light of my life. I could never do without you." Horace brought his arms around her.

She allowed a kiss, but then pulled back to push her case. "Horace, she will never let us be happy. She needs to be out of Denver," Baby said.

"Maybe she can go on one of those grand tours of Europe, London, Paris and Rome."

"When she returns, we will be in the same predicament again," Baby said. Horace had no answer. "Darling, when you run for senator next year, when you vie for the White House after that, who will be by your side? Who will happily attend your speeches? Who will plan dinners and receptions? Who will be your hostess, entertain politicians and make small talk with businessmen?" Baby asked.

"I want you," Horace said.

"Your wife," Baby corrected. "Your wife must do all of those things. A mistress cannot." Baby took Horace's craggy head in her hands. "Who could help you with your political dreams and make you happy at home? Who would be a better wife?"

"You. A thousand times you," Horace said.

"We must get a divorce from Augusta."

"I already had Billy give her a parting gift, but she said no to a divorce."

"We need to change her mind, to say yes to a divorce. And soon, before the campaigning for Senate starts. The newspapers will make a big to-do of this, but it will die down after she retires quietly somewhere far from here. The grand tour might get her out of our hair and away from reporters while we start the proceedings."

"I will tell Billy to get busy on this," Horace said.

"Tomorrow?"

"Tomorrow," Horace agreed. Baby rewarded him with something that Belle's girls at the Shoo Fly had called a French kiss.

CHAPTER 22

AS TABOR'S AIDE-DE-CAMP, Billy Bush had completed jobs large and small at the request of his employer, from million-dollar projects to shoeshines, but the assignments related to Tabor's other women left Bush holding his nose. Now Billy was being asked to secure a divorce from a respected married woman, who happened to have a backbone hard as iron rail and a tongue like a bullwhip. He felt nauseated. He decided to appeal to Augusta's logic and present the request for divorce in business terms. He debated going to see Augusta at her home, where he could leave as soon as he delivered the message, but in the end, he invited her to his office, a business setting. She was, of course, punctual and wearing a dull brown dress.

"Mrs. Tabor," Billy dove right in, "You are aware that Mr. Tabor wishes to terminate your marriage."

"We shall not divorce. It is shameful in the eyes of God," Augusta said, stating a simple fact.

"Mrs. Tabor, it is to your benefit to listen to all I have to say. I have done some research into this matter, and it is clear that a single woman enjoys more civil and business rights than a married woman, who in the eyes of the law, is chattel, simply baggage owned by her husband. If you petition for a divorce, you will be in a stronger position to negotiate the terms of settlement."

"Horace and I are partners in everything, and we have been for nearly thirty years. I deserve half of everything," she said, then waved that thought away. "It doesn't matter. We shall not divorce. We will simply live apart."

"Mrs. Tabor, if you persist in not recognizing the situation you are in, you put yourself in a very precarious position. If Tabor petitions for divorce, he can cut you off completely. You will be left, a woman of your age, without a dime."

"He would not do that. Why, even his fancy girls got a parting gift."

"One hundred thousand dollars will not last a lifetime."

"I will take in boarders. I am not afraid to work," she said.

"I have an attorney who has agreed to represent you in the legal proceedings."

"I have no need of an attorney."

"Mrs. Tabor, you do. Amos Steck was a judge in his own right and has some experience in these types of affairs." Steck had been Baby Doe's suggestion as he had been the judge that had granted her a divorce back in Central City.

Billy decided to try another path. "You know Mr. Tabor is eager to run for Senate. A prolonged court process would mean prolonged attention from gossips and reporters. The scandal could seriously damage Mr. Tabor's political career." Billy spoke more quietly now, "I know you want him to achieve his dreams. The best way you can help him is to quietly file for divorce and then retire somewhere away from the whispers." He paused, "It would be a good time to make a grand tour of Europe."

Augusta stared at the ceiling, seeming to chew on all he said. When she faced him to speak, Billy thought there might be tears in her eyes, but her voice was pure New England granite. "Don't worry yourself, Mr. Bush. There will be no scandal because there will be no divorce. I will take that European tour. By the time I return, Horace will have tired of the blonde. Then he and I will campaign for Senate."

Large feathery snowflakes fell on early April daffodils as Augusta's train headed east, cross-country, on the first leg of her grand tour.

CHAPTER 23

THE FIVE-STORY OPERA HOUSE took shape through the spring and summer. The stately red brick was frosted with gleaming white carved stone. Three grand entrances led to a rotunda with a stained-glass dome, seventy feet by twenty feet, bigger than Baby Doe's entire Blackhawk cabin. Soon patrons would step into the lobby and gape upwards at ceiling frescos of dancing nymphs surrounding an enormous glittering chandelier as their feet glided across parquet floors covered with thick Belgian carpets. Fifteen hundred plush mohair seats filled curving balconies and three tiers of box seats. Twinkling cut glass globes over the gaslights made the custom golden wallpaper shimmer. Tabor had ordered the best of everything from around the world: Italian marble, Japanese cherry wood, French silks and Honduran mahogany.

Horace thought it a fine idea for Baby Doe to accompany him on regular inspections as the building's interior took shape. Baby had seen the workmen's eyes widen at her first visits. She politely nodded and smiled, asking about and complimenting their fine workmanship. The men had responded by always treating her with courtesy.

Although Augusta was not in town, Billy had insisted that Baby Doe arrive at the opera house wearing the hated veil and in a hired buggy separate from Horace. She had grudgingly gone along with Billy's requests as the opera house neared completion and public interest grew for the new-world palace billed as the "crown jewel for the queen city of the West."

Eugene Hawthorne had been handing out silver dollars all over town looking for a rumor that could be spun into the next Tabor story, but Baby Doe was living quietly at the Windsor, Augusta was in Europe and Horace was keeping his nose to the grindstone. It seemed drearily dull when a freckle-faced newsboy told him of the crowds that gathered daily outside the Tabor Grand to watch the construction and gawk at the sumptuous fixtures, art, and furniture being carried into the resplendent entertainment house.

"It's a good corner to hawk papers. No other boys work it. You could probably get the deliverymen to give you a look at what's going in, if you shared another of those silver dollars."

"I'm not interested in looking at the artwork, unless of course, it was a painting of Baby Doe."

"I've seen her there in real life. The workmen say she often comes to look over the carpets and wallpaper and paintings and such." The boy snatched a dollar from Eugene's stubby fingers and ran away. A smile crossed Eugene's porcine face. The story was practically writing itself.

Baby arrived to oversee the installation of the Tabor nameplate on the front of Box A. The Tabor Grand would become the center of culture in Denver, maybe in the entire West. She wanted the nameplate to announce in a most extravagant way to all in attendance, Denver's highest social class, that it was Tabor's patronage that provided this for the city. She had ordered a two-foot-long plate of silver to be smelted from the Matchless Mine ore. The Tabor name was spelled out in raised gold letters. It would be displayed like a plaque at the base of a monument as Horace, Colorado's greatest benefactor of the arts, sat in the box above. Big and shiny, Horace thought it was perfect.

The stage curtain was also being hung. Baby was less enamored with the way it had turned out. When it was commissioned, Horace had suggested the artist paint a classic Roman scene. The artist, an insufferable snob who kept reminding all that he had studied in Europe, had smugly told Horace he must mean classic Greek since, as everyone knew, the Greeks were the better dramatists. Horace had replied that he and his friend Abe Lincoln on the hundred-dollar bill didn't know the difference between Greeks and Romans. The scene the artist had painted was Roman indeed, ruined temples and crumbling columns. At the bottom of the scene was a verse by Charles Kingsley:

So fleet the works of man, back to earth again;
Ancient and holy things fade like a dream.

Always superstitious, Baby Doe thought it seemed like a bad sign. "Horace, what do you think of the curtain?" she asked.

Horace gave it a once-over. "Looks like it's from Europe. You know these Denver society people like anything that comes from Europe." The newly-minted mining millionaires were sure that the East Coast elites looked down their aristocratic noses at the West; they reasoned one way to demonstrate culture and refined taste was to use their new money to buy stuff from the Old World.

"Does the saying seem a little grim to you?"

"Naw, its fine." Horace said. The artist gave Baby a stony look as Horace moved on from the auditorium to the lobby. Baby, Billy, the artist, and a host of decorators, contractors, and work supervisors followed. "Billy, did you get that singer we talked about booked for the opening?"

"Yes, Emma Abbott of the Grand English Opera Company. She'll be performing *Maritana,*" Billy said.

"In English, right? *Maritana* sounds Italian. I don't like it when they sing in Italian. Can't understand a word of it."

"Yes, Governor Tabor, it will be in English," Billy said. From the corner of her eye, Baby caught the curtain artist exchange smirks with a mincing man who bore a resemblance to Oscar Wilde and whom she recognized as one of the interior decorators.

"This is new. I don't remember ordering this picture. Who's this fella?" Horace asked, stopping in front of a portrait of man with a receding hairline and a large white Elizabethan collar in a gilded frame.

"It is the Bard of Avon," said the decorator waltzing forward. "Who better to grace the rotunda of this great theater than William Shakespeare?" Baby watched the decorator step behind Horace's back and roll his eyes at the curtain artist.

Baby felt anger rising up her neck and tinting her cheeks. "Horace Tabor, that's who is better," she said. *How dare they snigger at Horace? He was paying them for God's sake. They needed to treat him with respect.* "He built this theater; it's the finest in all the United States. And he built many other fine buildings here and in Leadville. He is the lieutenant governor and will be even higher soon. Take down this copy of a painting of a man long-dead and put up Lieutenant Governor Tabor's portrait." *Jackasses*, she thought.

Horace put his hand to his upper lip and pretended to smooth his moustache, smothering a grin. The rest of the men stared at the tiny woman, apparently unsure as to what had her so fired up. "Immediately," she said. Baby lifted her chin as high as it would go and stared down at the men.

Horace took her hand and tucked it into the crook of his elbow. "Better give the lady what she wants, fellas. Come, my dear, I hear they are serving pheasant at the Windsor tonight."

CHAPTER

24

TABOR'S CONCUBINE DECORATES NEW OPERA HOUSE

By Eugene Hawthorne

Crowds, which gather daily at the building site of the new Tabor Grand Opera House, report seeing many works of art and grandiose furnishings being delivered. The patroness overseeing the installation of these treasures is none other than Horace Tabor's kept woman, Baby Doe. She arrives veiled and by hired carriage as if to be anonymous. However, workmen and artisans confirm seeing her there and taking direction from her.

"Her taste in decor is really quite garish and she is often speaking with the coarsest of laborers," said one artist who did not wish his name to appear in this article.

Mrs. Tabor is still touring Europe and was not available to give comment on the situation.

Augusta could not believe the gossip she heard when she returned to Denver at the end of August. Her five months absence had not made her husband's heart grow fonder; indeed, the newspapers were full of stories that the blonde woman was more firmly attached to Horace than ever. More disturbing than the tales of romantic dinners out were the reports of that woman's influence in Horace's business; the floozy had made decisions regarding the opera house.

Augusta tried to remember the last real conversation she had with Hod. Was it when she berated him for the extravagance of the Tabor Grand? Or when she scolded him for the drunken bacchanal in Leadville? He hadn't come to the house to say bon voyage or the train station to see her off. That hurt. Augusta knew she had a sharp tongue, but she just wanted what was best for them, what was reasonable, prudent. She had always been the more practical partner in the marriage. No doubt, every word out of that blonde's Cupid bow lips was sugarcoated poppycock, but Horace did not seem to understand. Augusta missed the old coot. He won her over when they were young with his easy charm and storytelling and he had led her on a life of adventure. She had loved him then; she had never stopped loving him.

Augusta recalled years ago seeing an old prospector trying to lead a stubborn mule. The man pulled the lead rope, but the animal braced its legs and would not budge. Then he got behind the mule and swatted its rump with his hat. He swore at the animal until Augusta thought the poor beast's ears would melt. Finally the miner, threw down his hat in disgust and proclaimed the mule the winner. The mule gave the man a superior look and began to stride off down the path. The miner hurried to catch up and picked up the lead rope. The mule stopped and looked over its shoulder at the man. The miner gently put down the rope and the animal began to walk. Perhaps she should stop pulling on Horace's lead. Perhaps the best way to end this whole fiasco was to swallow her pride, humble herself and ask to be in his good graces again. She could turn a blind eye to that blonde, but she must stop all the talk of divorce and make sure the harlot didn't ruin Horace's finances.

Two days before opening night at the Tabor Grand Opera House, Augusta penned a note to Horace.

Dear Husband,

I have returned from Europe and would like very much to attend the opening night of the Tabor Grand. I am told the mayor of Denver will present you with a token of the city's appreciation. None will be more proud than I. Allow me to accompany you and put an end to the gossip.

I have said many things in the heat of passion, but please know that I always spoke and acted with your best interests in my heart. I am sorry for our estrangement. Can we bury the past and start anew? My life was always and shall always be devoted to you.

Your wife

The note arrived at the Windsor suite while Horace was out, busy at the opera house making last minute preparations. Baby Doe could not leave a letter with such fine feminine writing unopened and lifted the wax seal. She had not expected to read such sentiments from Augusta. She was unsure if the old girl had a genuine change of heart or just a change in tack, turning to catch Horace's wind instead of fighting against it. Whatever Augusta's thinking, Baby was not going to let Horace see the note. Wadding the fine linen paper into a ball, she tossed it into the basket at the side of her desk.

CHAPTER 25

NONE OF THE WINDSOR EMPLOYEES ever admitted going through the Tabor's wastepaper basket, but the entire staff of the hotel had heard about Augusta's letter. The whispers made their way down the ever-crowded mahogany bar, past the ears of political friends and foes, businessmen and reporters, and then carried out to the lobby and to the lips of ladies at tea and out to the street, so that even the most disinterested citizen knew of Augusta's heart-felt plea to forgive and forget. On opening night of the Tabor Grand, 1,500 pairs of eyes watched the Tabor family box, decorated with the two-foot silver nameplate and dozens of red roses and white lilies. No one sat in the white satin chairs.

Horace was in the wings all evening, stepping out to receive an unusually large watch fob presented to him by the mayor, in gratitude for all his fine works. The gold and silver bauble was a golden ladder with Tabor milestones on each rung. There was an ore bucket filled with gold nuggets, a pick, a shovel, a mule, a relief of Tabor's store, an etching of Tabor Block woven with Tabor's monogram. It was so heavy it would have torn any watch pocket off its vest.

Baby sat amid the other patrons on the orchestra level and applauded wildly as Horace thanked the mayor and said a few words about the bright future of the opera house and Denver. She hadn't tried very hard to remain an anonymous face in the crowd, in a turquoise gown and diamonds, so many diamonds: in her hair, around her wrist, draped over her bosom, in her newly pierced ears. She was just missing one on her hand. *When I have that one, I'll be sitting in the Tabor box*, she thought.

The next day the *Rocky Mountain News* crowed:

PERFECTION! TABOR'S GREAT TRIUMPH
OPENED LAST NIGHT

America's favorite prima donna, Emma Abbott and the Grand English Opera Company fittingly dedicated the magnificent new Tabor Grand Opera House.

Eugene Hawthorn also wrote of the evening in the *Denver Star Ledger*.

TABOR GRAND OPERA HOUSE
PREMIERE - FAMILY BOX EMPTY

By Eugene Hawthorne

Fifteen hundred of Denver's well-heeled attended the opening night of the Tabor Grand Opera House. However, Mrs. Augusta Tabor was not among them. The only empty seats in the house were in the Tabor family box. Horace Tabor graced the stage before the start of the performance to receive a gold watch fob from the mayor as a token of appreciation from the citizens of our great city. He was not seen after that. Maxcy Tabor and his fiancé, the lovely Luella Babcock, were seated in Box H. It was whispered that Baby Doe was in attendance, viewing from the orchestra level.

Baby Doe read the morning newspaper with disgust. That odious pig, Eugene Hawthorne, had gotten it all wrong again, making Augusta and the empty box the essence of the story. Loads of people had noticed her attendance at the opera house last night; of course, no one could comment, but she knew they had admired her diamonds and the turquoise gown. "I was the one there," she said aloud, shaking the paper.

CHAPTER 26

1882

THE WHOLE TOWN HAD BEEN ABLAZE with gossip when Augusta didn't show up at the opening of the Tabor Grand, so Baby Doe agreed to lie low. Since having tea in the Windsor lobby was a favorite activity of Denver ladies and the long mahogany bar was the de facto Colorado state legislature where Horace's whiskey lubricated the wheels of government, Billy suggested she eat all her meals in the hotel suite and give up her daily strolls.

Fall came and went and only the leaves changed. Augusta, Horace and Baby continued their unhappy merry-go-round ride with Baby pushing for divorce, Augusta ignoring entree of the subject, Horace asking Billy to figure out another plan and Billy delivering another request and receiving another dismissal. Horace spent every night with Baby Doe, but the short winter days seemed to last forever in the confines of the suite.

"I am so sorry to keep you cooped up here, like a pretty songbird in a cage," he told her again and again.

If this is a cage, at least it's gilded, she thought. Life could be worse, and in fact, it had been when she lived in Blackhawk. Horace seemed genuinely worried that she would tire of the situation and just walk out, but the idea never crossed her mind. Horace was good to her, he never balked at anything she asked, and he was the richest man in Colorado. She would never willingly leave. Besides, this couldn't go on forever. She would have liked to be out in society and resented Billy's suggestions to avoid being seen in the Windsor lobby and dining room; however, she would do this for Horace. He was pleasant company and tried to think of small entertainments to keep her occupied. Little gifts arrived daily, including books of poetry and illustrations of flowers and birds and bric-a-brac to fill her scrapbooks. An art master was hired to give her painting lessons. Horace sent seamstresses to her, laden with sketches of the latest fashions and bolts of fabric.

"As soon as Augusta files for divorce, we can start living life. We'll get married. I'll take you out every evening. We'll throw grand parties. We will do whatever your heart wishes," he told her.

Meanwhile, she painted landscapes she could not visit, clipped newspaper stories of events she could not attend and designed dresses that would not be seen.

Several days of sparkling blue skies and summery temperatures made Baby Doe restless. She and Horace both needed an afternoon away. So she ordered a picnic basket from the dining room and a carriage from the nearby stable, put on the hated veil, slipped quietly past Billy

Bush's office and set out with Horace west toward the foothills and Clear Creek Canyon.

The aspens waved their bare branches in a light March breeze and snow still lay in the shadows. Clear Creek tumbled past in mesmerizing rapids and falls while rainbow trout lolled in gentle eddies. Spring in the high country was a seesaw of big snows followed by pleasant days. Baby Doe thought there was nothing more glorious than an afternoon spent in the warm sunshine and cool, pine-scented air of Colorado.

"Ah, this is living," Horace said as he stretched his lanky old bones on a broad, flat boulder heated by the sun. "Out here in God's country, with nothing but my best girl."

That thought made Baby shiver. Best not to tempt God by mentioning His name in the same breath as her relationship with Horace. Better to change the subject.

"So now that President Arthur has appointed Senator Teller to his cabinet, how does that affect your campaign for Senate?" she asked.

The assassination of James Garfield and the elevation of Chester Arthur to the presidency were impacting politics across the nation. Colorado's senior senator, Henry Teller was joining the new president's staff as Secretary of the Interior, and someone would need to fill his vacant seat. Since the illiterate public could not be trusted to elect the right man to the esteemed U.S. Congress, the state legislature was responsible for selecting someone worthy of a national seat.

Horace answered, "Senator Teller won't start his work for the president until January. That's about the same time our state legislature will meet. They will appoint someone to fill the empty seat for sixty days until the newly-elected senator starts in March."

"But don't the state legislators elect the new senator, too? Would they appoint one man for a few weeks and elect another for six years?"

"That could happen. They'll probably give the sixty-day seat to someone who has done some favors and deserves a little reward. I am the lieutenant governor and I've been lubricating that state legislature with money and whiskey for years. They should give me the six-year seat."

Horace grimaced and rubbed a hand over his face, growing pink in the sunshine. "Fact is, we need to settle this problem with Augusta. Some of those fellas are acting squirmy, saying their wives are giving them a hard time about you and Augusta."

"Horace, what if, instead of begging Augusta to file for divorce, you did? I mean, what if you filed for divorce?" Baby knew this was a bold move, but during the past months Billy hadn't gotten anywhere in his many conversations with Augusta.

"I don't know, Baby," Horace sat up and stared across the water. "I thought if she was the one asking the court it would help her keep her dignity. Hell, nobody would ever believe that Augusta broke her marriage vows and gave cause for me to divorce her."

Anyone who spent a moment with that woman and her bullwhip of a tongue would say you had cause, thought Baby.

"Besides," he continued, "most of the judges are members of one morality committee or another. They say they are trying to raise the tone in Denver and leave the mining camps behind. But I think those judges are getting their ears chewed by their wives, who are scared that husbands all over town are going to want to run off with a pretty thing like you." Horace gave her a wink and a grin.

Baby gave him a rueful smile thinking, *Horace, you have hit the nail on the head.* But it sparked an idea. "What about a judge in Leadville or another mining town? Someone you are friendly with, that might see your side? Maybe someone without a wife or a widower?"

"Baby, you are a smart little cookie."

A week later, Billy was on his way to the far southwest corner of the state, to the little mountain town of Durango to meet with a judge that Horace had played cards with one time a couple of years ago. Horace owned some small mining interests there, and Billy might have implied that Tabor was looking to expand business interests in the area. He gave the judge a bare bones version of recent events and explained that not serving Augusta with official divorce papers would help keep this delicate family matter private. The judge called the court clerk into his chambers. The door was firmly shut. A few minutes later Billy emerged with a divorce decree, and that day's court record had accidently been glued to the page before it. The local newspaper reporter assigned to review court records would not see the entry. Horace and Augusta's marriage was over, and no one but Billy and the judge knew.

CHAPTER 27

BILLY LOOKED FORWARD to ending the torturous visits with Augusta where he asked her to compromise her morals, jeopardize her finances and deny her social standing so that his boss would feel better about bedding a pretty young divorcée. Frankly, Billy thought Augusta had played her cards right, not giving in to endless requests for a divorce, instead waiting out another of Horace's indiscretions. Now with the Durango divorce decree, Billy could put an end to this ridiculous circus, avoid the emotional conversations with Tabor's wife and begin the business-like talks about a settlement with her lawyer.

Billy had not anticipated Amos Steck's outburst of righteous ire on behalf of his client.

"This decree is worthless. Worse than worthless, it is fraudulent." Steck was a large-boned man given to making great flourishes with his hands. His face was bright red against his snow-white muttonchops. "Mrs. Tabor was never served papers. She is entitled to have a say in court." He slapped the table. "What cause was presented as reason for divorce? The woman has a spotless reputation. Whatever accusations were cast, certainly nothing was ever proven." He raised a finger to heaven in emphasis.

Having faced Augusta herself on numerous occasions, Billy's hide had grown pretty tough. His black eyes blinked merely once before he asked, "Mr. Steck, do you remember who it is that is paying your fee?"

"The funds may come from Mr. Tabor's bank account, but Mrs. Tabor is the client to whom I have a duty to represent zealously," Steck shook his fist in indignation.

"I asked you here to discuss the settlement terms."

"Mrs. Tabor is entitled to half of everything."

"The house on Broadway and a small yearly alimony," countered Billy. "And I will buy out her third of the Windsor Hotel for fifty thousand dollars."

"Ha!" Steck threw both hands in the air. "The house plus half of everything, all the assets, which I estimate at nearly ten million dollars according to newspaper reports, as well as, half his projected income, which is currently one million dollars per year. And I will ignore your insulting offer regarding the Windsor shares."

Gliding a hand over his slicked back hair, Billy knew this was undoubtedly an opening bid. The final settlement would look much different, but this was a long way from Horace's original parting gift of one hundred thousand dollars a year ago. "Tabor has made most of his money since 1878, when he stopped living full time with Mrs.

Tabor. The years they were together were hardscrabble years with no real money to speak of."

"That is precisely my point," Steck roared, pounding a fist on the desk. "Is there no appreciation for her work, her sacrifices, her loyalty?"

This settlement was not going to be the quick and quiet agreement that Tabor, and Billy, had wished.

Although Mr. Steck was on Augusta's side, he faced her with as much trepidation as those who crossed her. She had agreed to meet him in her home, but told him not to expect any refreshments. He planned to garland news of the Durango divorce with his demand that she receive half of the Tabor fortune. "So, because you were never served the decree, it is worthless. Tabor will be willing to pay dearly to keep the fraudulent divorce out of the public eye. You, dear lady, are sitting in the catbird seat. You can demand the choicest of Tabor's many assets."

"The divorce is fraudulent?"

"Yes, procedure wasn't followed, and you never had your say in court to refute the charges which, I might add, are ludicrous and would never be proven." Steck shook his white head, dismissing the thought. "Now, may I suggest that you request your Broadway home and several income producing properties. I believe the Matchless Mine is his best producing mine."

"The divorce decree is not legitimate? There is no true divorce?"

"No."

"I am still married to Mr. Tabor?"

"Yes, but let us not lose sight of the opportunity we now have. We can propose that, in exchange for a generous settlement, you will not file criminal charges for fraud against Mr. Tabor."

"Pffft," she snorted. "Don't be ridiculous. I am not charging my husband with anything. Go tell him and his little toady, Bush, that their shenanigans change nothing. I will remain at the Broadway Avenue house and I will work at the Windsor Hotel." She straightened her shoulders and looked down her long nose at her attorney. "What you fail to understand, Mr. Steck, is that my husband doesn't stick to things for very long. He plunges from one business venture to the next, one romantic affair to the next. I am sure the blonde woman is finding being confined to a hotel room very tiresome. Things will straighten themselves out without added melodrama from you. Now, see yourself out."

Steck sat gap-mouthed for a moment and then gathered his papers and top hat while Augusta stared out the window, pointedly ignoring him. As he reached the door, he thought he heard her softly say, "Tell him I will be waiting."

CHAPTER 28

THROUGHOUT THE SUMMER Augusta continued to play her waiting game. She began attending the Unitarian Church and took a position on the committee to raise funds for a new building. She attended performances at the Tabor Grand when she was sure Horace would not be there. She began accepting invitations to tea from the Denver social circle that she had previously thought of as uppity do-nothings, but now found the women to be very sympathetic to her situation. It made Augusta's teeth itch to hear strangers whisper, "Poor Mrs. Tabor" as she passed, but her new friends were not shrinking violets who "tut-tutted" behind their hands. Many had come to the West with husbands who were building a nation, and these ladies keenly felt their role in the Manifest Destiny of America.

Senator Teller's wife, Harriet, became a particularly close friend. Henry Teller practiced law in the early ruckus days of Central City and became the state's first senator. Mrs. Teller and Augusta had much in common as pioneer women that helped settle the mountains and, now, as political wives of millionaires, they shared a sense of civic duty to bring morality to the West. Mrs. Teller was tall and thin to the point of gaunt, a pious woman who dressed in sober colors, but had a particular weakness for overly large hats.

Over tea Mrs. Teller explained, "Ladies in the West have a divinely ordained duty to guide the moral development of not just our homes, but the entire region. We have to be as a lighthouse in the dark, unwavering, lighting the righteous path for others less fortunate."

Augusta didn't comment while Mrs. Teller mounted her soapbox and continued to expound on women's role in the expansion of the West.

"If your husband wins the Senate seat next to mine, we will be in positions to bring civility to the wilderness together."

Augusta gave her head a rueful shake. "Horace is not doing himself any political favors keeping that blonde around. There are endless stories of her in the newspapers. No one will vote for a senator with such a flamboyant mistress."

"Perhaps you should have your story told in the newspapers."

"Oh no, it will only provide more grist for the rumor mill."

"Perhaps," Mrs. Teller tapped her lip with a finger, "you could speak with a carefully chosen reporter, one who would tell your side of this sordid tale with some dignity. The public would see that blonde for the adventuress she is and recognize your selfless devotion to Horace."

Augusta could see the plans hatching beneath Mrs. Teller's bounteous flowered hat.

"That blonde would be driven out of town," said Mrs. Teller.

"It will hurt Horace's political ambitions, and I do not want that."

"No." Mrs. Teller reasoned, "Everyone knows men are base creatures who cannot help themselves. The blame will be placed at the feet of that woman."

Mrs. Teller arranged for Augusta to meet a reporter from the *Denver Republican* named David Jones. He was a thin young man with dark circles under his eyes and quiet manners.

"What would you like readers to know about you and your marriage to Horace Tabor?" he began.

"Well, Horace and I were married in 1857 in Maine. He worked for my father as a stonecutter. I wish we had stayed there and built our life." Augusta stared at her hands for a brief moment then cleared her throat and went on. "But Mr. Tabor is a restless sort. He tried farming in Kansas, but joined the rush to Colorado when gold was found in '59. I was the first white woman at Gregory Gulch. That's near Central City; of course, there was nothing there then. Horace's diggings there didn't amount to much, so we moved on to California Gulch."

"That's Leadville now, correct?"

"Yes. We did quite well there. I took in boarders, did laundry. I owned gold scales and a safe, and I was the postmistress. We were very happy."

"Was Mr. Tabor prospecting at that time?"

"Yes, but not with any success. He eventually put it aside to help me open a general store. I am sure you know the story of how his fortune began with him grubstaking the two Germans."

David Jones nodded slowly. "Mrs. Tabor, I was hoping to hear more about current events that surround your marriage. Do you know Baby Doe?"

Augusta flushed, embarrassed and angry. "I do not know her."

Jones said nothing, but frowned at his notepad and then looked at her with his dark eyes, quietly waiting for Augusta.

"I understand she is blonde."

The silence grew, seeming to take form and sit at the small table with them. Jones mutely nodded.

"She paints her face," she said.

Jones murmured his understanding.

"She is only interested in his money. When the money is gone, she, too, will disappear. She won't want a poor old man." Perhaps it was rash to speak so candidly to a reporter, but she had said these very words to Harriet and Billy and even Horace. The young man seemed to appreciate the absurdity of the situation.

"But he is not such an old man."

"Yes, he is. He used to have gray hair at his temples. He dyes it now to give himself a rejuvenated appearance. I am sure it was done to impress her." She seemed suddenly to lack the discipline to stop talking; yet, everything she was saying was true and all of Denver already knew it. "He used to be a forthright man, salt of the earth. But he is changed now; she has changed him. The divorce decree from Durango is completely false. My attorney, Mr. Steck, says it is invalid and based on fraudulent claims. I do not consider myself divorced from Mr. Tabor. The whole proceedings were irregular."

Jones' head shot up from his notes. "Divorce decree? What decree?" He caught himself and said in a quieter voice, "Our readers are not familiar with the Durango divorce that you mention."

David Jones' darkly circled eyes glittered with interest. Augusta thought he suddenly looked like a raccoon, cunning and devious, and she had just let him into her house to dig through the trash. The interview was not going as Harriet Teller had implied it would. "He is quite changed from the man I married all those years ago," was all she could say.

A few days later all of Denver read the *Denver Republican's* two-column story with the headline:

TABOR FILES FOR DIVORCE. DETAILS "SEALED." FRAUD SUSPECTED

Mrs. Teller was pleased with the way the reporter insinuated Baby Doe was the source of the change in the problematic behavior of Horace Tabor. Attorney Steck was delighted the secret was out. It would play well in any true divorce court, and his professional ethics had not been compromised. Eugene Hawthorne growled in anger that his sources had missed this development. Billy did not think this would help the settlement negotiations. Horace was surprised that Augusta would air their dirty laundry, and Baby couldn't believe anyone who had actually met the tart Augusta could write such a sympathetic story toward her. Augusta had to chew mint to remove the bad taste from her mouth.

CHAPTER
29

THE LATE SEPTEMBER AFTERNOON was as crisp as a fresh apple. Shimmering golden aspen trees gilded the foothills and a few bright white clouds scuttled across the blue sky while Baby Doe sat in her suite at the Windsor Hotel trying to fill her afternoon. She was confined most of the time now. Reporters were slinking around, eavesdropping for gossip since Augusta had begun taking afternoon tea in the Windsor's lobby with her new society matron friends. After tea, the reporters would slouch along the mahogany bar letting Horace buy drinks and listening to him and fellow politicians pontificate about the affairs of the day. Augusta would march over to the hotel business office to grill Maxcy and Billy about everything from the dining room menu to the accounting ledger. Baby Doe had to hand it to the old battle-axe. Augusta was winning: running the

Tabor Empire, managing businesses and meeting with political wives, all while keeping Baby stuck away and out of sight.

A political wife needed to be knowledgeable in current affairs, so Baby Doe had taken up reading the newspaper every day. While she could make light conversation as well as any debutant, she wanted to be Horace's trusted advisor. That meant keeping abreast of the state and national stories that could impact Horace. Of course, she also read every word the gossip columnists printed about Horace, Augusta and herself. The *Rocky Mountain News* was fairly kind to Horace and, by extension, "Tabor's Veiled Woman," unlike Eugene Hawthorne's yellow rag, the *Denver Star Ledger*, that printed all manner of lies. That was why only the *Rocky Mountain News* was available at the Windsor Hotel now.

Much of today's front page was devoted to the failed attempts of the Utah Territory to be considered for statehood. Most Americans considered Mormons with suspicion. Brigham Young claimed to be a modern prophet who had marched his followers into a hard barren wilderness. Young encouraged multiple wives and allowed women to vote. It was the behavior of the deranged. Now Congress had passed the Edmunds Act outlawing polygamy and banning polygamists from voting or holding office. In an adjoining column, the editor of the *News* wrote that the Mormons were twisting the teaching of the Old Testament for their own grotesque tastes. He claimed Mormons treated women more as livestock and did not treasure them as the heart of the home. The editor went on to call polygamy the twin of slavery and congratulated Congress for having the moral strength to stand against this perversion.

Baby snorted. She had seen many self-proclaimed Christian men treat their livestock better than their wives. She really didn't care what the Mormons were doing out there in the desert but, of course, Horace would have to speak on the right side of the issue. *Funny thing is*, she thought as she turned the page, *practically speaking, Horace has two wives.* That was when it hit her like a lightning bolt from heaven, an idea so clear, a plan so fully formed that it could have come direct from a Mormon prophet. Horace had to marry her. Then Augusta would have to recognize the Durango divorce decree or she would be participating in polygamy, breaking the laws of God and man. Baby laughed out loud. It was truly this simple. She wanted to marry Horace, so she would.

As soon as the train stopped moving, the hot humid air of St. Louis settled over the passengers like a sodden horse blanket. Perspiration pooled in every crevice and Baby's blonde curls began to lift from her head in a rebellious frizz. The jaunty feather in her hat wilted.

Getting married by a Justice of the Peace while wearing a rumpled traveling suit was not the wedding of Baby's dreams. She had made it clear to Horace that this elopement to St. Louis was just to force Augusta's hand. He promised her a grand affair in a ballroom filled with flowers and an evening of dancing to an elegant orchestra as her gorgeous gown twirled around her. "With a priest," she insisted. It was not going to be easy to get a priest to marry a divorced woman, but Baby didn't want to take any chances that her marriage to Horace be called fraudulent like the Durango divorce. She didn't want to repeat her mistake of marrying without a priest, and reasoned that a Catholic wedding could be a fresh start in the eyes of God. She would go to confession and seek forgiveness for her sinful life and then, with a clean soul, a clear conscience and a different priest, she could marry Horace. Although she hadn't been to Mass in ages, Baby did not like being on the wrong side of the Lord. One never knew when one might be made to reap the oats one had sown.

Horace had arrived in St. Louis by separate train two days earlier. That had been Billy's idea, in an effort to throw the reporters off this new chapter in the Tabor scandal. Horace had gone to the courthouse to get a marriage license and paid off the recording clerk to ensure that their names were not included in the daily list of transactions that were sent to the local newspapers. He ordered a nosegay of pale pink roses and calla lilies surrounded by lamb's ears and ivy, wrapped in a lace doily and tied with a long pink ribbon. Pacing like an expectant father, he waited for Baby Doe at the St. Louis train station.

"Baby," he called and waved without an ounce of discretion as she alighted from the car. "You look wonderful. These flowers are for you. We can go right now, to the justice's office. I have a driver and coach." He was as excited as a kid with a nickel at the penny candy counter. He directed a boy at his side to collect her things and take them to the hotel and bustled her into the carriage.

Horace talked the entire way to the justice's office. Baby couldn't get a word in, so sat in quiet delight at his exuberance. "Today is the day, Baby, the start of our life. Things are going to be different after this. We are going to live life to the fullest. Champagne every day," he declared. He wrapped an arm around her and smooched her cheek. "You're my little champagne bubble."

He let out a long, contented breath. "Baby, you have not been living the life I have wanted for us, with you being cooped up in the Windsor and people saying rough things, like I bought you and the only reason you would want to be with an ugly old coot like me is because of all the money. I want you to know that I intend to make it up to you because you are. . ." he hesitated, large ears turning pink. "Aww, I don't know any poetry, but I want you to know. . ." again, an embarrassed pause. "I wake up happy and I go to bed happy because I am with you." Horace shook his head slightly. "I wasn't speaking of that. Well, yes, but I mean to say you give me a new vigor. You are like fresh air and sunshine. The road hasn't been smooth and easy for us, but I will move heaven and earth to keep you happy and by my side for the rest of our days. I just love you more than anything." Horace pinched the bridge of his nose, but tears escaped and slid down his laugh lines and into his moustache.

Baby put down the beautiful nosegay and took Horace's craggy cheeks in her hands. She gave him the sweetest wedding gift she knew. She said, "I love you, too."

The newlyweds returned to Denver a few days later, and Horace announced to Billy that they had "got hitched without a hitch." They were going upstairs to rest from their travels and, with a broad grin and a wink, Horace asked that they not be disturbed.

"One more thing, Billy, I want you to go see Augusta in the next couple of days to let her know about all this," Horace said. "Make sure she understands the consequences."

"What about Maxcy?" Billy asked.

Baby Doe thought she saw Horace flinch. She had always tried to keep a distance between her and Maxcy, never wanting to put Horace in a position to choose between them. She didn't want to test the power of her female charms to overcome parental love. When their paths crossed at the Windsor, Maxcy had treated Baby Doe with a cool, but polite, reserve. She didn't expect much more. Maxcy was a dutiful son to his mother, staying by her side and obeying her in all things, yet never criticizing his father. For most of his life, he had been a silent witness to his father's philandering and his mother's loyalty. Baby knew that Maxcy had probably read the shrieking headlines and salacious stories, too. Maybe this was another reason why Augusta clung so hard to this wreck of a marriage. Perhaps, as much as moral righteousness or social indignation, her denial was a shield to prevent Maxcy from being hurt by the gossip. It dawned on Baby that she and Augusta probably shared a dislike of Eugene Hawthorne and his ilk.

CHAPTER 30

WHEN AUGUSTA CAME INTO the Windsor business office later that day, Billy asked if he could call on her at her home the next day. "Why?" Augusta asked. "If you have something to say, then out with it. Or do I need Mr. Steck with me?"

"No Steck," he replied with equal bluntness. Billy needed her to realize that this was the end, not another stunt, not a legal hurdle. He smoothed his hair and tried again. "Mrs. Tabor, we need to speak frankly, and I think it would be better in the comfort and privacy of your own home."

Augusta received Billy the next morning in her library. She had made coffee.

Billy wasted no time. "Mrs. Tabor, your husband and Baby Doe were married in St. Louis last week."

She snorted. "Poppycock, he cannot marry her as he is married to me. Steck has proven the Durango divorce decree to be fraudulent."

"They were married by a justice of the peace. There is a valid marriage license."

"Just more shenanigans."

"No ma'am, this is different. Mr. Tabor and Baby Doe are married; and if the divorce is fraudulent and you are also still married to him, then you are in a polygamist marriage."

"What?" Augusta looked like she might jump up and throttle him. "That's preposterous. Ridiculous. We are not polygamists."

Billy continued, "With the passing of the Edmunds Act, no polygamist can hold political office. Mr. Tabor will have to give up the lieutenant governorship. He can no longer run for Senate."

"No, no. That has been his dream for so long. Why would he throw it away like this? This could completely wreck his future. That blonde is ruining everything," Augusta said, frowning so deeply that her eyebrows came together and down the bridge of her nose. "He will tire of her."

"Perhaps," Billy allowed. "But the state legislators will be voting on the Senate seats after the New Year, only a few weeks from now. There is no more time to wait her out." He let her think on the point for a moment. "You can fix this. In fact, I believe you are the only one who can save Tabor's career."

Augusta twisted her hankie, tighter and tighter, around two fingers and glared at the floor. After a long silence, she looked at Billy, "How?"

"You must file for divorce now. Let him be elected and go to Washington. Then when the blonde leaves him, you can remarry him." She turned in her chair and stared so hard out the window Billy thought it might cause birds to fall from the sky. Again, he let her think.

Augusta slowly untwisted the hankie and dabbed at her eyes. "There is one thing..."

"Mr. Tabor will not disinherit his son," he said quietly.

Augusta shook her head and blinked back tears. "No, Maxcy will be fine. He is a good man. He's smart and he works hard. I rather he not be poisoned by wealth like his father. It is that," she rubbed her forehead with a spotted hand, "I do not want to cite adultery as my cause for divorce. I will not publicly acknowledge that woman in a court of law."

Billy was surprised. All of Denver knew Horace had been living with Baby Doe and had entertained a stream of floozies before that. Augusta, herself, had given a newspaper interview and discussed Baby Doe. "What about abandonment? He hasn't lived with you in two years."

Augusta nodded. "I will have Steck file the papers and get a court date before the legislature meets. Now please go, Mr. Bush. I'm not feeling well."

CHAPTER 31

1883

ON JANUARY 2, Augusta and Steck walked into a crowded courtroom; newspaper reporters filled the gallery and Horace's attorneys were huddled on one side of the aisle, but he was not with them. Judge Benjamin Harrington scowled at the crowd, causing everyone to hush. He wrapped his glasses around his prominent ears and read aloud Augusta's petition for divorce, then asked if this was correct, and if she was willing to proceed. Augusta closed her eyes and Steck answered for her, "Yes, Your Honor." The judge asked Horace's lawyers if they would be challenging the petition or disputing the charges. A tall, thin man with a deep voice answered for the group, "No, Your Honor." The judge then reviewed the settlement. Augusta would keep the Broadway home, an apartment building west of Capitol

Hill, a share of the Tam O'Shanter Mine in Leadville and a quarter of a million dollars.

"Very well, since all are in agreement, I declare this marriage dissolved. Madam, please sign here." The judge pointed to the bottom of a document.

Augusta held the pen above the paper, hand trembling. "I don't know my name," she said, her voice barely audible.

"What's that, madam?" the judge asked.

Augusta looked at the judge with wide eyes. "What is my name? What name shall I sign?"

Your name remains Tabor," Judge Harrington said. "It is legally yours to keep if you so wish."

"I will keep it," she declared. "I took the name as a young woman and I shall be Tabor until I die" She shakily signed the paper. "I suppose etiquette requires I thank you, Judge, but I cannot. I am not thankful. I did not do this willingly. Please put that into the record—not asked for willingly." A sob caught in her throat. She swallowed it back down and with the last remnants of her dignity hanging in tatters about her, marched slowly through the crowded courtroom, past the shouting reporters and out into the cold, bright sunshine.

Eugene Hawthorne couldn't hold back a chuckle. He could imagine the fit Baby Doe would have when she learned that Augusta would always be called Mrs. Tabor. He could practically hear her ranting, "There can't be two Mrs. Tabors. I am the wife, now. I am Mrs. Tabor. *The* Mrs. Tabor." That would make a very entertaining story. He headed back to the office to write it.

CHAPTER 32

THE GRAY CLOUDS HUNG LOW in the sky and fits of small, hard snow blew sideways when the Republican legislators gathered a few days later to select their nominee for the U.S. Senate. Since there was no vote by the general public and the Republicans held a majority in the state legislature, their caucuses would, in essence, be choosing the next senator. Three men were given consideration. Frederick Pitkin was the current governor, a law school graduate and a churchgoer. Educated and pious, he was the antithesis of carefree Tabor. Tom Bowen was an ambitious man new to Colorado politics. Whispers of "carpetbagger" had followed him out of Arkansas where he had gotten himself appointed to the state's Supreme Court after the war. Wily and cunning, he too, stood in contrast to the often-guileless Tabor.

No one expected any candidate to receive the twenty-seven votes needed on the first ballot. The first rounds of voting were simply the opening negotiations before the real wheeling and dealing began. Tabor was sure that his good nature and his money would insure the loyalty of all those politicians who spent their evenings in the Windsor Hotel bar; nevertheless, he made the rounds through the room, glad-handing and giving cash campaign contributions to those with upcoming elections. Billy was also there with a checkbook, ready to provide larger gifts after the first rounds of balloting determined who was firmly in the Tabor camp and who was on the fence. Several hours and thirty ballots later, the Republicans were no closer to having a clear nominee. Officials in charge decided no more secret ballots. All voting would be done by voice. Perhaps this would clarify the battle lines and allow candidates to better hone their lobbying efforts. Balloting continued for hours more, patience grew thin and decorum was tossed aside like a jacket in a stuffy room. Campaigning deteriorated into impolite whispered innuendo and, then shouted hostile accusations. On the ninety-seventh ballot, Tom Bowen received a majority of votes and became the Republican nominee for the U.S. Senate. With the party's majority in the legislature, his formal selection was ensured.

Baby Doe woke to raucous whooping coming down the hallway of the Windsor. She had dozed off sometime in the night waiting for the balloting to finish. Fortunately, the whalebone stays in her corset had kept her from slumping over and getting rumpled. Her hair and her gown still looked fine. Horace had said they would first accept congratulations from a few special friends privately here in the suite and then together make their first public appearance as a couple at the larger party in the Windsor's bar. She had chosen her dress and jewelry for the evening with care. The gown was a rich emerald velveteen with a rather modest neckline, nothing too low cut. The pearls around her neck, wrists and at her ears were elegant, but not flamboyant. She was dressing as Senator Tabor's wife now.

Horace came in alone. "Oh Baby, you look lovely, like a storybook queen."

"Like a senator's wife?" she asked with a seductive smile.

"Ah, well hell," Horace sighed. "They elected Tom Bowen to the six-year seat. That's his celebration party you hear down the hall." He collapsed into an armchair, the many hours catching up to him. "They gave me the sixty-day seat as a sop."

Baby Doe was flabbergasted. "After all you have done? You built firehouses and post offices and opera houses. You stopped the miners' strike. You built beautiful office buildings. You have given money to every charity cause in town." Her temper was lit now and counting his numerous accomplishments fueled the fire. "Those ungrateful vermin," she fumed. "Where is their loyalty? Their honor? Why, some of those men haven't paid for a meal at the Windsor in a year. I just want to slap their silly faces." She strode across the room. "Tom Bowen? He was a profiteer during the reconstruction of the South. He is not half the man you are."

She turned to look at him, "Horace, are you laughing?"

"No Ma'am," he said with a grin. "I'm just glad you are on my side." He pulled her onto his lap. "Here's what we are going to do. I need to leave for Washington right away. When I get there, I am going to book the grandest ballroom in the fanciest hotel. I'm going to buy every flower in town. Then I'm going to invite every congressman, every cabinet member, the vice president and the president himself to see me marry the most beautiful woman in the world. Meantime, you have the best seamstress in Denver make a wedding dress that will make every lady in both cities turn green."

"I want my family to come."

"Of course. I'll send you in a private rail car to pick them up in Oshkosh."

"And a priest, I want Mama and Papa to see me married by a priest."

"That might take a little doin,' but Billy and I will figure it out. After the wedding, I'll serve the sixty-day term in such high style it will leave them talking until the next election. When we come back to Denver, you can throw the fanciest parties those high society ladies ever saw. Then I'll work on getting elected governor and making you the first lady of Colorado." They sat in silence for a long moment. "Do you know the story of the guy who sold me a salted hole?

"I read it in the newspapers," she replied. A scoundrel named Chicken Bill Lovell had dug a shallow shaft back on Fryer Hill in the early Leadville days. When the going got tough, Lovell snuck over to a nearby working mine and, under the cover of darkness, stole a load of high-grade ore and dumped it at the bottom of his shaft. He took a sample of the ore to Tabor and offered to sell the shaft for $40,000. Tabor bit. Lovell took the check and quickly left town. When Tabor discovered the con, he ordered his men to keep digging. A mere eight feet further down lay one of the richest bodies of ore found in Leadville. That mine now brought in one hundred thousand dollars each month.

"Well, the Tabor luck turned that hole in the ground into the Chrysolite Mine. Trust the Tabor luck to turn this around, too." He patted her hand. "But right now, Baby Doe, I am so tired. I feel like I've been slinging a pickaxe in a mine all day. Let's hit the hay, and tomorrow when we wake up, I will make love to you, and then we can start fresh."

CHAPTER 33

HORACE AND BABY DOE exchanged telegrams and letters between Washington and Denver daily. There was so much to plan. Invitations needed to be engraved, in silver naturally, and then hand delivered to the president, his cabinet and the entire Senate. The Willard Hotel was reserved and food, champagne and flowers were ordered. Horace purchased a lovely sapphire and diamond wedding ring to decorate Baby's tiny hand and was talked into buying an enormous diamond necklace to be displayed on her ample bosom. For ninety thousand dollars, Horace's bride would walk down the aisle wearing the "Isabella necklace," part of the Spanish crown jewels that the queen had hawked to finance Columbus' voyage to the New World. Or anyway, that was the story the salesman told Horace; the letter of authenticity would be sent from New York City, soon.

When not working on the wedding of the year, Horace did some politicking. He introduced a bill establishing an army post in western Colorado to protect the forest belonging to railroad companies. He voted for a bill exempting jute from import tariffs, so that there would be "enough rope to hang those fellers who didn't elect me for six years." After hours, he practiced the brand of politics that had made him mayor of Leadville, buying rounds of drinks at the nearest bar and generally throwing money around. Horace could not be conceited or uppity if he tried; however, in a few short days he had gained a reputation as an ostentatious boor among the more starched members of the decorous Senate.

"Sweetest heart of my heart," he wrote to her, "watch the Associated Press dispatches. I am dining with some fellow senators and other bigwigs tonight."

"My Dearest Darling," she wrote back. "You have so little time in Washington, you must make the grandest, most memorable of impressions right away in your actions and appearances. I know you intend to wear the diamond ring, the diamond pin for your shirtfront, and diamond and onyx cufflinks on our wedding day. But I encourage you to unpack them and wear them when you go out in the evenings. The other senators must see what a great man you are."

Horace thought that was a fine idea and took to wearing his diamonds on the Senate floor as well. The sight of a senator wearing that many carats would have raised eyebrows among the staid Eastern gentlemen had they not been squinting against the glare.

Washington reporters jumped to learn more about the flashy new senator from the Wild West and they were waiting at the station when

Baby Doe's private train car, as luxurious as a velvet-lined jewel box, arrived. They shouted questions at the McCourt Family as Mama, Papa, two brothers, two sisters and their husbands climbed into a coach. Horace helped Baby into an elegant Victoria carriage with liveried driver he had reserved for her arrival. Porters struggled to load the wagon needed to transport the numerous trunks and bags required for the fanciest wedding of the year.

Although Baby Doe had written to her family about Horace's wealth, the elaborate plans for her wedding left them slack-jawed. Their set of suites at the handsome Willard Hotel became a hive of activity as the ladies bustled about with final preparations. There was so much to accomplish in just a few days. Final decisions about the floral arrangements and dinner service had to be made. Baby's sisters quickly realized their Oshkosh finery was too sedate for such an extravagant event. Colleen wanted a seamstress to add large bows to the shoulders of her dress and Claudia desired a cascade of ruffles attached to her bustle. Baby requested a hairdresser come to the suite that afternoon with drawings of hair arrangements. It was all too much for the men. Papa had lain down for a nap, and the younger men had gone for a stroll about town when there was a knock at the door.

"Oh, it must be the hairdresser," Baby said going to the door. "She is early."

The uniformed Negro whom Horace had hired to deliver invitations stood holding a small silver tray. He looked uncomfortable. "Madam, Senator and Mrs. Teller asked me to return this to you," he said in a quiet voice. On the tray was the wedding invitation, torn in half.

She grabbed the invitation and crumpled it in her hand, before Mama and her sisters could see. Quickly reaching for her coin purse, she tipped the man and shooed him out. Baby worked to swallow back her anger. That sanctimonious Mrs. Teller had sat in the Windsor lobby and whispered in Augusta's ear, prodding her to fight the divorce and running down Baby, and there was little doubt that the Tellers had worked against Horace's election in the Senate. Now this.

"What was that about?" asked Colleen.

Baby crushed the invitation even smaller and tucked it in her pocket. "A stroke of luck," she declared. "Washington's meanest woman won't be able to attend the wedding."

She and her sisters fell about laughing.

CHAPTER 34

THE DAY THAT BABY DOE had been working toward for years had arrived. By evening she would be declared the wife of one of America's richest men. The wealth alone would secure her a spot in the highest circles of society, but with a husband with the title of senator, governor and, perhaps someday even more, no one would dare exclude the Tabors.

Holding Papa's arm with one hand and a bouquet of white roses with the other, Baby stood around the corner from the Willard Hotel's largest salon, awaiting the cue for her entrance. Her gown was brocaded white satin with lace lingerie underneath. A train longer than Baby was tall trailed behind her and fluffy, white marabou down accented the shoulders, tiny waist, and plunging neckline where the Isabella necklace lay perfectly. Baby had encouraged the hairdresser to talk to the newspaper reporters that were loitering in the Willard lobby. "They'll want to know any details you can tell. Be sure to describe what the gown looks like and tell them it cost seven thousand dollars," she had told the woman.

Papa patted her hand and smiled at her. Baby's letters home over the past few years were very thin on details about the disappearance of Harvey, the kindly shopkeeper who helped her or the family history of this new love. She knew Papa had been skeptical about her marrying a man twenty-five years her senior, but the fact that a Catholic priest would be performing the ceremony gave him peace. "We are happy for you, Dearie. Your Horace seems like an admirable man. I pray he'll make you happy all the rest of your days."

The string quartet struck up a processional, and Baby Doe and her father entered the room as the guests stood. Baby looked to the cardinal red table at the far end of the room. There with the priest stood Horace whose smile was so broad it lifted his moustache and crinkled his eyes. Billy Bush and the other Colorado senator, Tom Bowen, attended him. Baby had objected when Horace told her Bowen would stand up with him. But Horace had said, "Politics is a funny thing. A fella can be your rival one day and your supporter the next. You have to let a lot roll off your back and just wait for the next time." Baby did not see the world that way. She would not forget Tom Bowen and the others' traitorous behavior, but she would ignore it—for today.

Baby's sisters awaited her on the left side. She turned to smile at her guests as she advanced down the aisle. Gentlemen in formal evening dress smiled and nodded. But something was amiss, like a picture askew. Everything looked marvelous, the candles were lit, her husband was waiting and the people were elegant. Baby looked over both sides of the aisle to a sea of black suits and stiff white shirtfronts and suddenly realized what was wrong. No colorful dresses or hats dotted the room. There were no women at all. Not a single congressional wife was to be seen. The most glamorous wedding that Washington would ever witness was to be attended by the bride, her mother, two sisters and one hundred men.

Baby Doe's smile wobbled and threatened to drop as she continued to walk forward. Her mind was whirling. *Why would these women snub me? They've never even met me. They're not friends of Augusta.* Baby was young, beautiful and now rich. *Are they jealous? Are they afraid I will steal their husbands? On my wedding day*? Hot, angry tears filled her eyes and threatened to spill onto her cheeks. She took a deep breath and blinked the tears away. *Did they think they would shame me? Teach me a lesson? Did they think I would run away crying?*

This day was everything she had ever wanted. It was her destiny. She had known from the moment she first spotted the Rockies from the train with Harvey that she was meant to live a charmed life. She had worked so hard for this, waited so long, and now it was all coming true. And she was happy, damn it. Yes, she was happy and she was going to let everyone know it. She would be happy to spite them. *I am not going to let those old envious bitties ruin my day.* They would not make her feel shame for the path she had taken.

Papa gave her hand to Horace. His droopy face fairly shined with pride and happiness. Three years ago, she had been drawn to his handsome bank account, but it was his heart of gold that had won her. She knew Horace's love was true, and on this day, she would devote herself to him for all time. She would be more than his lover and heart's desire. She would be his helpmate in all things. She would support him, defend him, be a bulwark against ill winds. She would be his ally and partner as they built a future together as kindred souls.

The priest was a small man with a big voice that carried to the back of the room as he asked, "Do you take this man for better or for worse, in sickness and in health, for richer or poorer, until death do you part?"

More than anything, Baby Doe had desired the marriage bonds as security in a man's world; now, as she recited them before Horace, she knew she had the rare privilege of marrying for love. "I do."

"If anyone has objections to this union, let him speak now or forever hold his peace."

A nervous trill shot up Baby's back, uncertain if any scandalmongers had followed them from Denver, but the crowd remained quiet.

"I pronounce you man and wife," the priest said and Baby laughed with equal measures of relief and joy.

President Arthur, whose young bride had died of pneumonia a few years earlier, immediately stood from his front row seat to offer his congratulations. "There has never been a more beautiful bride," he declared. Baby coquettishly lowered her eyes and snapped a rose from her arrangement. Rising on tiptoes she fastened it to the president's broad chest.

Horace whooped, grabbed Baby's hand and shouted, "To supper." They led the crowd through just-opening folding doors to a second salon sat for dinner. A six-foot centerpiece, so large it needed its own table, dominated the room. A heart fashioned from red roses was pierced by an arrow of violets shot from a Cupid's bow of heliotrope, hung over a wedding bell made of white roses. Each dinner plate and champagne bucket was surrounded by a halo of violets and every column was roped with garlands. In a nod to the famous Tabor luck, two giant four-leaf clovers fashioned from roses and edged in shiny green smilax leaves sat at the ends of the head table. The wedding cake, looking a tad plain in the surrounding anarchy of blooms, sat under a canopy of woven flowers trailing ivy. In the far corners of the room, greenery had been shaped into life-sized replicas of the boxes at the Tabor Grand Opera House. Even gentlemen who did not usually notice such fripperies were made to gasp by the floral riot.

Dinner was exceedingly gay with much laughter and champagne. The Willard staff had discreetly whisked away the tables and chairs intended for the absent women and made larger servings of the food and drink. The president and other guests stayed until after midnight.

Scandal broke with the dawn. A *Washington Post* reporter, after receiving a telegram from Denver—from a fellow by the name of Eugene Hawthorne—waited outside the hotel and sidled up to Father Chappelle as he was leaving in the wee hours. "Father, has the Church changed its doctrine on marriage as a holy unity for life? How was it that you were able to marry two divorced people?"

Father Chappelle gave the reporter a full interview right there, in the dark of night on a street corner. "I was completely duped. Deceived," the story read in the next day's paper. "I was not acquainted with either Tabor or the bride's father, McCourt. When I asked if there were reasons they should not be joined, not a word was spoken. I shall be returning the fee the bride's father gave me to perform the ceremony."

Baby Doe was a hot-pot mixture of anger and disappointment when the morning papers did not describe the most elegant wedding ever to be witnessed in Washington, but instead rehashed the same old salacious stories: the Durango divorce, Augusta's outburst in the Denver courtroom crying the divorce was "not willing," and how

Baby's own divorce proceedings included entering into a bawdy house with a policeman to catch her first husband committing adultery. They hadn't printed a single word about her fabulous dress or the Isabella necklace.

"Throw out that old rag," Horace said when he saw her frowning over the Monday morning newspaper.

"You're right, my dear husband," she said, forcing a smile and trying to erase the lines on her forehead. "I don't need to read about our wedding; I was there and it was wonderful."

Horace looked at his new bride with earnest respect. "I love you, Baby. You always face the world with a brave smile. There is nothing in this world I will dread with you by my side." He wrapped his arms around in her a long, hard hug, then kissed her head.

"I am going to the Capitol building a little early today. I'll round up the fellas in the cloakroom and explain this little dust-up. This is just a misunderstanding. That padre never asked if we were divorced; we would have told him," Horace said. "Beside I thought everyone had heard about us, you being the most beautiful lady in Colorado and me being the luckiest man alive." He grinned. "Are you still coming to watch the proceedings from the gallery with the other wives?"

"Nothing could keep me away," she said. She had been planning her entrance into the Senate gallery for weeks, no abominable newspaper story was going to keep her from it. She was finished hiding in hotel rooms. People could say what they want, but she was Mrs. Tabor now.

The ladies were seated and the senators had filed into the chamber and were preparing to take their places when a murmur arose from the upper level. A few men turned to see what was causing the stir in the usually sedate chambers. When they could not stop staring, more men turned. Baby Doe arrived wearing a glossy brown silk ensemble the color of a chocolate drop. A bejeweled girdle shaped as a serpent with emerald eyes and ruby tongue writhed around her slim waist and accented the curves above and below. The Isabella necklace highlighted her lush décolletage. Horace turned, and beaming, gave her a hardy wave. She smiled and wiggled her fingers in a small wave, making sure her new engagement ring, a huge diamond surrounded by sapphires as blue as her eyes, flashed in the light.

The hurt and anger she felt at the wedding had tempered and hardened into something new. As a blacksmith strikes red-hot iron, hammering it into a new shape, the slights and the snubs had battered Baby. However, now sitting apart from the other wives in the Senate gallery, she was calm and cool. No one was going to beat her down.

Let the reporters write about this, she thought. *These old crows sitting beside me can use those puckered faces to suck lemons.*

CHAPTER 35

WHEN CONGRESS RETIRED from sweltering Washington for the summer, Senator and Mrs. Teller returned to the cool, dry breezes of Denver. Mrs. Teller's first order of business was to host a tea for the wives of the city's upper crust. Augusta would not be in attendance as she was a divorcée now and that was a social condition best avoided. A group of three dozen of the city's better families had begun calling themselves the Sacred 36. It was these wives, and a few more women striving to be included, that Mrs. Teller entertained that afternoon.

"Ladies, we can never allow our husbands to feel any comfort around a divorced man. Tabor," Murmurs floated through the room at the mention of his name, *Poor Augusta*. "Tabor," Mrs. Teller resumed, "may have used his fortune to buy a divorce and a re-marriage, but he cannot be allowed to feel any ease living this new life. We must shut them out socially. We cannot be seen to approve of this kind of disrespectability. Heaven forbid, this disposing of a wife in favor of another becomes acceptable. We must protect our marriages and defend moral living. It is up to us, ladies, to stop any contagion of immorality as any one of our husbands could fall victim to an adventuress, a gold digger like Baby Doe."

Heads bobbed in agreement, a quiet "Hear, hear," was heard, and the most delicious shortbread cookies were served.

After a tour of New York City, the newlyweds returned to Denver to start their new life of domestic happiness. Their first order of business was to inform the state Republican party that Tabor's stint in the Senate was a great success, and he would be available to finance campaigns in upcoming local elections with an eye on the next open gubernatorial or senatorial seat for himself. They instructed Billy to explore all sorts of diverse new business ideas, from fire insurance to a new railroad. Billy shared the latest news of Augusta. She had sold her share of the Windsor to Billy and was planning a move to California to enjoy warm weather and anonymity. Baby Doe thought that was the perfect wedding gift for the couple who had everything. She could settle back in at the suites at the Windsor and become the only Mrs. Tabor of Denver.

Each morning Baby Doe prepared to receive social calls from the wives of the city's elite. She completed her toilette with care, readying her hair, clothes and jewelry, expecting calling cards to cover her suites like a mountain snow. None came. The new Mr. and Mrs. Tabor went out to restaurants and to the theater, but were not asked to be guests at parties or dinners. Invitations to dine with the Tabors at the Windsor were returned with stiffly worded regrets.

"There she is," whispered a woman as Baby Doe glided down the stairs and into the lobby of the Windsor.

"Who?" her friend asked.

Baby could hear the women and knew they were talking about her. She had begun going downstairs to take afternoon tea in the Windsor lobby, but most of the ladies of the smart set now took tea at the nearby American Hotel. The few women present these days were not in the highest circles and had not heard that it was no longer fashionable to frequent the Windsor.

"Tabor's blonde. Goodness, look at the size of those bows on her bustle."

The two women gawked at Baby as though she were a curiosity in a circus side show. She crossed the room and sat down at a small table without returning their stare.

"I always thought purple was a very garish color," declared the first woman referring to Baby's newest dress in a voice that Baby imagined was loud enough for the kitchen staff to hear.

"Poor Augusta."

"I heard she wasn't a very pleasant person."

"I would think she was quite unhappy being married to a philanderer."

He's not her husband anymore, she screamed in her head. She had been sure that money and marriage were the keys to her acceptance. She had both now, but still the Denver ladies were turning up their noses.

A waiter approached and asked if she would like tea and sandwiches. She could imagine the delight of the petty women at the next table if she got up and left. Well, they would be sorely disappointed. She was Mrs. Tabor now, and she wasn't going anywhere. "Yes," she said. "And one of those lovely little cream puffs." She smiled broadly at the waiter. She turned her gaze to the two women who continued to stare and gave them a dismissive up and down glare. Those harpies were no better than Eugene Hawthorne. *Even the Shoo Fly girls were more gracious than Denver women.*

When a calling card did arrive, it was from a reporter, a Mr. Samuel Baker from the *Colorado Journal*, requesting an interview. "Tell him I am much too busy to see visitors today, but he may return tomorrow," Baby Doe told the bellhop. As he took his leave, Baby Doe got busy preparing. She pulled a thick handful of blank envelopes from her desk. Over and over again, she wrote *Mrs. Tabor* or *Mr. & Mrs. Horace Tabor* on the front. She sealed them with wax and then cut them open with a letter knife. She pawed through her stationery to find blank pages without her new name engraved on top. She wrote an imaginary invitation to an intimate dinner for friends and another for an afternoon tea. She set these on top of the blank papers. She reviewed her handiwork and then folded a dozen sheets in half, opened them again and shuffled them with the envelopes into a messy stack.

The next day, Baby Doe made Mr. Baker cool his heels for nearly an hour before she called him up, letting him surmise she had graciously made time for him, squeezed in a few minutes from her frantic social calendar. Baby knew every detail would appear in the newspapers, so she took care to make sure the suite looked lovely and she looked even more so. Fresh flowers perfumed the room, roses competing with lilies and dahlias. She styled her hair in a long cascade of ringlets flowing down her back. Her peach-colored dress with train was originally designed for evenings at the opera, but no one had seen it yet. She thought that emeralds went well with the ensemble, but diamonds went well with everything, so she wore both. She positioned herself at her writing desk, as if answering correspondence, the stack of fictional envelopes and letters within eyesight, but not too close to the edge.

"I am sorry I kept you waiting," she said as he was seated. "I simply had to answer my correspondence. You see, we have received so many invitations to attend all manner of affairs from all the very best people." She waved her hand at the pile of papers. "Regrettably, we cannot accept every invitation, so we are not accepting any invitations currently. We wouldn't wish to create any hard feelings among the city's social set." She sighed at the burden of it all. "So I really can't comment on any social affairs."

"Perhaps you can tell me about you and Mr. Tabor, how you met," young Baker prompted.

"Oh, I remember well the night we met," Baby clasped her hands to her bosom and she stared into the distance. "We were both in Leadville at the time and Mr. Tabor's business associate, Mr. Bush introduced us over dinner. It was love at first sight. We both felt an instant bond, deep and true. It is unfortunate that neither Mr. Tabor nor I are poets, because it is hard to describe how our hearts sang at that first meeting. We knew at that moment we must be together and never part, no matter the obstacles." She gave a joyful sigh.

"Our recent wedding in Washington was the perfect demonstration of our deep affections. President Arthur attended, as well as, his entire cabinet and the Senate. The president was a charming man. He graciously complimented my appearance, and said he had a wonderful time."

"What does the future hold for you and Mr. Tabor?" the reporter asked.

"Oh, we are so happy. We would be content to live every day like this one, for the rest of our lives," she beamed. Then turning her eyes shyly down, "Of course we do hope to have children soon."

FIRST INTERVIEW WITH SILVER QUEEN.
TABOR'S NEW WIFE LIVES IN LUXURY.

Horace read of the instant affinity at their first star-crossed meeting and remarked, "That sounds about right." He handed her the paper and chucked her chin, "Silver Queen, I kinda like that name."

"Oh, there are a few liberties with the facts in the story," Baby said. "He writes I had rings on every finger, and I was really only wearing two on each hand." Baby cut the article out for her latest scrapbook and glued it beside chronicles of so many soirees to which the Tabors had not been invited. "Horace, when do you think those old crows will stop looking down on me and come calling?"

"Aw, it breaks my heart to see you worry about them." He came up behind her chair and wrapped his arms around her. "Maybe this newspaper story will help and, you know, some ladies might not like coming to a hotel for social visits."

"Oh Horace, of course. It's unseemly for married ladies to frequent the upper floors of a hotel without their husbands." Baby clasped her head. Why had she had not thought of that? "We need a house, a fabulous house, one that everyone will want to see."

He grinned under his shaggy moustache. "A place to start that family? Maybe have a little girl with blonde curls?"

CHAPTER 36

1884

THE YEAR 1884 STARTED with another Tabor family wedding and Billy Bush again was the best man. In January, young Maxcy wed Luella Babcock in a modest church service. As Baby Doe and Horace made their way down the aisle to the second pew, she could feel the chill of the assembled women as bitter as any Leadville winter wind. Luckily, Baby Doe wore her new full- length ermine opera cloak with matching muff and towering hat.

The Tabor house exemplified all that its owners were—brash, rich and completely lacking in subtlety. The Italian villa-style mansion was the largest in the Capitol Hill neighborhood, the home and gardens taking up an entire city block. The green velvet grounds were attended by five gardeners and surrounded by a three-foot brownstone wall. One driveway passed the front verandah, and a second took visitors under a portico, in case of inclement weather. Inside the floors were covered with Oriental rugs. Crystal chandeliers hung from decorative pressed tin ceilings. Heavy walnut furniture filled rooms stuffed with all manner of Victorian bric-a-brac. Mirrors, tapestries, flocked wallpaper and oil paintings—five of which were portraits of the Tabors favorite subject, Baby Doe—embellished the walls.

The extravagance was not limited to the house. The stable and carriage house held three carriages and twelve horses. Four snow-white horses were often hitched to the dark blue enamel landau trimmed with gold and upholstered in light blue satin. This was Baby's favorite conveyance as it highlighted her blue eyes. But there were some of Baby's dresses that simply coordinated better with the more open, brown, Victoria-style carriage with the red trim pulled by the sorrels or the black carriage with white trim and white satin upholstery drawn by a team of gleaming black horses. Baby Doe had spent too many sunny afternoons hiding in the Windsor Hotel as Horace's mistress. Now as wife, she wanted to get out and be seen, and she made sure every appearance was jaw dropping. The neighbors would never be able to claim that she wasn't good enough.

"I tell ya, Jimmy, it was the fanciest rig and horses I ever seen. Those horses was so shiny I had to cover my eyes," said a boy in a flat cap and short pants to his buddy. Eli and Lil' Jimmy had finished their deliveries to the Capitol Hill neighborhood and were meandering back to Mr. Perkins' grocery store.

"Did ya see Baby Doe?" Lil' Jimmy asked, panting to keep up with the long legs of the older boy. "Did she look like a living doll?"

"I just saw the Negros. They was gettin' the horses hitched up when I delivered vegetables to the back of the house. They say she goes out for a ride every day around Capitol Hill and through downtown. If we hurry, we can see her and the rig."

The boys hotfooted down 13th street until they came to the main driveway attended by two dainty bronze deer. They sat down against the brownstone wall to wait, pitching pebbles into the street.

"I hear she has a carriage to match every dress," Lil' Jimmy said.

"That can't be true," Eli scoffed. "I bet she's got a hundred dresses. Where would she keep all those carriages?"

Jimmy's mother owned only a couple of dresses. He knew someone nicknamed the Silver Queen would have more, but he really couldn't imagine why a woman would need more than a house dress and a church dress. "Maybe she has a carriage for every day of the week," he suggested.

"Yeah, that's probably true."

Then the boys heard jingling bridles and hooves shuffling through gravel. They hopped up as four glossy black horses pulling an ebony carriage bore Baby Doe, dressed in bright yellow, and her coachmen in scarlet livery, out of the driveway and down the street. The boys, having lived their entire short lives in the mountain West, only knew a world covered in dust, mud or snow. They had never seen anything so luminous. The rig, the animals and the passenger all shone in the sunshine. Eli and Jimmy trotted alongside with mouths gaping. Baby Doe smiled and gave a small wave; the boys waved back wildly with both arms overhead. Laughing, she reached into her purse, found a couple of pennies and tossed them to her new admirers.

Like ducks homing to bread crumbs in the city park pond, the next day there were several children waiting at the end of the driveway for Baby Doe's afternoon excursion. Each day there seemed to be a few more in the scrum. She scattered mostly pennies and nickels along the way, but every afternoon one lucky scamp caught a silver dollar. She loved the smiling laughing children, their eager faces peering over the stone wall as she came down the drive, their short legs running down the street alongside the carriage and their cheerful voices calling to her. At least someone in Denver liked her.

Eugene Hawthorne wrote about it, calling her little outings "Tabor's Traveling Circus" and the children "street urchins." Baby decided his poison pen could drain the happiness out of most anything.

"Ma'am, there is a visitor," the new maid stammered. Bridgette's round Irish face blushed furiously below her orange hair.

Baby Doe hopped up from the burgundy camelback sofa. Her first caller. *Where was the butler? Why hadn't he announced the guests?* Baby Doe had found it hard to hire help as the Denver matrons had already snatched up the experienced servants and the new domestics arriving in town with good recommendations were wary of working for a home tainted with scandal. So, the Tabors were left with a staff of questionable experience or work ethic. Baby hoped the minor chaos that seemed to occur daily within the house would not ruin her first social call.

"Tell Cook to make a tray with coffee and cookies. No, tea," Baby ordered. "I don't know where the butler is, so please show our visitor into the south drawing room." Bridgette's brow furrowed in confusion. "The room with the green draperies," Baby prompted.

"But Ma'am, she won't come in, and Cook already offered her a cuppa," the little maid said. Now Baby's forehead wrinkled in bewilderment. Bridgette looked down and said, "She's the housekeeper from across the avenue. She is waiting at the backdoor with a message for you."

A tall, bony woman was standing just inside the delivery door, her hands clasped primly at her waist, apparently convinced by Cook to at least come in out of the wind. "How can I help you?" Baby asked.

"Madam, I am Mrs. Morgan. I am the housekeeper at Senator and Mrs. Teller's home," the woman began.

The Mrs. Teller who ripped up my wedding invitation in Washington, thought Baby, struggling to keep a smile on her lips.

"Mrs. Teller is greatly distressed by the goings-on here. The children that gather at the gate each day are very noisy. Now, there are naked figures on the lawn. They appear to be dancing and cavorting," the woman said. "It's indecent."

Bridgette looked confused again, but a snorting laugh came from Cook. Baby Doe bit the inside of her cheeks to keep a sharp retort from escaping. When she was sure she could speak politely, Baby said, "Perhaps Mrs. Teller is unaware that the bronze statues are Psyche, Nimrod and Diane from Greek mythology."

The woman lifted her chin and stated, "The Tellers do not condone idolatry."

"It is art," Baby said, in a voice louder and higher than she wished.

"It is shocking to Mrs. Teller's refined senses."

"They were cast in Paris." Baby knew every lady in Denver looked to Europe, the center of sophistication and culture, to dictate what Coloradoans thought tasteful.

"Nonetheless," the woman answered, implying that was all to be said.

Baby Doe clinched her fists in the folds of her skirt and took a breath. As sweet as Cook's snickerdoodle cookies she said, "Please assure Mrs. Teller that we did not mean to cause her any disquiet and that we will take care of the statues right away." She turned on her heel and strode out of the kitchen, calling after her, "Bridgette, find that butler. Tell him to fetch my dressmaker." She would give Mrs. Teller and her friends something to look at.

The tiny French dressmaker thought she had seen every eccentricity in the new rich of the Wild West, but this defied belief.

"My neighbor doesn't like seeing them unclothed, so we will clothe them," Baby said as she, the dressmaker and the head gardener, a mumbling Englishman with the bulbous red nose of a drinker, toured the front lawn. "I want a jacket, pants and riding boots for Nimrod. And a derby hat. I think a flowing chiffon dress would fit Diana, don't you? Of course, she will need pantalets and a chemise underneath. Psyche should be in a stiff satin. Please make two outfits for each so we can change them. No one wants to be known for wearing the same dress every day."

CHAPTER 37

"AREN'T YOU EATING BREAKFAST?" Horace asked as a steaming plate was set before him.

The smell of Horace's bacon and eggs sent Baby Doe's stomach spinning. She covered her mouth and held her breath in a vain attempt to calm her insides. "Just toast," she said when she could speak.

"Darlin', are you sick? I'll send for a doctor."

"Oh, I will need a doctor, but not just yet." Baby gave her husband a feeble smile, "I'm with child."

Horace's whoop could be heard down the street.

More heartwarming news came with the spring winds. Baby Doe tossed the letter she was reading into the air and gave a small shriek of joy. "Horace, they are actually coming. My family is moving to Denver. Well, not everyone. My brother Peter, you met him at the wedding, he is my favorite. He is coming first. Maybe by summer." She picked up the stationery and read, "And Colleen and her husband want to come. You met them, too. Oh, they liked you so much." She ran on, "I have missed them, I really have. I don't have any friends in Denver. It will be so nice to have family around, especially when the baby comes." She hopped up and began charging around the room. "Peter can stay here in the beginning," she swept her arm around and laughed. "We have plenty of room." Another thought struck her. "Do you think you can help Peter find a position?"

Horace smiled, "Sure. What does he do?"

"He can do anything. He is so smart and charming and handsome."

"I'm not sure what job you get for being good looking," Horace laughed. He reached out and caught Baby, pulling her into his lap.

"Oh, I know! Peter can manage the Tabor Grand Opera. The actors would love him."

"I don't know about that. The opera house is Billy's little darling. He spends a lot of time there, likes keeping company with the performers, playing cards with the men and trying to romance the ladies. I don't think he'll want to give that up."

Baby tsked. "Billy has lots of irons in the fire. He runs two hotels and oversees all your new business ventures. Your next election, whenever that is, will keep him busy, too. He'd probably like to lighten his load a little."

"I don't think Billy is going to like it, but if it will make you happy, I'll give Peter the job." Horace's craggy old face stared into Baby's peachy smooth one. "Because my sweetest heart, I will do anything to make you smile."

"Horace Tabor, I love you." She really did. She was not sure when it happened, or even how. Maybe it was because Horace had proven himself to her a hundred times over. She trusted that he wasn't running around with other women anymore, he always took her side when people spoke against her, and she could see his hurt when folks were cruel to her. She believed him when he said he would make her life easy and beautiful. He cared about her. He was her best and only friend. He loved her with his whole heart, and it made her love him.

"I know," he grinned and his moustache wiggled. "I read it in the newspapers."

She kissed him softly and led him upstairs to their overstuffed feather bed.

Horace thought it would be best if Peter started as an assistant to Billy, like Maxcy was doing at the Windsor. Once Peter had learned the ropes, then Horace would broach the subject of Peter running the show, so to speak. They would go out to dinner at Windsor Hotel restaurant and stop at Billy's office to let him know he had a new aide coming soon. But Billy had been playing Horace's abettor for a few years now and his distrust of the "good news" showed on his face.

"Are you planning to make him manager of the Tabor Grand?" Billy asked bluntly.

"Well, let's see how things work out," Horace said.

"Yes," interrupted Baby with equal bluntness.

"Sir, I have done a good job at the Grand, getting it built and up and running. Managing the Leadville opera house was my first position with you; the theaters have been my greatest successes for you. I am the most qualified person to run the opera house outside of New York or San Francisco."

"Yes, you are very good at this job. That is why we want you to show Peter the ropes," Horace said.

Baby wanted to end this conversation. "Besides you have many other duties for which the senator depends on you." She slipped her hand through the bend at Horace's elbow and turned him to go.

"No," Billy said, slamming shut a ledger on the desk. "I have spent the past five years developing business plans, finding new investments and managing several businesses in multiple towns, only to be pulled away time and again to clean up your personal messes." He pointed a finger at Baby. "Messes caused by you and your grabbiness." He made snatching motions with both hands. "If you hadn't cooked up the Durango divorce, if you hadn't insisted on a secret St. Louis wedding or deceiving the priest in Washington, Tabor would be a senator or governor or, or, or . . . anything he wanted. But, no, you couldn't be the discreet paramour. You are so head-strong, plowing through without a thought of others or outcomes. You have to have it all your way, all of the money, all of the attention, all of Tabor." He stopped, gasping, seemingly out of steam.

Baby was speechless. She knew Billy disliked her, but she was shocked that he spoke to her so rudely in front of Horace.

"Now, Billy, that's enough," Horace said, holding up a hand.

"Yes, it is enough. I have had enough. I have a fine business mind and I should be focusing on that, not running sordid errands between wives and mistresses and political hacks. I should be managing the Tabor Grand."

"Ha!" Baby cried. "So you can hobnob with the performers after the show? Chasing skirts and playing cards?"

Baby knew by the way Billy tightened his lips under his thin moustache that she had poked a sore spot.

"You, of all people, dare to accuse me of impropriety?" Billy asked. "Don't forgot I knew of you in Central City, and I was there on the night you met Tabor in Leadville. I saw the ambition in your face."

Oh, you will be so sorry you spoke like that, Billy Bush, because I am the wife now.

The Tabors would not eat at the Windsor's fine restaurant that night, "nor ever again," Baby Doe declared.

Horace was slow to enter into conflict, preferring to ignore situations that couldn't be solved by throwing money at them. But, much as during the miners' strike, once a line had been drawn, Horace would doggedly stand to it. Billy's outburst made it impossible for them to work together. It was time to end the partnership and remove Billy from his role in all of the Tabor business ventures. However, that wasn't enough to soothe an infuriated Baby Doe; she could not let it drop and move on.

"We need to let the Denver businessmen know that Billy Bush no longer has your ear. It would be like just like him to trade on your name. Maybe we could get a reporter to write a story about him. I want everyone to know he is a snake." Baby Doe was spending her day nurturing her grudge against Billy when the new accountant entered Horace's office.

"Excuse me Mr. Tabor, but there seems to be a small problem with the petty cash fund at the opera house. I spoke with your son about it, and he told me that Mr. Bush would often use the funds when playing poker with the actors after shows. Maxcy thought the funds were usually replaced within a couple of weeks."

She knew it! "How much money is missing?" Baby Doe asked. She felt her burning anger cool to something like satisfaction.

"Two thousand."

"We can have him arrested for theft," she cried.

"Actually, I think the charge would be embezzlement," droned the accountant. "And that would be difficult to prove. It might be more expedient to file a lawsuit."

A few days later, at Baby Doe's insistence, Horace filed a lawsuit charging Billy with embezzling two thousand dollars from the Tabor Grand Opera House till to settle gambling debts.

Billy had treated Baby poorly for years. He had hidden her in the Windsor, humiliated her with that stupid veil and conspired against her with Augusta. Now, as Tabor's wife, she could balance the scales. *This lawsuit will paint Billy with the blackest of brushes, gambling, theft and low morals all splashed together*, she thought. The problem was that it is hard not to splatter paint on one's self.

At the end of the week a letter arrived from a law firm. Billy counter-sued Tabor to the tune of one hundred thousand dollars for illicit activities performed for which he had not been paid. His deposition before the court was lengthy and in it, he detailed bribes paid to various legislators during the Senate election. It explained how ten thousand dollars was spent to pay off public officials and secure the Durango divorce, to assist in procuring a marriage with "the woman commonly known as Baby Doe," and to find witnesses against

Augusta's character. Bush asked for seventy-five thousand dollars for injury to his business enterprises, having sacrificed his own interests to put Tabor's forward. Bush's final stroke would be to call Augusta and Maxcy to testify on his behalf.

The claims were so sordid that Eugene Hawthorne didn't need to write suggestive stories about the trial; he merely printed the court filings, including lists naming state legislators bribed by Billy. All of Denver settled in to watch another Tabor scandal play out on the public stage. The family was once again the topic of every conversation from dusty pool halls to posh parlors. Mrs. Teller tsk-tsked with the other doyennes of Capitol Hill, and Tabor's political friends distanced themselves as his adversaries realized the best time to kick a man was when he was down.

Everyone was unsatisfied when after one day of trial the judge declared, "This courtroom is not a school yard. I will not abide name calling and stone throwing. I am dismissing both suits as indecent and irrelevant."

"Well, the bright side is that Eugene Hawthorne and his cronies won't have anything to write about now that the suits have been dismissed," Horace said as the couple breakfasted in the morning room. Horace slurped his coffee and shook open the *Tribune*. He gasped as he saw the headline and swore under his breath as he leaned in to read a letter to the editor. Without a word, Horace stood and walked slightly hunched, like he had been punched in the gut, from the room. Baby snatched the paper her husband threw on the table.

TABOR UNFIT FOR PUBLIC OFFICE

By Senator Nathaniel Hill

Horace Tabor is a disgrace to Colorado. His private life is a disgrace and his public life is a disgrace. He spreads his money attempting to buy his way into office. He seeks not to serve the public, but collect titles. He has, again, caused a public scandal in this latest legal dispute with his business partner William Bush. Denver society has spoken its verdict regarding his life, siding with the gracious lady whom he cast aside. Tabor is an outcast in every sense of the word, socially and politically. The Republicans' gentlemen should look to their wives as examples and shun the rascal. The GOP must ensure that he never hold office again.

Baby Doe had become a bit jaded to the Denver newspapers' sensational stories of her and Horace's love affair, but the vitriol pouring from the pen of Senator Hill—a former colleague, a recipient of Tabor campaign funds, a supposed friend left her shocked and angry. She sputtered with rage, tore the paper into shreds and was stomping on them when Bridgette appeared at the drawing room door and asked, "Ma'am?"

"They knifed him in the back, just like Caesar," Baby cried and rushed out to find her man.

Bridgette picked up the mess. She liked the Tabors; they were good to the staff. Nobody deserved to be treated like those uppity Capitol Hill stiff-necks and snake-in-the-grass politicians treated

Mr. and Mrs. Tabor. The worst of the lot were those horrid reporters, sidling around the backdoor asking personal questions about the couple. Bridgette wasn't a good reader, but from now on she would look for the Tabor name in the papers before she brought them into breakfast and throw out the mean ones. Cook would help her.

Baby Doe found Horace in the library leaning over his broad mahogany writing desk. With head hung low and shoulders hunched, he looked like a broken man. She slipped up behind him, wrapped her arms around him, and lay her head on his back.

"I loved being the mayor of Leadville," he said softly. "I helped build that town, started the post office and the firehouse. I liked meeting people, talking with them and helping them solve problems."

The hurt in Horace's voice cut her like a jagged knife. She bit back the sob threatening at her throat.

He shook his big shaggy head. "Politics at a higher level is a nasty business."

"They are all snakes," she cried. "They just want your money. They take advantage of your good nature."

"It is pretty clear the pols in this town are not going to let me be governor or run for president."

"That letter is an outrage, Horace."

He turned around and gathered her in his arms. "I honestly thought that the good I could do for the state of Colorado would outweigh any gossip." He held her out at arm's length and looked into her tear-filled eyes. "I don't want to put us through this anymore. I know I promised you could be the first lady of Colorado and more, but would you be happy just being Mrs. Tabor?"

Baby had been full of ambition when she climbed out of the stagecoach in Leadville. She had set her cap for Horace Tabor and spent years devising schemes to marry him. Becoming first lady of the state hadn't even been a pipe dream then. "Horace, being your wife is all I ever desired."

CHAPTER 38

IN MANY WAYS, Peter and Baby were different sides of the same coin. Like her, he was fair-haired, good looking and had come to Colorado to seek his fortune, but Peter was more amiable. He didn't have a temper; his aspirations were more modest and cloaked in charm. Bankrolled with a generous Tabor paycheck, Peter quickly became the most eligible bachelor in Denver. He received invitations for dinners and balls from all the matrons with marriageable daughters, even those who had turned their noses up at Baby Doe, which put her nose firmly out of joint.

"I hear that crowd is calling themselves the Sacred 36," Baby said after Peter had received another invitation, this time to a summer garden party. "I imagine Horace and I won't be invited since he has left politics and leads a private life now." Baby knew that they probably would not have been invited even if Horace had been made senator or governor, but she didn't want Peter to know the lack of acceptance bothered her.

"Why do you want to spend time with those old harpies?" Peter asked.

She reached out and rubbed the leaf of a potted ivy that grew up and over a trellis surrounding the sofa. She had read of the popularity of indoor gardens among the English and had turned the drawing room into a veritable thicket full of ferns, primrose, rubber trees, African violets and potted palms. She sighed, she didn't know why she desired their respect, demanded their attention, wished for inclusion. People had long looked down upon her. Mother Doe had thought she wasn't good enough for her son. In fact, all of Oshkosh thought she had married above her station. The citizens of Central City had held her at arm's length; only the Shoo Fly girls had been amicable. She was tired of the critical stories and judgmental looks; she craved approval. She had been sure that demonstrations of the Tabor wealth—the mansion, the jewels, the opera house—would confirm their worth as Denver's finest citizens. She had thought that after the wedding people would warm to them, but at every turn the upper class rejected them. The best she could do was inspire jealousy.

"Wouldn't you rather spend evenings in the company of more interesting people? Well-traveled, well-read people?" he asked.

"Where would I find these people?"

"The theater."

The Tabor Grand was an oasis of culture in the vast West, the most important theater for a thousand miles. If Denver's elite wanted to attend a play, lecture, concert or ballet, they had to go to Tabor's playhouse and every actor on two continents was eager to perform on its glamorous new stage.

"Of course," she exclaimed. "What a brilliant idea, dear brother." After the next opening performance, she and Horace would invite the stars to the Capitol Hill mansion for late night champagne suppers, and the society reporters would have to write about every detail. While she would be nibbling cold roast beef sandwiches with world famous actors and actresses, the Sacred 36 would be eating their hearts out. It made her smile just to think about it.

Baby and Horace rarely missed a performance. Baby would time their entrance into Box A after everyone was seated and just before the house lights went down. Opera glasses would turn to see Baby Doe's latest gown. Horace would open champagne bottles, shooting the cork over the audience below. Baby would toss her head and laugh, fanning her bosom so that that her gems twinkled like stars in the gaslight.

Eugene Hawthorn snidely wrote that the Tabors surely felt a kinship with the scandalously four-times-divorced beauty Lillian Russell and her special friend Diamond Jim Brady. But it was with Sarah Bernhardt, whose mother was a Parisian courtesan, and Lillie Langtry, who had been the subject of several scurrilous newspaper stories regarding her relationship with the Prince of Wales, that Baby Doe developed a rapport. The three women agreed that living with a very rich man was the sweetest revenge against a pudgy toad that wrote defamatory stories for readers whose minds were smaller than his manhood.

CHAPTER 39

NO ONE WAS MORE SURPRISED than Baby Doe at the ferocity of a new mother's love when on a hot July afternoon she gave birth to a little girl. She had heard of mothers performing great feats, fighting off animals or starving themselves to save their child. She realized now that wasn't dime novel melodrama; she would do anything to keep this wee one safe and happy. She had not felt this way when she had the baby boy in Leadville. The stillborn child was a sign from God that she was on the wrong path with Jake. But this bundle of pink perfection, all silk and cream, was an angel brought to earth, a living confirmation that her marriage to Horace was blessed. If Eugene Hawthorn ever—ever—wrote anything to hurt this child, she would march down to that newspaper office and tear his heart out.

Horace, like most men, had never been enamored with infants, leaving Maxcy in Augusta's capable hands. He had never shared anything but work with his son, but he wanted to hold and spoil this little cherub, kiss the wispy hairs atop her head. "She looks like you," he told Baby Doe. "She is going to grow up to be the prettiest little thing you ever saw and I am going to buy her every dress in Paris."

Indeed, no infant had a finer layette. Baby had ordered fifty velvet and lace gowns, accessorized with embroidered booties and felt hats with fluffy marabou feathers. Every diaper pin was garnished with a diamond.

Instead of printing birth announcements, Horace had one hundred solid gold medals struck. Elizabeth Bonduel Lillie Tabor's entire name would not fit, so the quarter-sized medallions simply read: *Baby Tabor, July 13, 1884.* Horace instructed Peter to deliver them to the one hundred finest homes in Denver, adding "Mrs. Teller can't tear this up."

TABOR LOVE CHILD BORN

By Eugene Hawthorne

The Tabor house was made happy last Saturday with the birth of a baby girl. It is reported that numerous flowers and congratulations are arriving; however, this cannot be confirmed as no visitors have been received. The christening will take place in the mother's hometown of Oshkosh, Wisconsin, as Denver's esteemed Bishop Machebeuf will not allow the scandal plagued family to purchase a pew in the diocese.

"Horace let's go to the theater tonight. We haven't been in months."

"Alright, Nanny can watch the baby,"

"No, I want to take Elizabeth." If Denver's doyennes would not come to see little Elizabeth, Baby would take Elizabeth to them. "She is such a good baby; she hardly ever cries. We can take Nanny, too, in case we need her."

It took a little longer than usual to get out the door that evening. Bridgette had to place her boot in the small of Baby's back to pull the laces of the corset tight enough to fit into the emerald green gown and Nanny required an extraordinary amount of supplies to escort one tiny person to the theater. Horace muttered about getting by on less for a whole month in the mountains.

Edwin Booth was already performing the dramatic opening monologue from *Richelieu* when they arrived. Even though the house manager had readied the Box A as usual, with champagne chilling in an ice bucket, fresh white lilies woven in a garland in front of the box and an extra chair for Nanny, the family caused quite a ruckus as they settled in. Edwin Booth glared up at the box. "Do you mind?" his baritone trembled with indignation.

Baby Doe flushed crimson with embarrassment as the crowd tittered, while Horace waved him off. "Well, that fella' seems to think he's pretty important."

"He doesn't know who he has insulted," Baby fumed. She silently nursed her outrage throughout the first act. At intermission, Baby Doe jumped up and headed to the lobby. Nanny, carrying tiny Elizabeth, struggled to keep up. In her anger at Booth, Baby had forgotten her plan to parade through the lobby showing off her beautiful infant.

Peter was glad-handing with a middle-aged couple that excused themselves when they noticed Baby Doe, with a face like a thundercloud, making a beeline for her brother.

"Don't invite that actor to the house tonight for supper," she told him. "You know his brother killed President Lincoln."

CHAPTER 40

1885

JOSÉ ANTONIO ALTAMIRONO ESPINOSA was the fanciest dresser that Horace had ever seen. The Mexican businessman's stiff white collar gleamed above a dark silk tie. A high-crowned beaver top hat, brushed to a sheen, sat on his knee and he held a walking stick crested with a golden eagle. An unusual ring encircled a finger; Horace could not figure out the motif. Señor Espinosa's dark hair was carefully oiled and gray had just begun to tint his full moustache and sideburns. He wore elegance like a cape.

"Señor Tabor," he began in an accent cloaked in dignity and money, not the broken English of the Mexican cowboys that sometimes rode into Denver. "Have you heard the story of the Aztec treasure?" Horace shook his head no. Espinosa spent the next hour spinning a fascinating tale of an Aztec emperor trying to buy the good will of the invading Spanish with never-before-seen riches, the ultimate victory of the conquistadores, and the enormous treasure that was shipped out of Mexico to Spain.

"However, Señor, the Aztecs only mined a small fraction of the gold and silver. Great veins of silver still wind through the Yucatan jungles, and gold still lays hidden in the mountains of Chihuahua." Espinosa pulled the unusual ring from his finger and handed it to Horace. It was a large gold nugget soldered onto a band. "This is a sample of the ore coming from the northwestern mountains of my country."

Horace whistled. "That is quite a rock."

"Keep it. Take it to your assessor. He will tell you how pure it is." Espinosa leaned in as if there might be someone else in the office listening. "Señor, this is the opportunity of a lifetime."

In the blink of an eye, a million of Tabor's dollars went south of the border. Unfortunately, no gold, no silver and no one named José Antonio Altamirono Espinosa ever came back out of Mexico.

Where he had once relied on Billy's intellect, Horace now counted on the famous Tabor luck to guide his decisions. It had been Billy's job to weed out the con men from the legitimate businessmen and take care of the swarm of details required to keep dozens of business ventures operating smoothly. Things were starting to fall through the cracks without him.

"Please tell Cook dinner was delicious. Thank you for having me," Peter said.

"You're family; you're welcome anytime. This evening, however, Horace has a little something to discuss with you," Baby Doe said as the new butler took away empty plates.

"I'll get right to the point," Horace said, putting down his wine glass. "I sure do like the look of the mahogany I had put in the opera house. So much so, that I had Billy buy the whole forest down there in Honduras. It's very beautiful wood, and I think people would love furniture made from it. Problem is that I haven't received enough wood out of there to build a tree house."

Peter nodded. "I know it is a poor country and conditions are primitive. I imagine it is difficult to get lumber out of the jungle and to the shore."

"I have been trading telegrams with a business agent down there. He always has some excuse. The roads are bad. A railroad needs to be built. Docks need to be enlarged. There are not enough ships. Now, he says he needs another two million dollars." Horace shook his head. "Aw, hell, I don't know what's going on." He looked up at Peter, "I need someone I trust to go down there."

Peter took a long, slow sip of wine before he answered, "I agree that you need someone trustworthy to help you with your foreign investments. However, I don't know anything about jungles, railroads or steamships. I am better suited to managing the opera house. I am not your man."

"I just bought a yacht from a fellow in New York City. I've never seen it. I hear it is real nice. Would the prospect of sailing the coast and living on the yacht change your mind?"

Peter again politely declined.

Seeing no other possible course of action, Horace sent the business agent the money. No wood was ever harvested from the Tabor jungle. Horace developed a real distrust of foreigners.

Perhaps, Horace thought, it would be better to keep his money within the United States. Over the next five years he went on a shopping spree. He bought gold and silver mines throughout the Southwest and an additional 175,000 acres in Texas rumored to be rich in copper. In an effort to divest some of the mining income, he purchased grazing rights on a half million acres in arid southern Colorado and dabbled in wheat and corn speculation. He bought interests in hotels, banks and insurance companies. Upon seeing the fortunes being made in railroads, he sunk several hundred thousand dollars into a non-existent transcontinental railroad. Horace jumped at nearly every business opportunity that crossed his path, reasoning that diversifying his investments would increase his chances of getting lucky.

The baby was tucked in bed and the servants had retired for the evening, leaving Baby Doe and Horace alone in front of toasty fire.

"I have decided to cut my losses on the Lake Michigan venture," he said with a sigh. Horace had given over a million dollars to a canal and dock company to build a great manufacturing and shipping center on the shores of Lake Michigan. Unfortunately, Chicago was only ten miles away and had a lock on that type of business.

"I hear all the politicians in Chicago are corrupt. It is just as well you not get involved in Illinois businesses." She frowned, "There are so many shysters; it is difficult to know a sound investment from a swindle. I do wish Peter would help you more with your business ventures."

Horace smiled and patted Baby's hand. "Don't you worry. Silver is pouring out of the mines in Leadville with no signs of stopping. Why, the Matchless Mine alone will make me a million dollars this year and I have a least a half dozen other silver mines."

"What about the talk of falling silver prices?"

"The government buys four and a half million ounces of silver every month to make coins. That is never going to stop. People don't trust paper money. They like the feel of a silver coin in their pocket."

"I don't understand the debate in the newspapers about a gold standard and demonetizing silver."

"It is just some scheme cooked up by eastern bankers. I'm not sure anyone understands it. I do know that I have more money than could be spent in a lifetime." He wrapped her in a bear hug. "But it sure will be fun trying."

CHAPTER 41

1889

THE NEW BABY ARRIVED shortly before Christmas and was christened with the spectacular name of Rose Mary Silver Dollar Echo Tabor. This babe had her father's dark hair and chocolate eyes, but her mother thought she saw her own Cupid lips and turned-up button nose in the tiny face. Baby Doe had a new layette sewn for the infant, no hand-me-downs for the Tabor girls. She did reuse the diamond-garnished diaper pins because, of course, gems never go out of style. Five-year -old Elizabeth was not particularly impressed with little Silver Dollar, in spite of her mother's assurances that given time the sisters would be the best of friends. Elizabeth found the baby messy and loud. She would have preferred a kitten.

Famed Polish actress Madame Modjeska had thrilled the audience that evening with her portrayal of Desdemona in Shakespeare's Othello and was now enchanting Horace and Baby at another Tabor après-theater dinner. Several cast members, as well as Peter and his bachelor friends, rounded out the party. It rankled Baby Doe that these young men always appeared when there was food and drink offered at her table; however, their mothers would never offer a crumb of hospitality to Baby and Horace. For now, she bit her tongue. She continued to hope that perhaps one of the fellows would tell his parents what a lovely time he had at the Tabor mansion and they would feel obligated to reciprocate.

Nanny had taken little Silver Dollar to bed. Pretty and well-behaved, Elizabeth was allowed to stay up and mix with the guests.

The lass climbed into her father's lap and began to eat small ruby-colored strawberries from his plate as he listened to Madame Modjeska's tales of adventure from Europe. Elizabeth was mesmerized by the actress's hat, a blue velvet cap featuring a bird sown from iridescent beads and three towering peacock feathers which bobbed as she spoke, glimmering in the gaslight. A tiny hand, fingers sticky and red, reached out to touch the plumage. Horace caught his daughter's arm just in time, admonishing, "You can look, but don't touch."

"What kind of bird is that?" Elizabeth asked.

Madame Modjeska touched the beadwork. "It is very beautiful, no?" she asked in accented English. "It is the peacock, the most majestic of birds."

"Have you seen one?" the little girl asked.

"Oh yes, many times. Many royal palaces have them."

"Do the peacocks play with the princesses?"

"They are not playthings; they are simply meant to be admired. The males glide through the grounds and when they see a female they want to impress they spread their tail feathers like a great fan," she said, spreading her fingers to demonstrate.

"Papa, may I have a peacock? Like a princess?"

"Well, Little Missy, I don't know. A big bird like that would have to be kept outside."

"He can sleep with the horses."

"Mm, birds tend to do better in flocks than by themselves."

"May I have a flock of peacocks?"

Horace kissed the top of her curly blonde head, "All right, little Cupid. You can have whatever your little heart desires."

"What in God's name is that noise?" Horace said. He and Baby were rousted from sleep by a loud honking *wa-wa-wa*.

"I think it's the peacocks," Baby said.

Horace hadn't been sure how many animals were in the average flock of peacocks, but one hundred was a fine round number, so he ordered twenty-five cocks and seventy-five hens.

"It sounds like a cat stuck in a trombone. Why, it's not even dawn yet."

"Maybe they just need to settle in, get accustomed to their new home."

"I hope so," Horace said, running a hand over his sleep-tousled strands of hair.

The birds had only arrived the day before and already they were the talk of the town. Eugene Hawthorne had found out about their arrival and had penned a story about the "Tabor Menagerie." The head gardener had greeted the new pets with much swearing and muttering before locking himself in the tool shed for the afternoon.

"You know," Baby said with a mischievous grin, "if Mrs. Teller complains about these peacocks, I'll never get rid of them. We'll have to keep them forever."

Horace laughed and covered their heads with a large down pillow.

CHAPTER 42

1891

WHEN ELIZABETH TURNED SEVEN, Baby Doe decided it was time to hire a governess to educate the girls in the same manner as upper-crust East Coast children. On her first day, Mrs. Winkle let it be known that she would be making all the decisions regarding the education of little Elizabeth.

"My late husband and I came to Denver to establish an academic academy. It would have been the city's leading institution had he not died. I am left to carry on our mission alone, but I am well trained in the very best techniques of pedagogy."

Unsure what pedagogy was, Baby Doe said. "Elizabeth will offer you no trouble. She is a reserved, obedient girl." She added with a laugh, "Not sure where she got that from."

Tall and thin as a broomstick, Mrs. Winkle held her chin very high as she spoke. "In addition to lessons in history, arithmetic and grammar, I will instruct Miss Tabor in my philosophy called the 'discipline of dignity.' There are three guideposts to ensure a young lady always acts with dignity." Long, boney fingers began to tick them off. "A respectable woman never laughs aloud. A respectable woman never shares strong opinions. A respectable woman never calls attention to one's self." Mrs. Winkle's eyebrows arched to put an exclamation mark on her little speech.

Baby Doe's eyebrows went up as well. She enjoyed being the center of attention, and she attributed her success in landing Horace to her ability to laugh and have a good time. Although, it could be said her inability to hold back an opinion may have ruffled a few feathers. *Mrs. Winkle's disciplines might be fine little girls*, Baby thought. *But I can't imagine living my life that way.*

The governess quickly recognized that, more than anything, Elizabeth wanted approval and acceptance. Mrs. Winkle motivated her charge by explaining all eyes would always be watching a loveliness such as hers and she wouldn't want to embarrass herself due to a lack of social graces. Elizabeth soon thought the governess a great authority on all things and the little girl wanted desperately to please her. Quiet and observant, she watched Mrs. Winkle's sterling example of refinement and her mother's disregard for social expectations that did not suit her. Elizabeth noted the cutting looks from other women when they dined out or attended the opera and she came to understand why other children were not allowed to play with her.

Elizabeth did well with her deportment lessons, to Baby Doe's chagrin. With Horace away looking into a new business scheme, Baby had suggested she and Elizabeth could play cards, but the little girl had replied that Mrs. Winkle would think her time would be better spent doing schoolwork.

"I have always found the ability to make conversation and shuffle cards valuable skills," Baby replied. Elizabeth gave a long sigh that gave her an uncanny likeness to Mrs. Winkle and said it was past her bedtime, leaving Baby Doe alone to stew over this and other slights.

Of course, Baby Doe wanted Elizabeth to be accepted into the better circles, but there might be such a thing as being too straitlaced. Following social constricts never did anything for Baby and she didn't want her daughters to grow into doormats to be walked on. It also seemed to Baby that Mrs. Winkle spent too much time looking down that long nose, never criticizing aloud but her face speaking displeasure nonetheless.

A gust of laughter blew up from the dining room. Peter was again hosting his bachelor friends for poker and supper in Baby Doe's home. When her brother first asked if he and his friends could have their card party at the Tabor mansion, explaining his new little house was too small, Baby Doe had eagerly agreed. More than a year had passed and the card games had grown to include supper with unlimited wine and whiskey. The butler, when they had one, was called to serve and the maids spent the next day cleaning up. No return invitations were ever issued to Horace and Baby Doe. It was all beginning to vex her.

Curious about the festivities and aggravated that she was excluded in her own home, Baby drew on her dressing gown and went to the top of the stairs. A slightly drunken toast was offered to Peter's generosity. *Peter's generosity?* she thought with pique.

She heard the crunch of breaking glass and a slurred, "Oh, sorry."

"Don't worry, accidents will happen," Peter said. "Bridgette, bring a fresh glass and clean this up. And fetch more whiskey, the good stuff in Horace's library."

Baby Doe's displeasure flamed into a rage. She flew down the stairs and into the dining room. The young men stared at the tiny, angry woman with wild hair and checks burning who had appeared at the end of the food-laden table.

"I am not good enough for any of your mothers to call on, but my whiskey is good enough for you to drink?" she demanded.

She pointed at Jack Moseby, who was caught with a ham biscuit in his mouth. "You come here again and again and eat my food, but your mother has never once invited us to dinner."

"Will Macon," she declared, turning on another young man. "I have seen your sisters with their opera glasses examining my gowns at the Tabor Grand. They will not ask me to tea, but they will appear in copies of my dresses."

She glared at each of them, "Hypocrites, one and all."

The men gaped in stunned silence. It took a moment for Peter to close his gaping mouth and get to his feet. "Gents, my sister is not herself tonight. Her husband is away on business and the loneliness is very taxing on her and her children. I am afraid that, with the lateness of the hour, she is overwrought. I think we should adjourn for the evening."

The men shuffled to the door like scolded schoolboys as Baby Doe watched with hands on hips and Peter murmured apologies. When the door closed behind the last guest, Peter whirled on her.

"What was the meaning of that outburst? I'm shocked at your rudeness to my friends."

"My rudeness?" Baby Doe asked with heat. "Those men and their families have never been anything but inconsiderate and disrespectful to Horace and me."

"Scenes like this one will not win anyone's friendship."

"All of Denver acts as if they were great friends with Augusta and that gives them license to treat me poorly. Let me tell you, no one liked Augusta. She was a mean old woman."

"I think you are treated poorly because you are overambitious and garishly flaunt your wealth."

"If I were a man no one would say that of me."

"But you are not a man. You would do better to constrain yourself and act more reserved. You don't live in a wild mining town anymore."

"Most of the money in Denver came from those wild mining towns. Those women act like they have a fancy East Coast pedigree, but they were dust-covered miners' wives just a few years ago."

"And they are eager to brush off that dust and improve themselves, as Mrs. Winkle is doing with Elizabeth. People think your ways are too flamboyant, too ostentatious."

Baby Doe crossed her arms. She could not argue that point, but she would not concede it either.

Peter continued, "You must think of the consequences of your actions, for the sake of your daughters. I have done my best to achieve some measure of social acceptance in Denver and I believe that Elizabeth and Silver can benefit from my improving position."

"I am a good mother. I make sure my girls have the finest of everything," she fired back.

"Having the finest of everything will not gain them position. You can't buy respect. Refinement will gain them respect." Peter sighed, "You are your own worst enemy."

CHAPTER 43

1892

IT HAD BEEN A QUIET DAY at the Tabor house. With no performance at the opera house and no late supper planned, Baby thought it was a good afternoon to teach Elizabeth the messy basics of watercolor painting while Silver Dollar napped. She gave the governess the afternoon off and Nanny watched over the sleeping infant while Elizabeth and Baby Doe ventured to the front lawn in aprons and sleeve covers to attempt to capture the beauty of the peacocks in the late afternoon sunlight.

"Ho," Horace hollered and waved as he entered the driveway in a small gig pulled by a dapple-gray gelding. He used the small buggy to run about town, letting Baby chose from the more elaborate carriages and drivers for her daily excursions around and through the Capitol Hill neighborhood.

"Papa," Elizabeth dropped her paint brush and ran to greet her father.

"Afternoon, Mr. Tabor," called Abraham, the Negro groom, running from the stables to fetch the horse.

"A welcoming committee just for me," Horace said handing the reins to Abraham, scooping up his little girl and heading for his beautiful wife. "I ran into a fella I knew back in Leadville. I hope you won't mind Baby, but I invited him to dinner."

"Oh Horace," she said, a slight frown crossed her face. "You know I love to entertain company, but I need time to make sure everything is just so. I can't throw together a dinner party."

"It's just one fella and he is not the sort to go to dinner parties. He is kind of an odd bird. A venison steak and fried potatoes eaten with just us would be all right with him."

"Do I know him?"

"I don't think so. Winfield Stratton? He did some carpentry work for me at the First Bank of Leadville when I opened that up. You know that three-foot liberty silver dollar that hangs above the door? He carved that and covered it in silver-leaf."

"Oh, I remember that. It's beautiful. Do you have a new project that you want him to work on?"

"He isn't doing woodworking anymore. Struck a nice vein of gold last year, down by Cripple Creek, south of Pikes Peak. He's a smart fella, but," Horace repeated, "he is an odd bird."

The Tabors were again without a butler so Bridgette showed Winfield Stratton into the drawing room when he arrived for dinner promptly at

6 p.m. He was a small man with neatly trimmed white hair and moustache. He wore a blue suit with shiny, new cowboy boots and a big white Stetson hat. Baby Doe thought he looked perfectly respectable.

"Welcome to my home, old friend," Horace boomed in his usual jovial manner. "Let me introduce you to Baby Doe."

Win Stratton took off his hat and nodded to Baby. "Nice to meet you, Mrs. Tabor."

Horace held up two crystal decanters. "Let me pour you a drink? What is your preference Irish or Tennessee whiskey?"

"Nothing yet," Win replied as he looked out the window. "I don't drink during daylight, but I sure would like some of that Tennessee whiskey after dinner if I may."

Bridgette stuck her head through the doorway. "Cook said to say, dinner is served, Ma'am."

"Thank you, Bridgette. We'll be right in. Can you take Mr. Stratton's hat, please?"

"I'll keep it with me." Win clutched his hat to his chest.

"Of course," Baby smiled. This gentleman had visited their home when polite society refused to and he called her Mrs. Tabor; Baby would be happy to overlook his little idiosyncrasies.

The trio all sat at one end of the long dining table so they could speak without shouting to be heard. Win carefully placed his hat in the empty chair beside him.

"That is a fine hat, Mr. Stratton," Baby said. "I can see why you are fond of it."

"Thank you, Ma'am. I bought it and these boots with the first payout from my mining claim."

Horace tucked into the roast chicken, mashed potatoes and young carrots set before him. With a full mouth he asked, "So how's the world treating ya', Win? I read different things in the newspapers, but you can't trust those fellows."

"After I left Leadville, I took classes in mineralogy at the School of Mines. That's how I knew where to stake my claims. People in Cripple Creek laughed at me for digging on the side of Battle Mountain, but I knew I was on to something. I knew." He suddenly looked up at Baby. "Mrs. Tabor, do you pay attention to your dreams? Do you think it is possible to receive information from another realm through dreams?"

"Why yes, Mr. Stratton, I do listen for messages in my dreams." Every prospector had his own intricate system of charms and superstitions to help him locate pay dirt, and to Baby that seemed as reasonable as saying a prayer and lighting a candle in the church vestibule.

"At the college, I learned the science to figure what area was likely to bear gold, but my dreams told me exactly where to dig, under a ledge. I dreamt my Independence Mine is going to be the biggest gold mine in Colorado," Win said. He thoroughly chewed a bite of chicken. "I am going to use that mountain like a bank vault, only taking out a few thousand dollars of gold at one time. I'm living in a shanty up at the mine, part-time, in the warm weather, and supervising the work myself, you know, to keep an eye on things."

Baby looked at Horace, and he gave her a wink, his droopy moustache hitched up at the corners in a secret grin. *I can't imagine Horace sitting in a shanty, guarding a buried hoard. Odd bird, indeed,* she thought.

CHAPTER 44

1893

THE TABORS RANG IN 1893 in their usual style, extravagant but alone. They feasted on oysters, beef steaks, champagne, cake and ice cream. At midnight, Horace kissed all his girls and they pulled English crackers filled with sugared almonds and a fortune.

"My fortune is dull," Baby said. "'*Failing to prepare is preparing to fail.' Benjamin Franklin.*"

"I think I got your fortune," Horace said. "'*Your beauty should come not from fine adornments. Rather it should be the unfading beauty of a gentle spirit.' Peter 3:3-4.*"

Baby hung her arms around his neck and said, "I don't think I like that fortune either. I like fine adornments."

"And I like you with fine adornments." He leaned in and kissed her ear. "But I mostly like you without adornments."

The couple weaved arm in arm upstairs, leaving Nanny to put two overexcited little girls to bed.

By February, it was clear that 1893 was not going to be a happy new year. The world's largest company, the Philadelphia and Reading Railroad, had greatly overextended itself expanding into coal mining and steel production and had to declare bankruptcy. The P&R Rail collapse was a stone thrown into the center of the American financial pond. The ripples caused numerous adjacent businesses to fail. Rumors of shaky finances at the nation's largest employer, National Cordage Company, caused lenders to call in the loans of numerous adjacent businesses and the mortgages of thousands of employees. NCC went bankrupt and the resulting chaos caused the stock market to crash. In the ensuing months, five hundred banks closed, fifteen thousand businesses failed and four million workers were put out on the street. European investors left the United States in droves.

Newly-elected President Cleveland needed to reassure the world that the United States was stable and restore trust in the monetary and banking systems. He declared that every U.S. dollar would be backed by the most precious and valuable of metals, gold. No longer would the government purchase silver and citizens could not request their silver bullion be minted into coin. President Cleveland then borrowed sixty-five million in gold from Wall Street banker J.P. Morgan and the Rothschild family to prop up the Federal Reserve. The panic was abated, but the country was left in a deep depression.

Almost overnight the price of silver dropped from $1.29 an ounce to less than fifty cents. Silver had no value as money, just a pretty, shiny metal suited for jewelry and tea sets. Soon it cost more to pull the silver from the ground than it was worth, and ninety percent of the working population of Leadville became unemployed.

While J.P. Morgan made a staggering fortune, Horace Tabor lost one. Like the drought in the plains states that was withering the livelihoods of farmers, the lifeblood of the mines was drying up. There was no income coming from the Leadville mines and when ten Denver banks closed in three quick days, Tabor's cash on hand went as well. The remaining Denver banks wanted to know how Horace planned to repay loans he had incurred to finance his building sprees and the wild purchases of businesses and land. The future mine incomes he had used as collateral were non-existent.

Augusta sat on the front porch of her new house in Sacramento, a pretty little Victorian painted a happy blue with bright white gingerbread trim curling around the eves. She had found some contentment in her anonymous life far from Colorado, but she couldn't help but look back, to keep tabs. She ordered *The Denver Post* and the *Rocky Mountain News* be delivered to California. The news was always old by the time she received it, but she nonetheless scanned the pages for news of Horace. These days, the front pages of the newspapers across the country were covered with stories of the economic crisis and the plunging value of silver.

Augusta was surprised when wet drops appeared on the newsprint; she hadn't realized she was crying. Horace would be ruined by this, his entire fortune wiped out with the stroke of President Cleveland's pen. Tears came rapidly now, tears of relief. It was finally over. The blonde would leave him and he would come home.

Horace's happy-go-lucky nature didn't allow him to worry too much in the first months of the financial crisis. When bankers seeking mortgage payments knocked on his door, he told them, "Everyone needs to just give this a little time. Congress will surely repeal this ridiculous anti-silver law and everything will work itself out." When that answer no longer appeased the moneylenders, Tabor began a carousel of transactions, mortgaging one property with another, selling properties at fire sale prices, robbing Peter to pay Paul.

As they watched the latest carriage-load of angry bankers depart the mansion's long driveway, Baby Doe turned to Horace. "I thought those men terribly rude, coming to our home and demanding money. I nearly bit my tongue in half to keep from telling them off."

"Aw, they're just nervous. They're trying to keep their businesses afloat."

Good natured Horace excused their behavior, but Baby Doe was upset by the lack of obsequiousness with which the bankers had conducted themselves. In previous years, those men had fallen over themselves to get a bit of the Tabor Empire. In recent months the bankers had become increasingly ill-mannered.

"Are things as terrible as they made them out to be?" she asked.

"I just need to figure a way to ride out the storm. I was thinking I'd try to keep three properties: the opera house, because you love it; Tabor Block which has business tenants with paying leases and the Matchless Mine, because there's still silver in there. The Matchless will be the source of our comeback." He wrapped his arms around her. "I don't want you to worry about any of this. I'll always take care of you."

She looked at him with solemn eyes. "I believe in you Horace, you and the Tabor luck," she said.

Horace grinned and hugged her, "Always a smile and a brave face, no matter the trouble. You're a treasure, Baby."

CHAPTER 45

1894

THE DAY HAD STARTED HOT AND CLEAR. By mid-afternoon the usual puffy white clouds began to build over the city, but a short cooling afternoon shower did not come. Instead the clouds continued to rise higher and higher into the sky, their flat bottoms turned darker and ominous. Animals and men alike could feel the change in the air as the wind picked up and the thunderhead blocked the sun, bringing evening hours early. Housewives hurried to bring in laundry from the line and shopkeepers rolled up awnings; horses pranced and threw their heads, while dogs and cats headed under porches and through open barn doors. The first drops fell slowly, huge splats landing just here and there. Then the sky above the far eastern plains lightened into a sickly green and a storm rose from the depths of hell and fell upon the city. Blinding lightning flashed and thunder rolled without pause. The wind whipped and lashed at trees and houses, hail the size of hen's eggs crashed into store windows, sheets of rain turned the streets into rivers.

Horace and Cook hustled the family and most of the staff into the cellar. Bridgette whimpered, earning a pinch from Baby Doe, who hissed, "Not in front of the girls." Elizabeth and Silver sat on their father's lap, round eyes enormous with fear.

The furor lasted less than an hour. The Tabors slowly emerged as the sun peeked out from behind clouds that raced onward, north along the Front Range, leaving a wake of destruction in their path.

Abraham had refused to leave the horses alone in the stables and was already surveying damages when Horace climbed from the cellar.

"How'd we do?" Horace called.

Abraham trotted over, shaking his hairless black head. "Not too bad, Mr. Tabor. The horses are still fretting, but they not hurt. Looks from here, the house and stables in pretty good shape. But Mr. Tabor, the birds, the peacocks," Abraham hesitated, trying to choose the right words. "They all gone."

"What do you mean gone?"

"Looks like some drown in that low corner by the street. I think a lot was beat to death by the wind and hail and some just gone. There's feathers and dead birds ever where. I don't think the little ones and the women should be seeing it."

"Thank you, Abraham." Horace climbed back into the cellar and carried his girls out, his coat thrown over their heads. He trotted into the house as quickly as his old legs could carry them, followed by Cook, Nanny, Mrs. Winkle and Bridgette, but Baby Doe stood in the yard, slowing taking in the ravages.

Horace came back outside, "Baby, why don't you come in the house? The men will get this cleaned up." He put an arm around her shoulder, leading her in. "I think the old Tabor luck held. You and the girls are all right, the horses and the staff are okay. We didn't lose anything of any great value."

The English gardener pushed past, muttering, with a wheelbarrow full of dead birds.

"Well, the peacocks are gone, but I wasn't sure how we were going to afford to keep feeding them anyway," Horace said.

This is surely a sign from God thought Baby Doe. The beautiful, useless creatures had been throttled to death by the fierce wind and hail, but the house, their home, remained strong and their family unscathed. Maybe God was reminding her what was truly valuable and what was ornamental. She turned and looked Horace in the eye. "Are our finances really that bad?"

"I need to come up with some money to pay some bills, particularly the mortgage on the Matchless. It still has untapped silver." He ran his hand over his thinning hair. "But it is not sitting in the open, waiting to be picked up. I just can't make the bankers see the potential, with the anti-silver laws driving down the prices."

"We can sell my jewelry." Baby had been thinking of this solution for a few months, but now it was clear what God wanted her to do. She could rise above her vanity to save her family. They could use the many trinkets Horace had purchased over the past decade and a half to carry them along until better days, save what was left of the crumbling Tabor Empire. She understood it was better to have a producing mine than a necklace, but she loved Horace for not suggesting it first. Perhaps, too, God would reward her for such selflessness.

Horace stopped and stared at his shoes. "By God I hate to." He sighed and looked into her blue eyes. "I promise you I'll buy you all new jewelry when we get this thing turned around."

"I know you will." She slipped her arm around his back, and they walked into the house.

The next morning, Horace and Baby Doe went to the First National Bank of Denver. In the quiet marble confines, they pulled out diamond combs, square emerald earrings, dropped ruby earrings, gold bangles, silver cuffs, a diamond lavaliere, gem-encrusted brooches, the serpent girdle, the Isabella necklace and a dozen other baubles. Baby left a few memories in the box: her sapphire and diamond wedding ring, the watch fob the mayor of Denver had presented Tabor at the opening of the opera house and one set of diamond diaper pins. The proceeds would hold the bankers at bay and help the family get through 1894 without making any economizing efforts that the neighbors might notice.

CHAPTER 46

1895

"HITCH THE FOUR WHITES to the blue enameled carriage," Baby Doe told Abraham. They wouldn't be spinning aimlessly through the Capitol Hill neighborhood today, but going to see a young financier downtown. Just arrived from New York, Henry Bennett had bought the mortgage on the Tabor Grand Opera House from the bank and had sent notice to the house that morning that he intended to foreclose. Horace had gone into his study to write letters to bankers, politicians and anyone else who might listen that there was still tons of silver in the Colorado Rockies, and if the metal was re-monetized, the whole country could be lifted from the depression. He just needed a little time; silver would make a comeback.

Baby Doe had a different plan. She would use her feminine charms to sway the young financier to drop the entire foreclosure nonsense. She dressed with care in an ivory silk and chiffon dress with a square neckline too low for daytime. Over one eye she coquettishly dipped a small hat trimmed in silk flowers and trailing ribbons so long they sat on the ruffled bustle bobbing behind her.

Unfortunately, the meeting was not a success. Bennett was obviously some kind of deviant who did not even notice her overflowing décolletage and quickly sent her off, dismissing out of hand any extension of time or leniency. She ordered Abraham to take her to the opera house to see her brother Peter.

"Peter, you have to do something about the opera house. Horace got you this job as the manager, even though it caused that dust-up with Billy Bush. Now is the time to return the favor. You must loan Horace the money to save the opera house from foreclosure."

A small incredulous laugh escaped from Peter's open mouth. "I don't have that kind of money," he said. "That would take hundreds of thousands of dollars."

"We must hold on to the opera house in the Tabor family, and keep it out of the hands of that horrible Henry Bennett. I think he might be a homosexual."

"I have already spoken with Bennett. He seems like a reasonable businessman to me. He and I have a gentlemen's agreement to lease me the opera house and I will continue to run it."

"No, we must get Bennett out. The opera house is Tabor's. It is our family's crowning glory."

"Not anymore," Peter emphasized. "Even if I had the money, I would not give it to you. Horace would only mortgage the opera house to buy something silly."

"How can you say such a thing? After all he has done for you?"

"Horace has been very generous to me. He is a good man." Peter took a deep breath. "But he is not a good businessman. The opera house will provide me with a good job; however, it cannot be the basis for rebuilding the Tabor fortune. There is not that much profit in it."

"Judas," she hissed and stomped out of his office, through the luxurious lobby and out to her waiting carriage. She was so hot-headed she thought the silk flowers on her hat might catch on fire.

Tears filled Abraham's eyes as he led Samson the big black gelding from the quiet stable. Samson was the undisputed lead horse in the barn, kicking the stall if he wasn't fed first and nipping shoulders if a cinch was too tight. The horse sensed this morning was different, not the usual parade about town, and he balked, tossing his head and pulling against the halter in Abraham's hand.

"Easy, easy now," Abraham cooed, trying to calm the horse. "You going to a nice home, fine folks gonna buy you. But you gotta act like a gentleman now." The man's voice cracked with emotion. Abraham had worked hard to earn the animal's trust and the old Negro felt he was betraying the horse. Samson neighed and tried to sidestep away. "Shh," he said, "no use fussing. This my last day, too." Abraham mournfully handed the lead rope to the horse trader.

Three days earlier, Horace had announced he could no longer pay the staff and the beautiful carriages, silver-plated harnesses and gleaming matched horses were all to be sold. Horace would keep only the small gig and the dappled gray for getting around town. Even Elizabeth's pony and cart were to go. The three young grooms and the yard help had slowly walked away, joined by the muttering master gardener who had clearly said, "Good riddance to this crazy house."

The nanny and the governess were also dismissed. Mrs. Winkle, always efficient and disciplined, quickly and quietly packed her bag, said goodbye to her charges, instructing them not to fuss, and left via the back door. Baby Doe was not terribly sad to see the old broomstick go, but Elizabeth fought to hold back tears. When Nanny said her goodbyes, little Silver threw a histrionic fit, wrapping her arms around the young woman's legs.

Abraham had insisted on staying until the barn was empty. He couldn't just leave the animals, he needed to ensure they would be treated well. Besides, he had nowhere to go. "You don't have to pay me, Mr. Tabor. I'll just work for room and board," Abraham said.

Horace told him that was fine, but Cook and Bridgette had left after breakfast and Baby Doe would be doing the cooking. Abraham was welcome to come eat in the kitchen with the family. A couple of weeks later, Abraham too, walked away.

Baby Doe barely managed to hold her tongue and her tears when a weasely little man came to pick through the mansion's furnishing and buy the choicest pieces. He toured through the entire house, inspecting, valuing, judging and touching everything with his long fingers. Baby felt queasy when he groped the blue satin tête-a-tête with the ornate carved rosewood and then murmured, "Oh yes," as he stared at the coordinating blue lacquered glass chandelier hanging above.

"There are a few more items of value, personal items, the silver vanity set and the ebony inlay armoire and others, in which I am interested. Let me know when you are ready to liquidate the house," he said, standing on the front step as the vans heaped with elegant furniture, beautiful paintings and objêts d 'art rumbled away.

Baby slammed the door in his little rodent face. She hadn't seen the curtain drop back into place in the window across the street at Senator and Mrs. Teller's house.

Horace had taken to going out each day, prowling the streets of Denver for work, hitting up old friends for investment funds, any way to make money. Baby Doe was not sure where he went or to whom he spoke. She was secretly relieved that each evening when he returned for dinner, although he might be dejected, he was sober. She hadn't thought of Harvey Doe in years, but she couldn't help but compare her two husbands as they faced adversity. Harvey had been quick to give up, surrendering to whiskey at the first sign of hardship, unable to rouse himself to go anywhere but a saloon. Horace got up every morning, kissed his girls, hugged his wife, put on a cheerful face and went out searching for a way to take care of his family.

Strange male voices came from outside the house. Baby knew it wasn't Horace so early in the afternoon. She pulled back the lace sheer to see two workmen fiddling with the gas line to the house. She flew from the house, "What do you think you are doing?"

"Turning off the gas and water for non-payment," said the bigger man, his teeth brown with chewing tobacco.

"Well, stop that right now. Do you know who lives here? Horace Tabor, one of the most important men in Denver. You can't turn off his gas and water. He helped start the public utilities in this town."

The workman held up a grimy hand, "Orders is orders, Lady."

"How dare you? He has done more for this town than any other man."

But the deed was already done. The workmen threw their tools in the back of the wagon and drove off, leaving Baby shouting at their backs.

That evening when Horace got home to a dark house, Baby and the girls had prepared a "pauper party." Candles stuck on the saucers from the everyday china lit the dining room. A picnic sheet covered the middle of the floor where a mahogany dining table used to stand on an ornate rug. A steaming pot of beans and a pan of cornbread sat waiting to be served on tin plates. Baby had read that at the height of the depression in '93, New Yorkers threw these kinds of parties, drinking beer out of tin cans and such. Silver Dollar thought it all great fun, gobbling up cornbread slathered in butter and honey and clapping with delight when Horace formed hand shadow animals along the bare walls in the candlelight. Elizabeth missed Cook's cornbread and thought it wasn't a very nice party if one had to sit on the floor.

CHAPTER 47

1896

IT WAS ALL GONE NOW. Tabor Block and the Tabor Grand Opera had been auctioned on the courthouse steps. The Clarendon Hotel and the opera house in Leadville were also lost in foreclosure. The Capitol Hill mansion had been stripped of its elegant furnishings by bargain hunters and opportunists and finally sold by the bank. The Honduran mahogany operation, the prairie grazing lands, the Texas copper mines, the Little Pittsburg, and the Chrysolite, all of the mines had been seized. Of the once colossal Tabor Empire only the Matchless Mine remained, now shut down, her timbers rotting and her shafts filling with water.

Horace settled them into a small house on the west side of Denver. There were few opportunities left for him in the city. Old friends never seemed to be available to see him anymore. A dispirited Tabor left his family and took a train to Leadville to try his luck in a town where he still knew people and they remembered the Tabor name. The mountain people would not turn their back on one of their own.

The girls were enrolled in a nearby neighborhood school. It was a beautiful red stone building; but it was filled with the children of laborers, kids who generally had shoes and coats, but not new ones and not always the right size, having received an older sibling's hand-me-down.

Silver Dollar was excited to go, skipping and chattering as Baby Doe walked with them on their first day. "I am going to learn to read today," the little girl declared. "I already know how to count and how to write my name. Oh, and I want to make a best friend, too."

"That sounds like a very busy day," Baby said. "Now, stop hopping about. You'll ruin your curls." Baby had washed the girls' hair the night before, then sat them on the floor between her knees and wrapped long pieces of hair in strips of rags that formed perfect sausage curls this morning.

Elizabeth walked more slowly, careful not to disturb her shiny blonde ringlets tied up with sky blue satin ribbons, less eager to arrive at the new school, the first she had ever attended. The twelve-year-old girl had faced many loses in the past months, but the most stinging had been the release of her governess, Mrs. Winkle. Elizabeth's life had been filled with an excess of objects, but she did not have a treasure trove of people in her life. She had sometimes attended the après-theater parties with the adults, but no little girlfriends came over to play. Her parents, her sister, Nanny, and Mrs. Winkle had been her whole world. As she had departed, Mrs. Winkle reminded Elizabeth to always act in a dignified manner and mind her posture. This morning Elizabeth was working hard to keep her chin up and her back straight.

Dozens of eyes followed them as they entered the schoolyard. Jump ropes suddenly stilled, the marbles rolled to a stop and a ball dropped unnoticed. The Tabor girls' ensembles, although not new, were far more elegant than anything even these children's mothers owned. The Tabors hadn't bought new dresses in a year, maybe longer; Baby Doe had let out hems and added cuffs to the stack of older dresses that had once filled armoires, then covered the re-work with decorative ribbons, lace and ruffles.

Baby smiled and said, "Good morning," to a group of girls surrounding a circle of jacks and they murmured a shy reply. She looked back to make sure her more reluctant daughter was still following. Elizabeth looked past the other girls, her head high and mouth in a tight line. Baby Doe sighed; Elizabeth looked just like Denver's society ladies whenever she passed by.

SILVER QUEEEN DETHRONED

By Eugene Hawthorne

Oh, how the mighty have fallen! Silver Baron Horace Tabor has lost his Capitol Hill mansion to foreclosure. Neighbors report that creditors and merchants have emptied the large house of all valuables. Baby Doe Tabor is currently living in a working-class neighborhood on the west side. The man, who was once the richest in all of Colorado, is now camped in Leadville and works as a slag boy, pushing a wheelbarrow. Rogues on Larimer

Street are taking bets on which millionaire Baby Doe will set her sights on now that Tabor is busted. Could it be true that she is interviewing rich young bachelors to be her next husband?

Baby Doe crushed the newspaper into an angry wad as she read Hawthorne's latest slander. She stopped by the library each morning to read the local news these days, since a newspaper subscription was an expense she could not justify, especially when it contained trash like this. A throat clearing reminded her that this was the library's copy. She put the paper on the long table, smoothed the wrinkled edges with her hand and gave the frowning librarian an apologetic smile.

What kind of wife do they think I am? she thought. It riled her that after thirteen years, she still had to prove her love and loyalty. She was not a fickle butterfly, flitting off to the next rich man. She had fought so hard to win and marry Horace, and he had shown himself to be a treasure beyond mere dollars. The world may have treated her unkind, but Horace never raised his hand, never spoke a hurtful word, always strove to make her happy. When Augusta refused to divorce, when that viper Hawthorne wrote hateful stories about her, when all of Denver turned up their noses, Horace was with her. When the depression hit and they lost all their worldly possessions, Horace didn't drown in whiskey and pity; he humbled himself to provide for their children. He never lost heart, he never lost faith, and she wouldn't either. Fate had conspired against them, again and again, but Horace never wavered, and now when he was down on his luck, she would be steadfast for him. The Tabor luck couldn't be kept down for long. She would take pleasure in proving all the gossiping crows wrong, Baby Doe would stand with Tabor through good times and bad and in good times again.

She strode with purpose to the librarian, handed her the paper, looked her straight in the eye and said aloud, "What kind of wife do they think I am?"

CHAPTER 48

CHRISTMAS OF 1896 was a meager affair, with the few items in the girls' stockings of a practical nature, an orange, a new school pencil and a length of ribbon for each, pink for Elizabeth and green for Silver Dollar. Baby Doe and the girls collected pine boughs and wove them into garlands to surround the doorframe and the fireplace mantel.

Baby Doe said that Horace's homecoming was gift enough for them, but Horace knew she didn't really mean that and arranged a special treat for his ladies, a trip to Leadville to see the Ice Palace. The frozen boondoggle was a scheme to draw sightseers and their pocketbooks to help revive Leadville's fading fortunes. Constructed of a wood frame and ice block walls the whole structure was covered with water that quickly froze, sealing the blocks in place like chilly stucco. Ninety-foot towers greeted guests at the entry. The sprawling five-acre complex included a skating rink, a carousel, and toboggan runs to entertain the children. Adults enjoyed the restaurant, gaming rooms, a theater and a ballroom. Electric lights twinkled inside and large search lights shone along the massive outside walls, illuminating the diamond like ice crystals and refracting into hundreds of rainbow prisms.

The Tabors took the train from Denver and spent the night in the tiny room Horace rented in a boarding house, all crowding into a single bed. "Better to keep warm," Baby Doe told the girls as they squeezed together under the blankets. "It gets very cold up here in the mountains."

The next morning they walked to the ticket booth, fifty cents for adults and a quarter for children. Silver Dollar had no chance to feel the cold as she bounced with excitement, clapping her hands with delight and impetuously hugging her parents. Even Elizabeth, who thought it improper to gape, stared open-mouthed at the spectacle.

"Come on, 'Lizbeth," Silver said, pulling on her sister. "Let's go ride the merry-go-round." She dashed toward the turning carousel, weaving through knots of visitors with her older sister in tow, their parents trailing behind. Baby Doe was just able to see Elizabeth's blonde head careening through the crowd.

"Whoa, slow down," said a man who narrowly missed crashing into the girls. The stranger did a double take and pushed his bowler back on his head, staring after Elizabeth as she followed her little sister. He shook his head.

"Girls, stop running," Baby Doe called. "I'm so sorry," she said to the man. "My girls are overly excited."

"I thought I was seeing things," he said with a short laugh. "I saw your girl and said to myself, 'There's Baby Doe. No, can't be.' Then I turned around and there you were."

"Ho, is that Tabor?" another man exclaimed. "Should've figured they couldn't have a Leadville celebration without Tabor and Baby Doe."

"The Silver Queen's come to the Ice Palace," hollered an aged miner, who limped over to shake Horace's hand.

Elizabeth stopped and reined in Silver. A group of people was forming around her parents, shaking hands with her father and tipping hats to her mother.

"Look at all the friends Mama and Papa know here," said Silver Dollar.

"I don't think they know Mama and Papa; I think they just know *of* them."

A small frown skipped across Silver's tiny mouth as she thought what her older sister meant, but it was quickly gone. "Come on 'Lizbeth. Let's get in line."

Horace and Baby Doe watched the carousel as it carried the girls round and Silver Dollar waved each time her parents came into view. As the girls bobbed around and out of sight another well-wisher approached, a middle-aged man wearing a suit of clothes that looked several years old. The coat was clean but worn shiny at the elbows and frayed around the collar, probably purchased before the depression, when times were better. It was the look most Leadville citizens carried. "Mr. Tabor, good to see you." He offered his hand to Horace who shook it hardily. "Ma'am," he said, nodding at Baby Doe. "I hear you are working at the smelter." He shook his head. "Well, times are tough for everyone."

"Mama, Papa," Silver Dollar shouted from the back of a brightly painted horse, waving so vigorously she looked like she might topple off. Elizabeth sat sidesaddle on a tiger, trying to impersonate ladylike decorum, but appearing closer to sulky adolescent indifference.

"Hang on, Silver," Baby Doe answered.

"Pretty girls," the man said.

The ride slowed and stopped and Silver bounded off and toward the adults, "Now the toboggan runs."

"I'll leave you to enjoy the day," the stranger said. "I wish you well, Tabor." He tipped his hat and walked off toward the ice sculpture exhibit.

"Who was that?" asked Elizabeth.

"Not sure," Horace answered. "Maybe he worked in one of my mines."

"Everyone knows your father. Horace Tabor founded Leadville and he is the most well-liked man in this town," said Baby Doe.

"Well-liked is not well respected," murmured Elizabeth.

"What do you mean by that?" demanded Baby Doe.

"Toboggans," Silver Dollar declared and ran to a long line of children.

Elizabeth avoided her mother's eyes and followed Silver at a more reserved pace.

"Let it go," Horace said quietly to Baby Doe. They followed the girls and settled onto park benches set near the end of the toboggan runs for parents to wait as their children climbed stairs to the top of the runs and then shot down the icy run with delight and terror.

Horace and Baby Doe sat quietly for a long moment before Horace said, "Being here brings back a lot of memories. We had some big times in Leadville, didn't we?" He took her hand from her muff and tucked it through his elbow. "Seems I always had more luck than smarts. Maybe that's why I haven't always made the best decisions, but there is one decision I made that was right—marrying you."

He sighed. "I have always just wanted to be happy, have a good time. Giving you and the girls trinkets and dresses and such made me happy because it made you happy."

"We are certainly having a happy day today. Silver is grinning so big that her little cheeks are going to ache tonight."

Horace chuckled and nodded then said, "I haven't seen Elizabeth smile much since... well, since we had to move to west Denver."

"Part of that is the age. Let's hope she outgrows it soon. She is so worried about what other people think of her and of us. Sometimes I think that governess did too good a job teaching her to be a proper lady. I want her to have fine manners, but sometimes you just have to nail a smile to your face and say 'to hell with you.'"

Horace laughed out loud, and Baby Doe scooted closer, looping her arm through his and tucking her hand back into the muff. It was chilly in a building made of ice in the middle of winter in the high mountains. "I'm glad the girls are getting to see how the people here regard you. That is what is making me happy today."

"You always manage to see the sunshine through the clouds." Horace pulled her hand from the muff and kissed it.

Silver Dollar came rushing over, "Did you see me? I went very fast."

Horace patted her head and asked Elizabeth if she had fun too. "Yes, Papa," was the polite answer.

"How about ice skating next?" Baby Doe asked. "Did you girls know that I won a skating contest when I was young?"

"You did? Tell us about it, Mama," said Silver Dollar, grabbing Baby Doe's hand.

"This was back in Oshkosh. The Protestants held a figure skating contest to raise money for their charity fund, but the Protestant girls wouldn't enter. They thought it wasn't ladylike to lift their limbs in public. So I entered under the name L. McCourt and your Uncle Peter signed me in at the judges table." Baby Doe did not mention that the church ladies gasped as she skated out and her father had made all Baby's brothers and sisters cheer as loud as they could to cover the disapproving silence. "I twirled and jumped and finished by gliding past the judges in a perfect arabesque. I won a blue ribbon and a box of candy."

Silver Dollar clapped with delight, and Horace laughed at a story he had heard many times. Elizabeth muttered something about "quite a spectacle."

Elizabeth proved to be a natural, skating gracefully away from her parents. Silver took a few tumbles, but fearlessly hopped up and tried again. Baby Doe glided in time with the orchestra making slow circles and figure eights, before flowing into Horace's arms.

"Skate with me," she whispered.

Horace wrapped an arm around her waist, pulling her close and she rested her head on his chest. A waltz began to play. Baby Doe closed her eyes as they skimmed across the ice. She felt a lightness in her physique and spirit that had been long missing. She could almost imagine it was a decade ago, an earlier time with problems that seemed small now. They had lost so much during the past couple of years, but no banker could ever take the happiness Baby Doe felt on this day.

The lovers floated around the rink, unaware of other revelers, lost in a time and place of their own.

CHAPTER 49

1898

SENATOR EDWARD WOLCOTT was a man of great intellect, graduating from Yale and then Harvard law. He was also practical. He realized early in his career that the East was full of smart, well-educated young men, and opportunities often went to the sons of well-placed men. His father hadn't been particularly well-placed and with nine children there were not going to be opportunities for young Edward and the younger siblings. He and four or five of his brothers would have to make their own way. Edward had thought over several plans. In 1875, he decided to move to Colorado, where the economy was booming, and a young man could create his own future. It had been a brilliant move. He started a successful law practice, was quickly elected to the Colorado state Senate and then to the U.S. Senate.

Wolcott's intelligence had taken him far, but it was his practical nature that made him board a train to Colorado Springs and answer the summons from Winfield Stratton. The eccentric Stratton had become almost a recluse, spending most of his time sequestered in his office claiming he couldn't step outdoors without being accosted by shysters, huskers, and preachers all asking for money. Wolcott had never met the strange little man, but through a friend of a friend, Stratton had contributed money to Wolcott's various political campaigns. Wolcott supposed this audience with the millionaire would be some kind of calling in of the chips.

A young male secretary showed Wolcott into the modest office behind a huge oak door. A corner coat rack held a single hat. Wolcott had heard about Stratton's hat. According to legend it had been snow-white, but was dingy now, its band dark with sweat and dust. Wolcott tried to peer under the desk to see if the old man was wearing the pair of boots he bought with the hat in 1891.

Win began without preamble, "I was in Leadville recently. I saw Horace Tabor. He is doing odd jobs up there, anything he can find. I didn't even recognize him; I feel bad about that. See, he was good to me when I first came to Colorado. Gave me a job. He had me over to dinner once and his wife Baby Doe was as gracious a lady as I ever met. You could tell she was true to Horace, too." He looked at his hands on the desktop and frowned.

Loyalty was important to Stratton. Colorado newspapers had wrote many scurrilous stories involving Win's long-ago wife whom he accused of adultery and a son, whom he did not acknowledge, in spite of being a near mirror image of Win.

The older man shook his white head to scatter bad thoughts and proceeded, "I know people used to hound Tabor for money, and he would never tell them no. Now those same people act like they don't know him. I think that is a dirty shame."

Senator Wolcott spoke carefully, "I always liked Tabor myself. He was an amiable fellow, and he helped finance some of my earliest campaigns."

"And I have provided funds for your most recent campaign," Stratton said.

"Yes, and I thank you," Wolcott said. He started again, "Tabor was a kind and generous man, but with all the scandal surrounding his marriage and divorce—well, many of us had to distance ourselves.

"The first Mrs. Tabor has passed."

"Yes, rest her soul." Wolcott sighed, "I never felt good about it, but there was so much mud thrown at him that just being friendly with him was enough to ruin one's career."

The two men sat in silence for a long moment, Wolcott frowning at his shoes and Stratton staring at Wolcott.

"Senator, I believe the citizens of Colorado owe Horace Tabor a debt of gratitude for all he did in Leadville and Denver."

Another silence fell between them. Practical Wolcott sighed again, "What do you suggest?"

"The postmaster of Denver works in a building built with Tabor money, on land donated by Tabor. That man recently announced he is retiring. My secretary tells me that the postmasters for large cities like Denver are patronage jobs, appointed by the president at the recommendation of the Senate. I want you to submit Horace Tabor's name for the job."

Elizabeth wanted to fit in, but she hadn't made many friends at the school in west Denver. When she tried to act with dignity as Mrs. Winkle instructed, the girls thought her aloof and conceited. She thought them crass as they whispered behind their hands whenever she passed by.

"Females are jealous creatures," Baby Doe told her. "You are the most beautiful girl in the school. They will be petty. You must learn to rise above it. I've had to deal with this sort of thing all my life."

"It is not me they whisper about, Mama. It is you."

"Then I take it as a compliment that I have not lost my looks."

But it was not Baby Doe's looks they whispered about; it was her infamous history. "Be careful," the older girls would tease one another, "or Elizabeth's mother will steal your beau."

"Only if he has money," followed with cruel laughter.

When Horace announced to the girls his appointment as postmaster of Denver and they would be moving, Elizabeth was glad to bid farewell to the west Denver girls and their smirking smiles. Her father's new job was respectable, even honorable. The modest salary meant a comfortable life for her and her little sister, but not enough to indulge wild flights of vanity for her mother. Perhaps at the new school, she would be able to blend in.

Silver received the news of her father's new job with her usual enthusiasm. "The Master of the Post Office is a very important job," she told her friends.

Maxcy was now running the Windsor. The beautiful hotel had suffered in the depression of 1893, and Maxcy was still struggling to bring in guests and fill rooms. He offered his father a small set of two rooms at the back of the hotel, overlooking the alley. It would be temporary, just until Horace had saved enough money to purchase a home in a respectable neighborhood.

Baby Doe saw that all the pieces of her life were falling back into line again. Horace had been the postmaster in Leadville when the Little Pittsburg lode was found, and moving back into the Windsor was like coming home, all signs that God was smiling on her again. The Tabor luck was too strong to keep down.

The next fourteen months passed pleasantly. The girls liked their new school. Maxcy never hinted for them to move out of the hotel, and Horace was relieved, at age sixty-eight, to avoid the backbreaking physical labor demanded by mining and still provide for his family.

"This is not so bad," Horace told Baby Doe. "This job will tide us along until silver comes back. Then we can reopen the Matchless."

Baby economized just as she had in Central City all those years ago. She packed lunches for Horace and the girls each day, reworked skirts, yet again, into the simple flare of the more modern Gibson Girl style, and suggested charades to entertain them in the evening. She would never descend to buy inexpensive tickets to the upper reaches of the opera house or to ask Peter to allow them to stand behind the back row. The next time she attended the opera house she would be sitting in her usual seat in Box A and wearing a new dress. Meanwhile, she saved every penny. They would need it to reopen the Matchless Mine.

CHAPTER 50

1899

BABY DOE CAME TO REGARD warm April days as liars. They promised springtime, tricking children into taking off coats and forgetting them in the schoolyard. But the Colorado winter was not over, and snow could fall at any moment, crushing early daffodils under a heavy wet blanket. It was a deceptively mild day when a rented hack pulled up before the Windsor, and a bitter chill fell on the sunny promise of Baby Doe's new life. The driver called to the doorman to help. Horace, gray-faced and sweating, was slumped inside, hunched over in pain. The bellhop was sent to fetch a doctor, and Maxcy helped the others carry his father to the second-floor rooms.

"Appendicitis," the doctor declared. "It should be removed, however, that is not advisable in a man his age. I gave him a dose of laudanum to help ease his pain and I will send over more."

Her limbs moved stiffly as Baby Doe thanked the doctor and saw him to the door. She felt like a doll, overstuffed with cotton batting. Her thinking was slow and opaque. She couldn't interpret what the doctor meant. It would be the height of impropriety to question a doctor, but she didn't understand—would Horace get better without surgery? How long would this condition last? The doctor didn't mention any treatments other than the laudanum. She didn't know what to do, how to nurse him. The uncertainty was frightening.

She didn't leave Horace's side for the next few days, giving him the painkiller the doctor sent, begging him to take tiny sips of broth and then cleaning him when he vomited it back up.

During her early days in Colorado, a young Baby had stood in a large bucket while a miner secured it with a hemp rope and lowered her into the depths of the Fourth of July Mine. She had become dizzy as the bucket swayed and jostled into the increasing blackness. Baby had clung to the rope with white knuckles, summoning every ounce of her courage not to cry with fear in front of the miners. Now sitting by Horace's bedside, a disorienting darkness threatened to envelop her. Horace had been her bucket and rope, carrying her safely through the unknown. To what would she cling if he died?

As the week wore on, the knifing pain seemed to subside but his fever worsened, and she bathed his high white forehead with a cool damp cloth. He began to float in and out of consciousness. Occasionally, when his mind would swim to the surface, he spoke to Baby.

"There's my ray of sunshine." His smile so weak it couldn't lift his bushy moustache.

"Quiet now, darling. Just rest."

"No, there are things I need to tell you." He closed his eyes and let out a slow, shallow breath. He was still for so long that she thought he had drifted away again. But his eyes opened and he said, "You were the best thing that ever happened to me. Better even than striking it rich. I loved you with all my heart."

Baby noted the past tense of his declaration. Her throat clinched tight, but she managed, "I love you, too."

She kissed his burning head and patted his large paw lying atop the blanket. He grabbed her hand and looked hard into her eyes, "Hang onto the Matchless. It will make millions again."

He clutched her hand and held her gaze until she said, "Of course, darling. Of course."

He gave a small, slow nod and relaxed his grip. His eyes closed. Baby's world reeled and went black. The rope broke and with sickening speed the bucket dropped into obscurity. He was gone.

It was the largest funeral Denver had ever seen. Tabor's Light Militia dug out their old uniforms and contacted friends serving in the state's official militia to form an honor guard. Firemen from the houses founded and funded by Tabor in Leadville and Denver asked their fellow compatriots in the area to join them in the procession behind Tabor's hearse. The postal workers also formed a brigade. Four bands played dirges. The new Archbishop of Denver allowed Horace to be given last rites and a funeral Mass. The governor ordered flags be flown at half-mast and arranged for Tabor to lie in state at the Capitol.

Baby Doe's emotions spun like a tornado blowing in from the plains. She was dizzied at the outpouring of affection from people who had forgotten their friendship with Tabor after his fortunes fell. In turns she was resentful and grateful. Then as she, the only Mrs.

Tabor, climbed into the sober black carriage behind the hearse, she felt vindicated.

"Papa would have been so proud," Baby Doe told the girls as the procession moved from Sacred Heart Church to Calvary Cemetery through a throng of ten thousand onlookers lining the streets. "He was a truly extraordinary man. This is the prestige due a great man."

On the eve of a new century, all of Denver turned out to bid farewell to one of her most colorful citizens and the end of an era. The age of the adventurer conquering the West was over. Denver was now populated with business executives, bankers and railroad men. Billy Cody was calling himself "Wild" and paid a troupe of Indians and trick shooters to reenact the exploits of the trailblazers in a traveling vaudeville show. The frontier was dead; Denver had been civilized; and Tabor's life of unbridled exuberance had become a cautionary tale.

That summer Maxcy's generosity expired toward the woman who had ruined his parent's marriage, and Baby Doe was asked to pay the going rate for two rooms and board for three. She took the girls and moved to a rundown tenement near notorious Larimer Square, where drunkards and cheap whores walked the streets and the rats were as bold as highwaymen.

Baby Doe figured she had two options to provide for her little family. The first was to latch onto another rich man. All of Denver assumed she would; Eugene Hawthorne had written several stories insinuating that a few married millionaires were interested in her as a plaything. But without the security of marriage bonds, she would be trading one precarious situation for another. Her girls would have no social future if their mother was a mistress and with Elizabeth almost sixteen years old, there was no time to battle through another long divorce and then outlive the taint. Baby Doe had to insure there were no obstacles preventing a good match for her daughters. No, she would never settle for being anything less than a wife, and being the wife of Tabor, the state's wealthiest man at one time, had made her spouse *sans pareil.* She would never toss that away. She'd rather be the widowed Mrs. Tabor. So that left option number two: heed Horace's deathbed request and work the Matchless Mine. Being a widowed mother of two pursuing mining and business interests in a man's world would require every bit of her gumption.

CHAPTER 51

1901

SHE GOT THE GIRLS OUT THE DOOR early each morning, as it was two trams and quite a walk to get to their school. As soon as they were off, Baby Doe would put on her most respectable outfit and head to the financial district. She pounded on the doors of bankers and brokers to beg, cajole or harangue them into funding the reopening of the Matchless. She even wrote to her family in Wisconsin. Not Peter, of course, as he had proven himself an ungrateful traitor. She hadn't spoken to him since he sided with Bennett in the foreclosure of the opera house. She had nine other brothers and sisters who benefitted from Tabor generosity at one time or another. One of them could help her now. It was her sister Claudia who answered her pleas.

Dearest Sister,

June 1901

I have corresponded with our brother Peter regarding your state of affairs. We both agreed that it would be better if you and your children came back to Wisconsin and allow us to take you in. But I know this is not what you desire, that you wish to remain always in your precious mountains. Peter also spoke against providing you directly with funds. I agree, as banking is difficult for a woman without a husband. So instead my husband sent a check to the county treasurer in Leadville, paying off all back taxes on the Matchless. I understand from the treasurer this gives him ownership of the mine. I am here by transferring that ownership to you. It is our gift. I hope it provides you and the girls with the financial future of which you dream.

Claudia

Baby Doe gave out a Horace-like whoop as she read the letter. "Girls, we're moving to Leadville." A few days later a second letter arrived.

Dear Mrs. Tabor,

July 1901

Mutual friends have informed me that you are returning to Leadville and hope to reopen the Matchless Mine. Before his passing your husband had contacted me regarding a loan of fifteen thousand dollars. I have placed the funds in the First Bank of Leadville to be used to pay for any supplies. You may contact me after the mine is producing to discuss repayment terms.

Sincerely yours,
Winfield Scott Stratton

Winfield Stratton's secretary looked up from the page of dictation, one eyebrow cocked skyward. "Sir," the young man asked, "Is this wise? Do you think there is silver that can be reached for a profit?"

Stratton glared furiously. "Of course not. But I will not insult the lady's pride with an offer of a handout. Now, arrange some kind of trust with the manager at the First Bank of Leadville to pay her accounts at the local merchants and allow her a little pin money."

CHAPTER 52

THESE DAYS LEADVILLE LOOKED TIRED, like a two-bit saloon girl after a hard night. The edge of town was littered with abandoned mine head frames and tiny cabins tottering over with rot. There were as many boarded-up businesses as there were going concerns along Main and Harrison Streets. The glory days were over and the riotous cast had moved on. Only the toughest, craziest citizens remained, desperately trying to hammer dreams from dirt, pulling a little gold, copper, zinc and iron ore from the reluctant earth. A handful of merchants, saloons, banks and churches worked to keep body and soul together for these hardy folks.

Mrs. McGill had been the proprietress of the boarding house on Harrison Street since the boom days, in fact, Jake had lived there when he first arrived. Baby Doe was sure the stout woman with the graying hair remembered her, but mentioned nothing and welcomed her as Mrs. Tabor, tucking the first month's room and board into her apron pocket.

Elizabeth looked about the faded decor. The room was fairly spacious with two beds, an armoire, washbasin and a rickety armchair with one short leg. "Well, at least it's cleaner than the room on Larimer Street."

"It is just for the time being," Baby Doe said. "We'll buy one of those pretty little Victorian houses once the mine is producing." She pushed a steamer trunk to the end of one bed. "Let's unpack. Mrs. McGill will have dinner for us, then an early night. The thin air up here will make you tired and we have a big day tomorrow. I am taking you two into the mine."

Baby Doe dashed out after breakfast to meet with her banker to discuss the money Win Stratton had wired for her. The girls stayed at McGill's. Elizabeth said she wanted to write letters to her Denver friends with their new address, and Silver Dollar couldn't promise to sit still while at the bank.

"Look what I bought each of us," Baby Doe said, entering the room with a large bundle after her morning errands. She tore open the brown paper and held up three small pairs of butterscotch-colored overalls.

The next morning at the head frame of the Matchless, dressed in their new overalls, Baby intended to give the girls a lesson in the basics of hard rock mining and assess the condition of the mine. "The steam pumps haven't been run in a couple years, so I am guessing the lower levels are flooded. We can't get down there to find out until we are sure the framing timbers are sound. We can use this windlass and bucket to lower two of us down into the shaft." Baby Doe began a supply list in her head. "I need to buy a new rope; this one looks old. And picks and shovels."

"Mama, you cannot expect us to go down into an old, abandoned mine shaft and pretend to be miners. This is dangerous." Elizabeth said, hands on hips.

"You need to learn about mining, how it is done. You will inherit this someday and you'll need to know the business so you don't get cheated," said Baby Doe, her own hands going to her hips.

"Cheated out of all this?" Elizabeth asked, rich with derision. "Mama, there is nothing here. The silver played out years ago. You want us to go down there and endanger our lives for what? A new dress and our names in the gossip columns?"

Baby Doe's face flushed red with anger, "Listen here, young lady. The Tabor name and its legacy are yours to carry on."

"Oh, the Tabor legacy," she cried. "It's a legacy of bad decisions and fast living."

"Enough," Baby Doe shouted.

"Mama, there is no future here for us. We need to move back to Denver, where my sister and I can finish school."

"No, no, your future is here. The Matchless is the only way to regain our name and our standing."

"I want a conventional life. I want to marry a gentleman and have a family."

"This is how you will find a husband, with a fortune from the Matchless to entice a good proposal."

"No amount of money will clean the taint from the Tabor name. This is all just rot."

Baby Doe's hand shot out, slapping Elizabeth's face. They both gasped in surprise.

"You act like Papa was a saint and this is his shrine that we should all kneel before, but it is nothing but a hole in the ground." Elizabeth's eyes blazed with tears of hurt and anger. She turned and walked back into town alone.

Trying to wipe away the sting, Baby Doe rubbed her palm on her overalls and stared as her oldest daughter disappeared down the narrow road. She was sorry she slapped Elizabeth, but she could not abide the backtalk and disrespect. Baby felt as though they were teetering on the edge of a cliff, one wrong step and they all would fall. The Tabors needed to present a confident face to any potential investors; Elizabeth could not march about town calling the mine an empty hole.

Silver Dollar looked about at the refuse that had been discarded near the frame head. The twelve-year-old girl picked up a rusty shovel with a decaying wooden handle. "Mama, I'll help you. I think going into the mine will be exciting. I'm very strong."

Baby Doe grabbed her little one in a fierce hug. "You are my light, my sweetest girl."

"Where have you been?" Baby Doe asked as Elizabeth slipped back into the boarding house. They hadn't spoken since the day before, and after a silent breakfast, Elizabeth had walked out.

"To the library to write a letter and then the post office."

"Well, while you were taking your leisure, your little sister and I purchased some supplies and found a man willing to re-timber the mine. I am going to speak to another man tomorrow about getting the steam engine working. We can use it to run the water pumps, and then, when we are ready to pull ore out, it will turn the windlass."

Saying nothing, Elizabeth removed her gloves and unpinned her hat.

Elizabeth's air of superiority grated on Baby Doe. It was easy for the well fed to take the high road. The Tabor girls had always had the best the family could afford; that hadn't happened by chance. Baby Doe had worked and struggled to get ahead. Sometimes her schemes weren't strictly according to Hoyle, but she didn't regret any of her decisions, nor did she feel like justifying her life to a teenager. They were all going to have to pitch in to keep themselves afloat now. Elizabeth was going to have to get her hands dirty.

"I'm going to hire a small crew of miners to do the heaviest work, drilling and blasting. I'll manage them, but we will have do every bit of work we can ourselves, like mucking and operating the steam engine. I simply don't have the money to hire several men." *How do I make her understand that gentle living is a luxury we can't afford yet?* Baby Doe thought. *I need her help.*

The girl brushed at imaginary dust on her skirt.

"We will all have to work the mine until it starts producing. This may not be the life you once had; however, I have faith we can have that again. The Matchless will provide us with all those old comforts and enjoyments."

Elizabeth looked at her. "You completely misunderstand me, Mama. You think that I miss living in a mansion and being waited on by servants. That I want to wear expensive gowns and glitter with gemstones. But that's what you want. I want to live a quiet, respectable life. I am sick of people staring and gossiping. I am not risking life and limb in a dangerous mine shaft so you can have a bigger diamond."

"It is not immoral to want nice things, and it is not shameful to work hard." Baby Doe snapped. "You didn't know, but I worked in a mine in my first days in Colorado."

Elizabeth's head jerked up, blue eyes alight with anger. "Oh, I do know. I know you dressed like a man and worked in a mine. I know everything. I know how you got your nickname, Baby Doe."

"I told you, the Cornish miners thought I looked like a china baby doll. With their accent doll sounded like doe."

"No, Doe was your first husband's name, the husband you divorced." Elizabeth spit out with venom and then covered her face with her hands.

Baby Doe wasn't sure how Elizabeth had learned of her past; she had shown the girls only bits and pieces of her life before Horace, and even then, she painted it in watercolors, hazy and pretty, edges blurred. She looked across the room at Silver Dollar's wide eyes. She didn't want that sweet girl to see her mother's past with cold, sharp clarity, not yet. "So what of it? I met your father, and we fell in love. It was the greatest love story of the West. There is nothing more to be said about it."

Wanting to get miners working underground before the snow flew, Baby Doe hit the floor running each morning, overseeing efforts to install new timbers and pump dry the lower levels. She hiked the mile and a half up to the mine to figure out the day's plan and then dashed about town to buy supplies, hire help and try to arrange more operating money. Sometimes the girls helped clear slag or carry supplies from town, and some days it was easier to leave them at the boarding house than listen to Elizabeth's drama. At the end of every exhausting day, the air of the boarding house was filled with the prickly tension between Baby Doe and her oldest daughter. Baby stared across the dinner table at the beautiful blonde girl and wondered how this child could be so like her first husband, all good looks and no gumption, so concerned by the opinions of others. What kind of divine punishment was this?

After a long afternoon of hustling to and fro, Baby returned to the boarding house to find Silver alone in the sitting room.

"Where is your sister?"

Silver Dollar bit her lip, but didn't answer.

Baby tilted her head in the manner of all mothers that conveys "answer me."

Tears began to fill Silver's big brown eyes. "I told her she shouldn't. I told her not to go."

"What are you going on about?"

"Elizabeth ran away." Silver clamped a hand over her mouth, muffling the gathering sobs.

Baby Doe tamped down an uneasy feeling. She didn't have the time for melodrama. "Well, she couldn't have gotten far. She has no money and no friends in Leadville."

"Uncle Peter sent her the money for a train ticket to Denver. Then he is taking her to Oshkosh to live with Uncle Phillip. Everything has been arranged."

"Oshkosh?" Baby shook her head. She didn't understand. "Why would Peter take her to Oshkosh?"

Silver chewed on her knuckles as if to stop the hurtful message she was to deliver. "She said there was no future for her here. She said she wanted to live where no one knew her and our family. She said it was the only way she could become a respectable lady."

Fear shot through Baby Doe like a lightning bolt, and she whirled and ran from the boarding house. She had to stop Elizabeth from getting on the train. She picked up her skirts and tore down the street toward the train station.

Silver chased behind, "Mama, stop. Where are you going? The train left hours ago. Mama, please stop."

Baby couldn't breathe. She stumbled and caught herself. She turned to see Silver Dollar, the girl's fists clenched to her mouth and tears streaming down her face. "The train left hours ago," Baby repeated. A gasp caught in her mouth. "She is never coming back." Silver gave a tiny shake of the head. Peter had betrayed her again. This time he had taken her beautiful child. Without Horace by her side, she did not know what to do. Hopelessness smothered her, taking her breath, buckling her knees. She collapsed in the street.

"Mama, Mama," Silver said, wrapping an arm around her weeping shoulders. "Come on, now. Let's go inside here and sit down for a moment." Silver helped her up a few stone steps and into the cool darkness of the Church of the Annunciation. They found their way down a side aisle and Baby crumpled into a pew at the base of a statue of the Virgin Mary.

The serene face of the Madonna wavered through Baby Doe's tears. "Why?" She cried to the Holy Mother. "Why would he take her? Why would she go? Can't she understand what I am trying to do here in Leadville? Does no one see what I am up against?" She fell to her knees, clasped her hands and prayed, *Mother Mary, I have lost everything—my husband, my child, all of our worldly goods. Everything is gone. I have no one to lean on. I am surrounded by Judases, betrayed at every turn by my brother, by so-called friends, by politicians and bankers. Mary, what am I to do? I only want what is best for my children. Help me Mary,* she silently beseeched. But the Madonna would not look at her. She stared over Baby's shoulder. Baby followed the Virgin's gaze to the pew behind her and the dark doe eyes of sweet, sweet Silver.

Not all is lost, whispered the Holy Mother.

CHAPTER 53

1910

SILVER DOLLAR GREW PAST the awkwardness of adolescence and developed into a beauty of her own, with dark curls, big brown eyes that could be innocent or beguiling and the quick beaming smile of her father. She wasn't very tall, but her new woman's figure rivaled that of her mother's in younger days. She liked to be the center of attention and was chatty as a magpie. She loved writing poetry, reading romantic novels and wanted to become a famous authoress, like Jane Austen. Silver admired beautiful horses, but had to settle for riding a little burro Baby had bought cheaply for working the mine. She had become her mother's closest friend and confidant; and Baby had filled their solitary evenings with tales of her father's early days and Leadville's past wealth. As a teen, Silver spent the warm months helping around the mine in Leadville and when the snow began to blow, Baby would take her to Denver for a few months of schooling.

The money Win Stratton had left Baby finally dwindled away; and the once grand Tabors moved out of the Leadville boarding house and into a shanty at the mouth of the Matchless, a mile and a half from town up Little Stray Horse Gulch. Baby told Mrs. McGill that she needed to be closer to the mine, to oversee the miners and keep an eye on the silver dug from underground. In truth there had been little progress made and even less money. Work on the Matchless went on in fits and starts, depending on funding, weather and the availability of the men willing to climb in a bucket and be lowered into darkness on speculation.

The Tabor's new home was plain, a one-room, wooden slat building, about twelve by fifteen feet, which had been the foreman's office and tool shed in the boom days. The front entrance was through a lean-to constructed on the south end that prevented cruel winds from coming in with visitors. A good stove sat in one corner near shelves holding a mismatched assortment of plates and cups, a Dutch oven and three cast iron frying pans. Baby salvaged a kitchen table, a pair of stick chairs, an iron bed and two gently used wicker rockers with comfy pads made of a sturdy cotton canvas from the Sisters of Mercy Charity Shop. A small painted armoire and two steamer trucks held the women's personal possessions.

"Mama, I received a letter from Elizabeth," Silver said, rushing into the cabin and flourishing a torn envelope in one hand and a small note in the other.

It had been more than nine years since Elizabeth used Peter's train ticket to leave Leadville and her family. One brief note from

Baby's sister Claudia confirmed that Elizabeth had made it safely to Wisconsin and discouraged further correspondence.

"It says she married a very nice man and is living as Mrs. John Last of Milwaukee. She is expecting a baby," Silver hardly paused for breath. "She invited me to visit sometime after the baby is born." Her eyes raced across the page. "But I have to promise to behave appropriately and use my first name, Rose. She said it sounds less garish." Silver looked up from the letter with a small confused frown. "Why doesn't she like my name?"

"Oh, you know your sister. She likes all things to be prim and proper." Baby Doe tried to smile.

"When can we go visit her?"

"I think she means for only you to visit." It had escaped Silver's notice that Elizabeth had not included Baby Doe in the invitation to meet the new baby.

Silver looked at the letter, then the address on the envelope. Baby Doe's heart tugged as her eager-to-please child realized she had hurt her mother. Silver rearranged her features to present a superior air.

"Pffft," Silver said. "I would never visit. It sounds painfully dull. So dull that I fear it would ruin my creative spirit. After spending time in her drab little world, I might be struck colorblind or deaf."

Baby Doe smiled at Silver's attempted humor. She understood her younger daughter. Silver may have her father's coloring, but this lively sprite with the devil-may-care nature was Baby Doe's kindred spirit.

"She'll be sorry when the Matchless is producing and I write my first novel," Silver prattled on. "We'll move back to Denver and be the toast of the town. Elizabeth will write and ask if she can visit us, and I will tell her she can come only if she wears a sash proclaiming herself to be the Duchess of Dulldom."

This made Baby laugh aloud. She knew she shouldn't encourage such sassiness. Truth be told, she hadn't said a strict word to Silver in years, since Elizabeth left. Baby Doe had wanted Elizabeth to be refined, and the results had been calamitous. Elizabeth became a contrived goody-goody, contemptuous of her family, who ended up running away and disowning them. Baby Doe would not make the same mistakes with Silver Dollar; so, there were few rules for Silver growing up. The two were more like friends or sisters, sharing exploits, planning adventures and conspiring to try to recreate the lost glamour of bygone days. Baby did not want to lose her.

The women pursued fortune as best they could, Baby trying to scratch precious metal from the earth and Silver's scratching pen on paper. They just needed to find a rich vein of the precious mineral and get Silver's work read by someone other than her mother. So far, both exploits had cost more than they brought in. The mine was a continuous drain on their funds, always needing supplies, equipment or an extra pair of hands. Silver had written several poems that were set to music and published with the help of a man who had been a young house musician at the opera house. Now living in Denver, he called himself Maestro Lohmann and charged accordingly for his services.

"Oh, I have more news. I stopped at the library today, too. The librarian had a new book for me," Silver pulled a book from the satchel she had thrown down upon rushing in the door. "*Girl of the Limberlost,* I don't think I am going to like it, too much nature and bugs and not enough handsome men." Silver giggled. "But that's not the news. I saw in the newspaper that President Roosevelt is coming back to Colorado this autumn. He didn't have much time when he was here two years ago, but now that he's no longer president, he's going to tour around and hunt big game."

Baby nodded along, not sure why a twenty-year-old female would be excited about an old man's hunting trip.

"I had an inspiration," Silver continued. "I'll write a poem about Roosevelt's adventure and present it to him at the farewell celebration in Denver at the end of the trip." Silver clapped with excitement.

All the newspapers would cover such an event, this could be the spark to light Silver's literary career. The Tabors would be socializing with presidents again. Baby's mind whirled with possibilities.

"If we set your words to music, it can be sung in music halls, men's lodges and schools all over the state. If your song is well known before Roosevelt's farewell, the planners will have to present you to the president." Baby Doe set aside her darning, warming to the idea. "You get busy on the lyrics. I will write to Maestro Lohmann about the music. I will also write the mayor of Denver, I'm sure he remembers me. I'll let him know that the daughter of the great Senator Tabor has created a tribute to the president and should be in the front row at his farewell celebration."

Always a believer in audacious plans, Baby Doe's latest scheme had gone like clockwork. "Our President's Colorado Hunt" was printed with the dedication "In memory of the late U.S. Senator, Horace Tabor." The maestro played the tune nightly at Elitch Garden Theater and it caught on with the local crowd. The mayor wrote back that he, too, had enjoyed Silver's song and would be pleased to include her in the brief festivities at the train station.

A week before Roosevelt's going-away party, the Tabor women traveled to Denver where Baby Doe opened the long-forgotten safety deposit box holding the last remnants of the family fortune. Baby's past would help finance Silver's future.

"I'm sure you don't remember these," Baby said, handing wide-eyed Silver a pair of diamond encrusted diaper pins. "Oh look, your father's watch fob."

Silver gaped at the four-inch-long gewgaw depicting the highlights of her father's life, the store in Leadville, Tabor Block and the Tabor Grand Opera House. A tiny bucket of nuggets swung from the bottom. She turned it over and read, "'Presented by the citizens of Denver to H.A.W. Tabor.' Oh, Mama we can't sell this. It's our good luck charm."

"Honey, it's solid gold. It is worth a lot of money."

"Is it more valuable than Tabor luck?" asked Silver with a grin. "We need to keep this with us when I meet President Roosevelt and then take it back to Leadville."

Baby could never say no to Silver. "All right. I suppose we do need a talisman." She reached into the box for the last item, a large diamond surrounded by cornflower blue sapphires. "My engagement ring, this will keep us comfortable for quite a while."

After selling the gemstones, the pair headed to the enormous Denver Dry Goods Company on Sixteenth Street to buy Silver a new dress. Silver picked an emerald green ensemble with a draping V-neck, tailoring to the waist with a pale green straight hobble skirt that just reached her ankles. Silver inspected the ladies' hats lining an entire wall. She reached for one of the large brimmed affairs that were the fashion of the moment.

"No," Baby Doe said. "The crowd must see your pretty face." Baby chose a chic turban with a wide green velvet band. Silver tried it on. Her dark curls peeked from beneath in an intoxicating mix of sultry and innocent.

"Perfect."

"Your turn, Mama. I think the navy dress with the empire waist would look lovely on you."

But Baby Doe was not ready to be seen in Denver yet. Without a new, shiny fortune to capture their attention, the gossips and the reporters would revive the old scandals and delight in her store-bought wardrobe. It was better to use the money from the pawnshop to get Silver seen with the president and use leftover funds in the Matchless. Baby had only been able to fund a few repairs and the smallest of new diggings at the mine. However, once the mine was producing again, she could re-enter Denver society in a manner befitting Mrs. Tabor, widow of the great Senator Tabor, and leave the old crows speechless. Her wardrobe, jewels and purse would all declare that the Tabors were back on top of the world. If she couldn't have the very finest dress at the event then she would rather not go.

"This will be your day," she said. "We want all eyes to be on you."

Baby Doe feigned a headache the morning of the celebration and stayed in at their second-rate hotel. "I will read about it in all the newspapers," she told her daughter.

Judging from his toothy grin, the former president was happy to pose for a picture with the dark-eyed siren that sang a tribute to his hunting trip. The *Denver Post* ran a two-column article next to the photograph about the beauty and her budding literary career. It was noted she was the daughter of Senator Horace Tabor.

Baby Doe and Silver were thrilled with the publicity, but Eugene Hawthorne, in his new role as editor of the *Star Ledger*, cussed out his reporters for not recognizing a Tabor and failing to dig up any gossip about Roosevelt and the twenty-one-year-old songwriter, who happened to be the daughter of America's greatest floozy. Hawthorne hadn't written about Baby Doe since Horace died a decade ago, but he remembered the beautiful woman, her endless scandals that made his career and the embarrassing evening when he was tossed out of the Windsor Hotel. Much like Baby Doe herself, he never forgot a slight.

CHAPTER 54

SILVER'S MOMENT OF GLORY faded shortly after President Roosevelt's trained pulled away from Denver; and back in Leadville, life ground on as before. Silver bounced into town on the back of her little burro to pick up a few groceries. As was her routine, she first stopped at the livery stable to water her ragged little mount and pet the gleaming horses that she wished to ride

"I saw your picture in the newspaper." A tall cowboy leaned against the livery stable door. A black Stetson hat was pushed to the back of his head, revealing gray eyes and dark blonde hair.

The normally gregarious girl had suddenly lost her voice and her wit and stared mutely at the good-looking stranger.

"President Roosevelt seemed pretty taken with you." He pushed away from the door and strode across the corral with an athletic grace.

"I can see why." He took the reins from Silver and led the little burro to the water trough. He scratched the animal's head. "So Buddy," he said to the burro "is your mistress always so talkative?"

Silver gathered herself and said into the long furry ears, "Tell the gentleman no, that I am usually timid as a mouse."

His sensuous smile was so lazy it only lifted one corner of his mouth. "My name is Will Thomas. I'm new in town."

"I'm Silver Dollar Tabor."

"I reckon the entire state knows you."

"Is that horse yours?" Silver nodded toward a new horse in the corral.

"Yes ma'am." The gelding was tall and good looking like his owner, 17 hands high and the color of buttermilk.

Silver forgot about her little burro and eased over to meet the gelding. "You're gorgeous," she cooed. The horse, head held high, looked down his long nose and seemed to agree. Silver pulled a mealy old apple from her coat pocket and offered it to the quarter horse. Her little burro's head hung mournfully as the big boy stretched his neck out and plucked the burro's treat from Silver's hand. "What's his name?"

"I call him Major because he likes to take charge."

"I want to ride him."

"I don't think that's a good idea. This is a working ranch horse. He's strong and he's smart and he can be stubborn. He needs a firm hand. He is not meant for pleasure rides by little gals like you."

Major allowed Silver to rub his nose and pet his neck as he chewed the apple. Silver looked back over her shoulder with a coy smile. "I think he quite likes me."

"Well, I suspect," Will drawled, "that any male, man or beast, would fall for your charms."

"Let's make a wager. If I can ride Major all the way down Harrison Street and back, you will let me ride him whenever I want."

Silver stuck out her hand to shake on the deal.

Will held her hand and asked, "What do I get if I win the bet?"

Silver boldly met his sultry gaze. "If I fall off, I'll let you kiss my boo-boos." She pulled her hand away and held it at her décolletage. "I have to do some marketing. I'll be back in a bit." She turned on her heel and walked out of the corral. "Have Major saddled," she called back over her shoulder.

When Silver returned, both Major and the little burro were saddled and tied to the rail in front of the stable. Silver quickly secured her gunny sack of supplies to the pack animal and then petted and flirted with the large buckskin. "Are you ready, big fella? Let's go for a ride. Won't that be fun?" The smaller animal let out a long breath of resignation.

Tiny Silver needed a leg up to mount the huge horse. She took Will's black Stetson and placed it on her head. "Major wants me to look like a real cowgirl."

Will shot her his languorous grin, shortened the stirrups another notch and led them to the top of the street. "Just nice and gentle."

"Who are you talking to? Me or Major?" Before Will could answer, Silver took the hat from her head, whipped Major with it and kicked his flanks hard. The two shot down the street, Silver whooping like a warpath Indian and waving the hat. Curious citizens came out of shops and businesses all along Harrison Street to see what all the commotion was about. After about seven blocks, Silver pulled up on the reins and whirled Major around. They galloped back up the thoroughfare, Silver waving to onlookers.

Major shuddered to a stop in front of the small crowd gathered at the livery stable. Will reached up and grabbed Silver around her waist and pulled her from the horse's broad back. He held her, gazing into her flushed face, for far too long before he set her tiny feet on solid ground. The onlookers began to turn away and a couple of old women shook their heads. They weren't surprised by such a brazen display, after all this was Baby Doe's daughter and some rambling cowboy who was too handsome for his own good.

Silver Dollar trotted down the mountain to town every chance she got that winter. She told Baby Doe a variety of excuses, writing or reading at the library, picking up an urgently needed spool of thread, pencil, soap. When the weather was good, she, Will, Major and a borrowed horse would take a long, leisurely trail ride in the mountains. Other days, she and Major would simply circle the corral while Will did chores. Everyone in town knew there was some funny business going on in the stable loft, everyone but Baby Doe, who was preferring to stay close to the mine these days.

CHAPTER 55

1911

SILVER BELIEVED ALL THE SWEET honey that Will had whispered in her ears as they lay in the clean hay in the loft; so, she was surprised when he left town without even saying goodbye. The stable owner told her the South Park Cattle Company was looking for another hand to help with spring calving and then moving the cattle to summer high pastures.

She gave a small smile and tried to sound nonchalant, "That sounds like a good job for a wandering cowboy."

Bouncing back up the mountain on her faithful burro, Silver took stock of her first romantic experience. Although her heart was tender from his sudden departure, she felt much more grown up now. Will had been a lovely kisser, he had taught her about making love and given her a taste for whiskey. When the mine finally struck a rich vein and she and Mama moved to Denver, the city men wouldn't think her a witless mountain girl. She was a sophisticated woman now.

A couple of weeks later, Silver was thrilled when she was in town to run actual errands for her mother, and Zack and Adam Miller asked her to the Easter Ball at the Moose Lodge. The Millers were cousins whose fathers ran a hotel and restaurant and, by all accounts, were quite respectable for rough and tumble Leadville folk.

Baby Doe was not bothered that two young men would escort Silver Dollar, less opportunity for a hapless male to fall in love with her beautiful daughter. After all, the Tabors would be moving to Denver as soon as they hit pay dirt. There, Silver would meet more desirable candidates to be her husband.

"I have nothing to wear," Silver fretted.

"We can re-work the dress you wore to meet the president. Take off the sleeves and make a small ruffle over the shoulder." Baby would be the Fairy Godmother to Silver's Cinderella. From an old trunk of mementos she pulled the collar and cuffs of the ermine coat that had caused a stir at Maxcy's wedding all those years ago. The body of the coat had been sold long ago to pay the rent during a thin time back in Denver. "Let's sew these onto my good black wool. It will look like a new coat and so elegant." Looking beautiful was what Baby Doe did best.

The Miller boys called for Silver in a fine black buggy and brought a lovely spray of lily of the valley to pin to her shoulder.

Waving the youngsters off, Baby was in a stew of emotions. She was happy that Silver was getting out and having some fun, and the girl looked absolutely ravishing. Silver Dollar Tabor would be the belle of this Easter Ball. The whole evening threw a light on the fact that Silver was not a little girl anymore, she was a young adult. At her age, Baby Doe had married her first husband and traveled across country. Silver was adventurous like her mother. She would want to spread her wings soon, socialize with other young people and get away from the secluded life in the mountains.

Baby wanted Silver to enjoy the life of her dreams, a good husband and beautiful house. The precious metal of the Matchless was the key to financing such a dream. She continued to have faith that pay dirt lay very close, but she realized they needed to get the mine to produce soon. They had been in Leadville for nearly a decade, and neither she, nor her daughter, were getting any younger.

She rubbed these thoughts like worry beads late into the night, waiting for the girl. When the sky began to lighten to a lavender hue, she told herself that some family was probably hosting a breakfast for the revelers, but when the sun rose full in the east, she could no longer rationalize Silver's absence.

She wrapped herself in an old coat a long-ago miner had left in an upper tunnel of the Matchless. The dull black overcoat, with the sleeves pinned up and a pocket removed to patch an elbow, was ragged and ill-fitting to say the least, but it covered Baby from head to toe and was good for carrying wood or digging in the mine. She knew she looked ridiculous, but appearances be damned, she couldn't sit idle and wait for Silver. Baby needed to go into town and find her daughter.

A wagon came into view just as Baby set out down the road. It was Big Joe Johnson, a store owner from town. Joe was a nice man, a middle-aged, Midwesterner who desired to escape the life of toil on the family farm and earn his living using his head. He knew banking and law required more than his eight years of schooling, so he sought to become a merchant of some sort. He had moved to Leadville a couple years ago after answering an advertisement to "lease to own a mercantile in a fabled silver camp in the heart of the glorious Rocky Mountains."

"Whoa," he pulled the horses to a stop. "That you Miz Tabor? Didn't recognize you."

"Mr. Johnson, have you seen Silver Dollar? She went to the Easter Ball and didn't come home," Baby stopped. It sounded awful, as if Silver were the loosest kind of trollop.

Big Joe shifted uncomfortably. "I got her right here." He looked over his shoulder to a sleeping girl wrapped in a horse blanket.

Baby Doe dashed to the back of the wagon. Silver was a mess. Her hat was missing, her hair fell over her face and the narrow hobble skirt was torn. She was drunk as a skunk.

"Oh," Baby gasped. "Oh no. What happened? Silver, are you hurt?"

"Climb up, Miz Tabor and I'll give you a ride back home."

Silver's head lolled on her shoulders and she mumbled as Joe carried her into the cabin and laid her on the bed.

"What happened Mr. Johnson? Where are those Miller boys?"

"I don't know. Back home, I reckon."

"I am going to rip the hide off of them. Offering her drink. Not seeing her home—just leaving her. Was she at your store? How did it come to be that you brought her home?"

"I was heading to the sunrise Easter service when I saw Jesse Smith pushing her out of his saloon. Apparently, the Millers took her there after the ball, and there was a lot of drinking." Joe frowned.

"I don't know what all went on last night, and I won't repeat what that no-good Jesse Smith said."

The worry that had tightened Baby's chest last night fell to her stomach as nauseous despair. Big Joe didn't have to tell her Jesse's lewd boast or the sordid tales the townsfolk would be spinning by this afternoon. She knew how gossip spread.

Baby filled the wash basin with cool water and sat on the edge of the bed. "Mr. Johnson, we are very grateful for your help." She bathed the girl's face, forehead and neck and Silver shivered. "One last thing, Silver isn't wearing her coat. Is it in your wagon?"

"No, Miz Tabor. She didn't have a coat when she came out of the saloon this morning. I can ask around, maybe one of my customers knows where it is."

"No, Mr. Johnson, please don't mention the coat or any of this to anyone."

Silver slept until noon, then Baby roused her to eat lunch and drink all the strong coffee she could stand.

Silver slowly chewed on a ham biscuit at the small, rickety kitchen table. Baby Doe pulled up the chair across from her. "What happened last night?"

Silver stared silently at her plate. Finally, she gave a half-hearted shrug.

"Too much drinking, that's for sure." Under the table, Baby clenched her hands in her lap, "Was this your first . . . kiss?"

Silver gave a small rueful laugh, "No."

"Who?"

"Will, at the livery stable, he and I had an affair."

"What do you mean 'had an affair'?"

Silver looked at her mother with bloodshot eyes.

"Oh no, Silver. With a cowboy?"

The two women sat in silence. "My darling, I understand a romantic nature, the passions of the heart. I know how young people can get lost in a moment and fail to see..." Vocabulary escaped her. "Life is not a novel."

"Your life was," the younger woman said softly.

Over the years, Baby Doe had spun many fine tales, filling Silver's head with romanticized stories of her life; now how could she disclose the history of her heart to her daughter? How could she explain the bloodless marriage to Harvey and the reckless passion of Jake? How could she clarify the rationalization to leave both men and hunt for a man capable of taking care of her? How to describe searching out and seducing Horace like a general executing a battle plan? How to tell of how she fell in love with him? How could she explain that every sacrifice was so that Silver could live a more refined life and never have to make those kinds of choices?

She started over, "A woman must be careful. You are your own most valuable asset. You must withhold any affections for the right man. You cannot allow yourself to get into a compromising situation."

"Mama, I want to move to Denver," Silver blurted out.

"We can't leave the Matchless," Baby cried. She was sure that the latest efforts in the mine were very close to striking a rich vein.

"No, you don't have to leave. I will go. I'll get a job and I can send money back to help you with the mine expenses."

The man Baby had hired to dig had left for the winter, as she didn't have the funds to pay him. Spring was right around the corner, and she would need to find another old, unemployed prospector to help her, hopefully on contingency.

"No. Now is not the right time to move to Denver. Perhaps next year."

"Mama, I know this disappoints you," her voice trailed off. "I will go crazy if I stay here."

Baby didn't want to lose her precious girl, her friend, her companion; but perhaps it was best if she left town, at least for a while, and let the rumors she knew would be rife die down. She didn't want sweet Silver to be battered by the storm of gossip that was going to blow through town.

"What will you do in Denver?"

"I will get a job writing for a newspaper. I heard about girl reporters when I was interviewed about the president's visit." Silver reached across the table for her mother's hand. "I'm twenty-two-years old, most girls are married by that age. There are no prospects for me here."

"We don't have the money to get you moved and established in a reputable boarding house."

"I was thinking that Uncle Peter might help me with a train ticket and place to live for a little bit."

It galled her that Silver would ask that Judas for help. Peter had wounded her over and over. He had refused to help save the opera house. He had said he was the best chance for the girls to have a respectable future. But most devastating, he provided the means for Elizabeth to run away and bury herself in anonymous mediocrity. Now, Baby's second daughter turned to him. The thought of losing Silver to him wrenched her soul, but she couldn't deny Peter might be the girl's best hope. It broke her heart.

On a blustery morning a month later, Baby Doe and the little burro helped Silver Dollar carry her bags to the train station. Uncle Peter had answered Silver's letter with money for a train ticket and an offer to let her stay at his home until she was established. He had even arranged for her to meet with a newspaper editor regarding a position.

Silver chattered without stopping the entire mile and a half to town. "It is all so exciting, Mama. I feel like when I step on that train my life will, at last, start. Of course, I will miss you Mama, but not dull old Leadville."

"Leadville used to be far more exciting than Denver." Baby Doe stopped herself. She didn't want to sound like the old codgers that sit about clucking over the sad state of current affairs and remembering their better days. Of course life would be more fun for Silver in the big city and Denver certainly was the big city now. It was a bustling center of commerce and transportation with restaurants and theaters, lots of young people and parties, more opportunities and less snow. Baby Doe wanted all of those things for Silver. But she hadn't envisioned it coming to pass this way, with her daughter departing for the traitorous clutches of Peter to take a job in a viper's nest of a newspaper office.

Just as there was nothing in Leadville for Silver, there was nothing in Denver for Baby Doe. When she moved back to Denver, she needed to do so in a style grand enough to leave her critics gaping. She imagined a triumphant re-entry into the city worthy of the Caesars. She would arrive by private train car, dressed and bejeweled so finely that every female within the city limits would turn the color of emeralds. She would buy a new home on Capitol Hill and set to work finding Silver a nice husband. Finally, she would be received in society as the matrons who had given her a hard time were old, many were dead, and Baby was pretty sure she hadn't been mentioned in a gossip column in nearly a decade. The newspapers that gave evidence of her calumny had all rotted to dust, but the buildings that Horace had built were still standing. The Tabor name was still known, carved in stone across the facades of several prominent buildings. Things would be different in Denver. No one would know how she and the girls lived in Leadville, in a one-room shack whose walls could have been papered in promissory notes that she handed out all over town.

Baby Doe hugged her girl and kissed her cheek. She wanted to tell Silver to be careful, but also be bold, to work hard, but to enjoy life, to hold herself precious. The words stuck in her throat and all she could say was, "Remember, you are a Tabor."

CHAPTER
56

Dear Mama,

July 1911

I am writing from my new address. I have moved into a very nice boarding house for young women not far from the newspaper offices. Uncle Peter's house was lovely, but small, and he did not understand that as an adult I am capable of knowing my own mind. I am able to afford the rent here and am living and working as an independent woman.

I continue to work at the *Rocky Mountain News* writing obituaries, but make time to visit the reporters. I hope my cordial visits will earn me consideration when a position is available writing about fashion or gossip. Until then, my subjects aren't going anywhere. (Ha, ha.)

Much Love,
Silver

Dear Mama,

November 1911

Writing obituaries is contrary to my nature. I simply could not spend another day in such a grim position. My editor agreed and suggested I use my talents elsewhere. So I am going to publish my own broadsheet — just one page currently. It will feature news that young people, particularly silly young women, might find interesting, such as fashion and theater reviews and plenty of gossip about whom is attending which parties. Uncle Peter is providing me with a small allowance until I find paying advertisers.

Love, love, love,
Silver

Dear Mama,

June 1912

So much is happening! I had to shut down my broadsheet publication. It was great fun, I went to parties and performances and met lots of people, but I was never able to sell enough advertisements to make a profit, and Uncle Peter said he did not like me spending my allowance on frivolities. No matter, because I have begun writing my first novel! I am calling it the *Star of Blood.* It is a Western romance story about an outlaw cowboy and a high-spirited girl. It is very dramatic with a tragic ending. I think it will be quite good. I should have it finished by the New Year and Uncle Peter has arranged a publisher.

I have a new address, too. There was a mix up with the money that Uncle Peter gave me to pay the rent and the old bat that owned the house put me out. Again, no matter, I have a new room. It is small, but it has a lovely window where I sit and write and one of my housemates is a typist.

Love and miss you,
Silver

CHAPTER 57

1913

MONEY HAD GOTTEN PRETTY TIGHT. The Stratton loan had long dried up, the cash from the pawned jewelry was spent and Silver couldn't hold a steady job. That didn't stop Baby Doe from dolling up as best she could. She knew people were thinking her eccentric these days and she wanted to make a nice impression when she presented a copy of Silver Dollar's novel to the county library. Baby thought the novel was excellent, full of romance and action with a beautiful heroine. She was sure it would be very popular; Silver was very talented.

Baby wasn't much concerned with fashion and appearance anymore. She was sixty years old and rarely ventured into town; she had no need to worry about vanities. She hadn't bought a new dress for herself in years; in fact, any new additions to her wardrobe had come from the charity bin in the church vestibule. Although this was an important event, she would make do with what she owned. She washed and pressed an old but still presentable white blouse that she had owned since living in Denver and brushed clean a black skirt that had aged to a dull gunmetal gray. Lately, she had been wearing a pair of men's work boots given to her by the nuns for a poor old miner whom Baby Doe had employed for a short time. She had demanded the boots back when he quit for lack of wages. With a little newspaper stuffed in the toes they fit well enough. For today's trip to town, however, she pulled a pair of dainty black leather button-up ladies' boots from a trunk. Silver would not think them stylish, but they were in fine shape.

"I thought the local press would attend," Baby Doe said looking about the empty library. She was disappointed and bewildered that the town had not shown up for the dedication of young Miss Tabor's marvelous first novel. This had to be one of the most exciting things that had happened in Leadville in years.

The young librarian had told the editor of the *Leadville Press* that a hometown girl had written a novel and her mother, the infamous Mrs. Tabor, would be giving a copy to the library, but the editor wasn't much interested in attending a book donation. Miss Wilton brightly offered, "They promised to print an announcement; and as soon as I have read it, I can submit a review." She shifted awkwardly. "I think we should just go ahead."

"Miss Wilton, may I present the county library with a copy of my daughter Silver Dollar Tabor's first published novel, *Star of Blood*." Baby Doe proudly held out the thin book with two hands as if it were a rare and wonderful treasure.

It was challenging for Miss Wilton to write an accurate review of Silver's novel. The book was awful, melodramatic and meandering. The heroine possessed more than a passing similarity to the authoress and the protagonist was a mix of a young cowboy who had passed through town and Jesse James as described in the penny dreadfuls. The hero descends into a life a crime, robbing and murdering across the state and his doe-eyed lover, after collapsing with shock at his trial, dies alone and is buried in an unmarked grave. Miss Wilton wrote a vague essay about how exciting it was to see a local writer get published.

Eugene Hawthorne, now editor-in-chief for the *Denver Star Ledger*, didn't want his literary reviewer to mince words. "You know what I am paying you to write."

When the *Star Ledger* arrived in Leadville featuring a review of Silver's novel, Miss Wilton carefully cut the entire page out of the tabloid and threw it away. No one needed to read that vitriol.

CHAPTER 58

1914

BABY DOE SAT BOLT UPRIGHT in bed, her heart beating so hard it thudded in her ears. It was the second night that she had awoke from a strange dream about Silver. In her nightmare, Silver was lost; Baby stood outside the cabin and called her name, but got no response. The Virgin Mary appeared at the mouth of the mine. Baby cried, "I can't find Silver. Help me, Holy Mother." Mary had replied that the mountains were the safest place to keep a treasure.

She hadn't heard from Silver in months. Letters to her last address were marked "return to sender," and the letter Baby Doe had sent to general delivery went unanswered. Sitting alone in a cabin a hundred miles from Denver fueled her maternal worries. When she awoke, filled with a cold dread, she knew the dream was a premonition, a warning from Mother Mary. Something was wrong with Silver, and though she couldn't say what, she knew she had to get to her daughter.

A two-foot blanket of snow smothered the landscape between Baby and the train station in town. At first light, Baby Doe pulled on her patched-up coat and stepped into the old work boots. She wrapped old gunny sacks around her legs as an extra layer against the cold and wet. It was slow going to break a trail through the icy crust atop the thigh-high snow. She fell and struggled to find purchase to push herself up time and again. Puffs of breath hung like smoke about her face before freezing to her scarf.

It was midmorning by the time she arrived in town, sodden and exhausted. She made a fruitless stop at the post office, hoping against hope for an envelope addressed by Silver's childish hand, and then made her way to Big Joe's store armed with a proposition.

"Mr. Johnson, I have with me a very valuable piece of ore mined recently from the Matchless Mine. As it is in a very raw, unrefined state, I am willing to allow you to have it for twenty dollars."

Big Joe carefully studied the rock, turning it over in his hand.

"I do not have time to have it assayed as I will be leaving shortly to visit my daughter in Denver, but I am sure it is worth much more than that," she said.

He nodded, "Yes, Mrs. Tabor. This is a fine piece of ore."

Very well," Baby held out her hand to seal the bargain.

Big Joe pulled a twenty-dollar bill from the cash register and handed it to her. After she left, Big Joe tossed the rock to the stock boy. "Throw it out in the alley when you go to the backroom."

"Throw it out?" cried the boy. "But look at all that glitter. It's full of gold."

Big Joe shook his head slowly, "No son, those shiny specks are fool's gold."

"Why'd you give her twenty dollars if it is worthless?"

"Because, son, we mountain people take care of our own. Baby Doe was once an important lady in this state."

"She's just a crazy old bat now," the boy murmured.

"Well, she is our crazy old bat, and I won't see her go without."

Baby Doe hurried to the train station, her carpetbag bumping her legs. She had packed light, only two pair of wool socks, two pairs of drawers and a bit of hardtack. There was nothing left of her beautiful wardrobe during high times in Denver. That was fine, she told herself, those dresses would be hopelessly out of fashion now. She would buy all new clothes when she made her grand return. For this trip, her raggedy Leadville outfit would serve as an excellent disguise. No one would realize under those patches and tatters the little hobo was actually the grand Mrs. Tabor, the Silver Queen. She topped her ensemble with a motoring cap she had scrounged from the bin outside the Sisters of Charity shop. It was black with a short bill, a gauzy veil and a scarf sown to the sides. Baby Doe did not think she would be riding in an automobile anytime soon, but tied under her chin the scarf would keep her ears warm, and the netting would hide her face as well as Billy Bush's hated veil ever did.

The streets of Denver were bitterly cold and the room Baby Doe had rented wasn't much warmer. The boarding house, frequented by men working on the nearby railroad track, charged only two dollars a week. Baby eyed the dingy bedding and the smoky kerosene lamp and figured she got what she paid for. On the bright side, there would be no aging society dowagers having tea in the parlor or bitter gossip columnists lurking around the front door, as they did when she lived at the Windsor. She would find Silver and talk her into coming home to Leadville before the end of the week.

"Silver Dollar Tabor ain't here," said the frizzy-haired hag at the door. "Moved out." The woman shot a stream of tobacco-brown juice at Baby Doe's feet.

Baby clenched her arms to her sides to hold in the shudder of revulsion. In Silver's last letter home, months ago, she had written that her financial situation required she move and had given this address. "Do you know where she moved to?"

A claw-like hand wiped spittle from the hag's lip. "No, left in the middle of the night. Owes me money." Her dark eyes narrowed. "Do I know you?"

"No, we don't know one another," Baby said and started down the front steps.

"You're Baby Doe," the woman crowed and slapped her leg. "I shoulda known, last name Tabor. God, woman, you look like hell."

The short winter day had quickly faded into evening by the time Baby Doe had walked across town to Peter's house. She stood a long time at the small metal gate at the front of the garden. She hated to let him see her in this predicament, to admit that Silver may be in some kind of perilous situation and request his help, but she had no one else to whom she could turn. Then in the evening's gathering gloom, she spotted a lightness—a small grotto with the Madonna set under an evergreen tree on the edge of the yard. It was a sign she should knock on Peter's door.

Peter's blonde hair was white at the temples, wrinkles framed his blue eyes and comfortable living had rounded his frame, but he was still handsome. "Baby?" he asked.

"I am looking for Silver. She is no longer at the last address I have for her on Mercer Street."

"Would you like to come in?" he sighed.

"I have the most terrible feeling she is in peril. Do you know where she is?"

He was slow to speak, "No."

"Peter," she cried. "You are her guardian. I saw the last place she was living; it was horrible." Baby Doe's voice began to rise as the fear she had held down for hours crept up her throat.

He took her elbow and ushered her into the house. "I don't know where she is living, but I hear she is working at a hoochie-coochie dance joint off Larimer Street."

"That's not true."

"I'm sorry to say it is true. The drink has got a hold on her. She would tell me she needed brandy or whiskey for some medicinal reason or another, but it was all false. The broadsheet she wrote turned into an excuse to become a good-time girl carousing around town. We argued endlessly about it."

"No, no, this can't be. She is high-spirited, but she is a good girl."

"She has fallen. There was a parade of men who took care of her for a short time and then left her. Now, she cheapens herself dancing with scarves for the roughest of men."

"She never wrote about any of this. How could you let this happen?"

"She is an adult who has told me that she is capable of directing her own life."

"You were supposed to look after her. This is your fault," Baby spat at him.

"Oh no, this is your doing. She uses her looks and her body in a vain attempt to gain the love and security of a man. She thinks that her only worth is an ability to seduce males. These are the lessons you taught her."

How could Peter twist her parental guidance, her motherly advice into this vulgar paradigm? It was a man's world, so, of course, the best way to secure one's future was to become attached to a male of means and, yes, beauty was an advantage. She didn't have the time or patience to explain the facts of a woman's life to Peter. She pulled her arm back and slapped him as hard as she could and left.

The Knot Hole Saloon and Burlesque Theater advertised cheap booze and exotic dancing girls. Baby Doe stood blinking in the doorway, trying to see through the smoke and gloom. Two peroxide blondes listlessly waved scarves and twirled around a small stage illuminated by a few footlights while a dozen miscreants hooted and stomped their appreciation. A tall thin girl in a dirty chemise and a skirt so short that Baby Doe could see her knees leaned against the bar. Baby was not unfamiliar with the rougher side of life. She had visited the raucous saloons and gaming houses of the mining towns and was friendly with the night flowers of the Shoo Fly, but this place had none of the rowdy energy, none of the optimism of the boomtowns. Desperation hung in the air here. The girls wore hopelessness like a shroud. A fresh chorus of catcalls went up as a third dancer joined the stage, a curvaceous brunette. It was Silver.

"You can't watch the girls for free. You have to buy a drink," barked a large man from behind the bar.

The site of her precious little girl dancing in this pit of veniality horrified Baby Doe. She turned and ran from the building.

"What was that about?" asked the club owner, a greasy man, shiny with sweat even on this winter's night.

"Just some old hobo trying to warm up."

The freezing night air slapped Baby Doe out of her flight. She slipped down the adjacent alley to the theater's side door. *I'll wait for her here, out of the wind,* she thought and hunkered down behind a couple of broken old beer barrels. *My poor girl is probably scared and humiliated. She will be happy to go back to Leadville now. I'll take her home—away from this hell on earth—and we will just forget all about this. No one need know of how low Silver has fallen.*

A long strand of white twine lay neatly curled up near her feet. It was oddly clean in the frozen mud of the piss-soaked alley. Baby picked it up and, as her mind worked to untangle how Silver had come to this, her fingers tied small knots, one after another and another until she had ten. *A decade of rosary beads. Hail Mary, full of grace the Lord is with thee.* She tied a triple knot. *Our Father, who art in heaven,* she prayed and knotted. *Holy Mary, Mother of God pray for us sinners.* Ten more knots. *Deliver us from evil.* A triple knot. Her nerves quieted as she recited the rosary, fingering the knotted twine between her freezing fingers.

The side door swung open. The blonde dancers came out, and Baby Doe jumped to her feet.

"Off with you," one said to Baby Doe without paying her much attention. "Come back tomorrow night and buy a whiskey if you want to talk with us." They linked arms as they strode into the night.

The door opened again, and Silver stumbled out. Baby Doe reached out and grabbed her arm. "Get back. I have a knife," Silver growled.

"Silver, honey, it's me, Mama."

Silver squinted and leaned toward Baby's face, exhaling a fog of whiskey-soaked breath. "What are you doing here?"

"I have come to take you home."

"No," Silver pulled her arm from her mother's grasp. "Nope, not going back to that hole." She took a faltering step, shaking her head.

"Well, I have rented a room. Let's go there, get a good night's sleep, and we can talk in the morning," Baby said. There was no point talking tonight. The girl was soused.

"No, I won't go home with you," Silver batted at her mother like a petulant toddler.

"Alright, alright. Where are you staying? Let's go there and I will fix you some hot coffee."

"No, you can't come to my place."

"Why ever not? Silver, what is going on?"

"I live in a horrid little room, on a dreadful street. Tabor's great Silver Queen could never be seen there."

"Silver, you have had too much to drink."

"Yes, I always have too much to drink, Mama. It helps me forget about who I never became."

"I don't understand what you're saying. Let's get out of this stinking alley and go somewhere we can get warm and talk about this."

"We don't have much to say, Mama. You want me to go back to Leadville and I won't go."

"Well, you can't stay here." Baby Doe was now cold and tired. The fear that had driven Baby Doe here from Leadville and her revulsion at the Knot Hole Saloon had drained out of her, leaving her numb of emotion. "Just come back home, and we will think of how you can start over."

"You want us to sit around that rickety little shack and come up with a new scheme to become wealthy and respectable? We did that for years, Mama. You filled me with stories of you and your wonderful life with Papa. You taught me how to be a kept woman. The problem is that I have no man to keep me."

"You certainly aren't going to find any gentlemen around here. You cannot go on dancing in that ..." she couldn't even think of a word, "wretched place. You are ruining yourself and the Tabor name."

Silver's head lifted, her mouth hung open, then she began to laugh, a hysterical, unhinged laugh. "Ruin the Tabor name? Oh that's rich, Mama." Another peel of laughter, "Rich, it's a pun."

Baby grabbed Silver's shoulders and gave her a shake, "Stop it. Stop all of this."

Silver pushed her mother's hands away. "Don't you think I would if only I knew how?" desperation cracking in her voice. She began to cry, and Baby gathered her in a hug.

"Shh, now, honey child," she said. "The first step will be to get the liquor out of you."

Baby Doe managed to get her daughter back to the boarding house in time for a predawn breakfast with the railroad workers heading out for the early shift. The men had eyed the peculiar women as they ate, one dressed in a burlesque costume with face paint smeared around her eyes and mouth and the other in a baggy bundle of rags. No one spoke.

When the men left for work, Baby asked, "Why do your hands shake so?"

"I am just tired," Silver answered and hid her fists in her skirt.

"You can rest when we get home."

"Mama, I'm not going back to Leadville."

The women sat in uncomfortable silence for a long moment before Silver said, "I know some people in Chicago, maybe I can go there. They can help me find living arrangements. My book was well reviewed in one of the big newspapers there. I can join the press club and write again."

"Chicago? Who do you know in Chicago? Can they make introductions?"

"You don't know them," Silver said, her eyes sliding to the corner of the room. She rubbed her forehead, "Do you have any whiskey? My head aches so."

"Whiskey is what causes your head to ache."

"Mama, please, it's the best remedy I have found."

"I can't help you," Baby said. "I *won't* help you go down this path," she corrected. "The best thing for you to do is come home with me. Let memories of these misadventures fade. When the mine starts producing again, we will reintroduce you into Denver society properly."

Silver looked at her lap and sighed. "That is never going to happen. The mine will never run again. We will never be a part of polite society. It is all just a fairytale." Silver got to her feet. "I'll write to you when I get settled in Chicago."

"You can't just pack off to Chicago."

"I can. You said yourself that I am ruined here."

"Silver, wait."

But Silver was already at the door. "Go back to the mountains, Mama, and keep vigil over that empty hole in the ground. I have to go on living." With all of her usual impulsive energy, but none of the old gaiety, Silver walked out.

CHAPTER 59

1915

Dearest Mama,

May 1915

I am sorry I haven't written before, but life in Chicago can be quite exciting. I have a new beau, Billy Ryan, very handsome and dashing. I am settled into a hotel for women, but will move if Billy proposes. It is probably best if you write to me in care of general delivery.

I am embarking on a new career as an actress. Oh Mama, the theater life suits me. I am meeting the most sophisticated and worldly people and have been invited to many gay parties at cabarets and supper clubs. I am to appear in small roles in two motion pictures. I also have created a new dance act as a Cow Girl that I perform at a local variety hall.

Mama, you have always provided for me, and I can only hope to be successful enough to take care of you in the future. I have enclosed five dollars and will strive to do so again on a regular basis.

Much Love,
Rose (I am using this as my stage name—what would Elizabeth think?)

Letters did not come on a regular basis. Baby Doe continued to write to her daughter, usually narratives of the weather, Leadville gossip and the latest efforts to re-mortgage and open the Matchless Mine. As weeks stretched into months, Baby Doe's missives to Silver, or Rose, became increasing worried, begging for a note, any word that she was healthy and safe. Baby took to writing Hail Mary along the edge of her letters so the Holy Mother might intercede and Silver would respond. When an envelope did arrive from Chicago, it did not assuage Baby's fears. Silver's loopy handwriting was shaky and sloped down off the page.

Dear Mama,

1917

I am sorry I haven't written more. I never seemed to have time when things were going well and when I did have time, things weren't going well. My romances did not pan out with Billy Ryan or Carl Slanger (did I write to you of him?).

I have only a few more years before my good looks are gone. I've planned all along on getting a rich man and paying your mortgage, but I can't make the grade. I read the prayers you write on the edge of you letters and remembered you said Mary spoke to you. Perhaps she has spoken to me, too. I think I will enter a convent maybe that would be a solution to my life. If you do not hear from me, it is because I have taken a nun's vows.

Love,
Silver

CHAPTER 60

1924

BABY DOE FELL INTO A SOLO ROUTINE of trying to work the mine herself, talking a greenhorn into investing a bit in exchange for future earnings, or hiring busted old miners to work for a share of the coming strike, failing and then starting again to work on her own. The weeks and months began to blend in the solitary life, only light and temperature having meaning, working in daylight, hunkering down in the cold weather; and before she realized it, nearly a decade had passed.

Some thought she was getting a little soft in the head, maybe from the loneliness, maybe from drinking tainted mine water. Baby Doe knew her companionless life, appearing in town infrequently and dressed in the bedraggled garb taken from the charity bin, had turned her into the town character, an eccentric recluse, the odd hermit.

People had always whispered about her; they had tut-tutted when she wore glamorous gowns and jewels, now they gossiped about her black dress that had continued to fade, and the men's work boots that needed re-soling, the old miner's coat she wore in cold weather and the ancient driving cap with a now tattered scarf tied over her ears. Damned if she did, damned if she didn't.

The town's folk were friendly enough when she ventured into town, inquiring of her health, offering her a ride home. And the neighbors in the gulch would check on her after big storms. But there was no one to share the small delights and sorrows of life. The day a chickadee perched in her hand to eat breadcrumbs, only the magpies where there to laugh with her. When the sunset streaked pink and lavender and the snow caps glowed gold, no one sat with her to appreciate nature's handiwork. Only she knew of the frightful time when she slipped and tumbled down the rocky hillside narrowly missing sharp branches and hard ledges. There was no conversation at the end of the day. No recounting of the small happenings, the inconsequential observances that people share, tying their lives together, the insignificant occurrences and thoughts that are threads woven together into a blanket of common history. Baby Doe was a single strand on the frayed edge of the Leadville blanket, her colors intricate to the pattern of the past, but unraveling away.

Baby Doe sat on an old stump outside the cabin watching the sun drop behind the western peaks, sending up dying rays, tinting the cloud bottoms orange and pink as night darkened their tops. Although the long summer evening had been warm, the temperature would drop like a stone now. She pushed herself up and went inside to ready for bed. She washed her hands and face, hung up her dress and hat, pulled on a cotton night dress and wrapped her hair, now a dull ivory color, in a scarf. She brushed her teeth; she still had most of them, not bad for a woman nearly seventy. Perhaps she was already seventy, she really wasn't sure. She had shaved a couple of years off her age a few times as a young woman, not wanting to appear too old to land a second husband or to give birth to children. Now, the whole notion of age seemed too ridiculous to keep track.

Something drew her attention to the window, something near the head frame of the mine. She peered out but saw nothing. She thought it might have been the little black bear she had seen in the gulley a few days ago. She didn't keep much food around, so the bears tended to leave her alone. But the mountain lion that occasionally watched her, still as a statue up on the ridge, made Baby nervous. A few years ago, Silver's little burro screamed out in the emptiness of the night. At daybreak, Baby found a pool of blood and a few tufts of hair and she knew the lion had gotten the poor little beast. That was when she traded some Matchless ore for the rifle from Big Joe.

Baby scanned the hillside for yellow eyes, but saw none. She was about to climb under her quilts when from deep in the tunnel came a purple glow. It brightened and grew larger, then narrowed into an intense pinpoint. The light began to move down and to the left into the number three shaft, then disappeared in the blackness. She stood watching, waiting for the light to return, but it did not. She stepped back from the window, unsure of what she witnessed. The pale moon, still low in the early night sky, came through her window, illuminating the far wall and Baby's treasured picture of the Virgin Mother.

Baby Doe knelt on her old sore knees. "Mother Mary, is this a message from you?" The wind picked up and Baby was sure she heard "yes" whispered in the pines.

The next morning Baby hustled out to the mine, examining the shaft wall and picking out sample rocks, but she found nothing. Baby understood that Mother Mary knew where the silver was located and was trying to communicate this to her. Baby Doe simply needed to interpret the signs.

She remembered a long-ago conversation with Win Stratton; he had dreamt the location of his fortune. Baby began to record her dreams in a journal. Most often it was her daughters who spoke to her in the night, bemoaning the disappointments in their lives and offering no help with the mine. She prayed faithfully to Mary each night and watched out the window for the Holy Mother's guidance. Baby often saw white lights flashing near the tunnel mouth. "Mary, is that you?" she would ask. When no answer came, Baby knew it was just the spirits of old miners clamoring for attention.

CHAPTER 61

1925

BABY DOE WALKED SLOWLY AWAY from the post office with one thin envelope in her hand, a tax bill from the county. She wadded it up and threw it on the ground. She was sure the tax collector knew she didn't have the money. Even the bank no longer sent overdue notices of the mine's mortgage payments. Of course, there was no mail from Silver. Baby hadn't heard from her in ages. She had stopped sending letters to Chicago general delivery a few years ago in the hope that Silver hadn't written because she had taken a nun's vows.

Her next stop was at the Church of the Assumption to recite a decade of the rosary at the feet of the Blessed Mother. Baby had become an irregular attendee at the Catholic Church, coming and going on her own schedule to pray. Ever on the lookout for signs and dreams from Mother Mary, it didn't hurt to pay respects when she was in town.

"Hello, Mrs. Tabor," Father O'Malley whispered as he stepped out of the sacristy and came to kneel beside her. She nodded her greeting and continued to pray. He reached in his pocket, pulled out a set of cedar rosary beads and began to thumb them. Father O'Malley kept offering Baby new rosary beads, but she preferred the knotted twine she had formed in the cold alley behind the Knot Hole Saloon.

"Will you be staying for evening Mass?"

"Oh no, I'm sorry, Father. I don't have the time. Perhaps Sunday."

Father nodded, but they both knew she would not be in attendance on Sunday.

"I can hear your confession now," he offered.

Baby Doe gave Father a small smile and shook her head. She would never share her sins with this man or any other. God knew her story. That was enough.

"I can offer you penance and forgiveness. I can absolve your sins, cleansing your soul and putting you right with God."

In her advanced years she didn't need the priest to be her agent with God. She shook her head again and said, "I have made my peace with God. I will know when He forgives me."

She spent many long nights retracing the hills and dales of her life and knew God had done the same. He weighed her sins on His scales of justice, adding up every transgression and meting out fitting punishments. She knew that was why, after years of unimagined abundance, of sensuous luxury, God had taken it all away. Greed was a mortal sin, and her punishment was to live cold and hungry in a ramshackle shanty. She had been lustful and envied another woman's husband, and God had taken Horace, leaving her alone. She had been prideful, and her haughtiness had driven Elizabeth away to live in anonymous humility. She had desired the acceptance of society over communion with God, and He had made her and Silver to live as recluses, Baby at the mouth of the Matchless and Silver in her nunnery.

The Heavenly Father exacted a high price, taking her family, her home and her wealth. But He had not taken the Matchless. She had been able to rebuff numerous efforts by taxmen, bankers and other robbers to hold onto the mine for all these years. Baby Doe understood the message God was sending her: if she humbled herself, He would forgive her sins and if she lived a life of penance, dressed in rags and lived in the barest of circumstances, He would reward her. Alone in her cabin for years with only the wind for conversation, Baby Doe was sure that someday soon God would allow Mother Mary to speak to her, sending a light to show her the way to the Matchless silver.

After her prayers Baby Doe wandered into the library to read the latest newspapers. Miss Wilton did not greet Baby in her usual pleasant manner, but instead lowered her head and began stacking and restacking books at the far end of the counter.

"Good afternoon," Baby offered in a hushed voice, but Miss Wilton did not answer. "I would like to see the latest Denver papers, but they don't appear to be out." Baby pointed to the empty rack where the papers usually hung.

Miss Wilton paused, then reached below her counter and pulled out the *Rocky Mountain News*. She handed the folded paper to Baby, but did not meet her eye.

"You may wish to read in the reference room, Mrs. Tabor. I will make sure no one disturbs you," the librarian whispered.

Baby Doe nodded her thanks and took the papers to the vacant room. *Odd*, she thought.

VIOLENT DEATH OF SENATOR
TABOR'S DAUGHTER!

Silver Dollar Tabor was scalded to death under suspicious circumstances in a rooming house in Chicago's black district. Miss Tabor had lived under various aliases and was last known as Ruth Norman. Police are searching for saloon owner and local hoodlum, Jack Reid, with whom Miss Tabor had fraternized.

The article swam and swirled as Baby Doe's eyes filled and then overflowed, tears splashing on the paper, blurring the print. She took short breaths, trying to fight down the sob that threatened at the back of her throat. This could not be true. She would have known if Silver needed help. A good mother knows, can feel if her child is in trouble. The Holy Mother would have shown her warning signs. Baby Doe read the article again, but she still could not believe it. Shaking she stood and walked back to the library's front counter. Miss Wilton was a portrait of pity, her hand pressed to her mouth, her brow wrinkled with sympathy.

Baby Doe cleared her throat. "The poor young woman who died in Chicago is not my daughter. Silver is in a convent. I receive letters from her; I got one just last week. You can never trust anything you read in the newspapers, Miss Wilton."

"No, of course not, Mrs. Tabor. I am glad to hear that your daughter is well." Miss Wilton watched the little old woman leave the building and then she pulled out the *Denver Star Ledger*, Eugene Hawthorne's paper.

His front-page headline shouted:

DRINK AND DOPE BLAMED IN DEATH OF ONCE WEALTHY EX-HEIRESS.

By Eugene Hawthorne

> Silver Dollar Tabor, daughter of Senator Horace Tabor and his infamous second wife, Baby Doe, was found dead, scalded to death. She was nude. Neighbors in the squalid Chicago boarding house report that Miss Tabor was perpetually drunk and addicted to dope. She kept company with many men of the lowest order.

Smaller side articles revealed that Peter had sent two hundred dollars to Chicago to keep Silver's body from being buried in a pauper's grave and Elizabeth claimed not to have seen her sister in years. "I did not approve of the life my mother lived and I did not approve of the woman my sister became," Elizabeth told the reporters who had hunted her down. "I will not claim her now after this manner of death. She is no more to me than just a dead woman in the slums of Chicago."

Miss Wilton would keep this paper behind the counter, so Baby Doe would not accidently read the horrid details that Hawthorne's reporters had dug up. It was the least she could do for the poor old woman.

CHAPTER 62

1934

THE YEARS ROLLED ON, seeming to catch speed as they went, like an avalanche rumbling down a slope, blurring each passing day, leaving only distant memories clear. Baby Doe had poured all her energy into the Matchless Mine, continuing the strategy of obtaining questionable loans or talking old miners into working gratis and then promising everyone would be paid with a cut of the proceeds. But no one seemed to be able to envision the future quite like Baby Doe, and the results did not come fast enough to satisfy workers and investors. Eventually, they would drift away, and Baby would search out the next man to help with finance or work. With each passing year, she had fewer and fewer visitors, and she came to regard with suspicion most of those who made the trek up the gulch, men who wanted to buy her out or a rougher sort who came to see if she was dead yet. She stopped opening her door to strangers.

The summer sun had just slipped past its peak when Baby Doe heard a growling engine and grinding gears as an REO Speedwagon came bouncing up the road. She hurried into the cabin. Peering from behind a flour sack curtain, she watched two men climb out of the truck and look around. The driver of the truck was dressed in a Western-style shirt and denim work pants, but the passenger wore a fine gray suit and stylish fedora. They looked into the mouth of the mine and one gave the framing timbers a testing thump. They pointed at the electric lines that had been strung by a flush investor years earlier. At last, they walked over and knocked on her door.

"Who is it?" she called from behind the curtain.

"Mrs. Tabor, I'm Merle Green and this is my banker, Mr. DeWalt," called the man in work clothes. "We'd like to speak to you ma'am. I purchased the mine from the county for back taxes, and I want to reopen the Matchless Mine."

"Now is not a good time," she shouted through the door. The men looked at each other, but did not leave. "I am taking a bath." She hoped the men would feel so uncomfortable that they would scurry away.

"Sorry to bother you ma'am, but we have come all the way from Denver. If you don't mind, we'll just wait out here until you are able to speak."

"That's going to be a cold day in hell," she whispered to herself.

The men sat outside for the better part of an hour, before they knocked again. "Mrs. Tabor, could we speak with you now?"

"I am sorry. I am taking a bath. You can't come in," she hollered.

Huddling under the window, she could hear the men talking. "Water must be icy by now, don't you think?" asked Greene.

"Let's come back tomorrow," said the finely dressed banker. "No one around here takes a bath every day."

The men headed back to their truck. Baby Doe put a hand over her mouth to stifle a giggle, but Horace's braying laugh boomed through the cabin. His arm wrapped around her waist. She turned to fall into his embrace, but the cabin was empty. She stood motionless, suspended in time and place, trying to recapture the moment. Outside the truck clamored to life, gears ground into place and it chugged away. Still Baby Doe stood fixed, straining to hear Horace's voice, to feel the weight of his arm against her. After a long moment, she whispered, "I never gave up. I never left." Silent dust motes sparkled in a ray of sunlight from the window. "I am glad you're home."

CHAPTER

63

February 1935 - Denver

EUGENE HAWTHORNE sat by himself nursing a whiskey in a tall wingback chair of the Brown Palace Hotel. The Palace was currently the place to see and be seen for Denver's elite. The town's movers and shakers would recline in plush chairs and couches arranged in small clusters in the center of the opulent lobby, giving the illusion of privacy, while allowing all passers-by to see them. Now in his seventy-fifth year, Hawthorne still liked to keep his ear to the ground, keeping company with the politicians and newsmakers as they relaxed at the end of the day. He had no desire to retire, although, as owner, publisher and editor of his own newspaper, financially he could. To rest on his laurels would be to rot. Nothing pleased Hawthorne more than to charge into his newspaper's offices with a story lead that his young reporters had missed. After fifty years in the business, he still had a burning drive to get a story first, create the biggest sensations and write the biggest headlines. Some of his competitors had taken to printing uplifting stories to gladden readers downtrodden by years of economic depression, but Hawthorne knew that was a fool's errand. People wanted to read a story of someone who had it worse; they wanted the salacious details of how the mighty had fallen. He knew what made people feel better about losing their jobs and homes was to read the tale of the millionaire who had lost his factory, his mansion and his car. So Hawthorne, who spent his evenings at the Brown Palace noticing which banker drank too much and which business owner chewed his nails, perked up when he overheard the men sitting adjacent to him in the hotel lobby.

"I bought the property at a foreclosure auction. The taxes hadn't been paid in forever. I'm sure there is still money to be made there. I'm planning on reopening the works when weather warms up," one man was saying.

"What about the old woman? I thought she is living in the mine," another man asked.

"She's living in a supply shed and wearing rags. She wraps gunny sacks around her legs; I guess she's not got any wool stockings. It's a far cry from her old life, living in a Capitol Hill mansion and all."

Hawthorne leaned closer. 'From mansion to shed' would make an excellent headline.

"Where is she going to move when you start up the mine, Merle?"

"I don't think she has anywhere to go to. She seems pretty soft in the head these days. I'd let her stay in the shed if I could be sure she wouldn't get her shotgun and chase off my miners. I went up to Leadville to see her but she wouldn't come out and talk."

Leadville! They had to be talking about Baby Doe. He hadn't thought of her in years, but the old spite bubbled back up to the surface. He had hated that beautiful young woman and had wanted to humiliate and embarrass her as she had done to him. In the end, it was her own behavior that had proven to be her undoing. He had merely reported it, adding only a few garnishes to the endless stories that she provided parading around with a married millionaire twenty years her senior and flaunting his wealth in the most vulgar ways. Baby Doe became a social pariah, and thanks to her lack of refinement, he launched a successful career. The irony could have come from a Thomas Hardy novel.

"Meyers, I have a story that will make your career," Hawthorne said to the cub reporter. He could already see the layout in his mind, the pictures of the mansion and the mining shanty, a picture of Baby Doe in a fancy gown and one of her in rags. The headline would read "From Riches to Rags." He could hardly contain his glee. "I want you to get up to Leadville and find Baby Doe Tabor. She is living at the Matchless Mine. On his deathbed, her husband told her it still had millions in it and she promised him that she'd never give it up."

Young Wesley Meyers face lit up. "Oh yes, I know the story of Baby Doe. I saw the motion picture they made of her life last year. I read in Photoplay Magazine that the producers offered her a handsome check to come to the Denver premier but she refused."

"Now the mine has been foreclosed and sold. I want you to get the story of her being thrown off the property."

"I wonder why."

Hawthorne frowned. "Because it will sell newspapers."

"No sir, I wonder why she didn't take the money and appear at the premier if she is broke."

"I don't know, and furthermore, I don't care. I hear she's gone crazy. I'd go to Leadville myself, but winter travel in the mountains is for young men. So I am sending you. Get photographs and details, and I will assist you with the story when you return."

CHAPTER
64

End of February 1935

BABY DOE SAT AS STILL as a marble icon as the celluloid figures jerked and hopped on the bed sheet which hung against the mine's head frame. The producers had changed some of the names, but she could easily recognize Augusta, the German miners and President Arthur. Edward G. Robinson was a poor choice to portray Horace, much too short and his heavy features possessed none of Horace's natural lightheartedness.

She watched silently as the film reenacted her Washington wedding and the country's economic downturn when the gold standard was established. A penniless Horace stumbled into the Tabor Grand Opera House where he sees the specters of his past cheering him, including Baby Doe in Box A. The actor climbed onto the stage, collapsed in a melodramatic heap and died. The camera faded from

Horace to focus of the prophetic painted curtain. *"So fleet the works of men, back to earth again, Ancient and holy things fade like a dream."*

Wesley and Baby Doe both started when the film ran from the reel and whacked against the projector. "That is not how he died," Baby Doe shook her head. "That is not how we lived."

"Tell me your story, Mrs. Tabor, and then let me tell the world."

Baby Doe hesitated. If she had been born a man, she could have gone into business and people would have applauded her wits and ambition, but women were forced into limited roles and held to ridiculous standards. Those that strayed from the assigned course were labeled trouble. She realized now, after five or more decades, that her flaunting of convention played into the malicious hands of her detractors, and she had often let her emotions get the best of her.

"No," she shook her head. "This movie, all those stories about me ... it is all a pack of lies." *Why would anyone believe the truth now?* She could never make anyone believe that the comely young woman had grown to love the homespun millionaire. No one could understand her devotion to Horace and his legend, her trust in his vision, her faith in Tabor luck. People thought she had lost her mind living up here alone in the cold, barely existing on credit and charity. But she had endured the frigid desolation as a demonstration of her love and loyalty. To the world, she had been the beautiful butterfly that devolved into a homely caterpillar caught forever in its cocoon.

She shook her head again. "Mr. Meyers, please excuse me. I am suddenly very tired and need to rest."

"Mrs. Tabor, may I come again?" asked Wesley.

She did not answer him as she shuffled back to the cabin with the hitched gait of an old woman.

"What do you mean you didn't get a photograph of her?" Eugene Hawthorne shouted at the young reporter. The employees in the outer office buried their heads in work secretly relieved they were not the object of the boss's ire.

"I believe I am winning her trust. When we first met, she thought I was there to rob the mine. But I showed her the movie *Silver Dollar* and we established some rapport. I think on my next visit, she will be willing to speak to me of her life's story."

"I already know her life's story," Hawthorne roared. "Get me a photograph of that harlot."

The snow had fallen for two days and showed no signs of letting up. Looking out her window Baby Doe reckoned there was nearly four feet of snow on the level with drifts to the edge of the roof. She looked in the wood box again. She knew there were only a few small pieces of kindling left. She had wasted the last nice afternoon watching that ridiculous movie with that reporter instead of scrounging more dry firewood. It was going to be a long cold night.

Someone was out there. Someone was snooping around the mine. Baby Doe peered out the window; she could barely make out a tall figure through the blowing snow. It was Augusta, Horace's first wife.

"Shoo, shoo. Get out of here, you old bat," she shouted at the woman.

"Every sinner makes his own hell," Augusta called back over the wind.

Baby Doe jerked awake. She had fallen asleep in her rocking chair. It was nothing more than a dream.

Madam Modjeska stood preening in the middle of the room. She patted her cap with the peacock feathers, the one she had worn to midnight supper at the Capitol Hill mansion after starring at the Tabor Grand Opera House. She turned to Baby Doe and in her accented English asked, "Where have all your beautiful things gone? Where are your jewels?"

Baby looked down at the dingy black skirt and her legs wrapped in gunny sacks.

Again, Baby Doe awoke and surveyed the empty cabin. She looked out the bedside window. The storm had passed and the moon, bright in the inky sky, illuminated the snow drifts. She lay back down and pulled the quilts up around her ears.

"Did you tell Madam Modjeska about our peacocks?" Horace asked.

She rolled over to see Horace standing in the center of the little cabin. "Oh Horace darling, they are long gone. Everything is gone. Everyone is gone."

"You're still here."

"I never left the Matchless. It is my reason for living."

"I'm sorry that things ended up so hard for you, Baby. It is my only regret."

"I don't regret a moment I spent on this mountain. Horace, I am proud to be Mrs. Tabor. I love you, darling."

"Your love was made of kindness and loyalty and it's easy to be kind and loyal in good times, but hearts can harden when fortunes turn. All these years in this little cabin, you have proved your love."

Horace took her mitten-covered hands in his and helped her from the bed.

"Oh, I look affright," she protested.

"You are the most beautiful woman I have ever seen."

Baby Doe tucked her chin and lowered her eyes like the young coquette. Her hand instinctively smoothed her skirt. It was the golden satin dress that Horace had loved so much he had ordered a portrait painted of her in it, the gown draping seductively off her shoulders.

"Do you know what my fondest memory is?" Horace asked.

"Was it opening night of the Tabor Grand? The mayor of Denver gave you the largest watch fob to commemorate all your accomplishments. I was so proud of you that night."

"It was the day we went to the Ice Palace."

Baby recalled the afternoon. "Oh yes, the girls had a ball. We saw old friends, and you and I danced on the ice rink."

"That day was our golden mean, the perfect balance. We had a wealth of happiness and just enough money."

"It is all lost now. I thought if I could find the silver, everything would work out. I could restore your legacy."

"Oh dearest Baby, the real legacy of the Matchless is you and me. Our love is matchless." He gathered her in his arms and led her in a slow waltz about the room.

CHAPTER 65

EUGENE HAWTHORNE only packed one clean shirt. He didn't intend to be in Leadville for very long. He and Wesley would drive to Leadville, call the old woman out of her shanty, take a few fast photographs and get the hell out of there. The young reporter had been dragging his feet long enough, some excuse about snow in the mountains. If you want something done right, you have to do it yourself.

"Howdy," Big Joe called to the bundled-up figure stomping snow from boots at the front door to the Leadville General Store.

Under the tattered cowboy hat, scarf, coat, and coveralls was Tom French, a skinny old mountaineer as rugged as the country he called home. "Whew, getting to town was quite a project. The snow was higher than the belly of my long-legged mule."

The bell that hung above the door rang again as in came tiny Sue Bonney. "Hi, Big Joe. Hi, Tom. How'd everyone make out during the storm? I had a bad case of cabin fever." The gabby little lady lifted a lidded basket onto the counter and took out three jars stuffed with cookies. "I spent too much time baking. I made oatmeal cookies, ginger snaps and molasses cookies. Think you could sell them, Joe?"

"Sure," Big Joe answered. "I imagine your goodies won't last long. It has been pretty busy here. Everybody is wanting to get out of the house like you."

"Say, did you hear about the fella that died near Little Stray Horse Gulch?" Sue asked, her eyes wide.

"Yeah, he was here yesterday. Wanted to know how to get to Baby Doe's cabin. I told him he'd never get his car up that road in snow this deep, and she wouldn't talk to him even if he did. But he was hell bent on going up there. They say he tried to walk up there and had a heart attack," Big Joe said.

"Who was it?" Tom asked.

Joe shrugged. "Some big shot newspaper man from Denver."

"Has Baby Doe been to town?" Sue frowned with concern. "I can just see her chimney over the hill from my place, and I haven't seen smoke coming from there in a couple of days."

Tom shook his grizzled head. "Aw, she's a tough old bird." He always kept a respectful distance from that woman and her rifle.

"That old bird is pushing eighty," Big Joe said. He thought for a moment. "She hasn't been here to the store since before the storm, maybe two weeks."

Sue grabbed Tom's arm. "Come with me to check on her."

Tom started to protest, but Big Joe said, "I'll give you a few things for her." He grabbed a gunny sack and began to fill it. Into the bag went a jar of pickled beets that a young mother had brought in as barter. Joe filled a paper cone with some roasted coffee beans and cut off a hunk of beef plate, the cheap, fatty meat from a cow's belly. He added last week's *Rocky Mountain News*; he knew Baby Doe used old newspapers to insulate her thin cabin walls. Sue reached into the cookie jars, wrapped a couple in waxed paper and added them to the meager bounty.

Big Joe tied the bag shut with some twine, handed it to a reluctant Tom and said, "She won't take this if she thinks it's a handout. She brings me rocks from the mine as payment for groceries. Tell her she had some money on her account from the last ore samples she brought me."

Tom looked incredulous. "She's getting silver out of that hole?"

"No," Big Joe shook his head. "Just worthless rocks. But I won't see an old woman starve."

Tom led, breaking a trail through the hip deep snow, and Sue struggled to stay in his tracks, her stream of chatter only broken with gasps for breath. They were both drenched in sweat by the time the little cabin came into view. The snow lay undisturbed. No one had been outside since the storm's end.

"Baby Doe is wary of visitors. Best let me call to her from here," Sue suggested. "Baby Doe, it's me Sue Bonney. I brought you some things from the store. Tom French is with me."

No answer came from the cabin. The curtains remained still in the windows.

Sue and Tom waded closer. "Baby Doe?" Sue asked again. Tom began to dig snow away from the doorway and Sue trudged around to a window. A figure lay on the floor.

CHAPTER 66

BABY DOE TABOR FREEZES TO DEATH
WHILE ON GUARD AT MATCHLESS MINE

topped The *Denver Post* on March 8, 1935. The *Rocky Mountain News* had a similar banner across its front page:

BABY DOE DIES AT HER POST GUARDING
MATCHLESS MINE.

Entire pages were devoted to the life and death of Elizabeth McCourt Doe Tabor. Several reporters contributed articles detailing the riches and rags life of the queen of the silver boom. *Life of Baby Doe Was Tragedy of Riches and Rags, Queen of Colorado's Silver Boom*

Perishes After 36-Year Vigil, and *Two Dollars is Left of $11 Million Fortune* topped the dramatic stories. Coverage continued for days and featured interviews of Sue Bonney, Tom French and Leadville old timers who knew the Silver Queen. Some reports claimed the commemorative watch fob and knotted twine rosary were found clutched in Baby Doe's stiff fingers. There were images of a beautiful young Baby Doe and an old crone in rags shuffling down a Leadville street. A photograph of the Capitol Hill mansion was placed next to a picture of the mine shanty. Writers rehashed all the old scandals, the passage of time washing away much of the disgrace and turning the stories into the antics of a colorful woman. A legend was born.

Baby Doe Tabor, circa 1886

AUTHOR'S NOTE

BABY DOE TABOR WAS A REAL CHARACTER, in every sense of the phrase. Her behavior was quite scandalous for the time: she worked in a mine, she was divorced, she wore pants. She married both Harvey and Horace, became estranged from her two daughters and died alone at the Matchless Mine. She might have been born in 1854, but she shaved years off her age many times over the course of her life. She frequented the Shoo-Fly Variety Hall, but the residents of Leadville were steadfast in their claim she never worked as a sporting girl.

Most of the events I wrote about actually occurred, such as Alvinus Wood smelting lead carbonate into silver, President Arthur attending the Tabor wedding, and the Depression of 1893. Many of the people that live in my book also lived in Colorado during this time, including Augusta Tabor, Billy Bush, Jake Sands and Winfield Scott Stratton. Some characters are an amalgamation of my imagination and actual individuals. I created Eugene Hawthorne as an example of the newspapermen who hounded Baby Doe. Big Joe, Father O'Malley, the librarian Miss Wilton, and all the Tabor's employees are dramatizations of the people who helped her. I believe it was the wife of Senator Nathaniel Hill, not Senator Teller, who returned the torn wedding invitation, but I thought it might be confusing to introduce yet another mean society matron. The conversations, interactions and motivations of all the characters, whether real or imagined, were created in my mind.

Many of the legends that surround Baby Doe Tabor first appeared in 1938 as a five-part series in *True Story* magazine, written by Caroline Bancroft using Sue Bonny's name. Bancroft went on to publish a slim tourist pamphlet entitled, *Silver Queen, the Fabulous Story of Baby Doe Tabor.* If readers wish to learn more about the life of Baby Doe Tabor, I suggest: *The Legend of Baby Doe* by John Burke; *Baby Doe Tabor, the Mad Woman in the Cabin* by Judy Nolte Temple or *Augusta Tabor, A Pioneering Woman* by Betty Moynihan.

QUESTIONS FOR DISCUSSION

MANY OF THE EVENTS and people in *The Mrs. Tabor* are part of Baby Doe Tabor's true story. Do you find them realistic? Relatable?

How would you describe Baby Doe? An opportunist or a pragmatist? Reckless or plotting? What is her greatest strength and what is her biggest character flaw?

Do you think Baby Doe loved Horace Tabor or loved the idea of being Mrs. Tabor? Do you thinking her feelings changed over the course of her life?

Who was the antagonist of this story? Who was Baby Doe's worst enemy? Augusta? Billy? Peter? Herself?

Baby Doe marries for money and dies trying to restore the Tabor legacy. Which do you think was more important to her, the Tabor fortune or the Tabor name? Which would you choose: to be rich, but unknown or to be widely respected, but poor?

Modern women have more rights and opportunities than their counterparts from the late 1800s. Do you think ladies of that era had any advantages?

Did any of Baby Doe's behavior or decisions make you uncomfortable? Why? Would you have made similar or different choices given the same social constraints?

Baby Doe had few female friends, except the Shoo Fly girls. Why do you think they were accepting of her?

Elizabeth and Silver Dollar lead contrasting adult lives. Why do you think they turned out so differently? Was it possible for Baby Doe to have relationships with each daughter and work toward her goal of restoring the Tabor fortune and legacy?

Baby Doe was derogatorily called "ambitious." Do you agree? Is "ambitious" still an insult when it is used to describe women? Do you think Baby Doe could have been successful in today's world?

ABOUT THE AUTHOR

KIMBERLY BURNS grew up in Colorado hearing stories about the colorful characters of the Old West. She has a degree in journalism from the University of Colorado and a Masters in Organizational Behavior from the University of Hartford. While honing her skills writing dry corporate material, she joined numerous book groups where she indulged her passions for fiction, American history and storytelling. Kimberly lives with her husband in northern Virginia.

The Mrs. Tabor is Kimberly's debut novel. Her next book tells the story of Denver's most successful madam, Mattie Silks. A member of the Historical Novel Society and Women Writing the West, Kimberly is available to discuss her novel with book groups in person or online. Feel free to contact her at info@kimberlyburnsauthor.com.

ACKNOWLEDGMENTS

OVER THE YEARS, I have received much encouragement to write and tell stories. Many people will never know how I treasure their simple reassurances. I hoard them in my memory and bring them out on those days when nothing seems easy. To my sister Sheryl, my sisters-in-law, the yoga girls, the cul de sac ladies and my book group friends, thank you all. A special nod is deserved by Courtney Taliaferro, Melanie Muller, and Nicole Hipp for their extra help.

Kirsten Jensen at My Word Publishing held my hand through every step of the publishing process. Her patience and expertise were much appreciated. She brought me my wonderful editors, Bobby Haas and J.S. Burton, as well as the talented Victoria Wolf, who created the gorgeous cover. I must give credit to Caroline Hedges for tackling the messy first draft, Julie Pinches for help cleaning up my website, and Scarlet Heart Photography for the beautiful photos. The staff at Stephen H. Hart Research Center at History Colorado are so very helpful. I am forever indebted to the lovely ladies of Women

Writing the West; I learned much from their insights and experience.

Finally, I offer my deepest gratitude to my family. My children, Rob and Courtney, believed in me before I believed in me. My husband Robert, a man of action not words, put all the pieces in place so that I could accomplish my goal. I owe you everything.

Made in the USA
Middletown, DE
16 January 2022

58821249R10227